Felicity Hayes-McCoy

The

TRANSATLANTIC

BOOK CLUB

HACHETTE
BOOKS
IRELAND

First published in Ireland in 2019 by HACHETTE BOOKS IRELAND

First published in paperback in 2020

1

Cataloguing in Publication Data is available from the British Library

ISBN 9781473690332

Typeset in Bembo Book Std by Bookends Publishing Services

Printed and bound in Great Britain by Clays Ltd, Elcograf, S.p.A.

Hachette Books Ireland policy is to use papers that are natural, renewable and recyclable products and made from wood grown in sustainable forests. The logging and manufacturing processes are expected to conform to the environmental regulations of the country of origin.

Hachette Books Ireland
8 Castlecourt Centre
Castleknock
Dublin 15, Ireland

A division of Hachette UK Ltd
Carmelite House, 50 Victoria Embankment, EC4Y 0DZ

www.hachettebooksireland.ie

*For the members of the real transatlantic book club
in Clonmel, Tipperary, Ireland, and Peoria, Illinois, USA.*

Visitors to the west coast of Ireland or
upstate New York won't find Finfarran or Resolve.
The peninsula and its inhabitants,
and the Shamrock Club and its members,
exist only in the author's imagination.

PROLOGUE

PAT FITZ HAD HAD A WEDDING DRESS OF ivory-coloured poplin with a fitted bodice, a gored skirt and a stiff net petticoat. She'd made it on a sewing machine bought with savings from the summer she'd spent in the States the year she left school. There was a lace inset at the neckline but otherwise the dress was plain, except for the row of pearl buttons down the back. Her veil was sheer nylon, anchored by a band of artificial roses she'd bought in a place called Blanche's Bridal Bower, and brought home in her hand luggage wrapped in layers of tissue paper. Her shoes, which were ivory satin, were also from the States. She and Ger were both small and she wanted to keep things simple for fear she'd look like a cauliflower when they walked down the aisle.

In the end she'd been delighted with the result. The bell sleeves had made the dress fashionable and more than one person had asked where she'd bought it. There was a photographer from the *Inquirer* at the wedding breakfast, which was held in the function room at the Royal Victoria Hotel, and the group photo in the following week's paper was captioned *Finfarran Bride Designs Own Stylish Gown*.

Mary Casey was to have been Pat's matron of honour but, at the last minute, they'd decided little bridesmaids would be better. In a bit of a rush, Pat had run up a couple of frocks for her cousin's daughters, who were eight and six respectively and looked sweet. Mary, in her role as the bride's best friend, sat in the second row in the church in a feather corsage and a yellow coat dress she'd got from a shop in Cork. And Tom, Mary's new husband, had been Ger's best man.

Later on, the photographer had taken a shot of the four of them together, all eating a piece of wedding cake from the same plate, and the caption in the paper had been *Lissbeg Foursome Celebrates Pat and Ger's Happy Day*.

CHAPTER ONE

CASSIE FITZGERALD SHOOK OUT A PAPER tablecloth, thinking that this was going to be one hell of a farewell party. It was mind-blowing that everyone had responded so promptly to a text message, but apparently Resolve's Irish-American community always looked after visitors from home, and someone of Pat's generation would be especially fêted: most of the Shamrock Club's active members were seniors. Delicious smells were wafting from the kitchen and, at the far end of the dining room, a red-haired guy was setting up a microphone while an elderly man lifted instruments out of cases. Cassie threw a second glance at the sound guy. He didn't look much older than herself. Twenty-five at the most. But perhaps he was a hired electrician, not a member of the club.

As she looked at him for the second time, he gave her a shy, lopsided smile. His crinkly eyes were startlingly blue, and his typically Irish skin was a mass of freckles. Cassie smiled back, assessing his haircut with a professional eye. She decided he'd paid top dollar for it: whatever he was, he was getting a decent wage. As soon as the thought crossed her mind, she felt irritated. Her mom and dad might judge everyone they met according to their income, but she was supposed to have broken free from all that. That was why, as soon as she'd taken her high-school diploma, she'd decided to train as a hairdresser. Her sisters were shackled to a pre-defined career path, with no goal in life except to get richer. What Cassie wanted was a footloose life, full of risk and excitement, and to be free to take time to do stuff that mattered, like finding her roots in Ireland or making this trip to the US with Pat.

A voice from the kitchen announced that the savoury tartlets were out of the oven, and people went to lend a hand. Everything was being done by volunteers so Cassie had turned up early feeling that, though she was a guest, she ought to help. As the last platter was carried through to the dining room, she was squatting on her heels putting cutlery into the dishwasher when she looked up and saw the red-headed guy filling a kettle at the sink. He was tall and rangy, muscular, but not the type that spent time at the gym. Having switched on the kettle, he reached for a mug.

'D'you want a quick shot of caffeine before they throw open the doors?'

Cassie stood up and shook her head. 'I ought to go find Pat. I mean my gran.'

'There's plenty of time, don't worry. The chairman hasn't arrived yet and the quilting ladies still haven't hung their banner.'

'Do they need help?'

'Trust me, they do not. My grandma's the chair of the quilting guild. You don't mess with those ladies when they're focused on a task.'

So that's who he was, the grandson of a club member.

He leaned against the sink, waiting for the kettle to boil. 'Anyway, it'll take him about an hour to tune up.'

'Can you actually tune a tin whistle?'

'Actually you can.' He shot her an amused glance. 'Though I'm not sure Rambling Paddy knows that.'

'And he would be ...?'

'Your ambient music for tonight.'

Cassie giggled and the guy looked a bit guilty. 'That wasn't fair. He's a great entertainer. Probably played the ballroom when your gran was here before.'

'What – fifty years ago?'

'Sure. It was accordions back then, and an upright piano. No need for a sound system, my dad says. Just stamina and endless pints of Guinness.'

'Has your family been here long?'

'Five generations. Sorry, I should've introduced myself. I'm Jack Shanahan.'

'That's a good Finfarran name.'

'Like Fitzgerald.'

'And have you been to Ireland?'

He shook his head. 'Nope. Someday.'

'I used to say that too. I was born in Canada and the family never went home. But a few months ago, I just picked up and took off.'

'What about your job?'

Cassie explained about hairdressing. 'I've been working on cruise ships. You sign on for a couple of months, or even a few weeks, and plan as you go. Well, obviously it's not just cruise ships. You can work in salons as well. I love it. I'm a risk-taker. Anyway, I decided to spend Christmas in Finfarran. And then I stayed on.'

'Cool.'

'Um. I stayed because my granddad had died. But it is a cool place.'

'Losing a grandpa is tough. Mine was pretty cool.'

'I hardly knew mine. But that's not the point. The thing is, Pat was sort of in shock. So I hung around.'

When she'd seen him earlier, in the dining room, she'd thought Jack was shy. But now he seemed assured. He was lounging back against the sink, with his thumbs hooked into his belt and his weight on his elbows, and the hair on his freckled arms was bleached to gold. Irish-looking redheads weren't Cassie's type but somehow she found him intriguing. 'So what do you do?'

'I'm a computer geek. Started out working for my dad, now I troubleshoot for firms.'

'Not an electrician?'

'No. But if your family are pillars of the club, you're expected to pitch in.' Seeing the look on Cassie's face, he laughed. 'I enjoy it. It's not like I'm here all the time.'

'Only high days and holy days?'

'That's about it.' A blast of feedback from the other room made him wince. 'Oh, crap! Rambling Paddy must have moved a speaker.' He made for the door but, halfway there, he turned back. 'So have you decided?'

'Decided what?'

'What you're going to do next.'

'I'm going back to Ireland with Pat.'

He nodded, as if considering this carefully. 'Tomorrow?'

'Yeah.'

'Okay.' He nodded again, and turned away. 'Well, nice meeting you.'

Cassie took a step towards him and paused awkwardly. To her surprise, she found herself wanting to explain. 'It's just … my granddad died only a few weeks ago. And it was really sudden. Pat needs me around.'

'Sure.' His blue eyes crinkled as he gave her a lopsided smile. 'Like I said, it was nice meeting you.'

*

When Pat entered the building at five thirty-seven she could hear snatches of music from behind the dining-room doors, which had paper napkins over their porthole windows. Outside, women were easing themselves out of cars, balancing plates and Tupperware boxes. It looked as if half the households in town had been baking, and Pat knew that the cakes would be covered with lavish sparkly icing. The women of the sprawling suburbs of Resolve were mad for the sugar and glitter. Though here in the States, she reminded herself, they called icing 'frosting'. In the last couple of weeks little details like that had been coming back to her, maybe because of the other memories she wanted so hard to block out.

Moving past the dining room, she looked for somewhere to sit. They'd be expecting her to make a big entrance when the farewell party started, and she didn't want to spoil their fun by hanging about beforehand. So, as two women staggered past, weighed down by a trestle table, she slipped into a room on her right, which had a sign on the door that said 'Library'.

She'd been in the room only once before, on a whirlwind tour of the clubhouse fourteen days ago, when their guide had talked so fast you could hardly keep up. Now the room was silent, except for the ticking of a clock. The only occupant was a white cat, asleep on a sunny patch of carpet. There was an assortment of armchairs, suggestive of cosy reading, several stern, upright chairs around a square table, suggestive of study, and bookcases surmounted by donors' names in wreaths of carved shamrocks. And, bizarrely, an old-fashioned range with chipped enamel stood against one wall.

Sitting down, Pat considered a large computer on a side table. You could see it had been state-of-the-art in its time. With the exception of the recently refurbished kitchen, everything in the solid, well-kept building was like that – good quality, made to last, and slightly old-fashioned. And, wherever you looked, you usually found a plaque. The donors of the library furniture, the equipment in the gym, and the Lucky Charm bar had all made sure that their family names were given proper prominence. But, when you thought about it, why not? Each block and brick in the Shamrock Community Club had been paid for by public subscription, and the place had been built in the 1950s by volunteers who'd already put in long days on construction sites.

Pat was glad the window was closed and the room air-conditioned. Her holiday had been intended as a break from the last chilly weeks of an Irish February but, in fact, the heat had been wearing. People kept saying it was lucky they'd had such fine weather, and only that morning her cousin had announced that the lovely sunshine had done her the world of good. Secretly, though Pat had been longing for a good shower of rain.

There was a rattle of wheels in the corridor as a catering trolley went by. Cassie, who had driven over to the club ahead of her, was probably in the dining room laying tables. Pat's face softened at the thought of her. Small and feisty, with a snub nose, close-cropped hair, and a peacock-blue streak in her long black fringe, Cassie was one to dive head first into every situation, and usually found herself welcomed with open arms. It was she who'd suggested this holiday, bounding into the flat in Finfarran one evening when Pat had been sitting alone in the dusk, feeling sad. Five minutes after her whirlwind arrival the lights had been on, the range stoked, and a pot of tea made.

Then she'd sat down at the kitchen table fizzing with excitement. 'Right, I've had an idea. And I want you to hear me out before you say a word.' Linking her fingers around her mug, she'd leaned forward decisively. 'You're tired and don't pretend you aren't. You hardly slept a wink when Granddad was ill. Then there was the big funeral, and people turning up from all over the place – my lot from Canada, and all the cousins from the States, everyone needing beds and meals and attention.'

Pat had protested weakly that that was what funerals were like.

'I know. And I know you wanted to give Granddad a proper send-off. Which you did. But you had six people here in the flat, and masses of others staying at Uncle Frankie's.'

'Ah, yes, love, but I wouldn't begrudge them. Hadn't they flown thousands of miles to pay their respects?'

'I'm just saying it was a marathon, and that you're exhausted.'

There had been no point in denying that, or asserting that Frankie had taken care of the influx of relations. He hadn't. Anyway, before Pat could respond, Cassie was off again. 'Look, I know you turned down Mom's offer of a break over in Toronto. And why the hell wouldn't you after the last time?'

You couldn't argue with that either. The previous year Pat and Ger had spent a disastrous holiday in Canada. Sonny and Jim, their younger sons, had both gone there after they'd left university, while Frankie, the eldest, had stayed in Finfarran and worked in the family business. And, in the years that had followed, Sonny and Jim had never found time to come home. The flat over the butcher's shop where Pat had raised her children was poky and inconvenient, but it was where she and Ger had spent their long married life. So Sonny's large suburban home had felt alien, and the visit had revealed that Pat and Ger had nothing left in common with their middle-aged emigrant sons.

Worse still, Pat had discovered that the carefully chosen cards and gifts, which, for decades, she'd been sending to her granddaughters, hadn't been wanted. Instead of affirming her presence in their lives, they'd simply produced derision. Devastated, Pat had blamed herself and tried to get involved in their adult lives. But it hadn't helped. Two of the girls for whom she'd knitted sweaters and chosen birthday cards now had expensive homes of their own, and neither they nor their parents had had any time for their visitors. But Cassie, the youngest of Sonny's children, had turned out to be a maverick. Cheerful, forthright and sympathetic, she'd plunged into the vacuum produced by her siblings' indifference and forged a loving friendship with her grandmother. Then, when the painful visit was over, she'd accompanied Pat and Ger back to Finfarran, saying she planned to explore her Irish roots.

Her energetic presence had been a godsend when Ger was diagnosed with heart failure, and in the days after his funeral she'd displayed a fierce protectiveness that had sometimes brought Pat close to tears. And, when everyone else had left, she'd stayed put, still determined to help. 'Look, Canada's out of the question, we both know that. But here's the thing. I've been Snapchatting with Erin since she went back to the States after the funeral. And she says how about you and me take a trip over there?'

'To Resolve?'

'Sure. Why not? You enjoyed it before, didn't you?'

'But that was years ago.'

You could almost call it a lifetime. In the year of her engagement, Pat had spent the summer working in Resolve. Her passage had been booked before Ger proposed to her, and everyone had urged her not to waste the ticket. Besides, they'd said, a few months in the States would pay for a fancy trousseau.

Gently, Pat had tried to change the subject but Cassie had been unstoppable. 'Oh, come on, Pat, why don't we scoot over and see how Resolve has changed? Didn't you say you worked with Erin's gran in a clothing factory?'

'Well, yes, love. I did.'

'There's a whole garment district now. Great stores. Places to go. And since Erin's gran couldn't get to the funeral, she'd love us to stay with them.' Sensing reluctance, Cassie had hurried on: 'There'll be lots of people you know. Well, families, anyway. I mean, Lord knows why my lot chose Canada when practically every Finfarran emigrant takes off for Resolve.'

'I was only there three months, Cassie. Nobody would remember me.'

'That is *so* not true! Erin says you and her gran were

best buddies over there. And think of all the people who sent their condolences. Oh, Pat, let's do this. I want to meet my US relations properly. We'll have a ball. Say you'll come.'

That was Cassie. Her enthusiasms were so infectious that you always found yourself nodding. So, feeling uncertain but far too tired to argue, Pat had agreed. Now, in the silence of the library, the cat stirred as the clock struck the hour. Turning her gaze from a case of classic crime stories, Pat saw it was time to go to her party. Tomorrow, she thought, she'd be flying home to Finfarran and, despite everyone's kindness, crossing the Atlantic Ocean hadn't made things better at all. In fact, just as she'd feared it might, being in Resolve had stirred up memories she'd far rather forget.

CHAPTER TWO

MARCH HAD COME IN LIKE A LION, battering Ireland's west coast with a fierce Atlantic gale. The Finfarran peninsula had taken the brunt of it, and as Hanna Casey drove to her job in Lissbeg Library, the winding country lanes were strewn with debris blown from the hedgerows. In fields on either side of the roads, uprooted trees lay at crazy angles and, here and there, corrugated panels had been wrenched from the sides of barns. Yet, lying awake in her bed before dawn, Hanna had become aware of a change. The icy northerly wind had veered away from the peninsula, and now a southerly breeze had brought a morning as mild as milk.

This was typical March weather in Finfarran, what local people were accustomed to call 'four seasons in a day'. By this evening another storm could bring sleet, or even snow. But, for now, Hanna revelled in the rain-washed morning, the spangled celandines gleaming in the ditches, and the iridescent, mother-of-pearl sky.

She drove into Lissbeg, joining the flow of traffic streaming down Broad Street. Passing Fitzgerald's butcher's shop, she saw the upstairs blinds had been raised. Pat and Cassie Fitz must have arrived home from the States. Hanna was glad to see that the town had suffered little storm damage. It would have been awful if Pat had come home to find slates off her roof. Turning into the car park, Hanna pulled into the space marked 'Librarian', and went through an arched gateway into a paved courtyard. The town's former convent and school buildings were now the Old Convent Centre, home to a mix of amenities, including the public library and a walled park, which had been the nuns' private garden. An iron-bound door, once the school entrance, now led to council offices; a smaller door to the left accessed the library, housed in what had been the assembly hall.

At first Hanna had found it bizarre to work where she'd giggled and yawned as a schoolgirl. Her mother had been to the convent, too, as had every generation of girls in Lissbeg till the nuns had closed the school in the 1990s. Now the dark assembly hall had been extended to include exhibition space and a reading room, large windows and glass partitions flooding it with light. Glass-fronted cases incorporated in the heavy oak panelling still contained books left by the nuns, but the public library's collection was kept on metal shelving ranged in parallel rows down the room. Hanna's desk was at the front, its back to the glass wall that divided the library from the exhibition space. Next to the staff loo at the end of the hall there was a slip of a kitchen, where she and her assistant brewed tea and coffee and hung their coats.

With an eye to the weather, Hanna had worn a warm jacket this morning, and put a folding umbrella into her bag. Having hung both in the kitchen, she plugged in the public-access computers, then went to her desk to log onto her own and check the morning's emails. She'd hardly sat down when the door opened and Cassie Fitzgerald came in, looking remarkably wide awake for someone who'd flown from New York.

'Welcome back! When did you arrive?'

'You know what? I have no idea! It felt like we landed in the middle of the night, and then we had the drive from Shannon.'

'You must be exhausted.'

'Well, I crashed for a couple of hours and now I feel fine. Pat's still asleep, though.'

'How was the holiday?'

'Good. Great, in fact. I guess if I didn't feel needed

here I might even have stayed on.' A look of surprise crossed Hanna's face and Cassie went on hastily, 'But you've still got a job for me, right? Because I'll definitely be around while Conor's away.'

Conor, Hanna's library assistant, was going on a course, and it hadn't been easy to find someone to take on short-term, part-time cover. There was one day based in Lissbeg on offer, plus two more driving the mobile library, and everyone available had turned out not to have a suitable driving licence, or wanted to change the hours, which couldn't be done. Then Cassie had suggested herself and Hanna had agreed at once. The timing was ideal and she had had a second reason to be pleased. She'd always been fond of Pat, who was her godmother, so it was great to hear that Cassie planned to spend more time in Finfarran. Ger had been a cross-grained, miserly little man and the marriage had never looked easy. But Pat was shaken by her loss and Cassie's company would help.

Hanna smiled at the eager figure by her desk. 'That's absolutely fine. I cleared the paperwork last week, so we're good to go.'

'Brilliant. And my whole week's sorted. The salon at the Spa Hotel has a vacancy for a stylist, so I grabbed that to fill the other two days.'

'The Spa in Ballyfin?'

'Yep. Pat's planning to sell Ger's car, but she's said I can use it while I'm here.'

'Poor Pat – she'll have plenty of decisions like that to make.'

'I know. Ger left her everything. I bet Uncle Frankie's nose is well out of joint.'

Aware that a woman reading nearby was in earshot, Hanna stuck to business and asked if Cassie could start work at once. 'Mobile days are Wednesdays and Fridays, when you'll pick up the van from the County Library in Carrick, so if you come in tomorrow you can get accustomed to how I run things here.'

'No problem.' Cassie took out her phone. 'I got some great pix over in Resolve. Look, that was the farewell party. Only forty-eight hours ago – no wonder Pat's still asleep.'

As Hanna swiped through them, the photos became more erratic. Decorous shots of smiling women with platters of food, and a musician in a bright green waistcoat, degenerated into increasingly crooked selfies of Cassie and Pat in party hats. 'It looks like you had quite a night.' The next shot was another selfie, this time of Cassie and a red-headed boy holding up pints of Guinness. 'Who's the young man?'

Cassie shrugged. 'Just the guy who set things up for the music. His name's Shanahan. His grandma runs the club's quilting guild. The family came from near Ballyfin, generations back.'

Faced with such a statement, the instinctive reaction of most of Hanna's neighbours would be to establish certain facts. Which branch of the Shanahan family was in question, what village the specific household had come from, and the exact date on which they'd left Finfarran. But Cassie had stopped abruptly, as if regretting having volunteered the information, and, having spent most of her adult life in London, Hanna had lost that particular native instinct and gained a cosmopolitan sense of tact. Instead she exclaimed at a photo of a large cake covered with glitter, held aloft by a lady wearing two bouncy shamrocks, like rabbit's ears.

Cassie giggled. 'It was humungous! And Pat had to cut it with a ceremonial knife. I mean, the whole thing was crazy, but people were so kind.'

'So the holiday was a success?'

'I hope so. I don't know, really.' Cassie's nose wrinkled. 'I haven't dealt with grief before. It has stages, doesn't it? Denial and anger and stuff. And, eventually, acceptance? I don't know how long it's supposed to take.'

Hanna suggested it might not be that simple.

Intent on what she clearly viewed as a project, Cassie frowned. 'I can't understand how Pat came to marry Ger. She's such a sweetie and he was just an old crab. Don't you think?'

Aware that the woman reading nearby was now unashamedly eavesdropping, Hanna hesitated. While enquiries about antecedents were the accepted norm in Finfarran, direct questions like this one were not Nevertheless, gossip, whether harmless or malicious, was an inevitable part of daily life. As a divorcée who'd returned to the town she'd grown up in, Hanna's own marriag had been the subject of covert speculation, and she knew how distressing it could be. She was about to issue a quiet reproof to Cassie when she was struck by a memory of standing on a dais, exactly where the library's Popular Fiction shelving stood now. She was a seventeen-year-old schoolgirl enduring reproof from Sister Consuelo, an ancient nun whose remit had included 'Pastoral Care'. The experience was humiliating, and as soon as Hanna had been released she'd forgotten whatever the lecture had contained. What had stayed with her, however, was a fierce sense of resentment. Eager to avoid a similar reaction from Cassie, she settled for a smile and the recommendation that she get a good night's sleep before coming to work.

For the next while, Hanna was immersed in emails, but later she wondered if her brisk change of subject been either kind to Cassie or fair to Pat. Many private dramas were played out in this public space, where much could be learned from people's choices of books and films, where they sat and who they met here and, like most local librarians, Hanna's instinct was to keep her eyes open and her mouth shut. But that was the wisdom of experience, and Cassie was impetuous and young. With a pang of fellow-feeling for long-dead Sister Consuelo, Hanna returned to her work. But the hamster wheel at the back of her mind kept turning. With luck, Cassie would have more sense than to go about asking indiscriminate questions. On the other hand, having not been warned, it was possible that she wouldn't. And what would happen then?

CHAPTER THREE

AS PAT CAME DOWNSTAIRS SHE NOTICED the guest-room door was open and, judging by the look of the kitchen, Cassie had eaten and gone out. It was practically lunchtime but Pat discovered she was craving a real breakfast. Not a fry or anything heavy but maybe some toast and an egg. She could scramble the egg, throw in a bit of parsley, and call it brunch.

Frankie had agreed to drop a few bits and pieces into the shop downstairs for her return, and Pat had fixed with Des, who worked behind the counter, to add rashers and leave the lot in her fridge before shutting up. She'd asked Frankie for milk, eggs and a loaf, but on opening the fridge she discovered it was crammed. For a moment she was surprised. Then her powers of deduction overcame her jetlag and she turned on her phone.

There was a text from Mary Casey, sent the previous evening. I GOT YOU SOME FOOD IN YOU COULDN'T TRUST FRANK%1E CHANCES ARE HE@LL FORGET

A second message had followed immediately:
YOU@@ BE DEAD TO THE WORLD AFTER
THE PLANE ILL BE OVER WHEN YOURE UP

Mary, Pat's oldest friend, never stooped to
punctuation in texts and only used capital letters. She
also held decided opinions on what other people ought
to want and need. Opening the fridge again, Pat was
dismayed by a large ring of black pudding, a dozen eggs,
a punnet of tomatoes, and far more milk and fruit juice
than she and Cassie could consume in a week. In the
breadbin she found a cake of Mary's homemade brown
soda bread and a box containing three Danish pastries.
No bread appeared to have come from Frankie.

She had the box of pastries in her hand when the
door opened and Mary entered the flat, complaining
bitterly, as she always did, about the stairs. 'I declare
to God, it's like climbing a ladder to get up here from
the shop! And that stairwell's black as the hob of hell! I
could've missed my step.'

'There's a light switch at the bottom and the top, as
well you know. And a window on the landing.'

'Ay, well, it's halfway up there's a nasty turn in the
stair.'

Dumping her bag on the kitchen table, Mary
nodded at the pastries. 'I got three of them because I

knew you'd fuss about keeping one for Cassie. Put two out on a plate now and let's have a cup of tea.'

Pat gave up on her vision of a modest egg on toast. There was no use arguing with Mary Casey, especially if you were tired. She was a woman who surged through life like a battleship, seldom regarding the trails of flotsam bobbing in her wake. But, also like a battleship, she exuded strength and inspired confidence, something Pat had learned at an early age. She and Mary had been to convent school in Lissbeg together, hung out round the horse trough in Broad Street with lads from the Christian Brothers, and married husbands who'd also been best friends.

Tom had died ten years or so before Ger, resulting in a slight coolness between Mary and Pat. The idea that her friend would retain a husband when her own had been snatched away had offended Mary. It was she who had been the golden girl of the foursome, a leader where Pat had been a mere follower. Yet Tom had been taken and Ger, who, in her view, was a poor stick, had been left. God's failure to recognise the accepted hierarchy had seemed to Mary to be a deadly insult, and in the first years of her bereavement a sense of outrage had made her less close to Pat.

But with Ger's death the relationship had readjusted.

Mary had surged back into Pat's life, brushing aside Cassie's presence as irrelevant. A granddaughter might be all very well, and blood might be thicker than water, but only Mary could truly understand Pat. And Pat, who had long since analysed their friendship, had come to the wry conclusion that Mary was right. No one left alive in Lissbeg knew more about the dynamics of that complicated foursome, and no one knew more than Pat herself how powerful an ally her oldest friend could be when times got tough.

'I saw Cassie leaving the library just now. Did we ever think we'd see the day, Pat, when your grandchild would be working for my daughter?

'I'm glad Hanna has a job for her.'

'I'd say Hanna was lucky to get her. I hear young Conor's left her in the lurch.'

Pat gave her a direct look and Mary immediately tossed her head defensively. 'I'm not putting words into Hanna's mouth. I'm only repeating what I heard on the street.'

'Conor's gone on a course.'

'Well, that's young people these days, isn't it? Never content with what they've got but off looking for more. Mind you, they have great energy. Look at those.' She waved her hand at the pastries. 'Not that

I'm that impressed by all this artisan nonsense but those girls at the deli make everything from scratch.' Beating Pat to the pile of plates on the dresser, she whisked the pastries onto the table. There was a moment of unspoken jockeying about who would fill the kettle but, conceding that this was Pat's home ground, Mary settled for a tart comment about keeping teaspoons in drawers. 'You want to put them in a mug by the teapot and have them there to hand.'

Pat thought the better of mentioning dust. Any suggestion of an aspersion cast on Mary's standards of hygiene could be lethal. Her bright pink bungalow on the main road to Carrick had been specifically designed to avoid the inconveniences of Pat's flat, where visitors were entertained in the kitchen and you had to switch on a standard lamp if you wanted to read or sew. Mary hadn't bothered with drains or that sort of thing. Those had been Tom's province. She'd made sure she had double glazing and efficient central heating, a hi-spec kitchen separate from her lounge, and a bright light in the middle of every ceiling. She wasn't getting any younger, she'd pointed out belligerently, and she was damned if she'd squint at a newspaper, or scrub an old range with a Brillo pad. She'd had enough of that in her youth when she and Tom started out.

Getting no response to her comment on teaspoons, Mary slammed the dresser drawer and took a seat at the table. Pat brought the tea and looked round for her phone. 'I suppose you want to see photos?'

'Don't you know I do! But, come here to me, how are you feeling?'

'Jetlagged. Fine, though. It was a great holiday.'

'And was the house nice?'

'It was lovely. Mind you, we hardly saw Josie's daughter, she works so hard. Erin's a pet and she gets on great with Cassie, and Josie has a lovely little granny flat in the house. All on one level and, God knows, the poor woman needs it. I wouldn't say she'd climbed a staircase for years.'

'Isn't that what I'm saying about Ger leaving you that stair to contend with?'

'Ah, Mary Casey, you're like a dog with a bone! There's nothing wrong with my legs, or my lungs either. Poor Josie's got emphysema and she's walking on a frame.'

'Are you serious?'

'Well, she's ten years older than we are, if not more. Didn't she leave Lissbeg in 1950? And Ger and I got engaged in 1962.'

Tom had proposed to Mary the same week, and

Pat had gone off to Resolve that summer with a list of commissions for Mary's trousseau almost as long as her own. Sweetheart necklines and Silhouette bras had featured, and, in Mary's case, a spandex girdle to produce the right effect under her tussore-silk going-away outfit. It was Josie, Pat's cousin, who'd fixed up the job in the factory and found Pat a place in the rooming house nearby. Meeting her again, Pat had been shocked by her condition. Since then she'd told herself that she ought to count her blessings. Her own health was grand and she'd no need to think about leaving her home. After a bottle of wine and a night of reminiscence, Josie had admitted she'd wept for the loss of her freedom, and feared becoming a burden to her daughter as she grew older.

Mary bit into a Danish pastry. 'And tell me this, was the Shamrock Club the way you remembered it?'

'Ah, listen, girl, some things never change. But you should see how big it's got! There's a new wing with a kitchen and a dining hall, and they have what they call a library now, where they run book clubs.'

Books weren't really Mary's thing. 'So they've built a restaurant?'

'Not at all, the dining hall's just for members. But

they had the kitchen redone lately and, Holy God, Mary, it must have cost a mint.'

'Ah, they get great tax breaks in America. They probably wrote the whole thing off as charity.'

'Well, you could be right because there was a plaque up saying the Canny twins had donated it.'

Mary's eyes narrowed. 'Are they Moss Canny's sons?'

The merest flicker of a repressive glance showed Pat wasn't going to be drawn into gossip, even if the story was more than fifty years old. Moss Canny had left Finfarran in the mid-1960s under a dark and unspecified cloud. Something about a property deal that went wrong. The word was that his family had clubbed together to get rid of him, possibly before the guards came knocking on the door. In America he'd become a solid citizen, and though he'd come back once or twice over the years, looking prosperous, he'd never stayed long. No one of Pat and Mary's generation in Finfarran was likely to forget his story, though, and, since factual details were lacking, it had been embroidered over the years.

Pat poured the tea. 'That's right. Moss died a while back and the twins fell in for his construction business. They paid to have the old fittings pulled out and the club kitchen remodelled. Hang on, I have a picture.'

She showed Mary a photo taken on the night of the farewell party.

Mary's eyebrows shot up. 'Jesus, that's some plaque, Pat. And wouldn't all those steel units take the sight out of your eye!'

'If you want to see plaques, take a look at this one in the library.' With a snort of laughter, Pat showed her a shot of the chipped enamelled range. It had iron feet, a polished rail, a rotary damper on the ash-box door, and a large brass plaque above it, looking disturbingly like a coffin plate.

Mary squinted at the plaque. '"Brought from Finfarran by Denis Brennan AD 1956." What's that all about?'

'Well, you can see for yourself. "Ancestral range of the Brennans of Crossarra". Denis was the chairman of the Shamrock Club that summer I was there. Ninety if he was a day and worth a fortune.'

'I suppose it might have come out of some house belonging to his people.' Taking another bite of her pastry, Mary flicked a drift of golden flakes from her blouse. 'Come here to me, though, what's it doing in the library?'

'Well, it used to be in the kitchen and they wanted it out when they did the renovation.'

'So why didn't they feck it in a skip?'

'It'd be a brave improvement committee that'd dump the Brennan range. I'd say putting it in the library was a compromise. There's a rake of Brennans still alive and kicking, and even the Canny crowd wouldn't cross them.'

'You're making it sound like the Wild West!'

'Ah, it's just that they're fierce invested in the Shamrock Club. Emotionally, I mean. It's their link to home.'

'But hasn't Resolve been their home for donkey's years?'

Pat laughed, but she didn't reply. Mary, who'd never left Finfarran, couldn't imagine the strange pull that the homeland had on an emigrant. Or the complex strands of guilt and resentment in the relationships between those who went away and those who didn't. But she, with two emigrant sons and one who'd remained to build the family business, had an inkling: a knowledge augmented by that long-ago summer in Resolve. There'd been a time when she'd thought she might stay in the States herself and never come home again. But, in the end, she hadn't been able to do that to poor Ger.

CHAPTER FOUR

BECAUSE OF ITS REMOTE LOCATION beyond the Knockinver Mountains, the tourist board sold Ballyfin as 'Ireland's Best-kept Secret'. In fact it was reached by a newly built road, which divided the southern and northern halves of the narrow Finfarran peninsula and was known locally as 'the motorway'. To accommodate its last few miles, the foothills of the mountain range had been blasted, and Ballyfin, once a little fishing port, was now a booming resort with jetsetters strolling its narrow streets and a string of fashionable restaurants where champagne and oysters were permanently on ice.

The Spa Hotel in Ballyfin crested a long golden beach, which curved away beyond a little marina. The doors were incised with a swirling pattern of seaweed and, on either side of the entrance, naked flames danced in shells supported by bronze mermaids. Fishiness was the core of the town's brand image, not because of its maritime history but because of *A Long*

Way to LA, the best-selling book that had turned the resort into a tourist trade phenomenon. It was the autobiography of a Hollywood star, who'd once spent a nervous breakdown angling in Ballyfin. Unaware that the town's name derived from that of a medieval saint called Finbar, the designer of the book's iconic cover had produced an image of a dorsal fin slicing through waves. Not to be outdone, the editor, who had written most of the text, had made it the story of the star's struggle with neurosis and really big fish. This not only gave the book structure but added stature to its subject, who emerged as a kind of Captain Ahab battling with madness and monsters.

In a year unaccountably lacking in celebrity misery memoirs, *A Long Way to LA* became a global bestseller, helped by the fact that its publication coincided with the star's marriage to a teenage singer with a huge online fan base. A film shot partly in Finfarran followed, in which the star was played by an actor half his age. The title song, performed by the wife, won an Oscar. And Ballyfin became a happening place. The star had long since faded, the singer had gone into rehab and, these days, Ballyfin had become a place to eat seafood expensively, rather than catch it. But the association with Hollywood, combined with stunning scenery, continued to draw phenomenal numbers of visitors.

Cassie ran up the shallow steps between the bronze mermaids. It would be a couple of months before the tourist season began in earnest, and most of the peninsula's B-and-Bs and guesthouses were still closed, but the Spa Hotel was open all year round. Margot Ryan, who ran the hair salon, met Cassie at the lift and led her up to the rooftop spa. The reception area was floored in yards of highly polished parquet. Wall mirrors framed by gauze curtains reflected the light from the ocean, and a mirrored desk faced the gilded lift, which opened onto a terrace with a pool overlooking the beach. According to Margot, the vast sliding glass doors had been designed to bring the outdoors inside. 'But there's a hell of an onshore wind blowing, so they're staying shut today. Come through to the office and we'll have a look at the roster.'

They entered a room so small that it made the space outside seem even more like the set of a Hollywood musical. Margot lifted a pile of cushions off a chair. 'Sit down. Sorry about the mess. We're desperate to finish a makeover before the season kicks in, but all the work has to be done when we're closed, so it drags on.' She frowned at the cushions, which were cerise velvet trimmed with gold tassels. 'What d'you think of these? They're samples for the banquettes.'

Cassie accepted the seat. 'I suppose it kind of depends on your overall theme.'

'Which, let's face it, is *The Great Gatsby*, not *Gone with the Wind*. You're right. They're cat.'

'I didn't say—'

'I know you didn't. But they are. They'll have to go back.' Margot wriggled behind the desk and sat down. She was blonde and efficient, and her smart knee-length uniform fitted her like a glove. Cassie had been rather pleased when she'd first seen the spa staff's uniforms. The short sleeved button-through dress with its narrow white belt and collar was more *Grease* than *The Great Gatsby*, but the styling and fabric were lovely. Back when she'd had her interview, Margot had asked if she'd like to wear green or black. 'We can choose. Mind you, they're both buggers in a hair salon. Dark colours always are. You can wear a coverall when you're cutting, though – they're nylon so the hair shakes off. The uniforms are more about matching the rest of the staff. We all wear the same – masseuses, beauticians, us lot. Makes for a joined-up ambience, I'm told. And the colour choice avoids the suggestion of guards in an upmarket prison.'

Cassie had opted for black and decided she liked Margot. Part-time work in a salon was very different from spending weeks cooped up on a ship, but it was good to have a boss with a glint in her eye, which suggested she might be fun. She was about ten years older than Cassie and had worked abroad before coming home to Ballyfin. Today she was chatty and more relaxed than she'd been at the formal interview. Among the clutter on her desk was a framed photo of her fiancé, sitting at the prow of a yacht wearing oilskins and a big smile. He was a solid, dependable-looking guy, the manager of the marina, and, according to Margot, they were saving up to get married. 'Well, for a deposit on a house. Property prices are mad here in Ballyfin. That's the downside of the booming tourist trade. Still, you can't have it both ways, and aren't we lucky to have jobs that allow us to save? Paul got a raise a while back, and the tips I'd get here in summer would almost double my pay.'

Cassie could believe it. She'd checked the hotel's room rates on the internet before applying for the job, and seen charges as high as those in London or Biarritz. The recently extended marina had brought a new level of wealth to an already thriving resort, and the Spa Hotel provided what the wealthy wanted.

Margot consulted the roster on her computer screen. 'You're still okay to start next week?'

'No problem. I'm in Lissbeg Library on Tuesdays and out with the mobile Wednesdays and Fridays. So, like I said, I'll take any shifts you've got on Mondays and Thursdays.'

'That works perfectly. But I might give you a shout at short notice. Would that be okay?'

'In principle, absolutely. My time's my own.'

'No boyfriend?' Margot checked herself hastily. 'Oh, sorry! I didn't mean to be nosy. And I'm not suggesting it's relevant ...'

Cassie laughed. 'No boyfriend. I'm staying with my gran in Lissbeg, though, and my granddad died after Christmas so she's kind of my priority.'

'That's Pat Fitz, right?'

'Yep.'

'Aw – she's such a dote. Listen, don't worry, we'll be grand. I'm happy to get someone with your experience wanting to do part-time work.'

Cassie had already gathered this was the case. The majority of the peninsula's part-time workers in the tourist trade were foreign students subsidising a holiday in Ireland or saving for their following term's tuition. Kids born in Finfarran were pretty much 'raised for export', an expression she'd heard a lot since she'd been here. There was no longer the steady exodus to Resolve, which had been the norm in Pat's day. Now people went off to college in Cork or Dublin, then on to work in the cities. But for every one who returned and settled in Finfarran there were six who found posts abroad that they wouldn't find at home. Margot and her fiancé were exceptions to the rule. Cassie asked if she'd been born in Ballyfin.

'Yeah. My dad was a fisherman. Well, he still is, but now he mainly does boat tours.'

'And this is where you always wanted to settle?'

'That's it. Went off to college at nineteen. Always knew I'd be back.' Her fiancé Paul was a blow-in, she explained. 'He started out in the Lifeboat Service. Then he came here to work at the marina. It was a bit of a risk throwing up his job and moving to Finfarran, but we'd fallen in love as soon as we'd met and it's worked out grand. I've told him there's a site up the mountain with my name on it, and that's where we're going to live and raise our kids.'

There was still workable farmland to the north and south of the peninsula, but its tiny mountain farms were now considered unsustainable, and many were being parcelled out as building sites for homes. Margot's had been left to her by an unmarried uncle. 'It's a gorgeous place. I used to go there a lot when I was a kid. Back up on the mountain where it's quiet, but close enough for work. There's a great school in Ballyfin, too, for the kids when they come along. This is a fab place to grow up. Sea, sand, freedom. Real food. God, I remember the meals we used to have at my uncle's. Spuds from the field and fish caught by my dad. Evenings on the front step drinking tea, gazing out at the sunset. That's my dream.'

Cassie felt a stab of envy. Being footloose and fancy-free was brilliant, but knowing you had a place to put down roots must be good as well. It hadn't really occurred to her to wonder where she might settle. Toronto had never felt like home, while Finfarran sometimes did, which was weird, since her dad had never brought them to visit Ireland. It seemed like he didn't feel any pull from the place where he was born. Uncle Jim had never come home either. Maybe the urge had skipped a generation and come to her.

When she left the hotel she wandered down towards the beach. The stone pier was still in use by fishing boats. Beyond it, where the seabed had been dredged, the shining white marina sheltered several large yachts. The beach, which curved away from the pier, was deserted, except for a child walking a puppy. Buffeted by the onshore wind, Cassie crunched over shingle onto sand. The tumbling waves were tipped with foam, and gulls tossed and wheeled, surfing on air currents. The wind brought the smell of salt from the Atlantic and ribbons of crimson and emerald seaweed were fast being buried in hummocks of fine sand.

Down at the shoreline, where the packed sand was easier to walk on, Cassie turned her shoulder to the wind and happily lengthened her stride. As she left the pier and the marina behind, the sound of cables rattling against masts began to fade. Soon she could hear nothing but the cries of the seabirds and the shrill yapping of the puppy. With her cropped hair plastered to her head and her long fringe flying, Cassie turned her back to the ocean and looked up at Ballyfin. Directly above the beach was the esplanade, with its row of modern hotels, including the Spa. Above it, the steep streets of the port climbed to the town centre, where a terraced Victorian square surrounded a green. Beyond that again, above the outskirts of the town, rose the foothills of Knockinver, where Margot's uncle had farmed.

The best school in Toronto, a luxurious home and expensive, exclusive summer camps seemed nothing compared to the freedom of life here in this lovely place. Margot had described fishing trips when she and her dad would spend whole days on the ocean, and nights lying on the beach with friends, counting stars. She'd helped on the farm, milking cows and feeding chickens, and carried bundles of straw for the thatcher, who'd come in a rickety car to patch a shed roof. Her uncle had refused to abandon thatch for corrugated iron, saying there were years left in the roof if it was properly repaired. So Shamie had arrived with straw in the back of the car, and an armful of scallops, narrow pliable hazel wands sharpened at either end, to secure it to the roof. Cassie had loved Margot's description of the old man's deft patching and the bottle of milky tea he'd kept in his pocket, wrapped in a sock.

The house planned by Margot and Paul was modern, but Cassie could tell that Margot would capture all the charm of the farmhouse she'd loved as a child; the old house and its tumbledown barn and sheds were long gone, but the new home on the mountain would contain warm memories of the past. Swinging round to face the ocean, Cassie found herself longing to do the same. Not now, of course, when there was still so much of the world to see and explore. But sometime in the future when, like Margot, she'd be ready to settle down. Then, as the wind hit her again, she realised ruefully that one vital ingredient was missing. Margot had Paul, that solid, dependable guy in the photo. Footloose Cassie Fitzgerald had no one special with whom to share her dreams.

CHAPTER FIVE

MARY CASEY FROWNED AS SHE STOOD AT her kitchen window. At this time of year you could never tell whether or not it was safe to hang out your washing and, despite a lifetime of coping with Finfarran's changeable weather, the lack of certainty always put her on edge. Tea towels and that class of thing didn't matter, but a good dress could get ruined if the wind caught it and twisted it round the line. Pat was always telling her she made mountains out of molehills but, whatever Pat might say, appearances mattered. To Mary's mind, you were what you wore.

She could remember exactly what she'd had on when she and Pat had met Ger and Tom. It was at a match. Tom was playing and Ger had been in the crowd. The nuns were never happy about girls going to watch football but, since most of the lads on the local team had sisters and cousins who went to school at the convent, they couldn't ban matches outright. But the girls were expected to wear school uniform, presumably in the hope that lace-up shoes and lumpy brown gym frocks would prevent lustful advances on the sidelines.

Mary hadn't cared. You couldn't expect sixth years to do the likes of that, and the bishop was her mam's uncle so who gave a damn for the nuns? Pat had been doubtful but, as Mary had told her sharply, she could afford to be. When your figure went straight up and down, like a ruler, you didn't have to keep hitching your gym frock down over your bust. The tunics had three pleats front and back and buttoned on the shoulders so, if you had any kind of shape at all, they hung four inches shorter fore than aft. There was a knitted sash too. The nuns called it a girdle, which always made people giggle because you'd see ads in papers for spandex girdles designed to hold you in. Though wearing one under a gym frock would have made no difference: with the pleats and the stringy sash, whatever you did you looked like a sack tied with twine.

Peering out of the window, Mary considered the dress she'd carefully washed on a delicate cycle. If she sat at the kitchen table she could keep an eye on the weather and, if need be, whip it onto the line. Pat had worn some class of a dress to the football match, but she'd lost her nerve and added her school gabardine. Mary had sported a wine corduroy skirt and a ribbed pink polo neck. Neither had deigned to wear the school beret, and they'd both worn nylon stockings and shoes with heels – which they'd regretted when they'd got to the muddy field.

Tom played centre forward. Mary had seen him before in Crossarra, where a bad-tempered old cousin of his had kept the village post office, but he used not to be round Lissbeg that much. Nuala Devane was on the sideline, wearing her gym frock and beret. She and Tom were doing a line at the time. Nuala's dad had the dancehall in Sheep Street, and her mam sold tickets at the door. You'd see Nuala herself there, selling Tayto and red lemonade through a hatch, and Tom would hang round chatting to her until she was free to come out. He had loads of friends. There were the lads in the GAA, and the crowd at the Brothers, and everyone seemed to know him from the post office, where he helped out. Mary, who was an only child, had never needed to work when she was at school. She'd thought about going to England to train as a nurse after doing her Leaving Cert. But that hadn't happened. Because, from the day she'd seen him shoot the winning goal, she'd known she'd marry Tom.

The day after the match he was hanging round the horse trough in Broad Street, with a crowd of other fellows from the Brothers. Pat didn't want to cross the road in case they'd be seen by Benny, who was always up at the convent window, snooping. But Mary didn't give a hoot for Sister Benignus. There was no harm in talking to a fellow bang in the middle of town in the full light of day. Ger had been there too, though by then he'd left school. He'd been put into the butcher's shop the day he'd turned fifteen.

Mary was amazed when she discovered that Ger was Tom's best friend. Their friendship had begun in their first year at the Brothers' school when Tom was already a football hero and Ger was a scrawny runt. Brother Hugh had nicknamed them The Warrior and The Weasel. The name had stuck because Brother Hugh kept egging the kids on to use it and, according to Tom, Ger had no way to fight back. So, being Tom, he'd stuck up for Ger in the yard. That was Tom. He was different to the other fellows, the way he'd be quiet and gentle. He was always off doing jobs for his aunt Maggie – setting her spuds, fetching her shopping, and sitting keeping her company by the fire. Her ramshackle house in its sloping field gave Mary the shivers in those days, and Maggie was a sour old besom. But Tom said she needed him and, apparently, that was that. He was a fool to himself but, in the big picture, that had never mattered to Mary. And he'd fallen for her just as she'd fallen for him.

A spatter of rain against the window caused Mary to cast a complacent look at the washing she hadn't hung out. It hadn't taken long for Nuala Devane to get the message. Indeed, if you wanted Mary's opinion, Tom and Nuala hadn't really been doing a line at all. Not properly. And if Nuala had really wanted him, she could have got out from behind the hatch when he came into the dancehall, and worn something decent when she went to watch a match. She could have kicked, too, when Mary moved in on him, instead of going round with a puss on her. Still, none of it mattered to Mary, then or now. She and Tom were made for each other and that was the end of that.

Except that Tom could never turn his back on a lame duck. One day, when they were all still at school, Ger was messing about over at the horse trough. It was full of water then, not planted with flowers like the council had it now. Ger was walking the edge of it, like a tightrope walker. He was a stringy little sliver of nothing, with a mean, wizened face on him, and you could see he was only doing it for attention, and no one had even glanced at him till another lad shoved him in. The crowd was laughing and jeering, and calling Ger a wet weasel, when Tom appeared from nowhere and grabbed the bully by the neck. He had twice his strength and he held the boy's head underwater till he was choking, and then he heaved him out and left him sprawling on the road. No one ever shouted, 'Weasel,' after that happened and, from that day on, Ger had clung to Tom like grim death. Which was fair enough when he was still at school, with Brother Hugh being a bastard, but not by the time Mary and Tom got engaged. If you asked Mary, that was taking liberties. Ger was just another Maggie Casey, needing care and demanding Tom's time.

Having said that, she'd loved the way Tom had always been popular. People didn't just envy her because of how he looked, or how he treated her: he was a good man, and everyone knew it, and Mary was proud to know she'd been his choice. Neither a day nor a night went past now when she didn't find herself missing him.

But sitting here remembering did no good. Crossly, Mary stood up and shook out her newly washed dress – you wouldn't want to hang it out all crumpled and half dry. She was glad Pat was home again and the evenings were drawing out. After Tom died she'd divided up the bungalow and taken Louisa as a lodger. But she was away seeing her own family in England. That was how it was with Louisa: she'd skite off if she fancied it. Still, whatever you might think of the way her rat of a son had treated Hanna, she was a decent woman, and company in the evenings, so you'd miss her. And however good Hanna herself might be, the fact was that she and Mary had never got along. Tom had been stone mad about the child and, by then, Mary had realised that he needed careful handling. The first time she'd complained about the hours he spent at Maggie's place, she'd thought she'd have him toeing the line at once. It had been the shock of her life when she'd found that, for all he was gentle, he could be stubborn. But, having lost a battle, she'd known better than to start a war. Instead, when Hanna got old enough, she'd fixed for her to go round after school each day to give Maggie a hand. It wasn't until the dark nights after he died that she'd confessed to herself how much she'd resented the time Tom spent with Hanna, and that sending her round to Maggie's place had killed two birds with one stone.

Draping the damp dress across the top of the laundry basket, Mary told herself firmly that things had worked out for the best. Maggie's will had left Hanna her house and the scrubby clifftop field. And damn glad of it Hanna had been when she'd needed someplace to live after her divorce. She'd stormed out on her cheating husband and turned up on Mary's doorstop when her poor daughter, Jazz, was only fourteen, and no one could say Mary hadn't thrown open her door. But, apparently, Maggie's dump of a place was preferable to life in her mother's bungalow: Hanna had renovated Maggie's and moved there as soon as Jazz finished school. People were never grateful, thought Mary. So, when you'd had a hand in the way things worked out, generally it was wisest to say nothing. And life moved on. Hanna's had and Pat's would now. The past was dead and gone, and best not thought about.

Nevertheless, with her eye on the rain, Mary kept on thinking. Being alone a lot made you do that.

Long before she and Tom had got engaged she could see how things would be when they were married. Ger would be turning up all the time and Tom would be telling her Ger was lonely and missing his only friend. It had taken a while to think of a way to get shot of him. Then she'd noticed Ger had developed a bit of a yen for herself. She hadn't set out to chat him up. She'd hardly looked at him, really. But she might have strung him along just a bit. Nothing that Tom could have seen, of course, because she wouldn't have taken the risk.

In the end, it had all worked out as she'd hoped because Ger had married Pat. That wasn't something Mary had fixed, of course, because how could she? But she'd known Ger would propose to Pat as soon as she herself had accepted Tom. He'd figure he might as well, since there was nothing left to hope for. It was a good thing for all of them, really, she assured herself, because it had meant the foursome remained together. It had crossed her mind that Pat might decide to stay in Resolve, where she was so great with Josie, and not come home at all. She'd even wondered if something might have happened to keep her over there. There'd been a queer look about Pat when she came back, and she'd hardly talked at all about who she'd met there. But she'd settled down quick enough once she and Ger were married and, from Mary's point of view, it was another case of killing two birds with one stone. You wouldn't want poor Pat left on the shelf when her best friend married, and if Ger had a wife and a home to go to, there was less chance he'd be hanging around demanding attention from Tom.

CHAPTER SIX

CASSIE WOKE UP IN THE ATTIC ROOM above the butcher's shop. Once it had been her uncle Frankie's bedroom, but now it was officially called Pat's guest room. There was a roof light in the sloping ceiling, and a comfortable bed with a patchwork cover Pat had made at Lissbeg Library's sewing circle. As Cassie sat up it occurred to her that the sewing circle had been a great source of entertainment for Pat. It was now in abeyance, though Hanna had told her it might be revived later in the year. It was a matter of keeping an ear to the ground and responding to what was required.

Checking her phone, Cassie opened an email attachment from Erin. They'd been Snapchatting late last night, and Erin had promised to send more photos of the party in Resolve. Several shots featured Pat and her cousin Josie, Erin's gran, deep in conversation. There was one of Erin herself, dancing with a dreamy smile on her face and wearing a feather boa.

Rolling out of bed, Cassie crossed the corridor to the little bathroom underneath the eaves. Then, having showered and dressed, she clattered down the attic stairs to the kitchen, where Pat was having breakfast. Cassie kissed her on the head. 'Morning. What's the weather forecast?'

'Mixed, by the sound of it.' Pat smiled as Cassie sat down with a coffee. 'At least you've only to pop across the road to get to the library.'

Cassie glanced out the window. 'It's sunny now, anyway. Do you have plans for the day?'

'Well, I ought to get on with sorting Ger's clothes.'

'Oh, Pat! On a lovely morning like this?'

'It's got to be done sometime, love.'

'But couldn't you leave it till later? I can help. You go out for a walk or something this morning, and we'll do the sorting together when I get home.'

'Well, I suppose we could.' Pat looked doubtful. 'Let's see how I go. I might get a bit done before lunch.'

Finishing her coffee with a gulp, Cassie buttered toast with one eye on the clock. 'I'd better go – I don't want to be late on my first day.'

She ate the toast hastily and ran back upstairs to brush her teeth. Coming down, she found her uncle Frankie climbing the stairs from the shop.

Pat's eyes brightened. 'Now so! Here's Frankie and he'll give me a hand, won't you, son?'

Cassie had spent very little time in her eldest uncle's company. When she'd been to his home with Ger and Pat shortly before Ger was hospitalised, she'd gathered it stood on a site on the family farm. Pat had explained that a full-time manager lived in the old farmhouse. To begin with, as they'd driven west through rich farmland, Cassie had just been enchanted by the beauty of her surroundings. Then she'd begun to realise that what was involved was a serious amount of real estate. Uncle Frankie's house had been a revelation too. It was built on a height set back from the road and surrounded by a concrete plinth and green lawns. Ger had swung the car between gateposts topped with pineapples, and up a curved gravel drive to double doors surmounted by a portico. The contrast between this and Pat and Ger's flat couldn't have been more extreme.

Uncle Frankie and his wife Fran had been on the step to meet them. He was a short guy, older than Cassie's dad and Uncle Jim, but easily recognisable as their brother. Over tea, she'd realised that the Fitzgeralds' empire-building wasn't confined to her family in Canada. The farm didn't just supply Ger's little butcher's shop: stock was bought and sold constantly, and meat provided to retail outlets right across the county. And Ger seemed to be into commercial property-dealing as well. Later, Cassie had asked Pat why she and Ger had never moved out of the flat above the shop. 'Ger never wanted to, love,' was all she'd got for an answer.

This morning Frankie seemed surprised to see her. Then he smiled and said he'd thought she'd be at work.

'I am. Well, I'm just going. It's my first day at the library.'

'So I heard.'

It was odd that he didn't wish her luck, but he'd never struck Cassie as friendly. His smile didn't seem to reach his eyes. Still, they hadn't met on particularly smiley occasions: at the tea party he might have known that Ger was concealing an illness from Pat, and the next time Cassie had encountered him had been at the funeral Mass.

Grabbing her bag, she gave Pat a hug. 'Don't spent the whole day cooped up in here, will you? See you this evening – I'll get us dessert from the deli.' She edged past Frankie, whose bulk nearly filled the doorway, and descended the dark stairwell to the shop.

Pat began to clear the breakfast table. It was good of Frankie to drop by, she thought, and quite a relief not to have to cope with Ger's clothes on her own. Perhaps

Frankie might even like to take a jumper or a scarf. Ger was tight-fisted in many ways but, when he'd spent money, he'd always bought the best. And, though he'd never been much to look at, he'd always dressed smartly, cutting a good figure among his business cronies in Carrick and clapping the backs of the boyos at the mart. Frankie might well like the scarf she'd bought to go with Ger's tweed overcoat, or the blue pullover she'd got for him on their holiday in Toronto. It was cashmere with a lovely casual V-neck. Not Ger's usual sort of thing, but she'd bought it to surprise him.

Pat's eyes filled with tears and she shook herself crossly. It was silly to get sentimental about a pullover, but Ger had worn it on Christmas Eve when he'd first told her he was ill, and, only a week or so later, they'd taken him out of the place on a stretcher and, after that, he'd never come home again. They'd had a dreadful job getting the stretcher down the stairs from the flat and through the shop to the waiting ambulance with herself and Cassie coming down behind.

Blinking away her tears, she offered Frankie a cup of coffee. 'I made it for Cassie's breakfast and it's still hot.'

'No – well, yes. Thanks, Ma, I'll have a drop.'

He sat down at the table, shrugging off his Burberry trench coat to hang on the back of the chair. He was a good lad really, Frankie, even though he'd been a bit spoilt. Pat supposed that an eldest son was always the apple of his father's eye. She poured the coffee, thinking it was nice to see him sitting in Ger's place at the table. When she'd married she'd thought the flat a poky place to be rearing children, so it was strange how big and empty it felt now.

The shop and the flat had been left to Ger by his father. His brother, Miyah, had fallen in for the farm. When Miyah died everything came to Ger, so life got easier, and by the time Frankie and the lads were in their teens he'd trebled the size of the holding. He'd bought sites, too, that developers came round later from Carrick and paid him a fortune for. In fact, if you could believe the gossips, he'd banked enough to buy and sell half of Finfarran. Pat had never been certain that she did believe the gossips, because Ger was a great one to puff himself up. You could never be sure that he wasn't just striking attitudes. Still, plenty of money went into the till, and she and his growing sons were well taken care of. As a matter of pride, he'd made sure that Pat had a new coat each winter, even though, in the early days, they'd been hard put to make the shop pay. It was one thing to have a reputation for being a close man, but another to let yourself down in front of the neighbours. Ger wouldn't do that. And if he wasn't quite as rich as people said, sure it made him feel good to act like it.

It had been a bit of a shock to find Ger had left her everything. But, of course, the will had been drawn up years ago, before the children were born. Anyway, it made no difference because they'd agreed that the lads would end up with equal shares. She'd thought he'd have added that to the will, or made a new one, but the end had come so quickly that perhaps he hadn't had time. He'd have known anyway that she'd see things right.

It was because of Ger that Sonny and Jim had taken off for Toronto. He'd announced that he hadn't worked his arse off to see a grand, growing business broken up between his sons. So, as soon as Frankie had left school he'd been put in charge of the farm and, when the time came, Ger had paid for Sonny and Jim to go to university. Then, with nothing for them at home, they'd gone abroad as soon as they'd graduated. Their impressive qualifications had ensured that they'd prospered, just as Ger had said they would. But Pat had missed them terribly. And they'd never come back. Still, as Ger had pointed out to her, they had their own families and businesses to think about, and they'd done well and had their health and strength.

The thing was that Pat hadn't known if Sonny and Jim had resented Frankie's cushy life at home. And there was no denying it was cushy. The manager ran the farm and Ger had kept his hands on the reins when it came to the shop, so Frankie, with his big house and car, did little enough. There was no harm in him, Pat told herself, but you had to admit he was lazy. Yet maybe that wasn't fair. Here he was, on her second day back, dropping round first thing to give her a hand. It was nice of Cassie to offer, but somehow it seemed more fitting that his son would help take Ger's jackets, slacks and suits off their hangers, sort through those pathetic piles of shirts and socks and underwear, and bag them up for the St Vincent de Paul.

Sitting at the table, Pat watched Frankie drink coffee. Ger had been such a little fella compared to this heavy-set man with his broad shoulders. You'd hardly believe they were father and son, except for the look Frankie had when he was crossed. He was the spit of Ger then, with his mutinous face on. Pat knew little enough of Ger's business, but she was well aware of how badly he'd needed to get the best of a deal. She'd often wondered if that went back to the time when Brother Hugh had encouraged the bullies. The lads who'd seen Ger's humiliation at school had grown up to become the men he did business with, and it seemed to Pat that doing them down had always meant more to Ger than the money he'd made at their expense.

Smiling at Frankie, she mentioned the blue pullover. 'And if there's anything else you'd like of his, you know you've only to say.'

Frankie stood up and put on his coat. 'I'll need to be getting on now, Ma. I only dropped in to say I'll be round shortly to clear Dad's desk.'

'Well, yes, no, of course, there's that to be done.' Pat touched his sleeve. 'But there's all his clothes and personal things, Frankie. I'd like to make a start on those first.'

'You can get someone in to help you, surely. Or Cassie will give you a hand.'

'She would – I mean, she's offered. But I'd prefer if it was you, son.'

Pat could see that he wasn't really listening. Instead, he frowned and gave her a sharp glance. 'How long is Cassie going to be here, anyway? I thought she was only supposed to stay for Christmas?'

'Well, yes, but then your poor dad died and she didn't want to leave me ...'

'Ay, well, she can't expect to sponge off you for ever.'

Pat was shocked. 'Ah, Frankie, that's no way to talk about Cassie. She's only here out of kindness, and she's not sponging at all. She has two jobs.'

He gave her a bit of a smile and turned to go again. At the top of the stairs, he paused and said he'd a busy week ahead of him but he'd give her a shout before he came round to clear Ger's desk. He was gone before she could say a word, and Pat sat down at the table. How stupid she'd been, she told herself, to imagine Ger's blue pullover would ever have fitted Frankie. There was some cold coffee in her cup, so she drank it slowly and finished eating her corn flakes. She left the dishes on the table because she couldn't face washing them. But she stood up and went to sort Ger's clothes.

CHAPTER SEVEN

CASSIE'S WORK ON THE ONE DAY A WEEK she spent in Lissbeg Library would mostly consist of manning the desk when Hanna was otherwise engaged. The basic procedures were straightforward, and the vital thing to remember was to keep the desk in your eye line should you leave it. Some people, Hanna explained, took the view that they had a right to personal service. 'The different sections are clearly indicated and, obviously, the books are shelved in alphabetical order, but they'll still want you to find things and place them in their hands. Just be polite and help, okay? It's always quicker and easier. But, if I'm not at it myself, you mustn't forget that the desk is your primary responsibility.'

'Okay. Got that.'

'You'll need to check the returns for unexpected bookmarks.'

'Like what?'

'You'd be surprised. Anything from a rasher to a ten-euro note.'

'Seriously?'

'Absolutely. Now, some readers will ask for book suggestions.'

'Really? Because I can deal with bacon but I won't have a clue about that. The last proper book I read was *Wuthering Heights* at high school. That was cool but it's pretty ancient, isn't it?'

'Usually they're just looking for what they call "a good read". There's a display here at the front where I put the new bestsellers, and a shelf marked Recommended Reading. There's more eclectic recent stuff there, plus a few classics, and I change the books every Monday morning.'

'What if somebody wants to look something up?'

'I'll talk you through the reference section later, and you can familiarise yourself with our online resources. Spend some time on that today and tell me if you have any questions. But don't worry, people will know that you're a replacement. They won't expect you to have the answer to everything.'

'Cool.'

As they made their way between the shelves Hanna

smiled. 'You'll need to be aware of our resident eccentrics.'

Darina Kelly, a ditzy middle-aged mum, and Mr Maguire, a retired teacher, were serial joiners. If a club was set up, or a group formed, they were always first in line. Neither would have expected to be bracketed with the other, but Hanna always thought of them with the same resigned frisson of dread. On good days, she recognised that their eagerness was admirable. On a busy day, or during an interesting session, she frequently cursed Darina's non-sequiturs, and Mr Maguire's pedantic affectations. She knew, however, that Darina struggled with the pressures of late motherhood and that Mr Maguire was lost without his classroom.

Cassie grinned. 'No problem. I'm used to dealing with rich weirdos on luxury cruises.'

Hanna remembered that her daughter Jazz, who'd worked for a budget airline, often said the same thing about dealing with difficult customers: 'Don't worry, Mum, I've coped with plenty of weirdos on late flights to Málaga!' Evidently you got eccentrics at both ends of the economic scale.

Over the next couple of hours she showed Cassie how to find books in stock and to input requests on the inter-library loan system; walked her briskly round the audiobooks and music section; warned her that toddlers in Children's Corner must be accompanied by a responsible adult; and concluded by showing her where the mugs and biscuits were kept in the kitchen. 'And remember this. The public mustn't bring food and drink in, so you and I don't have tea breaks at the desk.'

'Got it.' As they stood in the kitchen doorway, Cassie looked down the oak-panelled room, which was flooded with morning sunlight. 'It's a nice place.'

'I like it. Well, actually, I love it, so I hope you'll be happy while you're here. By the way, you needn't worry about the exhibition space: in the summer we've got volunteer guides but, ultimately, it's my responsibility. And the gift shop isn't open at this time of year.'

Back at the desk, Cassie studied a list of online resources. After a few minutes, she swung her chair round in surprise. 'Wow, libraries offer a shedload of stuff.'

Hanna laughed. 'It may look daunting but you'll soon get up to speed.'

'I'm not daunted, I just didn't know you could access so much. Dumb of me.' Cassie wrinkled her nose. 'I've been wondering if Pat could join a club here again. Something exciting to take her out of herself.'

'Well, we do have a book club but I'm not sure I'd call it exciting.'

Cassie looked at her anxiously. 'She was still in shock and pretty miserable, but Pat got out and met people at the Shamrock Club. I think it was good for her.'

'There's a leaflet about it there. Why not take it home to her?' Hanna was tempted to add that dealing with loss would take more than just joining a book club. Nevertheless, one had to start somewhere, and she understood Cassie's sense of being on a mission. Unlike Pat's quiet stoicism, Mary's grief when Tom died had expressed itself in loud demands for attention and, irritating though these had been, Hanna had felt it was her job to make things better. Mary had moved on since then but, emotionally, she was still high-maintenance, relying heavily on family for company, and texting neighbours with fussy requests that were largely calls for attention. Pat, who was far more self-contained, would never make demands on neighbours or family, but perhaps that was all the more reason to fear that she'd become reclusive.

Then again, Pat had Mary. Until recently Hanna

had assumed their friendship was one-sided, with Pat offering constant support and Mary being a trial. But since Ger's death Pat had increasingly turned to her oldest friend, who'd responded with a warmth that Hanna saw as uncharacteristic. Perhaps, she told herself wryly, there was still hope for herself and her difficult mother. Maybe, at this late stage in her life, the leopard was changing her spots.

By the end of the day Cassie had successfully issued loans and received returns under Hanna's supervision, and the library's regular users were clearly enjoying her presence. As Hanna unplugged the computers and lowered the blinds, she asked about Cassie's plans for the rest of the evening. 'Have you recovered from the jetlag?'

'You don't get much coming in this direction. But I did spend ages last night Snapchatting with Erin.'

'She's your cousin?'

'Her gran, Josie, is Pat's first cousin. I don't know what that makes Erin and me. Thirds or something? Anyway, Josie got Pat the job in Resolve when she went there a million years ago.'

'Nice that you and Erin get on.'

'She's fun. I like her a lot.'

'Do you think you'll go back and visit?'

They had strolled down to the kitchen where Cassie bent down to take her bag from the locker under the coat-rack. 'Could do. I dunno.'

As she stood up her face was flushed and she seemed slightly forlorn. Hanna felt a rush of sympathy. 'It's a shame there isn't more family here to help Pat.'

'Yeah. Well, my mom and dad had to go home directly after the funeral. So did Uncle Jim and his lot. It was a big deal to take time off work.'

'Of course.' Hanna reached for her jacket. She hadn't had any intention of criticising Pat's family. The remark had been prompted by her reflections on her own problems with Mary. Lifting her own bag from the locker, she leaned against the door jamb. 'Everyone here in Lissbeg will want to do their best for Pat. She's well loved. You mustn't think there's no one around to give you and her a hand. My mother can be difficult but she'll always be there for Pat. They go back a long way.' Taking the library keys from their hook, Hanna grinned at Cassie. 'Actually, Mary's at a bit of a loose end, these days. My daughter, Jazz, is away with her other gran, and Mary's missing them. So you may find her at Pat's quite a lot.'

Cassie laughed. 'I'm kind of fond of your mom. She's feisty.'

'That's one way of putting it.' Hanna checked the kitchen switches and led the way to the door. 'The point is that you're not alone, Cassie. The whole town will be looking out for Pat.'

Cassie nodded thoughtfully. 'I know that. You're right, though. It's at times like this that families need to face stuff together. I hadn't thought of it that way before.'

CHAPTER EIGHT

HAVING CROSSED THE ROAD TO PICK UP cheesecake from the deli, Cassie went home with the leaflet about the book club, intending to entertain Pat with stories about her day. There was plenty to tell. Darina Kelly's kids, who were famously undisciplined, had arrived on their own, saying their mother had told them to read a book while she had her hair done. Setanta, a burly five-year-old, had announced loudly that his mum was having her roots touched. 'When she doesn't, she looks like marmalade on toast.'

Gobnit, Setanta's eight-year-old elder sister, had hushed him fiercely. 'You're not allowed to say that, Porky. Shut up.'

'And *you*'re not supposed to call me Porky. If you do, I'll call *you* FartFace.'

Several respectable ladies had looked round in horror, and Setanta's voice had risen several decibels. 'You're not the boss of me, GobnitFartyFartFaceKelly! You're a *pig*!'

Despite increasingly overt hints from Hanna, Darina often used the library as a crèche, so this was a scene that regulars had become used to. Ordinarily Pat, an inveterate people-watcher, would have been dying to hear how it had played out, but tonight she said she needed an early night. 'I'd say it's just the jetlag but I'm feeling a bit tired.'

'Have you eaten?'

'I have. I'm grand, love, don't mind me. There's dinner there on the range – you can help yourself.'

But the casserole was very nearly untouched. There were five bulging bin bags on the landing and, checking them out, Cassie found them full of Ger's clothes. She assumed that Frankie and Pat must have worked half the day to sort them, so no wonder Pat had been tired and a bit down. As she ate dinner, Cassie remembered her conversation with Hanna. Family needed to pull together after a bereavement, and Pat was going to need time and space. So perhaps, she thought, she and Uncle Frankie should talk about the process. Practical stuff like clearing the rest of Ger's things, and how to raise Pat's spirits on bad days. And how to share the task of keeping her going. Maybe they could plan some family outings to cheer her up.

Fired by the thought, she crept upstairs and found

Pat sleeping. So she left the flat quietly and went to get the car. She'd never had Frankie's number so she couldn't call to let him know she was coming, but it was still early evening so he wasn't likely to mind.

The Fitzgerald farm was on the southern side of the peninsula, where the cliffs were low and the land was most fertile. Ger had bought up neighbouring holdings, extending his property to the motorway in one direction and to the Atlantic in the other. Driving between miles of green fields Cassie was charmed by her surroundings. There was rain on the wind and sheep and lambs were sheltering against the hedges. As the watery sun began to set, the evening became chilly and, in dips in the road, Cassie's headlights pierced a drifting mist. Now and then they picked out a clump of tiny green ferns uncurling, like watch springs, against grey stones patched with white lichen. All this land now belonged to Pat. Eventually, Cassie supposed, it would come to her dad and uncles but, until then, she assumed, the farm would still be run by the manager. She couldn't see Dad or Uncle Jim developing an interest in farming.

Turning the car down the side road that led to Frankie's driveway, she wondered if her dad had ever worked in these fields when he was a boy. It didn't seem likely. The yard in Toronto was cared for by a gardener, who came each week with a mower and tools in a van; and, except for golfing, Dad never spent much time in the open air. Neither did Uncle Jim: he was always striving for weight loss but did all his bending and stretching with a personal trainer at the gym.

The gate was open so she drove between the fancy gateposts and pulled up on the gravelled sweep before the door. Frankie's wife, Fran, appeared on the steps. She was a statuesque brunette with brown eyes, long, curling lashes and the placid, benevolent air of a well-fed cow. Cassie slammed the car door and ran up the steps to greet her. Looking vaguely surprised, Fran offered her cheek for a kiss. Cassie pecked it obediently. 'Hi. Look, I'm sorry to turn up unannounced, and I hope it's not inconvenient.'

'Not at all.' Fran gestured towards the open door behind her. 'Would you like to come in?'

'Well, if you don't mind. I just thought maybe Frankie and I could talk.'

'We could sit in the conservatory, if you like.'

'Thank you. If you're sure you don't mind.'

They progressed down the hall to a vast white conservatory. On the way, as if she'd only just noticed, Fran remarked that Frankie wasn't home. Cassie felt flustered. 'Look, maybe I should come back another time.'

'No, sit down. I'll get you a vodka.'

She indicated a sofa upholstered in large chintz roses and Cassie sat down. 'Well, okay. Thanks. But I won't have a drink.'

'No?' Fran's big eyes widened. 'I always have a vodka at this time of day.' Fetching her drink from a miniature bar, she sat opposite Cassie in a vast rattan armchair. Cassie, who was wearing jeans and biker boots with a fleecy hooded sweatshirt, felt uncomfortably hot and underdressed. The conservatory was stifling, and Fran wore a flowered maxi dress with gold sandals, and a casually draped pashmina displaying her spray-tanned arms.

'So, will Frankie be home soon?'

Fran's vagueness became more pronounced. 'I never know, really. I'd say he might.' She leaned back and smiled. 'It's nice to have a visitor. Why did you say you'd come?'

'I didn't. I mean, I just said I thought we might talk. He and I. Well, you too, of course. About Pat.'

'She's very sweet, isn't she?'

'Well, yes. She is. And the thing is ... I wondered if you and Frankie and me could talk about the future.'

Fran sipped her drink carefully, as if it required concentration. Her face wore a puzzled frown. 'I'm not sure what you mean.'

'Well, just, you know, I thought we might talk about sharing things out.'

About to explain further, Cassie heard a step in the hall. Then Frankie came into the room and Fran's face rearranged itself in a smile. 'There you are! Look, Cassie's here.'

He was standing inside the arched entrance to the conservatory and, although the room faced the watery sunset, it seemed as if he'd blocked out all the light. Cassie wondered if she ought to stand up and kiss him. He didn't seem to expect it, because he crossed the room and stood by Fran's chair with his hand on her shoulder. Fran smiled up at him, saying Cassie had come round for a talk.

'Has she?' With his eyes on Cassie, he spoke to Fran. 'And you never offered the poor girl a drink?'

Fran looked hurt. 'I offered her a vodka, Frank. She said no.'

Before Cassie could say a word, Frankie went to the bar and came back with a vodka and tonic and a whiskey and soda, served in heavy cut-glass. Cassie found herself taking the vodka and tonic. It was far too strong and she put it down after the first sip.

Frankie had seated himself on the arm of Fran's chair. Again he looked at Cassie and spoke to his wife. 'And to what do we owe the honour of this unexpected visit?'

'She says she wanted to talk about sharing things out.'

For a second Frankie's eyes narrowed, but Cassie, who had plunged in to explain, didn't notice. 'What I thought was, we could talk about how we could tackle this together. I didn't want you to think I was taking over.' She stopped speaking, feeling that Frankie was looking at her strangely. Then, eager to make herself understood, she went on, 'I just wondered if maybe we ought to, well, coordinate. That's all.'

Fran smiled up at Frankie. 'That's kind, isn't it? We could do that.'

Relieved by her response, Cassie beamed at her. 'Pat loved it when we went shopping in Resolve.'

Fran looked at Frankie. 'Well, I like shopping.'

He laughed. 'I never knew a woman who didn't like spending men's money!'

Fran tittered and said he was a dreadful tease. Had the remark been made by anyone other than her uncle, Cassie would have jumped on it at once. But she was in his home, drinking his vodka, so it didn't seem the moment to call him out for dumb-ass misogyny.

Especially as Fran seemed happy to play along. 'The point is that I know you want to be there for Pat, Uncle Frankie, so I'd like to feel that you and I are a team. Fran too, obviously. You know?'

Frankie's face showed no expression. Then he knocked back his whiskey and put down the glass. 'Of course I do.'

'Great. So we'll keep in touch?'

As she reached for her phone to give Frankie her number, the atmosphere in the room still felt slightly strange. Cassie worried that what she'd said had been pompous. With a feeling that she was out of her depth, she said that her dad and Uncle Jim had wanted to stay around longer.

Keying her number into his phone, Frankie said he believed her.

Eager not to let the side down, Cassie assured him that Sonny had promised to call Pat often. 'Uncle Jim too.'

'I wouldn't doubt them.'

He handed her phone back to her and, with nothing left to be said, Cassie stood up. Frankie did too and his heavy arm swung around her shoulders. As he walked her to the door she could feel his fingers through her sweatshirt, and it struck her that he was twice the size of

Ger. Fran had remained seated in the conservatory, her beaded glass of vodka in her hand.

Cassie drove home in darkness, pulling up now and then to check the ghostly white finger posts that glimmered in the maze of country roads. When she reached the motorway she increased her speed till she came to the turn that took her back to Lissbeg. It was raining, so the streets were almost empty, but light shone from uncurtained windows, and in Broad Street music was playing in the pubs. Driving round to the rear of the shop, she left the car in the shed Ger had used as a garage, and crossed the cobbled yard to let herself in the back door, which opened onto a narrow passage. The blinds were down in the shop and, having turned the light off in the passage, she groped her way past the counter to the door at the foot of the stairs. Treading quietly, Cassie went up, thinking that, to be fair to Mary Casey, the steps were steep and the dogleg turn was awkward. There was a brave sliver of moon shining through the landing window, though; and, when she switched off the light at the top of the stairs and went into the warm kitchen, the old-fashioned lamp and the easy chairs, the seascape on the wall and the worn, scrubbed table seemed to be welcoming her home.

CHAPTER NINE

THE SUN SHONE BRILLIANTLY FOR CASSIE'S first mobile-library run. The following day, on her first shift at the salon, she described it to Margot. 'A girl from the County Library in Carrick came along to show me the ropes. That's where the van's based.'

'Where do you take it?'

'North side of the peninsula on Wednesdays. I love all the winding roads to the north, and the high cliffs beyond the forest. Don't get me wrong, the other side's cool as well. I just like the contrast.' She explained that on Fridays, when she took the southern route, her last stop of the day would be Ballyfin. 'That one's all winding roads as well, but on both days, once I've finished work, I shoot down the motorway, leave the van in Carrick and pick up my car.'

They were standing in the staff room, having met each other coming up in the lift. Cassie peered in the mirror at her fringe. 'Well, it's not actually my car. It was Ger's. Pat gave up driving ages ago. I'd hoped she'd want to take it up again, now she's on her own, but I don't know.'

'She's a bit old for that, surely? If she hasn't driven for years.'

'She's a very competent little lady under that sweet exterior. And getting out of the house would do her good. I'm trying to convince her to join the library's book club. She needs to get back in the swing of things.'

'Maybe what she needs is a bit of time.'

'Or a bit of encouragement. Like, she slotted right back into life over in Resolve. It was ages since she'd been there, but she remembered everything. The layout of all the streets and the numbers of buses. The whole thing.'

'It must have changed since her time, though?'

'Sure. Erin says it's probably doubled in size. Even the Shamrock Club's moved on a bit. Though apparently not that much!'

They went through to the salon, where Margot checked the appointments. 'The thing about a hotel salon is that guests expect us to be like room service. So we get more walk-ins than bookings. But there are some things you can anticipate. Obviously, if there's a wedding on, we know there'll be lots of updos. And hen parties often go for the whole hog – colour, perms, you name it. Then they're back next morning, hyper-ventilating, expecting you to put everything in reverse. If that happens, leave them to me. I'll put manners on them.' Margot scrolled down the screen. 'Otherwise, it's mostly wash-and-blow-dries and the occasional trim. Oh, and guys wanting cuts, but they never book.'

'And it's all guests?'

'Yeah. Even though there's times when we're practically sitting watching tumbleweed. I think it's crazy, especially in winter, because people from town would come in. But the manager's adamant. We've got to be "exclusive".'

Having dismissed the manager with air quotes, Margot suggested coffee. 'I have a lady at ten, so you'll be doing walk-ins. Sharon, the receptionist, should be here in a minute. She covers the beauty parlour as well as the salon, and her kid sister Kate is our junior. Keep the kid working – she tends to slope off.' Turning away from the computer screen, Margot grinned at Cassie. 'Let's have our coffee on the terrace. We might as well catch what sun we can, given the month that's in it, and I'll nip back in when I hear the lift.'

The terrace wrapped round two sides of the hotel's top floor and the view was spectacular. Leaning on the rail with her coffee, Cassie craned her neck to look at the mountains towering high above the little port. Beyond them were the roads she'd driven yesterday in the van, then the sparsely inhabited farmland between the ocean and Finfarran's ancient stretch of deciduous woodland, which was fringed with conifers tall as church spires. The mobile library had specific stopping places, not all of which had made immediate sense to Cassie. But she'd soon realised that a church had an adjacent hall, which hosted a day-care centre, and a guest house, which had once been a forge, owned a forecourt that accommodated the van.

Some of the villages she'd passed through had had few houses and no shop or pub. One, close to the end of her route, had a name that had caught her eye. She asked Margot about it. 'Do you know a place on the far side of the mountain called Mullafrack?'

'Well, yeah, but there's nothing there.'

'I know, but there must have been once.'

Margot shrugged. 'It's awful land that side of the mountain. There might have been people farming it way back. Not now.'

Mullafrack was where Jack Shanahan's people came from. He'd told her the name but she'd forgotten it till she saw the sign by the road.

Margot looked at her sharply. 'How come you're looking all wistful? Why did you want to know?'

'No reason.'

Burying her nose in her coffee cup, Cassie remembered the night of the farewell party. She and Jack had been sitting on the kitchen counter, taking selfies and drinking pints of Guinness. The evening was in full swing. The tables in the dining room had been pushed against the walls, Rambling Paddy had segued from 'Kathleen Mavourneen' to 'Finfarran's Forest', and most people were dancing and singing along. Through the door, Cassie could see Pat sitting chatting to Josie. As she'd watched, she'd felt a thump on her back as the club's cat leaped from a shelf and snaked down from her shoulder onto her lap. The shock made her lurch and almost spill her Guinness.

Jack had laughed and taken the glass from her hand. 'Whoa! That's a proper pint, don't waste it!'

'Yeah? Well, I'm told no one outside Finfarran can pull a proper pint.'

'Hm, pretty specific. Finfarran, not just Ireland?'

'That's what I'm told.'

He lifted the white cat from her lap. 'This guy is not allowed in the kitchen.'

Cassie scratched the cat's head. 'What's his name?'

'Pangur. He's supposed to be sixteen or something. King of the club. Descended from a cat who came here from Finfarran.'

'Seriously?'

'In the pocket of my great-great-grandfather's old frieze coat.'

'You're making it up!'

'That's the story. I've never believed it myself.'

The cat made another graceful leap, this time to the floor and, handing Cassie his glass, Jack bent to pick him up. 'Pangur always slept under the range when it was here in the kitchen. But since they remodelled he's banned, aren't you, big guy?'

When he'd turned round with the cat in his arms Cassie's heart had unaccountably lurched. At the time she'd told herself — with some truth — that she was tipsy. Now she frowned. 'Wistful' was a dumb word but, all the same, Margot was perfectly right. Ever since she'd left Resolve she'd found herself thinking of Jack. Constantly. Telling herself he wasn't her type made no difference. And what made matters worse was the fact that he hadn't seemed all that taken with her. He was friendly but not particularly attentive, and Cassie was used to making more of an impact on guys.

Carrying the cat, he'd gone into the yard and she'd followed, sobering up when the night air hit her face. She'd expected to find no more than a space for trash cans but, beyond the paving outside the kitchen, steps led up to a lawn surrounded by flowerbeds. There was a stunted apple tree in the far corner and Jack set Pangur on a bench beneath it. The cat shook himself violently and Jack grinned at Cassie. 'He's so mad now the kitchen is out of bounds.'

Cassie had put the drinks on the bench and tried to encourage the cat to allow her to pet him but, avoiding her hand, he'd leaped onto the grass and stalked off. Giving up, she'd sat by Jack and together they'd looked up at the night sky. And nothing at all had happened. He'd made some remarks about constellations and planets. She'd asked where his family had lived in Finfarran, which was when he'd told her they'd farmed in Mullafrack. 'I haven't a clue where that is, except it's somewhere near Ballyfin.'

It appeared that Ballyfin was the Shamrock Club's universal landmark. There must have been six editions of *A Long Way to LA* in the club's library, and several souvenir publications chronicling the shooting of the film. Signed posters of the book cover hung in the bar, and memorabilia from the shoot were displayed in a glass-topped case. Finishing his beer, Jack had held his glass between his knees. Then he'd stretched his arms above his head, reminding Cassie of the cat's indolent grace. She'd asked him why his people had left Finfarran.

'That I do know. Poverty. Hunger. They couldn't pay the rent, so the landlord threw them out.'

'But how could they afford to come over here?'

'Well, he wasn't a complete villain. There was some organised scheme to clear the land back in the late nineteenth century, and tenant farmers were given the price of their passage to the States. Could be they were actually given tickets, I don't know. Anyway, they had no choice, so they went. How about your folks?'

'Nothing so dramatic. My dad and his brother were raised in Lissbeg and went off to be computer nerds as soon as they left college. Like your dad is, I guess.'

'How come they went to Canada, not here?'

'My granddad knew some guy in Toronto, I think. I never asked.'

'Well, I gather my lot weren't exactly on coffin ships. But they had it hard.'

The cat had prowled back to them and Jack captured it. 'I'll take him indoors and shut him in the library. He still sleeps under the range.'

'I thought cats were put out at night, not shut in.'

'There's two schools of thought on that one. If you've got a good mouser, you might want to keep him indoors.'

'And he's a mouser?'

'I doubt if he'd bother – he's far too well fed.'

It was a pointless, inconsequential conversation, which had obscurely annoyed Cassie, though afterwards she'd taken herself to task. What more had she expected – some sort of starlit tryst? She wasn't looking for romance and, if she were, Jack Shanahan was the last guy she'd choose. There was a sedentary, comfortable quality about him that marked him out as a bore. Apparently, he'd never even left the town he'd grown up in. How could somebody his age have so little get-up-and-go? Now, she gave herself another mental reprimand. If he was such a bore, she'd better stop thinking about him.

There was a ping from the salon's reception area, and Margot hustled Cassie back inside. But the figures who emerged from the lift were Sharon, the receptionist, and her kid sister. Margot made the introductions and Cassie went through to the salon to check her chair and set out her gear. Pretty soon she was dealing with a woman who'd decided on a whim that she wanted a fringe.

'Nothing as edgy as yours, just something that makes me look like this.'

With a sinking heart Cassie took the proffered magazine and looked at a shot of Cher in a jet-black Cleopatra headdress. The woman, who had wispy fair hair and a square jaw, looked expectant. Cassie summoned professional tact, knowing as she did so that it would be wasted. 'Is it for a special occasion? Because the thing is, the hair in the shot is a wig. So maybe you could consider that as an option?'

The woman shook her wispy head. 'Oh, no, I don't think so. I'd like to go for a cut.'

'A cut and colour?'

'Well, colour might be a step too far.'

'Okay, but that does mean you won't look like the photo.'

'Oh, nonsense, dear, don't be so modest.' Thrusting the magazine into her bag, the woman sat down and beamed at Cassie in the mirror. 'This is my treat to me, and I know you'll work wonders! I can't wait to see my gorgeous new look!'

From the other side of the salon, Margot caught

Cassie's eye and made a poker face. Concealing a grin, Cassie summoned Kate to wash the woman's hair. Something told her that her first day in the salon was going to be way more stressful than driving the library van.

CHAPTER TEN

CASSIE AND ERIN HAD PROGRESSED FROM
Snapchat to Skype.

'What's the library like?'

'It's good. Taking the van around is pretty cool. So's
Hanna.'

Sitting cross-legged on her bed in PJs, Cassie
explained that today she'd driven the southern route
unaccompanied and, except for occasional glitches, it
had been wonderful. At one point, when she'd stopped
at a little two-room school, she hadn't been able to find
a book that had been on order. After a frantic search,
during which she'd knocked over the returns box, a
small boy had pointed out the book, dead centre on
a shelf at eye level. Cassie couldn't imagine how she'd
missed it. 'I guess the teacher unnerved me. She had
aggressive eyebrows.'

Erin giggled. 'But you don't just stop at schools?'

'Nope. Mainly it's parking lots. Way out in the
country. It's so gorgeous. There was misty, drizzly

rain today as I drove down to a village on the ocean, and then the sun came out and, right below me, this huge rainbow arched across the bay. Like I was in a movie. Some of the roads are awful, though. They're so narrow and you're steering between potholes. But it's so quiet. You can travel for miles and not see a single soul.'

'Spooky.'

'No, it's beautiful. Hanna says the hedgerows are full of wildflowers in summer. Right now they're kind of stark, a bit *Wuthering Heights*, but if you look closely there's a haze of pale green on all the bushes. Little leaf buds just beginning to appear. And the fields are full of lambs with squeaky high-pitched voices. It's really cute.'

'You can see and hear all that when you're driving?'

'No, but I do stop to eat.'

The sun had been out today when she'd taken her lunch break sitting on the step of the van by a ruined church. It was a tiny, roofless building, which, according to a nearby notice board, was nearly a thousand years old. Ferns were sprouting in the stonework round the entrance and the remains of a bird's nest were perched above the door. Sticks and tufts of dry moss had fallen from the forsaken nest to the threshold. Behind the building was a little graveyard where grey headstones stood at drunken angles among rough grass.

Erin's eyes widened. 'Oh, my God! That really is spooky.'

'No, it wasn't. It was cool. Like I was the only person left in the world.' Cassie rolled onto her stomach and adjusted her laptop against the piled-up pillows. 'Actually, no, it was better than that. Like being a Pack Horse Library woman back in the nineteen thirties.'

'Being what?'

'It was a thing. Part of the New Deal.'

'President Roosevelt?'

'Yeah. Probably. I've only seen photographs. You'll get it online if you google it. I think they went into the Kentucky Mountains. On horseback. Women with big saddlebags full of books. I guess it happened in other places too, not just Kentucky. They forded creeks and rode through storms with their feet frozen in the stirrups. And they wore long slickers and really cool nineteen-thirties hats.'

'Awesome.'

'It felt just like that. Me against the wilderness.'

Twenty minutes later she'd been parked beside a post office with a sign that read 'Wi-Fi Available' but, as she'd eaten her lunchtime sandwich, she had felt as if the church was some abandoned frontier dwelling and the graveyard full of the bones of pioneers.

Erin giggled again. 'Yeah, right.'

'Okay, that's a bit extreme. But, you know, people here are so grateful for the mobile-library service. I suppose it provides a social event as well as books and stuff.'

'How d'you mean?'

'Well, a gathering place. Especially for seniors. I see them hanging out after they've done the library thing. They combine it with a trip to pick up their pension or go for a coffee. Sometimes they just sit on a wall and chat. Moms with toddlers too. I guess it gets them out of the house.'

'Beats going to the gym.'

'Especially if you're ancient. I don't know, though – Hanna says the library did Read and Stretch sessions last year.'

'How the hell did that work?'

'I didn't ask. Touch your toes at the end of every chapter? She said the seniors piled in.'

'If it was my gran, it'd have to be something way less energetic.'

'Yeah, but that's the point, isn't it? According to Hanna, librarians keep an ear to the ground and respond to what's required. Someone comes in and suggests something and, if it makes sense and there's enough interest, she goes with the flow.'

Erin asked if Pat had liked the photos of the party.

'She loved them. I'm going to have one of her and Josie printed and put in a frame.'

'Gran was so excited to see her. Mom, too. It's crazy to think that the first time Pat met my mom was at the funeral.'

'Transatlantic travel used to cost a fortune.'

'Gran said that, when she came here, it cost a fortune just to make a phone call. She'd fix a time, like making a hair appointment. And she worried so much about the money she couldn't think what to say.'

'Wow.'

'Like, you and I can Skype without even thinking about it. But Gran used to save her wages up to afford a phone call home.'

'Imagine if you couldn't talk to your friends or family for months!'

'Crazy. And no email.'

'No Internet!'

'Just women in great hats carrying library books on horseback.'

Cassie grinned. 'I don't think Pat and Josie go back that far.'

Erin's face on the screen was thoughtful. 'Still, it's kind of sad that they hadn't met for ages and then they only hung out for a couple of weeks.'

They chatted back and forth a bit longer, and Cassie wondered if Erin had seen Jack lately. But, since she didn't know her well, she didn't like to ask. Anyway, it could be that Erin only knew him from the Shamrock Club, and Cassie had gathered that neither went there often. Most members appeared to be well over fifty, and anyone younger seemed only to be there because they'd been drummed up for a special occasion. So perhaps Erin hadn't seen Jack since the night of the farewell party.

She blinked, aware that her mind had drifted, and Erin laughed. 'You look like you're ready to sleep! What time is it over there?'

'Coming up to midnight and I had a long day.'

'Well, the night's still young in New York State and I'm going out to a classy restaurant.'

'Good for you.'

'I hope so. I've known him for ever and this is our first proper date.' Erin squinted at her own face in the corner of her computer screen, tugging critically at her long, fair hair. 'And you know what? I should be in the shower. Not sitting in my bathrobe talking to you.'

'Okay. Go. Have a good one.'

'I'll try. You get some sleep. Give my love to Pat.'

'Sure. Say hi to your gran and your mom for me. And let me know how the date goes.' Cassie closed her laptop, looking thoughtful. It was stupid to think that Erin's date might be Jack, and even dumber to want to hear that it wasn't. But that's how she was feeling. Which, she told herself crossly, was the stupidest thing of all.

When she got into bed she imagined she'd sleep as soon as her head hit the pillow. Instead her thoughts went round in circles, moving from her conversation with Erin to her day's trip in the van. At a stopping point that afternoon she'd encountered a woman who'd said she knew Erin's gran. 'Oh, my God, Josie Cox! I was at school with her. Mind, she was older than me but I knew her well. My dad and Josie's would give us lifts from Lissbeg. She married a lad called Fenton and settled down in the States and she never came back. She would have been a cousin of Pat's.'

'We stayed with her family when we were in Resolve.'

'God, I'd love a chance to meet up again with Josie! Actually, there's a rake of people I know over there. I'd send them a card at Christmas, say, and that's about the height of it. And I wouldn't be alone. The American post is a big thing here around Christmas. Well, for my generation anyway. It might be dying out.'

Cassie turned over in bed and tried to settle more comfortably. She remembered the woman's smile as she'd received her latest library book. The middle-aged daughter who'd been with her had placed it in her bag and winked. 'That's Mam set for the week with Catherine Cookson for company.'

Her mother had given her a shove. 'And isn't it better than sitting in front of the telly watching *Celebrity Something or Other*? Anyway, I do hate turning the telly off at bedtime. It brings it home to you that there's no voice in the house.' Then, seeing the look on her daughter's face, she'd turned to Cassie. 'Not that the family isn't great, coming in and keeping me company. And it's I that's insisted I want to keep my own roof over my head. Anyway, isn't it great to have winter behind us? There's a grand stretch in the evenings now, and fewer dark days.'

Cassie wondered how Erin was going to wear her hair on the date. American girls went in for long, flowing tresses. Lots of volumiser. Pushing her own hair off her forehead, she thought she might change the colour of her fringe. Metallic bronze, maybe. Or subtle streaks of silver. She'd anticipated that Margot might say her fringe was a bit out there for the salon, but Margot had been cool. Not like the manager on her last ship who'd said that Florida matrons wouldn't want a stylist looking like Björk. And he'd turned out to be wrong. Half the ladies on their way to gamble in the Bahamas had been a lot livelier than he'd thought. That was the thing about older people: far too many idiots wrote them off.

Rearranging her pillows, she looked at the clock by the bed. If she didn't get to sleep soon, she knew she'd be dozy tomorrow. It wouldn't matter, since it was the weekend, but she'd planned to see if Pat fancied a jaunt. Having visited Uncle Frankie's house, she'd imagined she'd touch base with him about that sort of thing from now on. Perhaps she ought to give him a call in the morning. But that might seem pushy. After all, Pat was his mom and – hang on – he, too, must be grieving for Ger, who, after all, was his dad. Feeling troubled, Cassie wriggled up against the pillows. Had it been insensitive to talk about Pat's loss and not even mention his?

Cringing at the thought, she turned her mind back to Erin, who was probably at the restaurant now, looking great in a gauzy dress and gladiator sandals. Erin had a pick-me-up-and-take-care-of-me quality. Nothing like a Catherine Cookson heroine. More like Cate Blanchett in *The Lord of the Rings*.

Determined to make herself drowsy, she set herself the task of matching the *Lord of the Rings* actors to their characters. Cate Blanchett as Galadriel. Liv Tyler as Arwen. Orlando Bloom as Legolas. Viggo Thing as Aragorn. This was rather good, like counting sheep. Ian McKellen (or was it McKellern?) as Gandalf. Elijah Wood was Frodo. Sean Bean was the guy in the huge cloak. Though they all had those. Huge black cloaks and filthy fingernails. Boromir! That was Sean Bean ...

Vaguely trying to list all the hobbits, Cassie found herself slipping satisfactorily towards sleep. Then, just as she drifted off, her eyes opened and she sat bolt upright, gripped by an idea. She knew exactly what was needed to take Pat out of herself, and it wasn't just a common-or-garden, run-of-the-mill book club.

CHAPTER ELEVEN

SATURDAY MORNINGS IN THE LIBRARY tended to be noisy. People who came to Lissbeg to shop dropped in to return or borrow books and stayed to chat with each other. When Hanna first took up her post she'd battled for months to maintain a conventional level of silence, gaining a dragon's reputation in the process. But the new reading room, with its sliding door and soundproof glass wall, had solved the problem. Those seeking peace and quiet could make use of it while their neighbours were more convivial in the hall. And that wasn't all. The state-of-the-art exhibition space was designed to house a medieval psalter gifted by a donor who'd also funded the library's renovations. So the reading room was expensively equipped with blackout blinds and a projector, and a screen that still gave Hanna a thrill whenever she hit the button to lower it from the ceiling.

The only downside was the effect of the sliding door on Darina's children. Setanta confined himself to creating sticky handprints on the glass, but Gobnit, if left unsupervised, would swing from the brushed-steel handle, using her weight to open and close the door. Today they were doing nothing worse than popping out from the shelving, making faces. Darina, who was selecting CDs, was oblivious to their antics, and everyone else appeared to find them amusing, though Hanna knew from experience that the mood could change in an instant if the children became too obstreperous, and that she'd be expected to cope, since their mother couldn't.

Darina was a tall woman, originally a blow-in from Dublin, with a high-pitched voice and a laugh like a horse's neigh. Mary Casey frequently dismissed her style as 'mutton dressed as lamb'. No one could argue with the description, but the tie-dyed smocks worn with Lycra leggings, and the hennaed hair braided with beads, appeared to Hanna, on her charitable days, to be brave as well as pathetic. Under Darina's assurance lurked a great deal of perimenopausal panic: she'd never really found her feet among her Finfarran neighbours, though her husband had made a group of breezy friends in Carrick's exclusive golf club. Now, as she approached the desk, her expensive scent contrasted oddly with her stringy hand-knitted scarf and paint-stained fingers. Remembering that her latest fad was art classes, Hanna enquired how they were going.

Darina looked troubled. 'I'm not actually sure that I've found my *métier*. Well, you know yourself I've a wonderful eye for colour. But perhaps my real canvas is my home and my own person.' She frowned at a splodge of Cadmium Lemon on her forefinger. 'Oils aren't easy, Hanna. But I did forget the primer, of course, and that was part of the problem. And landscapes are notoriously tricky for Leos and I'm on the cusp. Anyway, Gormfhlaith – she's my mentor – suggested I might seek out a different medium. So I think I'll step back from the course for a while. Well, she thought I should.'

Keeping a straight face, Hanna said that sounded wise.

'Do you think so? I do. I *really* think it's important to let one's juices flow organically.'

Gobnit was edging towards the reading-room door, so Hanna held out her hand for the CDs. 'Is that everything, Darina? Because I'll need your library card.'

'Oh, God, of course you will. I'm sorry!' Darina rooted madly in her bag before giving up and tipping its contents onto Hanna's desk. 'I have it here, I know I have.'

Hanna rescued an iPhone and an orange, which was

rolling towards her in-tray. 'I think yours is a keyring tag.'

'It is! You're right! You're absolutely right! And my keys are in my purse. Or, at least, they should be.'

As Darina searched wildly for her purse, Hanna noticed a library book in the pile of miscellaneous possessions strewn across her desk. It was a copy of E. B. White's *Charlotte's Web*. Picking it up, she saw it was weeks overdue. Darina's hand flew to her mouth in horror. 'Oh, no! *That's* where it was. I've been looking for it for ever. But you know me, head like a sieve and *so* much to contend with!'

'It's not a problem.'

'No, it is! I'm such a silly mare. But I could swear I searched my bag and it wasn't in it.'

The children were now watching from behind the shelving and Hanna suspected that *Charlotte's Web* had not been in the bag when Darina had searched for it. Directing a repressive glance at the two pixie faces, she said again that it really wasn't a problem. 'It's here now, so there's no need to worry.'

'Yes, but the fine.' Darina spotted her purse and made a pounce for it. 'I must owe you a fortune.'

Hanna replied that overdue children's books incurred no fines. It was something she'd told Darina more times than she could remember yet, once again, it produced a squeal of astonishment. '*Really?* How extraordinary!'

Fast losing any sense of charitable sympathy, Hanna explained again that this was a long-standing policy. 'And, actually, the entire fines system has been abolished. Though your membership card can be blocked if overdue books aren't returned.' She had explained this repeatedly too, and put up prominent signs about it, but it always took ages for people to grasp new systems.

The young woman behind Darina said it was more than time for the change. 'Fines only encouraged me not to bring books back at all.' Making a mental note to check her records, Hanna refrained from comment. An elderly man towards the back of the queue announced it was just as well that there was still some deterrent. The woman looked at him blankly. 'How d'you mean?'

'You'd have to have a proper deterrent or else we'll be facing a crime wave.'

'At that rate, you might as well advocate hanging.'

'For not returning a library book?'

'I never said that.'

A spotty boy chipped in: 'Well, that's what you

find at the end of the road when you get obsessed with deterrents.'

A middle-aged council official turned on the boy pompously. 'Hold your horses there, now. It's clear you're a stranger to logic.'

'As a matter of *fact* …'

With great relief, Hanna saw that Darina had found her keyring. Having checked out the CDs, she turned to the returns trolley, giving the book an automatic shake before setting it down. A bookmark fluttered from between the pages and spiralled to the floor, landing at the feet of the elderly man. As he bent down to retrieve it, Darina gave an embarrassed squeal and snatched it out of his hand. It was a voucher for a herbal product guaranteed to control hot flushes. Behind the shelving, the children burst into hysterical laughter, Gobnit leading and Setanta joining in without knowing why.

'*That*'s where this went to! *Gobnit!*' Grasping at dignity, Darina swept her possessions into her bag and marched out, hustling the children ahead of her. As soon as the door closed behind them, the queue began to discuss alternative medicine. There was no point in attempting to interrupt them, so Hanna decided to sit back and enjoy it. The personal anecdotes were riveting and at least the queue had abandoned the row about bringing back capital punishment.

A little later, when things were quiet, Hanna's thoughts strayed to a story she'd told Cassie. It was about a Scottish librarian who'd thought she'd uncovered evidence of a crime. 'She worked in a library in Dundee. And, one day, a reader asked her why the number seven was marked on page seven of all the books she took out. It was underlined in pencil.'

'In every book?'

'In each one this woman had chosen to borrow. She was a sweet little old lady. Probably had a blue rinse.'

'We had a library on a cruise ship I worked on, and half the books were romances set in World War Two. Which was probably the heyday of most of the female passengers. I spent that cruise up to my ears in blue rinse. So, what happened to the Dundee librarian?'

'She decided there was another Zodiac Killer on the loose. You know the Californian serial murderer? The one obsessed with cryptic numerology?'

'No.'

'It was a big case in the late 1960s. They never made an arrest, so this librarian got spooked. She'd gone through every book in the genre and they'd all had the same cryptic mark on page seven so she smelt a rat.

Maybe a new murderer. Maybe the one who'd escaped detection had come to live in Scotland. Maybe it was a case of espionage, or an international plot.'

'So what did she do? Call the police?'

'No, she had a bit of sense and told her supervisor. And then she discovered the secret of the Elderly Readers' Codes.'

Cassie had grinned at Hanna's dramatic pause. 'Okay. I'll bite. What was it?'

'Well, you're quite right. Some readers like to stick to a single genre. And ladies of a certain age do tend to gravitate towards World War Two romance. Authors like Ellie Dean, say, or Lizzie Lane. These days we've got digital filing systems, which link a person's library card to the books they've already borrowed, so you can check with your librarian if you're wondering whether or not you've already read a particular book. But the generation we're talking about predates digital filing. And before it came in, lots of people invented systems of their own.'

'But if you'd read a book wouldn't you remember it?'

'Maybe not if you only read one kind of book. So you devise a code.'

'That's amazing.'

'It's also defacement. But I do think it's charming and, apparently, it happens all over the world.'

'Even here?'

'A bit. There's one bedridden old lady who sends her husband to borrow books for her. Whenever she reads a novel, she puts a tiny star in the top left-hand corner of the title page, so he knows which books to avoid.'

'That is so sweet.'

'I can't be seen to encourage it, but it's a case for using discretion. I'm not going to interfere.'

'Not even to tell him she doesn't need to do it?'

'No, because it gives them a sense of control at a time when life is getting difficult. Anyway, no one wants to be told what they need, or how they ought to do things, and elderly people are just like anyone else.'

It struck Hanna that Darina's unfortunate bookmark was yet another instance of the importance of discretion in its other sense. The most unlikely personal revelations occurred in libraries, and in a small community it mattered greatly that, whoever else might gossip about them, readers could feel confident that library staff would not.

As Saturday morning ticked away, Hanna began to look forward to sitting down with a book herself. She'd planned to do some early seasonal clearing in the garden, but the weather suggested an afternoon indoors. With a pleasurable sense of the week winding down, she wondered if she might bake a cake and have tea by the fire. Then, as she finished her final tasks, the door swung open and Cassie bounded in, followed by Pat.

Cassie came to rest by Hanna's desk. 'I've had an idea!'

Pat intervened: 'Yes, but, Hanna, love, I've told Cassie it mightn't be something you'd want. I mean we can't just come barging in with some mad proposal.'

'It's not mad, it's sensible. And what's not to like?' Cassie's eyes were bright with excitement behind her flying fringe. She planted her hands on Hanna's desk and leaned towards her. 'You said you couldn't go round telling people what they needed, older people especially, that's what you said.'

'Yes, I did.'

'And you told me you couldn't demand that people turn up to clubs and things if they weren't inclined. It was a matter of keeping an ear to the ground, you said, and responding to what was required.'

'I know I did but, Cassie, what's this about?'

'Well, I've talked to Pat and she says she's sure people will turn up.'

'But you mustn't feel pressured.' Pat touched Hanna's hand earnestly.

Cassie was as tense as a fiddle string. 'And half of them won't have seen each other for ages. Oh, come on, Hanna, say we can have one.'

'For pity's sake, Cassie! Have *what*?'

For a moment the bright face under the peacock fringe looked astonished. Then Cassie laughed. 'Oh, of course, I haven't said, but wait till you hear! It's terrific. A transatlantic book club, that's what!'

CHAPTER TWELVE

CASSIE AND MARGOT WERE SITTING IN THE staff room at the salon.

'I talked to Erin after I cleared it with Hanna, and she's all for it.'

'But what's a transatlantic book club?'

'Well, just what it says. You set it up with members on both sides of the ocean. And you use Skype.'

Margot frowned. 'How? Everyone sits at home in front of their computers?'

'No, because the point is to make it communal. So, over here it's going to be based in the library, and over there they'll be in the Shamrock Club.'

'Right.'

'Well, we're calling it a dual-library thing but, really, the one in the Shamrock Club is just a room full of books.' She'd talked it all through with Erin, whose gran had got in touch with the club committee. 'The president or chairman, or whatever he is, was so up for it. And Erin emailed this morning to say the committee has waved it through, so we're good to go.'

'Hang on, let me get this right. Everyone gathers in the two venues at a certain time of day?'

'Exactly. Round lunchtime in Resolve, seven p.m. in Lissbeg.'

'And what? There's one computer?'

'One on each side of the ocean. With the image shown on two big screens. All that's needed is the Skype connection, plus a little camera and a microphone pointed at the group in each venue. And people just sit round in chairs, like a regular book club.'

'So, what'll they see on the screens?'

'It'll be like an ordinary Skype session. The group in Lissbeg will see the Resolve lot and vice versa. It should feel like two sides of a circle having a chat.'

'Won't people interrupt each other?'

'Probably. But they do that at any book club. And we'll have two facilitators – one here and one there.'

As soon as Hanna had grasped the idea, she'd said she'd be happy to facilitate the group in Lissbeg. She could set up the technical side of things too, and the reading room with its large screen would be the perfect venue.

Margot asked who'd do the facilitation in Resolve. Cassie shook her head. 'I'm not sure. They haven't got a librarian. Like I said, it's just a room full of books. Erin said they'd find someone.'

'And is Pat pleased?'

'She kind of wavered at first, but she does that. It was the same when I suggested that we take the trip to Resolve. But it's so not complicated.'

'How about the technical side over there?'

Though she hoped Margot wouldn't notice, the question made Cassie uncomfortable. Someone in Resolve would have to set up the camera and make sure the sound worked, so Jack might well be co-opted again by the club. But she hadn't been able to ask Erin about it. Not while she didn't know whether or not Jack had been Erin's date. It should have been easy to throw in a casual question about the restaurant. Had the meal been good? How had things gone? And, by the way, what was the guy's name? Yet she hadn't been able to find the right words, so she still didn't know if it had been Jack, which made her shrink from mentioning him to Margot. If she did, Margot would want to know all about him, and striking the right nonchalant note might be hard. The fact was that she still wasn't sure how she felt about Jack Shanahan. All she knew was she felt a tingle whenever his name came up. Daft, she told herself crossly, but there it was.

Fortunately Margot's next appointment had arrived. Cassie's shift had begun with two wash-and-blow-dries and a man who'd just wanted his beard trimmed. Margot and the girls in the beauty parlour had appointments through to lunchtime, and she was covering walk-ins to the salon. Now she debated whether to stay indoors with a magazine or to wander onto the terrace where the sun was glinting on pools left by last night's rain. The outdoors won hands down over the windowless staff room, so she crossed the highly polished parquet, indicating to Sharon that she was just stepping outside.

Leaning on the balcony rail, Cassie looked out at the ocean. There was little wind today and hardly any foam on the waves. Down in the marina the vessels rocked gently at their moorings. Among them was a small cruise ship painted in sparkling white and navy blue. Cassie reckoned it could carry about a hundred and fifty passengers, far fewer than her own last ship. Its shallow draft was designed to access small bays and communities, and she guessed it was on its way round Ireland, having already visited the Scandinavian fjords. The chances were that Ballyfin would be worth no more than an overnight, and that the schedule would include a Finfarran coach tour. Probably that would amount to a straight dash up and down the motorway, with shopping in Carrick and the option of a set dinner here at the hotel.

Remembering the rambling byways and the stunning views from the mountains, Cassie pitied the passengers, though, no doubt, they felt they were having a great time. And Carrick had plenty to interest visitors. Unlike Lissbeg, which had started out as the focus for cattle-dealing, it had grown up at the feet of an imposing Anglo-Norman castle. There was an early medieval cathedral, an old granite courthouse and a park where you could imagine Jane Austen's ladies taking the air. But its shopping streets were crowded with computer stores and sports outlets, and its slightly dilapidated Georgian squares and long Victorian terraces were cramped by ribbon development and out-of-town malls.

It also had the legendary Royal Victoria Hotel, an imposing building set in a terrace off Main Street. A curved flight of granite steps led to double doors with gleaming brass fittings – Cassie and Pat had been there on Sunday for tea. It could be had in the Royal Vic's conservatory but Pat said that the lounge was the better choice for the time of year. As they'd driven through heavy rain along the motorway, she'd told Cassie that, with luck, the hotel might even have lit its fires. And she'd been right. A large fire had been burning in the entrance hall, stoked from a shining coal scuttle and flanked by urns of dried flowers. Beyond it was the bar, approached through an archway, and at the far end of the bar was the lounge, where they'd found a table and two velvet chairs by another crackling fire.

As the waiter arrived with a laden tray, Pat had exclaimed at the sight of the cake. 'You're going to love the Sachertorte! It's been their speciality for years.'

'Is this someplace you and Ger used to come to?'

'Ah, no, love. Ger wasn't one for an outing.'

'So did you come here on dates with other guys back when you were young?'

'Ah, no, love. Mary and Tom used to come here to dinner dances. And Mary and I drop in still for tea when we're in town. I wasn't one to go dating in my young days.'

'You mean Ger was the only guy you ever went out with?'

Pat was inspecting the sandwiches with a smile. 'Do you know what it is, you're a dote to have thought of this book club. Did Erin say who's joining up in Resolve?'

'Well, it's early days, but her gran and her mom are in. And the chairlady of the quilting guild.'

'Mrs Shanahan?'

'I guess so.' It had felt as if each conversation she had always came back to that name, and the way Pat said it had seemed kind of weird. To avoid meeting her eyes, Cassie had reached for the milk jug. When she'd looked up, Pat had been adding boiling water to the teapot.

Now, as she leaned on the balcony rail, Cassie heard a ping from the lift and saw a man approaching the reception desk. As she left the terrace and went inside, her thoughts were still in Carrick. Had she and Pat been fencing with each other over the teacups, each unwilling to be drawn because both had something to conceal?

When she reached the desk the guy turned to face her. He was thirty or so, not tall but very tanned and handsome, with hair that looked as if he had it trimmed every week. He wore a well-cut business suit over a crisp shirt with an open collar. Sharon introduced them. 'This is Cassie. She'll take care of you. Cassie, this is Mr Miller. He just wants a trim.'

When he spoke it was in an American accent and, unlike a lot of clients, he held out his hand. 'Bradley Miller. Call me Brad.'

Cassie shook his hand and smiled back, deciding he was probably good for a fairly decent tip. She'd been a bit startled when she'd found that tipping wasn't an Irish thing or, anyway, not at the rates she was used to. But, as Margot had said, the Spa Hotel catered mostly to foreigners, and this guy looked a likely fifteen per cent.

As soon as his hair was washed, she settled him in the chair at her station. He smiled at her in the mirror. 'So where's home?'

'Toronto. How about you?'

'California. But I travel a lot.'

'Do you?' She ran her fingers through his hair, which was dark brown and sun-streaked, and asked him how much he wanted cut.

'Just smarten me up – don't scalp me.'

Some clients made it plain that they preferred her to work in silence but this guy seemed to expect a chat, which was fine with Cassie, who always found strangers interesting. She straightened the chair and asked if he travelled for his job.

'I work on cruise ships.'

'Wow, really? So do I.'

He raised his eyebrows at her in the mirror and she laughed. 'Well, not right now, obviously. But a lot. Is that your ship in the marina?'

'The *Wave Charmer*, that's her.'

'Cool name. So what do you do?'

The fact that he was staying in the hotel didn't suggest that he swabbed the decks. He shrugged.

'Itineraries, that sort of thing. Liaison with local tourist offices. Scoping places out.' It was an American cruise line, called Your World Awaits, he explained, and he'd worked for it since graduating college.

'So it must be good?'

'Yeah. The ships are small and the teams are really tight. Great people.'

But presumably he preferred to spend a night or two ashore. Of course, you might want some time away from your team when your ship was small. 'I don't know that I'd care to stick with just one line.'

'Well, I guess you like variety, since you're here.'

Cassie laughed. 'Obviously.'

'So, what, you got washed up by the tide? Or you're in Ireland to find your ancestors?'

'What makes you think it's either?'

'Well, it's usually one or the other. Sorry, I don't mean to pry.'

'No, that's okay. I have family here.' Cassie, who'd been wielding her scissors, picked up the mirror. 'Is that good, or do you like more off?'

He swung the chair, considering the back of his head, before he grinned and said he'd leave it up to her. 'It's really no big deal so long as it dries before I'm out of the gym.'

It was evident when he'd taken his jacket off that he worked out. Guys on the ships often did. The equipment was usually top notch and staff were allowed to use it. He wasn't insanely muscly, though, just fit.

'I'll take a bit more off, then, and you'll just have to towel it dry.'

As she worked, they chatted about the cruises she'd been on, and the talk suddenly made her miss the sea. When she'd come to Finfarran with Pat and Ger she hadn't intended to stay beyond the new year, and now she wasn't sure when she'd get away. Being stuck in one place had never been part of her life plan, which had always involved moving on to the next exciting thing. Yet recently she'd been half thinking of turning round and going back to Resolve. What was that about? Some vague urge to pick up where she and Jack had left off? But that was crazy, because there was nothing there to go back to. Nothing at all. Far better to find a new ship and return to the life she loved. Meeting Brad's eyes in the mirror again, she felt a rush of the old excitement that had first made her up sticks and leave home. Perhaps Fate had sent her someone who'd give her a few pointers. She'd never taken a ship to Scandinavia, but maybe, when Pat was settled and seemed happier, she'd pack her things and do just that.

CHAPTER THIRTEEN

THE FIRST MEETING OF THE TRANS-
atlantic Book Club was to be an inaugural discussion.
On Tuesday morning, with the Skype link yet to be
set up, it was clear that texts and phone calls were
producing mounting interest in Resolve. In Finfarran
Cassie had put an announcement on the Edge of
the World website, which was both a community
noticeboard and a tool to showcase the peninsula to
tourists. Within a few hours of the posting, Ferdia, the
website's administrator, rang the library to say he'd had
lots of enquiries. Cassie, who took the call, was elated,
Hanna less so. Lacking a book as a point of focus, the
meeting might be hard to manage if it turned out to
be large. But she reminded herself that enquiries didn't
guarantee attendance. It was easy to click on a website
but harder to put on your coat and go out if the evening
happened to be cold.

Ferdia, who worked in the management office
of the Old Convent Centre, had offered to oversee

the Skype set-up. As the equipment belonged to the county council, Hanna was glad to have it done by a full-time employee. He rambled into the library at lunchtime, saying he might sign up for the club himself. 'Though your interface could be a lot more sophisticated.'

Hanna laughed and led him through to the reading room. 'A Skype link will be just fine, so long as the blessed thing works.'

'Well, it's not exactly rocket science. You'll be grand in here, and I'll come and plug things up around six. Do you want to give me a contact for my oppo in Resolve?'

Hanna looked at Cassie, who'd followed them to the doorway. At first Cassie appeared unsure but then she and Ferdia sat down in a huddle over her phone. Leaving them to it, Hanna went back to her desk. She'd hardly reached it when her own phone bleeped. It was Mary Casey announcing her interest in the club: PAT SAYS UV AN INTERNET YOKE WITH THE YANKS8 ILL BE IN WITH HER

Hanna glared at the screen. Mary had been told a hundred times not to text her at the library but no amount of telling seemed to work. Her only response was to draw horrific word pictures of all that could go wrong if Hanna's phone was turned off. 'I could be stretched dead at the foot of a staircase.'

'You live in a bungalow, Mam, so that's hardly likely.'

'I could turn my knee in the street and be whipped into hospital.'

'Well, if you are, you'll be in good hands.'

'Holy God Almighty, that I reared a heartless daughter!'

'Oh, for Heaven's sake! If you fell in the street half the town would come into the library to let me know. Anyway, why should you fall?'

'You'll be old yourself one day, Hanna-Mariah Casey.'

'Don't call me Hanna-Mariah. And don't try to change the subject. You're as fit as a flea, and you know you always have been.'

After each row Hanna would get remorseful and try to explain that emergency texts would be fine. 'I won't turn my phone off if you'll promise not to text me unless you have to.'

Boot-faced and resentful, Mary would promise, and the following day a text would arrive declaring she'd bought a biro, or denouncing the postman for failing to shut the gate. The constant interruptions weren't appropriate in a workplace, yet Hanna always felt worried when her phone was off. What if this were to be the one day when something terrible happened?

Now, as she hesitated, the phone bleeped again: MAKE SURE YOU KEEP ME %GOOD SEAT YOU CAN DRIVE ME HOME AFTER

Stabbing the shutdown icon, Hanna cursed under her breath. Then, looking up, she found Pat standing by the desk. 'I thought I'd just drop in, love, and say how excited I am about tonight.' Pat nodded at the phone. 'Texts from Mary?'

'How did you know?'

'I had one myself this morning, saying she'll be coming to the club.'

Hanna struggled to regain a professional mindset. 'Well, I hope she'll enjoy it.'

'Do you know what it is? I often think it must be hard to be Mary Casey's child.'

As Pat was the soul of discretion the comment surprised Hanna. Pat gave her a slightly woebegone smile. 'I suppose it's one reason I've always tried not to put too much pressure on Frankie. You don't want your child cringing every time you call.'

'Well, I wouldn't say I cringe, exactly …'

'Of course you wouldn't, love, and I didn't mean to

suggest it. But no one can deny that Mary is demanding. God knows I've told her so more than once.'

Hanna laughed. 'So have I, but I'd say we've been wasting our breath.'

'Ah, well, sure we're all as God made us.' Pat paused, looking thoughtful. 'You know, that was a saying my mother had and I've always just repeated it like a parrot. But sometimes I wonder if it's not God that makes us the way we are. It's what life throws at us.' She looked at Hanna and her expression changed. 'You're thinking your mam had nothing much thrown at her.'

'Well, my dad did tend to wrap her up in cotton wool.'

'That's true, but you know, love, we all have our troubles. Not that Mary isn't a lucky woman to have a daughter like you.'

'You wouldn't say so if you could hear what I've been calling her mentally since I saw those texts!'

'Ah, Mary is Mary. You'd have to be a saint not to call her a cow the odd time in your head.'

*

Cassie had given Ferdia Erin's details as his contact in Resolve. So, unsurprisingly, when the Skype connection was established, Erin's was the first face to appear on the big screen in Lissbeg. The camera wasn't yet properly angled and, as her image settled, Jack's voice could be heard from out of frame. Then the angle shifted and Cassie found herself looking straight into his eyes. They were even more startlingly blue than she'd remembered but his face creased into the same lazy, lopsided smile. 'Hey, Cassie. How's it going?'

'Great. Uh, fine. How are you?'

'I'm good. This is some crazy idea.'

'Well, yeah ... I ... it's nice that you're on board.'

Erin appeared beside him and waved. 'He couldn't avoid it. His mom and me kicked his ass.'

Before Cassie could process this, Jack and Ferdia were fiddling with the cameras, checking that all the seating was in shot. Anticipating a turnout of about a dozen, Cassie and Hanna had laid out three rows of chairs in the reading room. The Shamrock Club must have come to the same conclusion because a similar number of chairs were set in front of the bookcases, with their carved wreaths of shamrocks and gilded donors' names. On one chair, comfortably curled against a cushion, Pangur the white cat was fast asleep. The domesticity of the club's library, with the Brennan memorial range standing in the background, contrasted sharply with Lissbeg's high-tech reading room, but the equipment there was just as good as Ferdia's, and the crowd beginning to arrive in Resolve was dressed in the height of fashion.

In Lissbeg, the first arrival was Pat. She was closely followed by Mary, who marched down to the front row and sat dead centre, where Pat joined her. They were both wearing their best coats, and Pat had washed her hair. Even though the evening had turned chilly, the room was filling up, and everyone appeared to have made an effort to look their best. It seemed that, on both sides of the ocean, people were treating this as a special occasion.

As Cassie slipped into a seat at the back, Mr Maguire strode into the room, with a lordly nod at Hanna. He was carrying a rolled umbrella, which he stood in a corner by the screen, nearly disrupting Ferdia's snaking cables. Then, obviously annoyed by Mary's commanding position, he went and sat on a chair by the door, as if expecting some pressing summons to a more important commitment.

The chairs over in the Shamrock Club were filling well. Like Cassie, Erin was seated towards the back. Jack was invisible, presumably manning the computer. Cassie wondered if Erin had helped him rig the screen and organise the equipment. His mother, a well-dressed, good-looking woman, came in and sat in the same row as Erin. But not next to her. The empty seats between them made Cassie feel better, and now they were claimed by two large men. Seeing them appear on the screen, Mary announced that they must be the Canny twins. Pat shushed her covertly. Minutes later, as Erin's mom and her gran, Josie, arrived, Pat herself squeaked aloud in happy recognition. The sound refocused Cassie's thoughts, reminding her of why she was here. Tonight was all about pleasing Pat, and Jack Shanahan's presence was irrelevant.

The majority of the seats in both venues were now occupied, and Hanna glanced at the clock. At that moment the door slid open and Darina Kelly edged in holding Gobnit by the hand. The entire room turned at the sound of the sliding door, and the group in Resolve, who had watched it open, craned forward to look at her. Darina froze in the doorway, mouthing regrets at Hanna. 'Too dreadful, I'm *so* late and I'm *dreadfully* sorry, but Gobnit got really difficult so I had to bring her along.'

Gobnit, who was wearing a Shaun the Sheep onesie, was clutching her mother's iPhone. Cassie could see people in Resolve asking each other who Darina was.

Slipping out of her own chair, she piloted the pair towards a couple of empty seats. Gobnit immediately slumped in her chair and focused her attention on a game she'd been playing on the phone. Darina remained standing. 'I feel so terrible, honestly, everyone. Do please forgive me. Is this where I should be looking, Ferdia? Is this the camera? Oh, and there you all are, over on the other side of the ocean! So lovely, and here I've kept you waiting!'

Hanna moved to the front and smiled at the faces on the screen. 'Hello, everyone. I'm Hanna Casey, Lissbeg's librarian, and it's a pleasure to be here on this very special occasion. I'm sure you'll agree that there's no need for our friend Mrs Kelly to apologise any further. So do sit down, Darina, and we'll get on with the introductions.'

Cassie saw Erin giggle. The rest of the group in Resolve was leaning forward, smiling, and Josie raised her hand and waved at the camera. 'Hi, Hanna. Hi, everyone. Hello, Pat! This is such a great idea and we're so pleased to be part of it. We don't have a librarian so I've been elected facilitator on this side. But we all love reading and, most of all, we're excited to see old friends and neighbours. I don't think I know Mrs Kelly ...' Darina attempted to get to her feet to say she was only a blow-in, but a woman beside her pinned her down with her elbow. Josie kept going. '... but I do see lots of familiar faces. Should we go round the two groups and say who we all are? Some of us may have gotten so old that we're almost unrecognisable!'

There was a burst of laughter and for the next few minutes Cassie's attention was half on the screen and half on the group around her. It was taking a while for people to grasp that they needed to raise a hand before speaking, and several tended to talk simultaneously. But everyone was good-humoured and Josie and Hanna were quick to work out ways of keeping control.

The introductions involved a great deal of exclamation and explaining, and extraordinary amounts of genealogical knowledge. With detailed reference to townlands and villages, people's relations were identified and traced back through generations. Ann Flood from the Lissbeg pharmacy was revealed to have a third cousin who worked in Resolve's uptown branch of Walmart. Those who'd been to the States and returned to live at home recalled names and asked about old acquaintances, and various people recited the dates and reasons for their departure from Finfarran.

It was a good half-hour before Hanna raised a hand

and caught Josie's attention. 'Do you think we should turn to the books we plan to read?'

Josie glanced round at her companions. 'Well, we've had some discussion over here but I'm not sure we've reached a consensus. And, of course, it depends on you guys as well.'

'Should we make it a recent novel? Maybe from a popular US author?'

One of the Canny twins rose to his feet and raised his voice. 'The committee suggested we might begin with *A Long Way to LA*.'

Cassie could feel the people around her telling themselves to remember that they were on camera. *A Long Way to LA*, which had drawn tourists to Ballyfin at the expense of the rest of the peninsula, wasn't a wholly popular book in Finfarran, but her visit to Resolve had taught her that the Shamrock Club's older members seemed to love it. Its descriptions of Finfarran's beauty, and the central image of the heroic fisherman, fed into their nostalgia for the land they'd left behind.

There was an awkward pause in which Hanna sought a diplomatic response. Then Mrs Shanahan looked up from a patch she was tacking. 'Well, the books in the case right here behind me were given to the club by my late husband. I must say it'd be very nice if we were to choose one of them.' Several women who'd been introduced as members of the quilting guild agreed, and Mrs Shanahan turned to Josie. 'It's a mix of authors from both sides of the Atlantic. Agatha Christie, Margery Allingham, Rex Stout. All classics. He was a lifelong collector of crime stories – I think he began with the Hardy Boys and the Nancy Drew books.'

Hanna looked at the camera. 'Well, that sounds like a good idea. What do you think over there?'

It was evident that the Canny twins weren't happy, but most of the other faces on the screen were enthusiastic. It wasn't quite clear to Cassie how Hanna clinched the deal but, all at once, everyone seemed to be in complete agreement.

Hanna spoke directly to Josie. 'Why don't you go through the books before our next meeting? Choose a few titles we could vote on?'

'Sure. I can do that.'

Despite Josie's smile, she looked slightly uncertain. Assuming she was concerned about ways and means, Hanna pressed on: 'Once we've made our choice, if it's something I haven't already got in stock, I'll order copies for readers over here. Will you be okay to source copies at your end?'

Josie nodded and said there'd be no problem. Amid the cheerful babble that followed, Mr Maguire stood up and cleared his throat. 'I hope you'll forgive me, but I need to be getting along.' He strode to the front of the room to retrieve his umbrella, approaching the camera at such speed that the group in Resolve saw him looming at them like the Creature from the Black Lagoon. Then, having achieved the commanding position he'd been thwarted of, he tapped the umbrella on a chair and addressed the assembled group. 'Before I leave, I'd like to offer a hearty vote of thanks to our facilitators. Well done, Hannah and Josie! Let's give them a big clap.'

Hearing the unmistakable voice of a schoolmaster, everyone broke into desultory applause. Mr Maguire paused, as if expecting a reciprocal vote of thanks to himself. Then, as no one rose to the occasion, he removed himself with a deprecatory bow. As he passed into the night, the two groups plunged back into animated discussion while, from the back rows on either side of the Atlantic, Cassie and Erin exchanged a triumphant thumbs-up.

CHAPTER FOURTEEN

AFTER THE MEETING PAT FOUND IT HARD to sleep. When they left the library, Cassie took her arm and insisted on fish and chips. They went to the sit-in chipper on Sheep Street, next to the place where Nuala Devane's dad had kept the dancehall, and ate smoked cod and chips with mushy peas. When they got home Pat regretted the two cups of strong tea she'd had with them. Climbing into bed, she switched off the light and, after half an hour's wakefulness, slipped into a shallow sleep.

In her dreams she was back in Resolve searching for something, but all the familiar landmarks had changed. Struggling to find the factory she'd worked in, she realised that it was long gone. But why was she wearing the dress she'd bought for her wedding trousseau? And here was Josie, coming towards her on a walking frame, while her own image, reflected in a shop window, was that of the slim girl she'd been at nineteen. Between sleeping and waking, she saw the faces of the book-club members mouthing silently from a huge screen on a high hill. Josie's eyes were fixed on her, looking troubled. Then she was stumbling upwards in her vinyl Cuban heels, and Mary was barring the way, holding a copy of Dorothy Sayers's *Murder Must Advertise*.

She woke to find herself curled up on Ger's side of the bed. It was the first time she'd ever lain there, and the shadows thrown by the furniture were unfamiliar. She'd always liked sleeping with the window open but Ger had preferred it closed. He didn't mind the light from the street outside, though, so the room had always been shadowy rather than dark. Lying on his side of the bed, Pat was aware of the pediment over the wardrobe and how its scrolled shape appeared black on the opposite wall. From her side you'd be more conscious of the way the light through the window made barred patterns over the bed. Feeling chilly, she reached out and found Ger's blue cashmere pullover, which, in the end, she'd laid aside when she'd bagged up his clothes. There was warmth in the wool when she put it on over her nightdress, and she slid back into his hollow in the mattress, pulling the duvet up around her ears.

As she drifted back to sleep, she remembered how, all those years ago, Josie had taken her shopping on her first weekend in Resolve. They'd caught a bus to a downtown branch of Macy's and bought ice-creams at a soda place before starting the search for a dress to wear on her honeymoon. Ger had decided they'd go to Kerry and have a couple of nights in Ballybunion. He wanted to visit some farmer his dad bought cattle from. Pat had heard good things about the strand, so she'd told Josie she fancied a dress that would look smart on a beach. And, though Josie had pooh-poohed Ballybunion, saying the beach near Lissbeg was far better, she'd joined in the search with enthusiasm. In the end they'd found a knee-length blue shift, with a pattern of white daisies round the hem. Pat had promised herself she wouldn't wear it until the honeymoon. But promises were one thing and what happened was something else.

*

She was eating breakfast when Mary arrived the following morning and called her a terrible slut to be sitting there in her dressing gown. Sticking out her tongue at her, Pat nodded at the teapot. 'That's still hot, have a cup.'

'I will, though I've only just had coffee at the deli. I got a lift in with Hanna when she came to work.'

'Was she passing your door?'

'Doesn't she always pass it?'

'She does if she drives a mile out of her way.'

Mary drank tea and examined Pat critically. 'You're looking rough, girl. Did you sleep last night?'

'I did and I didn't. You know yourself.'

'I do. But I'll tell you this, you'll feel better if you get on with things and get out.'

'I have Ger's clothes bagged up for the Vincent de Paul, anyway.'

'That's great. Though, mind you, I'm never sure I trust them. I read they sell most of the good stuff off to China.'

'Holy God Almighty, Mary Casey! Is there anything goes on at all that you don't find suspicious?'

Mary spread butter on a piece of toast and looked round for marmalade. 'Come here to me, though, what did you think of the crowd in the library last night?'

Pat brightened. 'I thought it was great, didn't you?'

'Josie's as bad as you said she was.'

'How d'you mean?'

'Well, the frame. And the state of her, Pat, she looks dreadful.'

Pat offered marmalade and said nothing. Mary had

taken a scunner to Josie years ago, when Pat had talked too much about her after spending the summer in Resolve. It was never wise to praise someone to Mary. She was like a child, the way she needed attention. It hadn't helped that, before Pat went home, it was Josie who'd persuaded the machine-room manager to give her a box of pearl buttons and a pattern for a wedding dress that, for style and modernity, had beaten Mary's cream-puff creation bought in Cork. Though, having held her peace for all these years, Pat wasn't going to open that can of worms now. Instead she remarked that Hanna had been a very good facilitator.

Mary dipped toast in her tea and brushed aside the comment. 'The place was exactly the way you described it. Though did you see the cat? I wouldn't let a cat up on a cushion. He'd shed hairs. Still, they'd have great attachments on their hoovers over there.'

'They call them vacuums.'

'Oh, I wouldn't doubt you. They'd always have to be different. All the same, they make great gadgets in the States. One of those quilting-guild ladies had a mother a cousin of mine who used to send presents over at Christmas. There was a great yoke for taking stones out of olives. Another was a wire thing you'd use to slice hard-boiled eggs.'

Pat remembered gadgets like those in Resolve in the 1960s. The rooming house to which Josie had introduced her had had a shared kitchen, and she'd hardly been able to credit all the things that were in the drawers. There was a big fridge-freezer too, like you'd never have seen in Finfarran. It made crushed ice that clattered like an avalanche into your glass, scattering bits that melted on the floor. And there was a salad crisper, though most of the salads she ate there were tasteless enough. They put celery salt and paprika on them to give them a bit of a lift, and a honey-mustard dressing that she'd ended up addicted to. Salad cream on hard-boiled eggs was never the same again.

Mary kicked her under the table. 'What did you think of your woman in charge of the ladies' quilting crowd?'

'Mrs Shanahan?'

'Very genteel. Is she English, Pat?'

'I think someone said she was old money from Boston.'

'Would that be English originally, so?'

'I wouldn't know.'

'And she married a Shanahan. Would they be the crowd from Mullafrack?'

'So she said.' Pat reached out and smacked Mary's

hand as she dunked more toast in her tea. 'Stop sticking marmalade in the teacup!'

'Why?'

'Because it's fierce bad manners.'

'Tis far from fancy manners we were reared. Anyway, isn't it only the two of us? Nobody'll see me.'

'Well, I'm the one that'll have to wash the cup.' Pat stood up and went to boil the kettle. 'You'll have another drop, now you're here.'

Mary took her cup to the sink and made a big show of washing it. Back at the table, they poured more tea and Mary asked if Pat had plans for the day.

'The Vincent de Paul woman's coming round for the bags.'

'But, sure, that'll take no time. She only has to get them downstairs.'

'There's a fierce lot more to be cleared out, though, Mary. All Ger's bits and pieces. And his papers. Well, they'll be fine, because Frankie's going to do them.'

'Is he now? And did he help with the clothes?'

'Well, no. He had things to do himself, so he had to get on.'

Mary pursed her lips but, for once, said nothing. Pat was glad. She didn't feel up to defending Frankie this morning. But that was the thing about Mary: she'd be kindness itself if she saw you were feeling weak. She'd back off now and probably offer to scrub out the whole flat. Or go home, make a pot of soup and force one of the neighbours to drive it round in their car. Pushing the last of the toast across the table, Pat asked what Mary had thought when your man mentioned *A Long Way to LA.*

'God, Pat, I nearly rose up and threw a chair at him! Was that Moss Canny's son?'

'It was.'

'Weren't there plenty there who could open their beaks that know far more than he does about Finfarran? Sure Moss hardly came home at all after he left in disgrace.'

'Well, the twins are on the committee.'

'And don't you know as well as I do the kind that get themselves onto committees? Aren't they only there for what they can rake back?' Mary put her elbows on the table. 'I tell you what, though. I haven't read a detective story for years. All those Golden Age books by people like Agatha Christie. I'd say I went through the whole lot back in the day.'

'Did you? Why?'

Mary, who, to Pat's knowledge, had never been a reader, gave a shrug. 'Tom's aunt Maggie was always

wanting them. He'd have to go into the library on the
way home from work. I used to have a read of them
before he'd bring them round to her.'

Pat managed to keep a straight face. Of course Mary
had claimed the books before they'd gone round to
Maggie's. She'd have felt that, by reading them first,
she'd kept Tom's aunt in her proper place. You couldn't
know Mary as well as Pat did without knowing the
way her mind worked. But that didn't matter. Before
they'd ever met Ger and Tom, she and Mary had faced
the world together, from their crocodile walks at the
national school to the last day at the convent, when
they'd burned their berets and cocked a snook at the
nuns. They'd linked little fingers at the age of six and
sworn eternal friendship, and look at them now, said
Pat to herself, still drinking tea and squabbling over
toast. They'd been a pair long before they'd been two
of a foursome and now they were back where they'd
started, without Ger and Tom.

CHAPTER FIFTEEN

DRIVING BETWEEN THE CLIFFS AND THE forest, Cassie was aware of new growth on the conifers to her right. Each dark branch had an inch-long, neon-bright tip, as striking as the peacock streaks in her fringe. The darkness and light on that side of the road contrasted with the unbroken blue above the ocean on her left. It was what Pat called 'a pet day', when the sun had new warmth and spring appeared to have taken hold overnight.

She had made good time since her previous stop so she slowed the van and dawdled, admiring the towering trees. The last time she'd been on this road was the week before Christmas, when she'd driven over in a borrowed car, seeking holly. Wearing a hooded duck-down coat she'd brought from Canada, she'd bumped slowly down a forest track and, seeing flashes of scarlet among the conifers, found three holly trees in a clearing, their leaves gleaming like candle-lit lacquer. Hanging from the branches of a nearby oak were long tendrils of ivy, some almost as fine as yarn and others clustered with black berries among green and gold foliage. She'd found no mistletoe, though. That had been brought to Lissbeg later by Fury O'Shea and The Divil.

Now, as she approached a roadside pub, she saw Fury's van parked up ahead. He lived only a mile away, so that wasn't surprising. Yet Cassie smiled. Somehow it felt just as it should that, as soon as you thought of him, Fury O'Shea would appear. Pulling in behind his van, she decided to stop for a pub lunch. The fresh air and sunshine had made her feel peckish earlier, so the sandwich she'd intended to eat at noon had been wolfed more than an hour ago, along with a chocolate bar.

The little building, probably once a thatched cottage, had a *faux*-rustic porch and a slate roof. Otherwise, it must hardly have changed for centuries. There was no pub sign but the name of the licensee was painted on the lintel above the door. The whitewashed stone was pierced by small sash windows and the walls were several feet thick. As Cassie approached, Fury appeared in the doorway, with The Divil, his elderly fox terrier, peering around his leg. Cassie waved and called hello but Fury didn't deign to raise his voice. He stood at ease in the entrance, a lanky man in his late sixties, wearing

a shabby, oversized waxed jacket, with the ends of his
corduroy trousers stuffed into heavy wellington boots.
When she reached the porch, he nodded. 'You're back
again, then.'

'It's good to see you. How's The Divil?'

'Game ball.'

Fury turned and went inside and Cassie followed,
briefly blinded by the change from bright sunlight to
Stygian gloom. Other pubs of the same design up and
down the peninsula had taken out their internal walls
to accommodate tourist parties but here there were still
two small low-ceilinged rooms, with a muddy-brown
varnished bar to the front and a snug to one side. A
jam jar full of wildflowers stood one table, dandelions,
marsh marigold and a sprig of shepherd's purse. The
windows were framed by yellowing lace curtains and a
TV hung on the wall above the bar.

Leaving her to give her order, Fury slid onto a bench
behind a table. Cassie had been here once before when
the owner had seemed surly but now, vouched for by
Fury, she was welcomed like an old friend. This was
Fury's local and the chances were that he ate here most
days, having whatever the publican's wife had cooked
for her own family meal. There was a large plate of
bacon and cabbage in front of him, and several potatoes

boiled in their jackets beside it in a dish. Under the table, The Divil had his nose in a saucer of cabbage mashed in gravy. Cassie asked the man if he could do her a ham roll. 'And a coffee? I'm driving.'

He nodded and disappeared through to a kitchen, and Cassie joined Fury on the bench. 'Has The Divil gone off Tayto?' The little dog was famous for his love of custard creams but whenever she'd seen him in a pub he'd been eating salt and vinegar crisps.

Fury kicked at the saucer under the table, splashing gravy onto The Divil's nose. 'He's on a diet. The vet said his teeth were banjaxed if he kept up the custard creams. I warned The Divil that, if he didn't take notice, the rats would be laughing at him. He saw the sense of that.'

'But the Tayto?'

'Ay, well, she was a bit down on his salt intake too. So I told him sodium taken with tea converts directly to sugar. He likes a saucer of tea, so that pulled him up. Mind you, I had to say I'd read it in a scientific survey.'

'And had you?'

'Not at all, girl. Sure I'm illiterate.'

This was a lie he had instigated, to avoid filling in forms and providing written estimates. A master woodsman and the best builder on the peninsula, he cultivated a reputation for eccentricity, turning up when and where he chose and never answering his phone. All the same, according to Pat, he wasn't called Fury for nothing. When he took on a job he wouldn't stop until it was done to perfection.

Cassie looked at The Divil, who was grimly chewing cabbage. 'And he believed you?'

'Ah, for God's sake, he's a dog, girl. He can't understand English. But he knows an ultimatum when he hears one, and you'd have to give him a logical reason, to save the poor fella's face. I mean, cutting back on the custard creams is one thing, but being in a pub with no Tayto is hard. But it was that or give up on the tea and he made his choice.' Fury lowered his nose into his pint. 'Mind you, I bet if you looked you'd find that somewhere on the internet. "Sodium taken with tea converts to sugar." But "depending on conditions" or "in sufficient quantities". Have you ever noticed they always add something to cover their arses in court?'

Cassie's roll arrived with a large unexpected tomato sliced into quarters, topped with a blob of mayonnaise and a jaunty sprig of parsley. The coffee was hot and strong and the ham, cut from the bone, had been glazed with honey, producing the perfect combination of savoury and sweet. Surreptitiously, she detached a piece of meat and edged it from her plate onto the floor. Under the table, with an air of elaborate nonchalance, The Divil neatly covered the scrap with his paw. Fury's face gave no indication that he'd noticed, though Cassie knew that he never missed a trick. Later on, behind closed doors, The Divil might be reprimanded, but in public, and especially in front of a woman, Fury wouldn't let him down. Besides, he had a fond appreciation of the little dog's resourcefulness, like a craftsman watching his apprentice display a complex skill.

As Cassie devoured her ham roll Fury raised his eyebrow. 'They say you've brought America back with you.'

'You mean the Transatlantic Book Club?'

'It's the talk of the seven parishes. I suppose people like it. Though when I took the boat I wouldn't have fancied waving at my old neighbours on a screen.'

'Did you go to the States?'

'No, I was in London, on the sites.' He looked at her quizzically. 'And, before you start doing the sums on your fingers, I'd be about six years younger than your gran.'

'Did you know her and Ger back then?'

'Not at all, girl. I left school at fourteen and went working for my dad.'

'So did Ger.'

'Ay, but he was older than me and, anyway, he was a townie. My dad was a forester, not a shopkeeper. But he died and I went to London around the time Ger and your gran set up house.'

'So you never knew my dad? Or my uncle Jim?'

Fury put out a foot and scratched The Divil's back. 'They were grown and gone before I came back. What is it you're fishing for?'

Cassie licked mustard off her knife. 'I guess I'm just wondering. My dad never said why he went away.'

'You could ask him.'

'But you don't, do you? Ask your dad stuff like that?'

Fury shrugged. 'I'm no expert. Mine was the silent type.'

'That's a Finfarran characteristic, isn't it? I like things above board and clear.'

The barman arrived at Fury's side with another pint. Fury pushed away the remains of his food and considered Cassie. 'Did you never think that some things might be none of your damn business?'

'Well, but this is family stuff.'

'I was thinking especially of family stuff. People leave for all sorts of reasons. I heard your dad and your uncle Jim were fierce well qualified, so they went off to get jobs they couldn't get here. I was the opposite. Well, maybe the other end of the scale. My dad died before he had half his trade taught me and, back then, there was nothing here for an unskilled lad. You could say the building sites were my university – you'd be talking nonsense, of course, but, sure, people do.'

Cassie was still pursuing her own train of thought. 'Back at Christmas, I thought I'd persuade my dad to come visit, and we'd do family things and hang out. I didn't know then that Ger was so ill.'

'That's an old story. People never making it back till they turn up to a wake.'

'Why?'

'This was a hard old place when I was young. No money, not much work, and too many priests and nuns.'

'Do you think that's what my dad thought?'

'I've no notion.'

Fury, who'd been sipping his pint, took another pull at it. Cassie remarked that Hanna thought she asked too many questions.

'Does she now?'

'She doesn't actually say so, but it's what she thinks.'

'Maybe she's right. I hear you've been showing an interest in Ger's will.'

Cassie sat bolt upright. 'No, I haven't!'

'That's good, so.'

'Seriously, Fury, honestly, I haven't.' Cassie stopped suddenly, remembering her conversation with Hanna in the library. Had she been overheard?

Fury looked at her sideways. '"Where there's a will, there's a relative," they say.'

'What does that even mean?'

'Don't get huffy with me, girl. You're a grown woman, not a child, so you should have a bit of sense.'

With an effort, Cassie controlled herself. After all, it was she who'd raised the subject, and maybe Fury had something useful to say. But when he spoke again his mind appeared to have drifted to something else. 'Come here to me now, with all your schooling did you never learn what "glamour" means?'

'You mean like models and movie stars?'

'That's what they use the word for, these days. People living the high life. What it really means is deception. A charm to make something look like something else.'

Cassie shot him a glance, wondering if he was coming over all puritanical. But that wasn't Fury at all and, besides, his expression was mischievous. 'You can look it up in a dictionary if you doubt me.'

'I don't. I just … How do you mean, a "charm"?'

'In the old days they would have called it a spell. Enchantment.'

Thinking he might be winding her up, Cassie bit into her sandwich and there was silence until Fury remarked that things weren't always what they seemed.

'Well, I know that.' Cassie frowned. 'Did *you* look it up in a dictionary?'

'I did not. I heard tell of it. There were O'Sheas living here in this forest long before a one of us round these parts thought of dipping a quill in ink.'

'Your family?'

'So my father said. He didn't say much but, when he spoke, I wouldn't doubt him. Nor my mother either, and she was a great storyteller. You have to mind a forest.'

'How do you mean, mind it?'

'I mean keep an eye on it. And maybe pay attention to it too. Wood can tell you things.'

Cassie wondered if two pints at lunch might be one too many. Fury was staring at the blank TV screen. 'I went away when my father died because I knew what would happen. My older brother had fallen in for all my father had. And by the time the same brother died of drink, the house was well-nigh fallen down and he'd sold off the forest.'

'That was tough.'

'It was worse than that. It was wrong. I'm not saying he hadn't a right to what my father left him. What I'm saying is that my father was a fool. He knew damn well my brother was a waster, and he didn't see where his real duty lay. People can take care of themselves. The land can't.'

'Who owns the forest now?'

'I do.'

Cassie was confused. 'But I thought you said— Oh, did you buy it back?'

'I did not. The title deeds belong to some fellow over in Australia who's never set a foot in the place. The forest belongs to me because I take care of it.'

'You mean you're his manager?'

Fury swallowed the last drops of his pint. 'I mean what I said. I don't own it. It belongs to me. Because I belong to it.'

'Oh. Right.' This was all getting a bit much for Cassie. She checked her watch and slid out from behind the table. 'You know what, I need to move on. There'll be people waiting for books.'

Fury stood up. 'We'll be away too. I've a tree to look at.'

He ambled over to pay for his lunch, then he and The Divil followed Cassie out into glorious sunshine. Beyond the conifers that fringed the forest, Cassie could hear birds singing in oak trees and alders. She remembered the shadows cast by their stark winter branches as she'd driven down the frosty track, seeking holly. She'd encountered Fury that day too, and he'd helped her to load armfuls of green and gold leaves and scarlet berries into the boot of her car. He hadn't replied when she'd asked him where in the forest she'd find mistletoe. But the following day he'd turned up in Lissbeg with a sackful on his shoulder, and a sprig of it had hung above the range on Ger's last Christmas Day.

CHAPTER SIXTEEN

THERE WAS A POEM BY THOMAS HARDY that Pat liked. She couldn't remember if she'd first read it in *Palgrave's Golden Treasury* but it seemed likely because that was a book the nuns at school were cracked about. It might have been somewhere else, though. Because when she'd looked Hardy up in the library in Carrick, she'd found he'd written a lot of stuff the nuns wouldn't have liked. Apparently, he'd lost his religion, picked up with a young one, and stopped talking to his wife, who'd ended her days in an attic. The poem was written after the wife died, when he'd been thinking of the past and remembering how they'd met. By then the young one had become the second Mrs Hardy, and Pat imagined she must have been pretty vexed when she read what he wrote. But maybe she'd known the bargain she'd made when she'd married him.

This morning Pat was determined to be properly dressed by breakfast time. She'd set her alarm and had taken a shower before seven. Then, having waved Cassie off to the salon, she washed up the breakfast things and got the flat straight by nine. It was another sunny day, so she planned to have a walk and do some shopping.

Climbing the stairs to her bedroom, she stepped into the second-floor room that had once been Sonny and Jim's. She'd moved the beds out years ago when Ger had decided to use it as an office. There was a big desk against the wall, with a roll-top and a brass lock, like something out of Dickens, and a row of metal filing cabinets he'd picked up at an auction. Looking around, Pat wondered what would happen next. She'd always been on at Ger to let her decorate, but he'd hated disruption so the room still had the paper she'd hung when the lads were small. You could see the marks where it had been scraped when the beds were pushed in and out.

The desk was locked, and so were the filing cabinets, and the keys were still on the ring Ger had kept in his trousers pocket. When they'd carried him down to the ambulance in his dressing-gown and pyjamas, Pat had followed them out through the shop and sat in beside him, forgetting she'd need her own keys to get back into the flat. But Cassie had kept her head. She'd taken Ger's car and followed the ambulance, having thrown her bag and Pat's into the back along with a couple of coats. By the time they got Ger to Carrick, he was dead. Though the paramedic hadn't told her so, Pat had known that well enough. She'd stumbled down the ambulance steps into sleet. They'd lifted out the stretcher, and Cassie had been there, wrapping her up in her coat. Pat had been wearing slippers. Later, in the hospital, when they'd told her Ger was gone, she'd noticed how wet her feet were. Cassie had rubbed them with a towel, but she'd had to put the slippers back on to walk to the car and go home. They were good for nothing by that stage, so she'd thrust them into the kitchen bin before going to bed. That night, because Ger had been so careful to keep his keys close by him, she'd taken his keyring out of his trousers pocket, and put it under her jumpers in a drawer.

This was the first time she'd been in the office since then. The sun showed up a lot of dust, and the faded paper looked awful, so she wondered if she'd look out for some paint. She'd meant to go by the hardware store anyway, to ask about getting a new lock. The shop was safe as a bank, because it had to be for insurance, and there was a Yale lock on the door at the top of the staircase that led to the flat. They'd always kept that one on the snib during opening hours, because anyone wanting to come upstairs had to pass through the shop first. But without Ger down below and coming up in the evenings, she felt she wanted the flat to be more secure. She'd stopped using the snib now, so visitors had to knock. And last night, when she'd woken up and found it hard to sleep again, she'd decided to get a Chubb lock for the door.

All morning her mind had been groping for the words of Hardy's poem. As she stood at the office window, a boy who'd been sitting by the horse trough waved to a girl on the other side of Broad Street. And the first lines of the poem appeared in Pat's mind.

Woman much missed, how you call to me, call to me,
Saying that now you are not as you were
When you had changed from the one who was all to me,
But as at first, when our day was fair.

That wasn't the verse that appealed to her. It was another one, with a wonderful line about a dress. She couldn't remember how it began, but she knew that it ended with the poet's wife wearing an 'air-blue gown'. It was a sad poem, though, about a thin wind oozing through thorns.

Down by the horse trough, the girl threw her arms

around the boy, and together they crossed the street to the nuns' garden. Up at the second-floor window, Pat could look down from above, as if she were God. The high convent wall facing Broad Street had been breached to give public access to the garden and there was another entrance as well, from the library courtyard. In summer flowering herbs softened the lines of the garden, but at this time of year, from Pat's vantage point, you could clearly see the design. Formal herb beds, edged by low walls and box hedges, were laid out in concentric circles between gravelled walks. In the centre, on a plinth in a wide granite basin, was a statue of St Francis with arms extended and water gushing from carved flowers at his feet. Everything radiated from the statue, which faced a row of stained-glass windows in the old convent wall. The glass produced narrow streaks of brightness in greyness, and below the windows was the nuns' graveyard, enclosed by cast-iron railings.

The sense of being the eye of God suddenly troubled Pat. It was as though life had been pulled inside out, and now it was she who was peering down at young lovers meeting, like Sister Benignus watching the world from behind panes of glass. Leaving the window, she went to get her coat. Last night Cassie had brought a message

from Fury O'Shea, saying he'd be glad to give a hand
if anything wanted doing in the flat. Pat knew that
trying to ring him was pointless. He never answered his
phone. Still, the lad in the hardware store would pass
on a message. She could drop in and order the Chubb,
and stroll round the town in the sunshine, and there
was a nice café now in the nuns' garden, so she'd go
there for tea and a bun when she'd been to the shops.

*

At three o'clock Fury stepped back and admired
the Chubb lock he'd just fitted to Pat's door. He was
flicking drill-dust from the paintwork when Frankie
appeared, mounting the stairs from the shop. Fury
held the door open and Frankie walked in with the
air of a man expecting an explanation. Pat beamed in
welcome. 'There you are, son! I didn't know you'd be
passing.'

Frankie turned an aggrieved eye on the door. 'I didn't
know myself but I'd business in town so I thought I'd
drop by. What's happening here?'

'Wasn't it great luck? I went out for a lock and who
should I meet but Fury?'

Frankie's eyes swivelled to Fury, who tucked his
polishing rag into his pocket and said he'd be getting

on. 'You're grand there now, Mrs Fitz. I've The Divil below in the van so I won't stop.'

'Ah, no! Would you not have a cup of tea after all your trouble? And the poor little dog must be dying of heat in the van. Bring him up and I'll give him some water.'

She looked at Frankie, invoking his support, but Frankie's face darkened. 'What did you want a new lock for? And, if you did, you could've called me.' He reached out and swung the door, as if inspecting the handiwork, sending a screwdriver skittering across the floor.

Fury stiffened almost imperceptibly. Then he smiled at Pat. 'I wouldn't say The Divil would refuse a saucer of tea.'

'He'd be very welcome to it. Bring him up and I'll put the kettle on. I've a cake here in the tin.'

'I will, so.'

Frankie looked blandly at Fury. 'I'm afraid we can't have a dog coming through the shop.'

Fury lounged across the room and bent to retrieve his screwdriver. When he stood up, his expression was equally bland. 'Is that right?'

Pat gave a little cry of distress. 'Ah, no, Frankie, it's only The Divil. And Fury went out of his way to give me a hand. I met him below in the hardware shop and he came straight round.'

Frankie reached for his wallet. 'What do I owe you, Fury?'

Briefly, Fury held Frankie's eyes before turning deliberately and addressing himself to Pat. 'I'll let you know in due course, Mrs Fitz. There's no hurry. I'll see you another day.'

'You will, of course, and you're very good, Fury, I appreciate it. Go below and get The Divil now, and put him under your coat when you're coming through the shop.'

Frankie interrupted her. 'These days, Mam, there's health and safety to consider.'

Pat grasped the corner of the kitchen table and two pink spots appeared on her cheeks. 'There is and there always was, Frank, I'm well aware of that – your father was ever a man to go by the book. But this house has never failed in common hospitality. Fury stepped in on his free day and did a job for me. And I've just offered him and The Divil their tea.'

Shrugging his arms into his jacket, Fury turned on his heel and went down the stairs. Pat looked at Frankie, recognising the stormy look she'd often seen on Ger. She was used to Frankie being what she thought of as 'a bit high-handed', and normally she wouldn't have crossed him. But to be so uncivil when Fury had been so kind was something else. She shot another covert glance at him, fearful that he'd march off in a huff. But instead, as Fury reappeared with The Divil under his arm, Frankie crossed the room and sat down at the table. With a sigh of relief Pat went to fill the kettle. Ever since Frankie was small, she thought, he hadn't been able to stand the thought of missing a treat, and now, even though she'd crossed him, he still wanted to stay for a bit of her cake. She was flustered, feeling that Fury might not want to sit down with him, but Fury strolled over, took a seat and perched The Divil on his knee. He seemed relaxed and unconcerned so, with luck, things were going to be fine.

CHAPTER SEVENTEEN

CASSIE WAS ON THE ROAD TO BALLYFIN when a text came through from Margot. She pulled in to read it and found she needn't have set out for work at all. Refurbishments in the salon had reached a stage that couldn't be completed in an evening so, to avoid paying overnight rates to the workmen, it was closing at the end of the morning shift. There were no afternoon bookings, which meant nothing would have to be cancelled, so this had been deemed the least disruptive plan. Cassie couldn't tell from the text what Margot thought of the decision, but no doubt she'd hear the whole story on Monday. And now she had an afternoon to spend however she liked.

Though the sun was shining, there was a chilly wind blowing from the east and she'd set out dressed in a fleece-lined hoodie with a warm jacket on top, skinny jeans and Doc Martens. Having got this far down the motorway, it seemed silly to drive back to Lissbeg, so she decided to turn inland to the foothills

of Knockinver. When she'd taken her northern route
last week in the library van, she'd noticed sheep tracks
leading into the mountains, so perhaps, since she was
suitably dressed, she'd take a solitary walk. There was
a ruined tower somewhere round there, high up on a
hillside, so if she could find the location again, she'd
park and check it out.

The mountain range was spectacular. It ran north–
south across the western end of the narrow peninsula,
and the peak of Knockinver was almost as high as
Ireland's highest mountain, Carrauntoohil. Its river
valleys were full of the sound of rushing peat-brown
water, and its upper slopes were often lost in mist.
Cassie was no mountaineer but she guessed that the way
to the tower would require only a steep, scrambling
walk. There might even be a proper car park, and steps
to take her up the slope. Then again, there might not.
Finfarran's ancient monuments were an odd mixture
of tourist traps with entrance booths and gift shops,
and deserted sites with little or no signage, protected
by nothing more than straggling barbed wire.

She found the tower more by luck than judgement.
It was further off the road than she'd remembered,
and to reach it she had to pass the sign that pointed
to Mullafrack. As she came to the signpost she could

see the roofless tower in the distance, a square building rooted in rock, with its back to rising ground. It was too early in the season for much sign of new grass, but golden furze blazed on the sunlit hillside. Cassie hadn't read a great deal but the dark tower and its gleaming backdrop made her think of a children's book, called *Elidor*, she'd been given at the age of twelve when she'd had flu. It hadn't been her sort of thing at all, and she'd never finished it. Instead she'd been left with a series of vague impressions, because the bits she'd read had turned up in her feverish dreams. There was something in it about two towers, called Findias and Gorias, one of which she remembered as dark while the other was made of gold.

The track beyond the signpost was longer than she'd expected and climbed higher than she'd thought it would. When she left the car the tower was still about a quarter of a mile above her and, beyond it, the foothills rose to where the rugged mountain peak was capped in cloud. There was a stile set in the wall that enclosed the scrubby car park. Cassie crossed it and began the ascent, feeling a bit like Emily Brontë all alone on the moors.

The chill wind was at her back and, all around her, insects buzzed in the furze. Tasting the sharp upland air, Cassie felt a rush of satisfaction. This morning she'd imagined that by now she'd be working in the salon, making inane remarks to her clients and breathing in the synthetic scents of hair products. Here, on either side of the track, the waist-high furze smelt of warm coconut and the narrow way beneath her feet was floored with soft turf. Tough roots crossed it, forming occasional toe and heel holds, and sometimes, unaware of one, she stumbled to her hands and knees. When she tripped, the track became a tunnel and, looking ahead, she could see looming masonry, and a single blank window, like an empty eye. Then, when she got to her feet again, her head emerged into sunlight, the tower was re-contextualised in the wider landscape, and she heard the sound of birdsong above the murmur in the furze.

The third time she stumbled she came down heavily and, inspecting her bruised hands, tried to place a new buzz that had sounded among the droning of the insects. After a confused moment she recognised the beep of a message alert and reached for her phone. Realising who it was from, she felt a tingle like an electric shock run through her body. Jack had never sent her a message before. Biting her lip, Cassie considered the screen. Ferdia had announced that syncing devices would mean he and Jack, she and Erin could all keep in touch about the book club but, in practice, there had been no need. The guys just did what they did and that was that. With no idea what to expect, Cassie opened the message and found a question for her to pass on for Ferdia, whose Wi-Fi had apparently gone down. Hitting the screen, she sent back a thumbs-up. The tingling feeling, she told herself, had been nothing more than the shock of landing hard on her hands and knees. With the phone back in her jeans pocket, she stood up unsteadily, licking the weal made by a twisted root across her palm. Then she kept climbing though the sun-warmed furze amid the song of the birds.

At the top of the track the ground widened into the plateau on which the tower was built. The rock was close to the surface here and growth was minimal, though around the base of the building, where fallen walls had trapped rainwater, the lower courses of stonework were dappled with yellow lichen and moss. Inevitably, the tower had seemed much smaller from the road. Now it reared three storeys above her, the ruined tops of its walls silhouetted against the sky. Beginning to walk around it, Cassie found a doorway blocked with rubble and, beside it, a large, rusty sign.

According to the mottled print, the Office of Public Works was responsible for the site's maintenance, which seemed to focus on preventing passing tourists suing for damages. Members of the public were forbidden to enter the tower, or to climb on its walls, and there was a stern warning about the dangers of the unlevel ground. Further along, a circle of blackened stones had once held a campfire, and abandoned beer cans and rubbish suggested that local lads might use the site as a place to party. The empty eye Cassie had seen from the tunnel was a mullioned opening high in the tower wall. The first-floor windows were narrow, and there were none at ground level.

Continuing her walk around the base of the building, she turned a corner and, to her astonishment, bumped into Bradley Miller. 'Wow! Er, hi ... I didn't realise there was anyone else here.'

'Nor did I. Hello there.' He held out his hand and, remembering his mixture of friendliness and formality, Cassie reached out to shake it. In stepping towards him, her foot turned on a stone and only the hand grasping hers kept her from falling. She righted herself and laughed. 'Dangerous ground. I should have heeded the notice!'

Brad glanced around disparagingly. 'What I want

is a notice that tells me what this place is. How come there's no information?'

'I suppose they don't expect many tourists.'

'Well, they sure as hell won't get them if they don't provide the infrastructure.' He stood back, looking up at the tower. 'Pretty amazing, isn't it? Anywhere else there'd be tearooms and guided tours.'

'I know. But I like it as it is.'

'So do I, actually. But tearooms make my job a whole lot easier.'

'How come you're still here? I thought the stop-off was only an overnight.'

'It was, but not for me. The company reckons Finfarran could be a pretty cool destination. You know, a few days with organised tours and options for nights ashore.'

'So this is reconnaissance?'

'Pretty much. I had some time due, so it's kind of a working vacation.'

As Cassie continued her walk around the tower he fell into step beside her. When she completed her circuit they stopped and took in the view. Looking east, back down the peninsula, she could see the edge of the green mass that was Fury O'Shea's forest. Brad produced an iPhone and began taking photos. 'God, wherever you turn round here, there's another amazing shot.' He put the phone back in his pocket and glanced down at Cassie. 'I read about that exhibition you've got in your library.'

'Not mine, exactly. I'm just a part-time temporary worker bee.'

'Sounds like a pretty cool book.'

'I don't really know much about it. You'd have to ask Hanna.'

'Is she your boss?'

'She's the librarian. There are volunteer guides who do tours of the psalter exhibition. But not at this time of year.'

'Could you organise private tours for groups?'

'Well, I couldn't, no. Like I said, I'm just an employee.'

He nodded decisively. 'I should meet with Hanna. Some of our cruises have cultural themes. Ireland and lectures on medieval manuscripts, that's a good fit.'

'Impressive.'

'Not really. I'm just the guy who comes up with suggestions. Actually, my most successful so far was tequila-drinking in Spain.'

'But do they make tequila there?'

'We had to import it from Mexico. It was worth it,

though. The Tequila Trail was one of our big hits.' Seeing Cassie's response, Brad grinned at her. 'Everything we do is tailored to its specific demographic. Medieval Irish literature would require a different approach.'

'So will Hanna. Don't start with the Tequila Trail. It wouldn't go down well.'

'I guess librarians like authenticity.'

'Don't you?'

He turned his brown eyes on her before he replied. 'Yeah, I do. When I find it, I think it's special.' Stepping back, he looked up at the tower. 'Like this place. It certainly feels authentic. I wish the Office of Public Works had felt we needed fewer warnings and more facts, though. How old would you say it is?'

'I haven't a clue.'

There was a sudden gust of wind and Cassie shivered. Brad immediately sprang into action. 'Are you cold? Come on, let's get you warmed up.'

He set off at a brisk pace and, following, Cassie found him raking out the remains of the campfire. 'What are you, a Boy Scout?'

'Endlessly inventive, that's me.' He made a neat structure of charred ends of plank and gnarled furze roots. 'Got any paper?'

'No.'

'Disaster. No, wait.' He pulled a bundle of fliers out of his pocket. 'God bless Ballyfin's Fish World Experience. Nice flammable paper, and they made me take half a dozen.'

Crumpling the fliers, he inserted them between the pieces of wood. Cassie hunkered down beside him. 'So now what? We rub two sticks together?'

'Nope. I'm a smoker.' Producing a cigarette lighter, he lit the paper, which flared up and caught the kindling at once. There was a rickety wooden box, which might have been used to carry beer cans up the track. Brad fetched it and set it down by the fire. 'Have a seat. We can burn it later if we still feel cold.'

Still hunkered down, Cassie looked up at him. 'Chuck it on and let's have a big blaze now.'

He stamped on the box and the slats cracked and splintered, then they both began to feed the crackling fire. As the flames rose, Cassie could see the view down the hill through a heat haze. Brad settled beside her, sitting back on his heels.

'Mind if I smoke?'

'No, of course not.' She could hardly object, she thought, with all the sluggish smoke billowing from the fire. The flames had reignited some plastic or rubber in the ashes, and the clean scent of burning wood had turned acrid. As it caught the back of her throat, it made her cough.

'Oh, shit, I'm sorry.' Brad stubbed out his newly lit cigarette.

'No, it's not you. It's just something in the fire.' Cassie stood up and moved upwind and Brad called across the fire to her. 'You okay?'

'Sure. My own fault for wanting a huge blaze.'

'Oh, come on, don't say that! A huge blaze is the only way to go.'

Laughing, she walked back to him, around the circle of stones. The smoke was thinning and the heart of the fire was glowing. Far below, there was a flash of light from a mirror as a jeep pulled into the car park. Brad pointed down the hill. 'We've got company.'

Cassie felt an unexpected mixture of shyness and guilt. Lighting the bonfire had probably been irresponsible and, for no reason she was prepared to think about, to be found here with Brad seemed kind of weird. Several people jumped out of the jeep and were pulling on jackets. She looked at Brad, who read her thought on her face. 'I left my car at the other side of the hill. What's up? Do you want to beat a retreat?'

He appeared so amused that Cassie's shyness

intensified. 'No. Well, yes. I don't fancy chatting to a lot of tourists. Do you?'

'Not when I'm not being paid to. How about we walk to my car and I'll drive you back round to pick up yours? Most likely they'll have moved on by then.'

She wasn't certain she wanted that either, but the sound of voices coming up the track unnerved her. 'Okay, if you're sure you don't mind.'

He stood up and kicked the fire, scattering the wood and stamping out the embers. Cassie helped, rolling stones over sparks. Then, as the voices got closer, he gave her a conspiratorial wink. 'If we're quick, they'll never even know we've been here.'

It was hard to tell whether or not he was joking, and Cassie suspected that, if he was, the joke might be on her. She knew her confusion couldn't have gone unnoticed. But perhaps he was just being funny to set her at ease. But this was no time to stand around wondering. As the first of the group of tourists emerged from the track onto the stone plateau, she ducked low and followed Brad around the dark tower.

CHAPTER EIGHTEEN

HANNA STOOD IN A GROUP OF SHOPPERS, all queuing for Sunday joints or the makings of weekend breakfasts. When her purchases were handed across the counter, she told Des that she'd slip up to the flat. He said she'd need to rap on the door. 'Herself don't leave it on the snib now, but I know she'll be glad to see you if you go up.'

When Hanna knocked Pat welcomed her in with open arms. 'There you are! I haven't seen you properly since I came back.'

Taking a seat by the range, Hanna looked round at the well-swept floor, the scrubbed table, the framed print of a Paul Henry seascape, the teapot on the range, and the glass-fronted press. Nothing had changed since the last time she'd been here, except for the presence of an ornate vase on the mantelpiece, which didn't seem to fit Pat's style. It was made of gilded pink and purple lustre, ornamented with flowers, and held a bunch of narcissi, their clusters of creamy, ruffled petals and deep saffron centres adding to the overblown effect.

Pat saw Hanna glance at it. 'Ger's mam used to have that on the mantelpiece back on the farm. It came here in a box of stuff when the poor woman died and, God forgive me, I never liked it, so I stuck it inside in the press.'

'I don't think I've seen it before.'

'No, you wouldn't have, love. It was at the back of a shelf. Ger took it out when Cassie brought mistletoe up to the flat at Christmas and, since then, I haven't had the heart to put it away.'

'Well, it looks great.'

'I don't know … I think those flowers make it a bit blowsy.' Pat cocked her head and considered the vase. 'But they were Ger's mam's favourites, you know. "Bridal Crown". She carried them on her wedding day, poor woman, and God knows she wouldn't have had much else.' Pat linked her hands on her knee and turned her wedding ring on her finger.

Feeling she'd led them into melancholy territory, Hanna remarked that she'd just bought black and white pudding. 'You must be glad to have Des below in the shop.'

'Ah, listen, Des is a great lad altogether. Though

why I still call him a lad I don't know. He must be pushing thirty. I'm a lucky woman to have him there to rely on.'

Her woebegone expression belied the statement so Hanna changed the subject to the book club. 'I think it's a brilliant idea. And several more people have applied to join.'

'I suppose there's a lot of us knew Resolve in the past.'

'Did you ever think of staying there yourself?'

'Ah, no, love. Sure I was engaged when I went.'

'And you were just there for the summer?'

'That's it. I worked in the factory with Josie. Your mam and dad were engaged too, and I'd a list as long as me arm of things to buy for Mary's trousseau. Then she decided she wanted a summer wedding, so I packed them all up and posted them home.'

'What was that about?' Hanna stopped suddenly, thinking it might have been about herself.

Pat laughed. 'Ah, no, love, she wasn't pregnant. She just took a notion. Ger and I got married in the autumn, when I came back.'

'Wasn't there a big thing about you being a foursome?'

'There was, and talk of a double wedding. But you know what Mary's like.'

Hanna, who had observed her mother with the cold eye of childhood, believed she knew exactly what Pat meant. At a double wedding, Mary would have had to share a spotlight, something she never would or could abide. For years Hanna had wondered why Pat put up with her. Now, unwilling to ask the question bluntly, she said she'd always been glad that Pat was her godmother. 'There were times I wouldn't have survived my mam without you!'

'Well, nobody had to twist my arm. I was glad to. And, later on, I'd say you almost saved my life. I was very depressed after Jim was born, because they'd done a hysterectomy. I'd signed the paper beforehand, of course, but they hadn't asked me to read it, and I'd never thought they'd do that while I was asleep.'

'God, Pat, that's awful.'

'Ay, well, that's how they treated women in the hospitals then. I don't know that they're much better now. Anyway, 'twas the right thing to do, I suppose, if I needed it. But the point is that your mam knew how much I'd wanted a daughter. And I was very down when I found I had no hope of one any more.'

Hanna didn't ask if Pat had had any counselling. At that time in Finfarran there would have been no such thing.

'It was Mary put the heart back into me. She turned up with a big box of chocolates and bullied me into eating them, and there was a nurse at the top of the ward with a face like a bag of spanners, glaring down at us. It was like being back at school, and the two of us got the giggles. And then Mary produced a picture you'd drawn for me.'

'Did I? I don't remember.'

'Ah, you'd only have been about six. Mary gave it over to me and said you were a lucky girl to have me as a godmother. I suppose it cheered me up.'

'She was right.'

'Well, she was no great hand at the mothering job herself. That's what she said.'

'Did she really?'

'She's not as insensitive as she seems, Hanna. Not all the time, anyway.' Pat paused. 'And then, when she was gone, I found she'd left a package. It was a knitting pattern for a little girl's jacket, and some needles and pink wool.'

'Was that the one with the cable stitches you knitted me for my birthday?'

'That was it. Of course, Mary was useless at knitting so, in one way, she was only getting the job done for her. But she knew how to set me back on my feet.' Pat looked at the vase of flowers. 'Mind you, Ger's mam was very good to me too. She had no daughter either, and I was always fond of her. I thought it might be the same way when Frankie married Fran. But that was a non-starter. Fran's a decent enough woman but, do you know what it is, she has no conversation. Either that or she's deep. I've never known which. And I hardly know Sonny and Jim's wives at all. No, you're more of a daughter to me than any kith or kin, Hanna – and Mary was wrong. It's I that was lucky, not you.'

Hanna was touched. 'You really were a rock during my childhood. I always knew I could run round to you when Mam got on my nerves.'

'Ay, if you weren't off slaving for Maggie Casey.'

'It wasn't as bad as that. Maggie was old and grumpy, but being out of the house gave me freedom, and it made for peace all round when Mam could keep Dad firmly at home.' Struck by what she'd just said, Hanna frowned. 'I know that sounds bad but, actually, he adored her.'

'Oh, there's no disputing that.'

'I hated to see him torn between Mam and the rest of the world. But then I'd see them sitting together in the garden, or jaunting off to Carrick for dinner, like a couple of teenagers out on their first date.'

'I'd say that's half Mary's problem. She never grew up. She doted on her own dad and he was a kind of a cold man, as far as I remember him. I've always thought she felt she was owed some imaginary debt of love.'

'God, isn't it scary how our neuroses get passed on to our kids? I grew up fantasising about the perfect family and, by hook or by crook, I was going to create it for Jazz. And look at her now, the child of divorced parents. Maybe if I hadn't been trying so hard I would have noticed I'd gone and married a rat.'

'Ah, Jazz is grand. She has a life of her own now, and a good job. Don't go putting yourself down. You're a wonderful mother.'

'Well, at least she spent her formative years feeling loved. Not that I didn't – I knew Dad adored me as much as he doted on Mam. It was just hard to see him punished whenever he dared to show it.'

Pat's face creased with worry. 'I didn't think you noticed that when you were young.'

'Kids often see more than they're given credit for.'

'I suppose that's true.'

'And people do the best they can, don't they? That's the lesson you learn as you get older and, if you've any sense, you stop looking back and move on.'

'You do, I suppose, if you're able. But it takes self-awareness, and Mary was never a great woman for that.'

'Maybe she's the one who should have gone to the States and broadened her horizons.'

Pat laughed. 'And take her eye off Tom for a whole summer?'

'Well, you trusted Ger.'

'Ger was a horse of a different colour.' Pat got up and said she'd boil a kettle. In Finfarran circles, the offer of a cup of tea at such a juncture meant one of two opposing things: either your company was appreciated or you'd stayed too long. Seeing Hanna hesitate, Pat gave her a playful slap. 'I'd love you to stay if you've time.'

'But don't you have things to do?'

'I have, and plenty of them, but I'd rather take my ease and talk to you.'

Hanna settled back in her chair and raised a subject that had struck her earlier. 'You have a new lock on the door.'

'And you're not to worry about it.'

'I'm not.'

'You are. But you needn't. I know you're all determined to take care of me, and it's very kind. It helps. But I have to find my own way through this,

Hanna. The new lock just gives me a sense of security. Well, that's not the whole truth, it's more than that. There was never a time in my life when I could look round and call a space my own. But I can now and I have to learn to live in it alone. It's not what I would have chosen, love, but it's how things happened. Ger used to say that in life you can only play the hand you're dealt.'

CHAPTER NINETEEN

FITZGERALD'S CLOSED AT TWELVE THIRTY on Saturdays. When Pat came downstairs Des was scrubbing the chopping blocks and the sign was turned on the door. 'Would you have a minute, Mrs Fitz?'

He came round the counter, looking awkward, and passed a very clean hand over his bristly head. He was a square-set man, light on his feet and quietly spoken, and the striped apron he wore over his white coat was tied low under an incipient paunch. 'I was wondering if we'd have the usual window display, or if you wanted to skip it this year with Ger's death so recent. I thought I might ask Frankie, but then it seemed best to come to you.' He gazed at her doubtfully, obviously concerned that he might have said something wrong.

At first Pat couldn't think what he meant. Then she remembered. 'For St Patrick's Day? Oh, yes, of course. No, we should have it, Des. We always do.'

The window display had been Ger's idea, a way of combating the Carrick supermarkets' St Patrick's Day offers. It majored on nostalgia in the face of commercial hype. Instead of neon harps and foil shamrocks, Fitzgerald's window sported a plaster wolfhound posed against a round tower, and customers buying their St Patrick's Day lunch were given a free bunch of shamrock. Pat didn't know where the slightly chipped plaster figures had come from, but they'd certainly been in the shop since Ger's father's day. The shamrock came from the farm. There were two or three places there where it grew profusely, and the idea of a giveaway that cost him nothing had greatly appealed to Ger. Each year he'd driven out with a knife and a plastic sack that had once contained sheep nuts, and returned with plenty for the customers and enough over to make a wreath around the wolfhound's feet. So long as they didn't lose by it, Lissbeg always liked to do down Carrick, and the free shamrock, as well as the saving in petrol, convinced many of the wisdom of buying local.

Pat hastened to reassure Des. 'I should have remembered myself, and you did right to come to me. I'll see about it.'

'Right so, Mrs Fitz. I'll put the dog on display at the start of the week. Wednesday's the seventeenth, so if you could get me the shamrock soon I'll be set for the rush.'

As he spoke, the door to the yard slammed and Cassie

came in from the passage. Pat beamed at her. 'Now! There you are, love! Are you busy this afternoon?'

'Not a bit. Why?'

'Well, I wondered if you'd drive me out to the farm.' Pat turned to Des. 'Ger would always check in advance to make sure of the shamrock. I know where to look and Cassie could take me today so we'd see what's what.'

Cassie pushed her hand through her fringe. 'No problem. Is this for St Patrick's Day?'

Pat explained and Cassie's eyes sparkled. 'I didn't know we grew shamrock on the farm.'

'Well, it wouldn't be in the fields, love. You find it growing thick round a gate or up along a verge.'

'You mean wild?'

Des chipped in. 'Like your gran says, you just have to know where to look for it. Some years it fails in one place and springs up in another.'

'Wow! So it's like a treasure hunt.'

Pat laughed. 'Sometimes it's more like an endless trek down muddy boreens. We've never had a year without it, though. Not while I've been in this house.'

'Okay. Let me find a pair of wellies and you can tell me where to go.'

*

It was what people called 'a soft day', half sunny, half misty. The bushes by the roadsides still wore a winter air, but the celandines gleaming against the stone walls had become flashes of gold in a carpet of yellow primroses. On lesser roads bounded by the banks of earth that Cassie had learned to call ditches, the primroses, fringed with pale green leaves, flourished behind a barbed network of dark, dormant briars. In damp corners between the stones, lamb's tongue fern grew in emerald clumps. Cassie lowered her window to look out at them. Then, as she turned down a boreen indicated by Pat, she gasped. A profusion of starry flowers powdered the blackthorn hedges, their white petals shining like snow against the stark wood.

Pat smiled at Cassie's reaction. 'I've never known a spring when I haven't gasped at the blackthorn flowers. I love the little catkins hanging from the hazel as well.'

'It's amazing how quickly everything's coming to life.'

Pat began to chant in a childlike sing-song:

'From Brigid's Day on,
The birds build nests,
The sheep drop lambs,
And the day gets long.

'I learned that from the nuns. Brigid's Day is February the first, and they say it's the first day of spring.'

'It was snowing this year on February first!'

'More often than not, that's the way of it, love. But that's what they say. When I was young we used make more of Brigid's Day than St Patrick's. Well, girls did, anyway. Maybe not lads so much.'

'What did you do?'

'You'd go round with a doll that was dressed up in lace and flowers.'

'What was the significance?'

'Ah, the custom was dying by that time, love, and I'm not sure what we were doing. There were all sorts of things they did in the past at the turn of the seasons. Dew gathered in Maytime was used for love potions, and there were herbs you could pick and put on your eyes to banish enchantment.'

'No! Did you do that?'

'Not at all, no one believed in that kind of stuff in my day. I think going round with the dolly was just about welcoming the spring.'

'That's cool.'

'You'd walk the bounds of your land at certain times too, and you'd light fires.'

'What for?'

'Protection, I think. From bad luck, you know, or a curse. An uncle of mine found an egg once, buried at a field boundary. He said someone had put it there to curse the land.'

'Wow! He believed that?'

'Land can bring out strange hatred in families.'

'He thought a *family* member did it?'

'I'm not sure, love. I was only a child, and they wouldn't talk where I could hear them. I'd say there was bad blood between him and his brother, though.'

Cassie drove in silence between the flowering thorns. Then she remembered her conversation with Fury. 'Did you know Fury O'Shea before he went off to England? He left after his dad died. His elder brother got everything so Fury just took off.'

'I suppose that's right.' Pat looked at her mildly. 'What's this about?'

'Nothing. Well, nothing much. It's just ... people here seem to have gone away a lot. And there always seem to be quarrels about land.'

'Plenty of land was hard got, Cassie, and if a farm couldn't feed a whole family, people had to emigrate.'

'Fury didn't want to go. Well, I don't think so. He just couldn't bear to see what would happen to the forest. In the end it got sold off. Was his brother an alcoholic?'

'You'd find plenty who'd say he was. Plenty of others who'd say he was just a man who couldn't cope with what life threw at him.'

'But how come he didn't get help?'

Pat pointed to an upcoming junction. 'Here we are. If you take this turn, we can pull in and look around.'

Cassie turned, bumped along obediently for several hundred yards, and pulled in where she was told, by a slender hazel growing out of the ditch. This was nothing more than a rutted cart-track running between small fields. Pat, who had also worn wellington boots, climbed out of the passenger seat and made her way to Cassie's side through a patch of young nettles. Their first furry grey-green leaves were springing through a tangle of last year's dead couch grass. 'There used to be plenty of shamrock down here. We'll be better walking – the car would only get filthy.' She set off carefully, picking her way between the muddy ruts.

Cassie crossed to a nearby gate and climbed up a few bars to get the lie of the land. The fields sloped upwards and, in the distance, she could see what she thought was the gable end of the old farmhouse. Catching up with

Pat, she asked if she'd been right. 'Is that the house Ger was born in?'

'He was born and raised in it, love, and never left till we got married. I remember it in his mam's day. She kept a lovely home. His granddad bought the butcher's shop, and the flat above it, way back in the thirties. Well, the upstairs was just storage then, no one lived there. But Ger and I were given the use of it and, later on, Ger got the shop and his brother got the farm. And then, after poor Miyah died, Ger kept the farm going. Even these days, people like to know where their meat comes from. Ger used to say he could name the field that raised every joint in the shop.'

'What happened to Miyah?'

'He was never strong. He had a heart attack. Maybe he had the same weakness Ger had, I don't know. We didn't have all the scans and things back then.'

'You didn't have modern stress and stuff, though, either, did you?'

'No, but I suppose we had stresses and strains of our own.'

Cassie gestured up the hill. 'But look at all that amazing gorgeousness! And listen to the birds!' She turned a slow full circle, the heels of her boots churning up the mud. 'How could you find a more stunning place to live?'

'I don't suppose you could.'

'Do you still notice it?'

'Gracious, child, I haven't lost the use of my senses yet.'

'That's not what I meant. I thought that maybe because it was all so familiar you, kind of, wouldn't see what's here any more.'

'No, I've always loved the countryside. I didn't know you did.'

Cassie wrinkled her nose. 'I didn't either. Not before I came to Finfarran. Now I don't understand how Dad and Uncle Jim could leave.' As she spoke she realised that, only the previous week when she'd first met Brad, she'd been pining to set off round the world again. Yet now, gazing through drifting mist at these rolling fields, she couldn't imagine a better place to be.

With a squeak of triumph, Pat pointed to the foot of a gatepost. Squatting down Cassie peered at the mass of green trefoil. Its branching stems carried clusters of leaves hardly bigger than a fingernail, and each was divided into three further leaflets. She looked up at Pat. 'Not like the lucky shamrock you see on a greeting card.'

'No, love, I think some people confuse shamrock with four-leaf clover. It's an easy mistake to make. Anyway, this is the stuff we call shamrock here. You'd wear a bunch of it on your lapel.'

'Or in your hat?'

Pat laughed. 'Not many do these days. Mind you, Ger's father did. Your great-granddad.'

Cassie stood up with a leaf in her hand. 'Do you think he picked it here?'

'I've no notion, love. He'd have got it on the farm, though, I do know that.'

They were admiring the leaf when a shout came from the direction of the car. Looking up, Cassie saw Frankie coming towards them. Irritated by the interruption, and concerned not to show it, she waved with more enthusiasm than she felt. Then, as Frankie approached within hearing range, she called out cheerfully, 'We haven't been walking the bounds!' Frankie's face darkened. Thinking that she'd said something wrong, Cassie hastened to explain. 'I mean we're not burying eggs or trying to curse you.'

By now he had joined them, and was looking sharply at Pat. Cassie wondered if speaking of curses was thought to be unlucky. Or maybe it was a male/female thing, like the St Brigid's celebrations.

Something women didn't discuss with men? Whatever it was, he didn't seem happy.

Pat smiled. 'Don't mind her, son. I was telling her all about pishogues. We came out to look for the shamrock and there's great growth this year.'

Cassie saw Frankie's shoulders relax. He glanced at the shamrock without much interest, and the smile that never quite reached his eyes spread across his face. 'Fran said someone saw your car passing. She has tea made in the house if you'd like to drop up.'

Pat's eyes lit up. 'Well, that's nice, now. Isn't it, Cassie? I could do with a cup of tea.'

Cassie sighed inwardly. Whatever else she'd inherited from the Irish side of her family, it didn't include this endless obsession with tea. Still, if that was what Pat wanted, she couldn't be churlish. She smiled at Frankie, aware as she did so of a dull, wary mulishness in his eyes. He turned on his heel and, as they followed him, Cassie wondered if he mightn't be very bright. Had he taken on the farm because Dad and Uncle Jim weren't interested, or did he end up working for Ger because he wasn't fit for much else?

CHAPTER TWENTY

CASSIE WAS IN BED WITH HER LAPTOP ON her knee when a Skype call came through from Erin. Accepting it, she noticed Erin's avatar had changed. In the new shot the silvery-fair ringlets that had cascaded round her face were combed up into a severe bun. When she appeared on the screen her hair was down and a bit straggly and she was huddled in a large bathrobe.

Cassie waved at her. 'Hi. What's up?'

'Not much. Whatcha doing?'

'Lying here trying to decide whether to sleep or listen to music. Nice avatar.'

'Do you think so?' Erin twisted her hair onto the top of her head, held it there for a moment, and let it fall onto the shoulders of her fluffy pink robe. 'I changed it to cheer myself up, but I'm not sure I like it.'

'I think it looks good. How come you needed cheering up?'

'Oh, just, MEN, is all.'

'What's happened?'

'He dumped me.'

Retaining what she hoped was an unchanged expression, Cassie repositioned her laptop against her knees. 'Who did?'

'Oh, for God's sake, keep up! Jeff did. The guy who took me out to dinner?'

Still working hard on her expression, Cassie nodded. 'Oh, right. Jeff.'

'That's him. Jeff-oh-my-God-Erin-you're-so-gorgeous-you-look-so-fantastic-in-that-dress.'

'So what happened?'

Erin pulled forlornly at her hair. 'Do you think I should get this cut?'

'No, I don't. Tell me what happened.'

'We went out again. I thought things were fine. Next day my phone buzzed.'

'Oh, God. He dumped you by text! I hate when they do that.'

'I hate *him*. Men are rats.'

'I'm sorry.'

'Yeah, well. It is what it is. You're absolutely sure I shouldn't get a haircut?'

'Totally. I see it all the time. Long-haired woman gets dumped. Comes in demanding a pixie bob. Wakes next morning and regrets it.'

Erin looked doubtful. 'Okay.'

'Delete all photos of him. It's a cheaper option.'

'I did that as soon as I got the text.' Erin pushed her nose to one side and pulled down her lower lip. 'Anyway, he was odd-looking.'

'There you go! You're on the mend already.'

'Sure I am.'

They chatted on, frequently reverting to the awfulness of Jeff. Fortunately, Erin did most of the talking, leaving Cassie to deal with her own thoughts. So, Jack hadn't been Erin's date after all. With that established, she realised how much the thought had troubled her, and how huge had been the wave of relief when she'd found it wasn't so. What she needed now, she thought wryly, was a confidante. But, nice though Erin was, she couldn't be that. Not when she could easily bump into Jack at the mall or somewhere, and say something that would let the cat out of the bag.

Later, lying in bed with the light off, Cassie decided she needed to get a grip. There was no cat. And no bag. Nothing to tell. Nothing. She repeated this to herself several times before facing the fact that it wasn't honest. Why hadn't she asked Erin the name of her date in the first place? And tonight, when she'd heard who it was, why had she felt so tongue-tied? If there was no reason for this horrible, cringey sense of embarrassment, wouldn't she just have spoken up and laughed with Erin at the joke? But she hadn't, dammit, and the current state of her mind showed how bad things had got. Turning over, she switched on the light and reached for her laptop. There was no hope of sleep at this point, she told herself crossly. Because now she knew for certain that Jack wasn't dating Erin, she was anxiously wondering whether or not he was dating somebody else.

*

When Cassie arrived at the library next day, Hanna could see that she hadn't had a good night. She was listless and pale and had dark circles under her eyes. Judging by her expression, though, she didn't want to talk about it, so Hanna sent her to set out the cushions in Children's Corner. 'There's a Tots Tell session booked in this morning, but the mum who was going to lead it has had an emergency.'

'What's Tots Tell?'

'Don't you remember? We went through the children's activities last week.'

'Sorry. Yes, I do. It's toddlers reading aloud. Is that right?'

'No, because not many toddlers know how to read.' It was the gentlest of rebukes, lightly spoken, but Cassie looked disconsolate. Hanna smiled. 'Look, don't worry, there's been a lot for you to pick up. The mums choose a suitable book – like *Piggies* or *Wolf in the Snow* – and hold it up, and ask the tots what they see in the pictures.'

'And that's it?'

'It's about socialisation, Cassie, and interaction. And familiarisation with the concept of books. All that stuff we talked about?'

'Yeah. Sure. I'm sorry. I'll go put out the cushions.'

'Do. And you'll be leading today.'

'I will?'

'Yes, because, as I said, the mum who was going to do it has had an emergency. It was Darina Kelly.'

'Oh, God, of course it was. What happened?'

'She thinks one of her kids has drunk nettle dye.'

'You make dye from nettles?'

'Shades of yellow and green, apparently. Darina was planning to tie-dye some muslin and Setanta assumed she'd been making tea. Which is exactly the same recipe, apparently, so I can't see what the problem is. Anyway, Darina's taken him to the clinic.'

'So what do I have to do?'

'Just hold up whatever book they select, turn the

pages, encourage chat, and try to make sure that no one pees on the cushions.'

'How?'

Cassie looked so aghast that Hanna laughed. 'Kids tend to wriggle before it happens. Admittedly, they tend to do the same if they love a picture. But you don't have to worry. The mums are a great bunch. They'll keep things on track.'

As Cassie went off to find the cushions, Hanna took her third call of the day enquiring about the Transatlantic Book Club. At this rate, she told herself, she'd need to set out extra chairs this evening. When she finished the call, the door opened and Pat came in, mobile in hand. 'I've just had a text from Mary. She says your phone's turned off. I'd say the second one there is meant for me, not you.'

Hanna smiled reluctantly as she read the first text.

TELL HANNA JOHNNYS GOING TO GET ME IN THE CLUB TONIGHT

The second, which had been sent moments later, read, TAKE THAT SMIRK OFF YOU%T FACE YOU KNOW WHAT I MEAN SEE YOU 7

Evidently Mary had cadged a lift to the book club from her neighbour Johnny Hennessy. Hanna looked at Pat anxiously, acutely aware that Johnny and his wife had a lot to put up with from Mary. 'Is Johnny going to join us?'

'Not at all, I'd say he's just coming into Lissbeg for a pint.' Pat nudged her. 'Don't you go feeling guilty, now. He'll save you driving out to pick Mary up and bring her in, but the chances are that you'll still have to take her home.'

'Actually, I'm glad to see her safe home when she's there in the house alone.'

'Ah, she was on her own for a good few years when Tom died and she was fine.'

'She's older now, though.'

Like every other woman with elderly relatives, Hanna fretted about the future yet tried to live day by day. She'd been relieved when Louisa, her ex-mother-in-law, had taken a flatlet at the bungalow, which had begun to feel too large for Mary on her own. Sharing was the perfect solution for two ageing widows, and Louisa, who regularly went to London, needed no more than a pied-à-terre in Lissbeg. She was a reserved, genteel woman with a shrewd sense of humour and, surprisingly, she and Mary got on well. Hanna suspected this had to do with Louisa's frequent breaks from her housemate, but the arrangement worked and she was glad of it. Having shared Mary's home herself in the first years after her marriage break-up, she knew that, whatever changes might have to be made in the future, she and her mother couldn't live under one roof. Jazz, to whom Mary was indulgent, could laugh at her grandmother's foibles, just as Pat could find Mary good company yet also call her a cow. But Hanna had watched the corrosive effect of her mother's jealousy all her life, and her relationship with Mary had always felt far closer to war than love.

Pat put her phone into her bag. 'Well, you'll have a break now between your day's work and the meeting this evening. Will you come up to the flat for a bite to eat?'

'I'd love to.'

'I'll see you later, then.' Pat turned to go, then jerked her head at Cassie, who was staggering towards Children's Corner with a basket of cushions. 'If I were you I'd get a strong coffee into that one. It looks to me like she's dying to curl up on that lot and go to sleep.'

*

In the end, Cassie made it through the day successfully, though she was yawning widely as she and Hanna crossed the road at five thirty. As soon as they got to the flat she said she'd nip upstairs and change. 'Could I just grab a sandwich, Pat, and take it with me?'

As Cassie disappeared upstairs with her sandwich, Pat gave Hanna a knowing wink. 'If you ask me she'll be fast asleep in five minutes. And down here at ten to seven, bright-eyed and bushy-tailed.' A delicious smell was rising from a saucepan on the range. Ladling soup into bowls, Pat carried them to the table. She pushed the breadboard towards Hanna, and indicated the butter dish. 'There you are now, help yourself.'

They chatted as they ate, but most of Hanna's mind was on the meals she'd eaten in this kitchen as a child. The hours she'd spent round at Maggie's place had come to an end when the old lady died so, from the age of twelve, Hanna had helped in the Casey family shop after school. It was a grocery on one side and a post office on the other. Kids would sit outside drinking red lemonade, and people who came to post letters would lean on the counter for a chat. If a horn hooted out in the road, Hanna would be called to cut cheese or slice bacon while her dad attended the petrol pumps that stood outside the door. She had quite enjoyed the work and the new closeness to her father. But in the evenings, and on Sundays, when Mary demanded Tom's undivided attention, it had always been best to slip away, lest her presence provoke a row. There was plenty of entertainment to be had on the beach and exploring the cliffs but, more often than not, she'd find herself here in the kitchen, chatting to Pat.

Time spent with her godmother was nothing like the time she'd spent at Maggie's place. Here she had never been asked to scrub the floor or peel spuds. Instead, sitting in the warm kitchen, eating drop scones with jam and butter, Pat would talk about the poetry books she borrowed from Carrick Library and kept on the shelf of the dresser among the blue-striped cups. And, between the recitations from old-fashioned poets she never heard of at school, Hanna would talk to Pat about paintings.

As a child, she hadn't been much of a reader, and when she'd found books it was pictures that mattered at first, not words. What had seized her imagination was a flier from the National Gallery, which she'd found tucked into a school library book. The exhibition was long over by the time she'd borrowed the book, but as soon as she'd seen the flier she'd been entranced. It was a reproduction of a painting of an eighteenth-century manor. In front of the house a young man stood at a horse's head, wearing a yellow coat and knee breeches with a richly embroidered waistcoat and a tricorn hat. The horse was harnessed to a high-wheeled open carriage in which a young woman in powdered curls and a pink quilted petticoat sat with a laughing toddler on her knee. To fourteen-year-old Hanna the painting had offered heart-stopping possibilities, though at the time she would have been hard put to articulate what they were.

During the summer holidays, she'd risked a row by persuading her father to take her up to Dublin. They'd walked the National Gallery without finding her painting, but when they'd emerged Hanna had a dream. She already knew she was useless with a paintbrush, but people created catalogues, and wrote the signs under the pictures and statues. Maybe she could find work doing that. Later, when she'd discovered that large galleries had libraries, everything had fallen into place. She would train as an art librarian and work in a thrilling gallery. And one day, beyond the confines of Finfarran, she'd find her own version of the life portrayed in her painting, complete with a beautiful home, the perfect husband, and a child who would never, ever feel unloved.

A gush of water in the downpipe outside the window indicated that Cassie was taking a shower. Pat laughed and stood up to make tea to follow the apple tart they'd had for their dessert. 'She'll be down now in a minute, all dressed up to the nines. God, wouldn't you envy her energy? She was awake half the night with her light on, I know that for sure. And do you know what it is, Hanna? I'd say she's in love!'

If this was true, thought Hanna, it was typical of Pat to be delighted. She'd always had a soft spot for a love affair. Hanna could remember confiding in her the first time her own heart had been broken, by a boy she'd met at a disco. And when she'd come back to Finfarran grieving for a broken marriage, for which she'd thrown up her dream career, Pat had told her roundly that life was complicated. 'So your husband turned out not to be the man you'd thought you'd married! Sure what matter? Didn't you give it your best shot, girl? And look at the lovely daughter you've come away with!'

Now Hanna smiled at Pat, whose eyes were shining at the thought of Cassie in love. 'So who is it? Do you know?'

'Not at all, love. I haven't a notion. But I haven't lived this long without knowing the signs.'

CHAPTER TWENTY-ONE

HAVING TAKEN THE BRIEFEST OF CAT-NAPS, Cassie found herself dressing as if preparing for a date. The jeans she'd worn to work were clean but, rummaging through her wardrobe, she took out a new pair and an oversized sweater, edgy and urban but also suggestive of the waif-like look she'd always envied in Erin. Not that Erin was competition. Definitely not. That had been established. Having indulged in a scented shower gel, which she'd had unopened since Christmas, Cassie sat down at the mirror and frowned at her hair. This was the moment, she reckoned. She'd add a touch of metallic pomade to the peacock flash in her fringe. Subtly different was the effect to go for. Nothing to elicit comment. Not with an audience looking on from both sides of the Atlantic.

The slightest touch of silver pomade produced a satisfactory background shimmer. Happy with the cut, which she'd trimmed only the other day at the salon, Cassie leaned forward and wondered about her eyes.

The cat-nap hadn't done much to mitigate her lack of sleep. Hesitating, she wondered whether a haggard look would be interesting or just hag-like. Then she decided not to take the risk. The combination of panda eyes and a huge grey sweater might be more Morticia than Galadriel.

Ten minutes later, discreetly made up, she shimmied into the new jeans and pulled on the sweater. It was fine-knit silk and wool and looked effortlessly cool worn with Doc Martens. As she gave a final twirl in front of the mirror, she remembered another book she'd had as a kid. It had been too full of magic hares and unicorns for her liking, but one line had apparently lodged in her mind. The Victorian heroine, who lived in a village called Silverydew, and had a governess with the twee name of Miss Heliotrope, was described as 'one of your true aristocrats for whom the perfection of hidden things was even more important than outward show'.

Remembering it, Cassie giggled. By that reckoning, she herself must be seriously aristocratic, since no one in Resolve was likely to see her footwear or smell her expensive bergamot shower gel. But that, she reminded herself, wasn't the point. Getting dressed up might partly be about Jack but, really, all she wanted was to make herself feel good. Seconds later, catching her eye in the mirror, she knew that it wasn't. But telling herself it was made her feel better – or, at least, less of a lovesick fool.

Grabbing her bag and the plate on which she'd carried up her sandwich, she clattered downstairs to where Pat and Hanna were still at the kitchen table. Neither of them remarked on her appearance. Unsure whether to be miffed or pleased, Cassie washed the plate and went to make herself a coffee. It was twenty past six and Hanna stood up, saying she ought to get back to the library. Switching off the kettle, Cassie said that she'd go along.

'No, don't, stay and have your coffee. You're not supposed to be working – you're a club member.'

'Yeah, but I'm happy to help.'

'There's really nothing to do. Ferdia's going to set things up.'

'I can put out the seating.'

'Well, okay, if you're sure you want to.'

Pat stood up decisively. 'Let's all go over now. I can help too.'

Cassie felt guilty. Her best chance of seeing Jack was during the set-up, but was it fair to drag Pat across the road so early, and to allow her to carry stacks of library chairs? Anyway, what could possibly happen if and when she saw Jack? She couldn't expect a chat in the midst of the technical stuff. About to say that she'd stay put and come over with Pat later, she saw that her grandmother had already gone to fetch her coat. Hanna, whose coat was on a nearby chair, was clearing the kitchen table. Unsure of what to do for the best, Cassie helped her. Then Pat came back, wearing a yellow anorak, and the three of them made for the door.

They paused on the landing as Pat turned the key in the new Chubb lock. It had come with two keys, which Fury had formally placed on the kitchen table saying that, when a workman fitted a lock, half the world complained that they'd never seen sight nor light of their spare key. 'And then,' he'd declared bitterly, 'they're up and down the town announcing you've probably sold it off to a gang of thieves!'

Pat had given the spare to Cassie, watching her fit it onto her keyring with the Yale key to the flat door, and the other which gave access to the shop. Now she checked that Cassie had the keyring.

'Yup. It's right here in my purse. Don't worry.'

'Because I turn this key when I go to bed now, you know that.'

'Yes, I do.'

'And you might want to go gallivanting after the book club.'

'Well, I might. But I think I'm far more likely to want to come home with you and crash.'

As they descended the stairs to the shadowy shop, Cassie wondered where Pat had thought she might go gallivanting. With the exceptions of her visit to Frankie and Fran and the fish and chips she'd had with Pat after last week's book club, she hadn't been out at night since they'd returned from Resolve. In fact, she'd never mentioned her visit to Frankie's – she wasn't sure why, but she'd felt she still needed to process it. Perhaps the bottom line was just that she didn't like her uncle much. He'd been weird again last weekend when they'd gone for tea after finding the shamrock. Fran had given them a great welcome, hugging and kissing them both and summoning scones and plates of cake. She'd ushered them into a living room full of over-stuffed armchairs, and fussed about bringing Pat a side table for her cup. But Frankie had simply sat and stared disconcertingly at Cassie, who'd hardly been able to wait to get away.

She set out the chairs for the book club while Ferdia fiddled with the computer and Pat and Hanna chatted with Mary Casey, whom they'd met as they came across the road from the flat. Darina arrived ridiculously early with Gobnit still in tow. The little girl was hunched over a game on her mother's iPhone. Sitting down, Darina rolled her eyes at Cassie. 'Isn't it dreadful? She won't give me the phone so now I have to take her wherever I go!'

Cassie decided that Gobnit's presence was Hanna's problem, not hers. Anyway, the child's iPhone fixation was keeping her quiet. With the chairs arranged, she went through to the library and found Pat asking which books the group in Resolve had chosen. Hanna said she didn't know. 'Josie and I exchanged email addresses, but I've heard no more.'

Mary swung her bag onto Hanna's desk and gave a derisive snort. 'Wouldn't you think Josie would get her ducks in a row!'

Cassie saw Hanna's flash of irritation before Pat leaned in to give Mary a push. 'Ah, for God's sake, she's not running a boot camp! They're probably still discussing it and haven't been able to choose.'

'Well, I've never known what anyone sees in that Josie Fenton. From all I've heard she's about as much use to the world as a chocolate teapot.'

Hanna intervened: 'Pat's right, Mam, and there's no hurry. It takes time for a club to get on its feet.'

Seeing Mary's eyebrows rise in massive disapproval,

Cassie edged away from the desk and went back to join Ferdia. As she'd hoped, he'd just established the link with the Shamrock Club. When she entered the reading room she heard Jack's voice and realised, with a sense of shock, that she'd know it anywhere. Yet they'd spent so short a time together that evening in Resolve and had hardly exchanged more than a sentence since.

Pausing just inside the doorway, she could see him on the screen. As he walked away from the camera on his side of the ocean, she realised he was taller and more muscular than she'd remembered. 'Rangy' was the word she'd used to describe him in Resolve, and it still seemed to fit. He moved with a grace that reminded her of Pangur, the white cat, and now, watching the steady way he went about his work, she wondered if the comfortable quality she'd dismissed as boring was actually effortless assurance. As he came back to adjust his camera he cracked a joke with Ferdia, his eyes gleaming like slivers of blue glass. Feeling she was acting like a stalker, Cassie moved abruptly from the door and walked towards Ferdia's camera. To her delight, Jack's face broke into its lopsided smile. 'Hey, you! Good to see you!'

But did he mean it? Or, more to the point, what exactly did he mean?

She stopped at what she hoped was a flattering distance from the camera. Last week, delighted by the sight of a woman she'd known at school, someone had rushed forward and bent down with her nose almost pressed to the camera in Resolve. The effect on the screen in Lissbeg was grotesque, and what ought to have been touching had provoked a roar of laughter.

Unsure whether to wave or not, Cassie tried to stick her thumbs into her belt loops and couldn't locate one through the folds of her sweater. Desperately, she clasped her hands behind her, then panicked because it might look as if she'd deliberately stuck out her boobs. It seemed an awfully long time since Jack had spoken so she raised her voice and called out, 'Hi.' Jack blinked and took a step back and, seeing his reaction, Ferdia frowned and reached for the volume control. Cassie wanted to crawl away and die. Obviously, she'd sounded like a foghorn, as weird and inappropriate as the lady who'd looked so grotesque last week.

But the guys didn't seem to be bothered. Each was fiddling with his volume settings, trying to establish balance, and when Jack looked up he just asked her to say something else. 'Could you speak again at the same pitch, Cassie? And move about, like you did last week?'

'Sure thing.'

Just as she'd done previously, Cassie moved from chair to chair, speaking from different positions. But last week had been different. Now she felt all arms and legs, and everything she said sounded stupid. Jack's encouraging attitude made matters worse. 'Don't worry, just keep talking. I need to get a level.'

Cassie promptly froze and couldn't say anything at all. Groping for words, she found Gobnit's eyes fixed on her, filled with scorn. At that moment Mary Casey surged into the room. 'What's the story here? It's nearly seven. Are you not ready yet?'

In fact, there were ten minutes to go, and even Resolve's punctual readers had only begun to trickle into the Shamrock Club's library. Jack's face on the screen broke into a smile. 'Oh, hi, there. Mrs Casey, isn't it? We're testing for sound. Could you sit down somewhere and say a few words? Maybe move around?'

'I'll sit where I'm going to sit, young man, and that'll have to do you.'

She ensconced herself in the front row and was joined by Pat, who was followed by a chattering group of others. Feeling relieved, Cassie edged out of camera-range and went and found Hanna. 'Would you like me to stay at the door and let latecomers in?'

'That'd be great. I'll go through to Ferdia now, and see what's happening.'

'I think they're pretty much all set up.'

Alone at the desk, she pulled herself together and, when the last latecomers had been sent through, slipped back into the reading room and found the club discussing its choice of book. As Hanna had guessed, the group in Resolve had been unable to agree. Josie was holding two books up to the camera, Agatha Christie's *And Then There Were None* and *The Moving Target* by Ross Macdonald. 'So it came to a toss-up between these two, or at least ...' Josie looked round nervously '... most of us accepted that it did.'

A hand shot up a couple of rows behind her, and Ned, one of the Canny twins, stood up. 'Actually, if you'll forgive me, Josie, that's not exactly the case. A number of us feel, Hanna, that an Irish author would be more appropriate. And many of us are still of the opinion that *A Long Way to LA* would be best of all.'

A large woman sitting by Josie turned and looked over her shoulder. Whatever she said to Ned was lost, because her back was to the microphone, but, judging by the faces behind her, it wasn't anything good.

Everyone sitting round Cassie was agog, some of them clearly hoping to witness a fight. Then Hanna cleared her throat. 'Can we all remember to raise our hands if we're going to speak, please? It makes things easier. And I do see what you mean about reading an Irish author, Ned, but I can't imagine you found many in your collection, did you, Josie? Vintage detective fiction isn't really an Irish genre.' Josie said, no, she hadn't, and Hanna went on briskly, ignoring the red herring of *A Long Way to LA*. 'Christie or *The Moving Target* look like great choices. And, after all, this is just the beginning. We might branch out into other genres later.'

Ned Canny looked unappeased but, before he could respond, Mary raised her voice: 'If you ask me, you can't beat Margery Allingham.' Everyone in Resolve leaned forward to see who had spoken and Mary waved her hand imperiously, summoning Josie's attention. 'Would you have *The Case of the Late Pig*, Josie?'

Josie said they had.

'Well, there you are, then. Why don't we go for a compromise?'

Having clearly worked hard to establish the options, Josie looked flustered. But Mary was now on a roll. 'I'd say that's the best way forward, wouldn't you, Hanna? We'll settle for *The Late Pig*.'

From the back of the room, Cassie saw Hanna stiffen,

but such was the force of Mary's self-confidence that, on both sides of the Atlantic, heads were beginning to nod. Looking a little bewildered and having taken the mood of her meeting, Josie smiled. 'Well, I guess it looks like we're all in agreement. Thanks, Mary.'

In the scatter of applause that followed, the sideways look that Cassie saw Mary throw at Pat spoke volumes. Whatever had been the outcome of their earlier spat about Josie, she had now triumphantly demonstrated how to get your all ducks in a row.

CHAPTER TWENTY-TWO

MARY AND PAT HAD A TIME-HONOURED tradition of watching Lissbeg's St Patrick's Day parade from the window of Pat's kitchen. The clock above the seed merchant's a few doors down from Fitzgerald's sported tricolour ribbons, while the deli had decked its shelves with rainbow colours and filled its window with pottery bowls overflowing with green and gold confetti. All along the parade route, volunteers were rattling boxes, collecting for the mountain-rescue team, the lifeboat service and other local charities. The shop window displays made a festive background for the marching groups with their streamers, the tractors pulling trailers crowded with musicians, and the floats carrying school kids in green hats and nylon beards.

Ger always used to stay open for late-night shopping on the sixteenth, and leave the blind up the following day to display his decorations. Pat had told Des to do the same this year. When Tom and Ger were alive they used to saunter round the town together, leaving the grandstand view from the kitchen to Mary and Pat. So, she didn't miss him in the flat today, though she'd felt lonely earlier, seeing the wolfhound and his round tower with the crêpe-paper-covered pots of shamrock at his feet.

Pulling a couple of chairs from the table to the window, she settled herself to await Mary's arrival. Across the street a marching band had assembled in the old nuns' garden. Along Broad Street, and over at the horse trough, people were claiming viewing points. Back in the day they'd all have been to Mass first thing in the morning and sat down to their dinner at one o'clock. Now the parade was held at noon because most people had their big meal in the evening and, though some made an exception for Patrick's Day, like they did for Christmas and Easter, not many households went to Mass these days. Neither did Pat. She'd had enough of the nuns' old guff at school, and the way the Brothers had treated Ger had put her off the lot of them for life. Besides, the clergy's abuse of kids all over the world made her sick, and the fact that they wouldn't admit to it made things worse. Since the revelations, she'd noticed plenty of her generation staying away from the sermons and sacraments they'd grown up with.

They might drop into the church all right but not if the priest was there. She couldn't tell if that made her sad or plain angry – because why should they have to do that at their time of life? But she didn't dwell on it. You lived out your time the best way you could and tried to do right by your neighbours, and if that didn't make you a good person, the belt of some bishop's crozier never would.

It was a grand day for the parade. The sun was glinting on the old convent building's stained-glass windows and striking light from the silver flutes and fifes in the kids' hands. The band wore white tops and black tracksuit bottoms and the colours made Pat think back to the past. When she was at school no one had been allowed in the nuns' private domain, but when she'd married and moved to the flat she could look down and see black-robed figures moving between the herb beds, their heads bent within their veils, which had starched white lining. That was before the school closed and the council bought the buildings and the garden.

As Pat watched, a pair of birds swooped over the horse trough. Curving across Broad Street, they rose, turned, and settled on a wire that stretched from a telephone pole on the street to the end of the library building. It was early for the house martins to turn up again in Lissbeg. These were the first she'd seen this year, and now they were joined by two others. As the newcomers turned in flight towards the wire, the white feathers on their underparts flashed. Then the curved claws fastened round their perch and, as they sat in a row on the wire, all Pat could see were four glossy backs, as black as the birds' cocked heads, and their long forked tails. Who could believe that these little bundles of bone, muscle and feathers had flown all the way to Africa and returned to their nests under the convent eaves?

There was another poem by Hardy she liked, about an old thrush with what was described as a 'blast-beruffled plume'. It had made Pat think about the house martins' journey across the windswept ocean, so she'd looked them up in the library to see how far they'd had to fly. The distances were mind-boggling, and it had pleased her to see that practically nothing was known about the life martins lived at the other side of the world. Though the eaves above the stained-glass windows were thick with their mud-built nests, she imagined the birds as jealous of their privacy – members of a community but protective of the secrets of their individual lives.

As though in response to a signal, the four martins rose from the wire and wheeled across the courtyard and the garden, darting towards the nests that clung to the old convent wall. Turning her head to follow their flight, Pat saw Mary walking down Broad Street with a bunch of shamrock pinned to her lapel. Mary, who was a great one for the Carrick shops, always said she'd rather be out of the world than out of the fashion. She had her good coat on now, the way she always did on St Patrick's Day, a new tweed three-quarter length with a plum-coloured velvet trim. The sight of her almost made Pat expect to hear Ger take his hat from the peg and go down to meet Tom. Instead she went down to let Mary in, and followed her up the stairs to the flat aware that – whatever you might say about her expanding figure – Mary had always kept her shapely legs. Among the things Pat had bought for her all those years ago was a pair of ten-denier tights to wear with her wedding dress. You wouldn't have found tights in Ireland in those days, which was why Mary wanted them. When they'd gone to the mall, Josie had had to tell Pat to ask for "pantyhose". That was Josie, she was one of those people who'd adapted to the States straight away, the kind that wouldn't always be looking over their shoulder towards home.

As soon as Mary settled in her chair by the window, she produced a packet of mint chocolate biscuits. Pat shook her head at her. 'Ah, for God's sake, you knew I'd have buns made.'

'I did, of course, but what harm? Can't we open these as well?'

That was how it was in Finfarran. You wouldn't want to go into a house with one arm as long as the other, so you'd always bring a bottle or some kind of treat. Still, Pat knew Cassie would be home at some point and make short work of whatever she and Mary didn't eat. She put the biscuits in a bowl on the windowsill, where their green foil wrapping looked the part. Over in the nuns' garden the band had begun to play. The parade was due to march down one side of Broad Street and back up the other. According to the programme, the band would join them on their final circuit of the town but, to begin with, it would play in the garden to entertain the crowds.

Mary gave Pat a poke in the arm. 'So what did we think of last night?'

'I thought you could've kept your beak shut, for one thing.'

They hadn't got much further with the book talk last night after choosing *The Late Pig*. Somehow they'd all got chatting about their St Patrick's Day celebrations and the fact that the Shamrock Club was planning a do. They were going to have a dance and a big meal in the evening, and Mrs Shanahan's latest piece would be presented to the club. She'd held it up to the camera, so the group in Lissbeg could see it, and explained that it was a banner for the Lucky Charm bar.

Picking at green-foil wrapping, Mary remarked that, as banners went, it looked like a lot of work. There was a pause in which they ate biscuits before catching each other's eye. Then Pat let out a yelp of laughter and smacked Mary on the hand. 'God forgive the two of us, would you stop it!'

'Ah, be fair now, I kept a straight face last night.'

The banner had featured a huge four-leafed clover, which Mrs Shanahan, who'd designed it, had called 'the sweet little emblem of Ireland'. With admirable politeness, the group in Lissbeg had said it was great.

Pat regained her composure. 'Ah, God help her, Mary, it's a lovely piece of work.'

'I never said it wasn't. But wouldn't you think that Josie would have put the poor woman straight? I mean, a four-leafed clover, Pat! "The sweet little emblem of Ireland"!'

'Josie's not in the quilting guild. And Mrs Shanahan's the chairlady.'

'I'd have said something if I'd been there, to stop her making a fool of herself.'

'Maybe she wouldn't have wanted you interfering.'

'Ay, well, you'll always stand up for Josie, we all know that.'

'Haven't I just said it's nothing to do with Josie?'

'Well, what call have you to stand up for that Mrs Shanahan, then?' Sniffing, Mary turned her attention to the window. The front of the parade had appeared at the far end of Broad Street. Swinging along at a great pace, school kids were marching to the beat of a drummer, in front of whom strode Mr Maguire, resplendent as St Patrick with a cardboard crozier and mitre. He was wearing green poplin robes with a sheepskin round his shoulders and a pair of hide boots. Some steps behind him was Darina, arrayed in sacking and more sheepskin. She was flanked by Gobnit, clutching the iPhone and wearing green face paint, and her hair was flying in green and orange dreadlocks. The previous night Darina had announced at the club that modern scholars believed St Patrick had a wife whose name was Sheelah. This had been met with blank stares on both sides of the Atlantic and, judging by his expression today and the speed at which he was moving, it wasn't a theory Mr Maguire endorsed. Behind the school kids, two abreast, came balloon-festooned tractors, and a van from which employees of the AgriCoOp were throwing handfuls of sweets. Behind them, more musicians were followed by the local fire engine in which crew members were wearing flashing shamrocks on their helmets.

Leaning forward, Pat spotted Cassie. There was a young man with her and they were walking along behind the spectators, trying to find a clear space on the pavement. Pat put her head out of the window and waved them up. For a minute Cassie seemed to hesitate. Then she nodded and spoke to her companion, who looked up at the window and waved back at Pat.

When they came into the flat Cassie seemed in great form. 'This is Bradley Miller. He's from the States.'

Mary turned round appraisingly and asked if he had relations in Lissbeg.

'I come from good German stock on both sides, I'm afraid. Not a single drop of Irish blood in my veins.'

'I'm not saying it's compulsory.'

Pat intervened: 'Indeed she's not. She's just being nosy. You're very welcome, Bradley. Are you here for the parade?'

'Yeah. I'm scoping out the area for work. I arrange tours.'

'Is that so?' Mary, who'd continued to stare at him,

raised her eyebrows. 'And how did you two meet, if it's not too nosy a question to ask?'

Pat nearly kicked her but the young man didn't seem bothered and neither did Cassie. Instead, they sat at the table eating buns and Cassie explained that they'd met in Ballyfin when she'd cut his hair. 'He works for a cruise line.'

Pat said that sounded glamorous. Mary nodded judicially. 'And that's why you got chatting?'

'I suppose you could say so, yes.'

You couldn't go staring at the poor lad the way Mary was, but Pat took a look at him while she was making the tea. He was wearing what Josie would call smart-casual clothing and had a great tan and a wide American smile. She wondered if Cassie had met him today by appointment, or if they'd just happened to meet in the street. As she poured milk into a jug, she decided to wait and see if that would come out in conversation. But Mary waded in with both feet. 'Tell me this now, Cassie, are you out on a date or how did you meet up today?'

Pat nearly dropped a cup, but Cassie just laughed. Bradley got up to carry the tray and said he'd come into town for the parade. 'And, next thing I know, there's Cassie. It wasn't too surprising. She'd told me she's staying here in Lissbeg with her gran.'

'You'll have to forgive me now, Bradley, but turning up where you know she lives sounds a bit opportune.'

He gave her a broad, infectious grin. 'Not guilty, Mrs Casey. But Cassie's gorgeous, so, yeah, I do see your point.'

It was said in such a charming, easy-going way that everybody laughed, and, though Pat shot a quick glance at Cassie, she could read nothing but good humour in her face. Later, when Bradley was gone and Cassie was upstairs in her bedroom, she gave Mary the kick she'd been holding back for hours. 'Honestly, have you no sense of how to behave?'

'And what have I done now?'

'Questioning Cassie and Bradley like that! I was mortified!'

'God, Pat, you're a terrible woman for fooling yourself. You weren't mortified at all! You were dying to hear the answers. Though I'll tell you this for free, girl, I'm not sure I believe them. If you ask me, that Bradley Miller's a hard nut to crack.'

Sticking to the habit of a lifetime, Pat didn't argue with her. Mary might get hold of the wrong end of the stick on occasion, but she was no fool and, this time, it could be she was right.

CHAPTER TWENTY-THREE

MARY'S VISIT EXTENDED INTO THE evening. When she left, Pat called Cassie down and they chatted. According to Cassie, Brad was surprised by what he'd seen in Lissbeg. It wasn't the kind of St Patrick's Day parade that he'd envisaged, and Cassie, too, had found it different from what she'd expected. 'I guess I'd imagined the sorts of things you see on TV. Majorettes and police bands and fountains spouting green water.'

'Well, no, love, we wouldn't go in for that.'

'And the mayor and politicians glad-handing. And multi-cultural stuff. In Toronto last year we had a dancing green dragon.'

'You'd get the odd politician out here, all right, but there wouldn't be much call for dragons. I'd say they'd be more St George's thing than St Patrick's. Snakes, now. You might get snakes in a Patrick's Day parade. Did you and Brad not enjoy yourselves?'

'God, no, we loved it. Well, I know I did, and he had a ball.'

Mary would have been sure to ask if Cassie had plans to see Brad again, but Pat had a feeling the question wouldn't be welcome. She decided to leave it at that. He'd looked like a decent fellow, very cheerful and charming but, like Mary said, there was something reserved about him. A kind of smoothness that seemed to keep you at bay. Pat wondered if Cassie wasn't aware of it, or if she simply had no reason to care.

Later, when Cassie had gone out again, and Pat watched the Dublin parade on the evening news, she told herself she was getting as nosy as Mary. Cassie's life was her own and she didn't need her granny sticking her oar in. On the other hand, there were times when she seemed terribly young and vulnerable. She was a girl who'd struck out on her own far too young, perhaps, and had missed having a mother she could talk to. Sonny's wife, Annette, was nice enough but, like Cassie's siblings, she was a full-on businesswoman. When the children were young she'd left them to a nanny, descending in a guilty whirl if they were ill or did badly at school, and otherwise being absent or unavailable. Cassie's career choice had made no sense to her mother, who saw her freewheeling lifestyle as irresponsible. If Cassie were in love, Pat was sure that Annette wouldn't notice, and if she'd fallen for a lad who worked on cruise ships he wouldn't be deemed good enough for her upwardly mobile family.

As she turned off the news before going to bed, Pat reflected that she'd been younger than Cassie was now when she'd spent that summer in Resolve. Ger had proposed to her on the beach where the four of them had gone to celebrate Mary and Tom's engagement. They'd planned a night at the pictures in Carrick after a drink in the pub, but the news of the engagement had put paid to that. Instead they'd taken a bottle of Blue Nun down to the beach near Lissbeg. It was a night of bright stars. They hung like jewels in an inky sky and their pale light glimmered on the waves. The boys went looking for timber on the shoreline while Mary and Pat went up to the dunes for handfuls of grass and dry seaweed to start a fire. Pat could remember sand sliding beneath her feet as she climbed the dunes. They were so steep she'd had to hold the hem of her skirt in her teeth, so she wouldn't walk on it. She'd pulled herself up by grabbing tufts of marram grass and a sharp blade of it had slashed a cut across the palm of her hand. The blood had tasted salty when she licked it.

When the fire was lit the four of them had sat there, passing the bottle round. After a while, Mary and Tom had started acting the maggot. She'd take a mouthful of wine and kiss him, and pass it on to him that way, mouth to mouth. Pretty soon they forgot the wine and started to snog. Pat and Ger were sitting across from them, feeling awkward and watching through the flames. It didn't matter, of course, because the other two didn't notice.

A bit after that, Mary had grabbed Tom's hand and run with him into the dunes. They'd taken the bottle with them, so Pat and Ger just sat by the fire, looking up at the stars. Pat could hear the sea and smell the tarry smell of the burning timber. She could sense the ocean stretching away for thousands of fathomless miles, black under the moonlight on one side of the world and sparkling under sunshine on the other. And Ger had said, without looking at her, 'Will we get married, so?' Pat had said yes at once because she'd known the question was coming. She'd known that Tom would ask Mary too, but she'd kind of been holding her breath in case he wouldn't. She'd told herself life was strange and that you never knew what might happen. But as soon as she'd seen Tom's face that night she'd known what he had done.

In those days Resolve had felt like a different world altogether. Looking back, Pat could see herself struggling with the door of the railway carriage, stepping onto the platform and seeing Josie standing there in a little shift dress and a pillbox hat. The hat was made of white petals, her hair was styled and her makeup looked great. Back then, women in the States never seemed to go out unless they were all dolled up – that was the first thing Pat had noticed when she'd got off the boat in New York. In Lissbeg you might run out to the shops with an apron over your frock, and you only got your hair done for special occasions. Most of the girls made their own clothes and no one had their legs waxed or their nails done in a beauty shop, like Josie did. That was for millionaires. Yet Josie just worked in the office at the factory, and lived in the rooming house nearby with a rake of other girls.

The woman who owned the house lived in the basement and Josie said it was great the way she never interfered. 'There's places where the landladies act like some class of mother superior, walking in and out of your room and telling you what to do.'

'But this Mrs Quinn doesn't do that?'

'Not at all. Mrs Quinn's sound. So long as you pay your rent on the nail, and don't be bringing in lads, she leaves you alone.'

They'd caught a bus to the house, which was on the outskirts of town, only a few stops away from the factory. Pat's face must have changed when she saw it because Josie asked if she'd been expecting a white picket fence. Pat said no but they both knew she was lying. What else would you expect if all you knew of America was what you'd seen at the pictures? She'd imagined something out of a Deanna Durbin musical or, idiotically, a wooden house like the ones they'd have on the main street in a cowboy film. Instead it was a brick-built, three-storey place with an attic. Josie said Pat was lucky not to have ended up under the roof. 'There's no air-con up there and it's fierce hot in summer. But someone's moved out of the second floor back, and I've got her to give you that.'

The second floor back was bigger than Pat's bedroom in Finfarran. You couldn't fault the bed and there was a table where you could sit to write letters. Josie warned her not to think she could eat there. 'Mrs Quinn's afraid of mice, but you can bring a cup of tea up. There's a dining room off the kitchen downstairs, where we have our meals.'

The girls in the house worked different shifts, so you never knew who'd be home. Pat soon got used to making her breakfast in the kitchen and sitting down with whoever else happened to be around. There was a lunch room in the factory where you could get a hot meal any time, and if she and Josie didn't eat in the Shamrock Club in the evenings, she'd have a snack at the house and take a cup of tea up to her room. A few of the girls kept biscuits hidden in their wardrobes but Pat didn't risk it. Josie had introduced her to Quinn's so she didn't want to bring mice and get the poor girl into trouble. To begin with, she was often too tired to eat anyway: her work as a sewing machinist was exhausting and she wasn't used to the long hours or the heat.

Other things were different too. Accustomed to Mary's overbearing manner, Pat had been amazed at how easy Josie was to get along with. Her room on the first floor was always full of chatter and laughter, as people ran in and out, sharing gossip and swapping clothes. She was happy to lend hats, shoes, and even her best jewellery, including the little string of pearls she'd had from her boyfriend on her birthday. Pat had been amazed, but Josie just shrugged. 'Sure, nobody's going to take off a necklace and lose it!'

'Wouldn't Donal be cross?'

'He'd have more sense. Besides, the pearls are mine to do what I like with, and I like to be good to my friends.'

It really was as simple as that. Josie was kindness through and through, and Donal, whom she'd married

a few years later, was the easiest-going lad you could
ever meet.

Josie and the Shamrock Club had made Pat feel safe.
The club was smaller then, and Denis Brennan, the
president, had been almost like the father of a family.
Most of Resolve's Irish-American community worked
either in construction or the clothing industry, and
Brennan was the largest developer in town. It was he
who'd provided the site the clubhouse was built on,
and many of the members worked for him and rented
houses he'd built.

Having turned off the television news, Pat locked
up and climbed the stairs to bed. As she switched off
her bedside light, she remembered buying Ger's blue
pullover in Toronto. Cassie had driven her out to the
mall and walked round the shops with her patiently, but
Pat had found herself wishing that Josie was there to
help her choose. It was strange, considering she hadn't
seen Josie for over fifty years. Then, only a few months
later, Ger had been dead and she herself had been back
in Resolve again, and, instead of wearing a white petal
hat, Josie had been using a walking frame. She'd always
moved like a dancer, running lightly down the stairs
in Mrs Quinn's rooming house, and whirling down to
the bus stop in the mornings, her feet in their cork-

soled strappy sandals hardly seeming to touch the hot, dusty sidewalk. Everything in Resolve that summer had seemed hot and dusty and very far away from Finfarran. And everything about Resolve last month had felt like a surreal dream.

At some point during the farewell party Cassie had introduced Pat to Jack Shanahan. He was the same height as his grandfather, with the same quiet assurance in his stance. The background music had been very loud and Cassie had had to shout his name. But she didn't need to. Pat would have known that lopsided smile anywhere.

CHAPTER TWENTY-FOUR

TO CASSIE'S SURPRISE, THOUGH THE SALON was fun, the library job was her favourite, especially the solitary hours she spent driving up and down the peninsula. When she mentioned this, Hanna said she knew what she meant. 'I drove the van myself before Conor took over, and I do miss those days out in the countryside.'

'I've never spent so much time alone.'

'What do you enjoy about it?'

'Space to think, I suppose. And the scenery. It's fantastic to watch the landscape coming alive again in spring.'

Now, bowling along on her southern route, she decided just to enjoy herself without trying to explain it. Lowering the window, she took a deep breath and realised how strongly the air smelt of salt. The ocean wasn't visible from the road she was currently driving along, yet the salty tang was a constant reminder of its presence. It was the same wherever you went on the narrow peninsula: even on the stillest of days, there was a hint of a breeze from the Atlantic.

Hereabouts the roads were bounded by hedgerows, not ditches, and all around her they were starting to bloom. It was too early yet for many new flowers, but tender leaves were budding and unfurling on trees and bushes. Two weeks ago, talking to Erin, Cassie had described them as a green haze. Now they grew thickly, hiding the briar's dark brown stems and softening the hard edges of stone walls. A speckled thrush called from a tree by the roadside as Cassie approached, and as she passed a house where flowerbeds edged the driveway, daffodils were poking through the soil, like green beaks.

Up ahead was the curve in the road that would take her down to a village. It was one of the library van's regular stops, home to half a dozen families with many more dependent on its presence. There was a shop that was also a post office, a pub, with a couple of petrol pumps, and a two-room school, which local children attended until they were twelve. Many of the kids walked to school, loitering in the lanes and running races, as their parents and grandparents had before them. Later, when they transferred to the secondary school in Lissbeg, they were picked up by a bus, which, like the library van, had stopping places all along the peninsula. In Pat's childhood, before the days of the school bus service, many families from outlying villages couldn't afford to send kids to secondary school. The cost of travel or of boarding in Lissbeg had been too high. Cassie thought of the woman she'd met on her first solo trip in the van. She was a pensioner who remembered Erin's gran, Josie, because her dad and Josie's used to take turns driving their daughters to the convent school in Lissbeg. Pat and Mary had met in the same way: Pat's father, who worked in Lissbeg, had driven them to school each morning and a friend's dad had collected them sharp at four in his Morris Minor.

As Cassie pulled in, the door of the village shop opened and a girl waved at her. 'Hi, I thought you were the post van.'

Cassie called to her through the window: 'I passed him a few miles back. He'd parked up to deliver boxes.'

'Ah, right. He won't be long, so.'

The girl waved again and went back indoors and, having opened her van, Cassie, who was ten minutes ahead of schedule, sat in the cab waiting for people to arrive. The village shop had a painted façade with the post-office sign prominently displayed. It was a modern building with a well laid-out interior, selling an array of groceries and hardware products, and an alcove with a computer from which you could go online and print screengrabs and files. Signs in the window offered a photocopying service and takeaway coffee, and there was a delicatessen counter with freshly made salads and sandwiches. Mentally, Cassie contrasted its modernity with the fittings in the butcher's shop in Lissbeg. You could imagine Fitzgerald's interior being produced by a designer who'd label it 'vintage' but, according to Pat, it was all the real deal. The tiles covering its walls from floor to ceiling were original, and their designs had already been old-fashioned at the turn of the twentieth century.

Ger's granddad had bought the business as a going concern sometime in the 1930s and seen no reason to make changes to the building. The tiles in the shop were cream, with a green-embossed band all around the walls at waist height. Above this, on the wall opposite the counter, was a series of rural scenes – a milkmaid with a wooden yoke and pails, her skirt looped up and her dark hair in ringlets, a group of men resting under a haystack, and a rosy-cheeked shepherd trudging home with a very clean lamb in his arms. From the wall behind the counter, framed in wreaths of buttercups, a cow with her calf, a large pig, and a herd of sheep stared out at the customers, relics of a time when no one had been bothered by the thought of their dinner grazing in flowery fields. Ger had installed electronic scales and tills and a cooler display unit, but the walls, the marble-topped counter, and the butcher's blocks, with their hollowed, scarred surfaces, were just as they'd been in his father's day.

Cassie had asked Pat if that was because Ger thought the place looked pretty cool as it was. But no, according to Pat, it was more that he didn't like change. 'I suppose it's the height of fashion now but I can tell you that years ago it got laughed at. No one wanted the old shop fittings then.'

'I bet they'd cost a fortune if you wanted to buy them now.'

The conversation had taken place in the kitchen over tea and cake with Frankie, who'd appeared, as Pat had said, 'as if he'd heard the oven door'. Apparently he was a sucker for his mom's baking. Cassie wasn't crazy about the way he walked in and out of the flat without warning but, of course, he had his own latch key. After all, it had been his childhood home. When she'd mentioned the cost of the tiles he'd turned and looked at her, his heavy jaw working on the cake, like a bull chewing the cud. Lately, most things about Frankie had creeped Cassie out. It felt like he was always staring at her. But maybe that was just stupid. Or mean. The fact was that Frankie was unattractive, much like Ger had been. But before Ger had died Cassie had got to know him a bit. She'd seen how he'd tried to protect Pat from his illness. Instead of improving on acquaintance, though, Frankie got worse.

The first person to arrive at the van was a farmer who'd promised to pick up a book for his wife. As Cassie scanned the copy of P. D. James's *Devices and Desires* he asked if he could order *The Case of the Late Pig*.

'I think most of the copies are out but I can put your wife's name on the list. Is she a member of the Transatlantic Book Club?'

'No, but she's heard of it. The word is that it's great craic altogether.'

Cassie was pleased. The book-reading bit hadn't even started but already the club had had word-of-mouth reviews. And the waiting list for *The Case of the Late Pig* was getting long. They'd agreed to discuss the book in a fortnight, to give people time to find copies. Though, apparently, the chances were that many members wouldn't read it at all. Hanna had told Cassie that always happened with book clubs. 'And with this one it's likely to be worse, since most people really just want to chat, not discuss books.'

'Oh, wow. Then maybe the library wasn't the right place to host it.'

'Not at all. It's a perfectly valid use of the facility. Things will settle down. We'll end up with a core group that enjoys reading, and others who drop in and out just to touch base with friends.'

Cassie added the farmer's wife's name to the waiting list, served two more arrivals, and sat on the step of the van to enjoy an unexpected burst of sunshine. A buzz from her phone alerted her to an incoming message, and she hesitated before unzipping her bag. Hanna had issued strict instructions about the use of her phone when she was on the road. 'It's no different from being here in the library, okay? You don't use your phone during working hours. Checking it out when you're driving is illegal, anyway. You can keep it on for use in an emergency but, otherwise, remember you're at work.'

It made sense, so Cassie hadn't argued, but now, glancing down at the screen, she saw the message was from Erin. The street was empty and there was no sound of any car approaching so, keeping the phone tucked into the bag beside her, she took a quick look.

The message that appeared beside Erin's latest drop-dead-I'm-a-free-woman avatar made her heart leap.

Jack wants to give you a Skype call sometime this evening. He says when you see it will you accept?

*

By 7 p.m. Cassie was sitting in her bedroom with her laptop open on her knee. Her last hour at work had been torture. Few people had visited the library van, and she was itching to get it back to Carrick before the rush-hour traffic held her up. But she stayed put, knowing it wasn't fair to do otherwise and feeling pretty certain that Hanna would hear of it if she left early. In the event, the roads hadn't been crowded and she'd dropped off the van, picked up her car and driven home to Lissbeg in record time. But what had Jack meant by 'sometime this evening'? Standing up, she walked round the room telling herself there was no need to sit staring at her Skype screen. The volume on her laptop was set to max so she'd hear Jack's alert as soon as it came. But taking a shower and changing was out of the question, and what if she was stuck in her bedroom for hours and needed to cross the landing to go to the loo?

As soon as the thought occurred, she found herself dying for a pee. But that was ridiculous. She'd been to the loo as soon as she'd got home. Deliberately, she set the laptop on her dressing-table and went to look out of the window. It was dumb, she thought, to allow herself to get wound up like a spring. There was a cat creeping along a wall below in the back yard. Would Jack call from the Shamrock Club's library, where Pangur slept under the range? It didn't seem likely. From his home, then? From his bedroom? How odd that their first date might happen in such an intimate space. But it wasn't a date. Of course it wasn't. It was probably just some question about the club. But, if so, why would he call her directly instead of getting in touch with the library? Swinging round, Cassie stared at her screen. She could have sworn she'd heard something. But she hadn't. For a minute she worked hard at not going to check the volume control. Then she gave up and made a rush for the laptop, picking it up and throwing herself onto the bed.

At that precise moment, the call from Jack came through. Certain that it would cut off if she didn't take it immediately, she stabbed repeatedly at the keypad and found herself looking at his face.

She couldn't tell where he was but it wasn't the

Shamrock Club library. Cassie scooted backwards and propped herself up against her bedhead. Jack smiled. 'Hey, you.'

Hastily, Cassie lowered the volume control. 'Hi.'

'Have I mistaken the time difference? Are you in bed?'

'No, I just thought – well, I thought I'd take the call here. I mean, it's private.' Her eyes flicked to the image of herself in the corner of the screen to see how she looked. Not great. Even if she hadn't had time to change her clothes, she might have fixed her hair. And she was sitting up in a bed with polished brass knobs, like something on a film set. To her horror, she realised she'd left a bra hanging from one of the bedposts. Oh, God, would he think she was some kind of weirdo expecting phone sex? Changing the angle of the laptop, she pulled herself together. 'So, what's up?'

In an attempt to avoid sounding sexy, she could hear herself sounding spiky. Jack's voice, which had been relaxed and intimate, became brisk. 'Just a question, is all. I've cut together a video of Pat's farewell party. If I put it up online could she access it? Or should I mail her a disk?'

'Wow. That's kind of you. Sure. Put it online – she's fine with the internet.'

'Okay. You got it. I'll send you the link.'

There was an awkward pause in which Cassie panicked, afraid that he'd end the call. Casting round for something to say, she told him she'd been to Mullafrack.

'Really? That's cool. How come?'

'Well, I saw a sign when I was driving the library van, and I went back later to have a closer look. The village is gone but there's this big tower up on the side of the hill.'

'Does someone live there?'

'No, it's ancient, Hanna says medieval. Brad's planning to take tourists up to see it.' Wishing she hadn't mentioned him, she rushed on, explaining that Brad was just a guy she'd met. 'I cut his hair at the salon.'

'And you met him in Mullafrack?'

'Yeah. Just – you know – coincidence.'

'Right. Well, it sounds exciting.'

'No, really, I mean … he's just a guy.'

Jack looked taken aback. Then he laughed. 'I meant that finding the tower must have been exciting.'

'Oh, God, well, yes, yes, it was. Maybe your ancestors lived there.'

'It sounds a bit grand for the Shanahans.'

'I guess. But I was thinking of you – I mean your family – when I was there.'

It was Jack who broke the pause that followed, asking her how she'd enjoyed St Patrick's Day.

'It was good. How was the Shamrock Club do?'

His eyes crinkled. 'Well, I videoed the ceremonial presentation of Grandma's banner.'

This was better. This was just ordinary chat, like you'd have on a date. Cassie relaxed and smiled back. 'Over here they dispense with ceremonial. There's just lots of marching and music in the street. And farmers parading on tractors. Brad thought it was weird.'

As soon as she'd spoken, her eyes widened in dismay. Jack had shown no negative reaction but, instinctively, she wanted to reach through the screen and grab his hand. Whatever about phone sex, Skype dating was horrible. And now they'd hit another stupid silence. Cassie contrived to keep calm, but in her head she was howling like a dog. How could anyone be so completely asinine? Why had she mentioned Brad's name again?

CHAPTER TWENTY-FIVE

THE DIVIL WAS ALWAYS WELCOME AT THE building suppliers in Sheep Street, to the extent that Colm, the manager, kept him a special tin of custard creams. In the circumstances, The Divil felt that sticking to his diet when he was there would be embarrassing, and Fury, being a reasonable man, agreed. They were sitting in the office, a shed at the yard entrance, and while Fury and Colm drank tea out of chipped mugs, The Divil was crunching a biscuit under the desk.

Colm looked down and nudged him with his foot. 'Will you have another?'

The Divil looked up at Fury, who shook his head. With a deep sigh, the little dog licked his whiskers and Colm gave Fury a shove that nearly upended his mug of tea. 'Ah, for God's sake, Fury, a bird never flew on one wing!'

'Fair enough so. Give him another, and you can come and catch my rats when all his teeth fall out.'

'You're a terrible hard man, do you know that?'

'I do. And while we're on the subject, you won't get round me on the price of that load of timber, so don't even try.'

'I've told you before, if you don't like my prices you're free to go elsewhere.'

'And I've told you there's no point in trying to call my bluff. And for why? Because I'm not bluffing, Colm. You can hike your prices once a year and you won't find me complaining ...'

'I will!'

'All right, fair point, you will. But I'll still pay. But snaking them up in mid-March isn't on.'

'It's not me, man, it's the suppliers.'

'Well, tell them where to stick their badly cured pitch pine.'

'If I did that you'd be in here complaining I didn't stock it.'

'No. If you did that they wouldn't waste their time trying to cheat you. They'd give you the stuff at a decent price and feck off and cheat somebody else.'

'You've no notion how this Brexit thing's been affecting suppliers.'

'No, nor I don't want to hear of it either, not with The Divil under the desk. The B word does terrible things to his blood pressure.'

'Well, lookut, I'll see what I can do for you on the load.'

Fury immediately produced a roll of notes. Shaking his head vehemently, Colm poured him more tea. 'No, no, no, not at all. I'll see you the next day.'

'Ah, take it now before I change my mind.'

'What do you mean, before *you* change your mind? Haven't I just lowered the price?'

'Get away out of that. It was too high to begin with.' With an air of great reluctance, Fury stuffed the notes back into his pocket. 'Oh, all right, I'll see you again.' Established procedure satisfied, and having settled the money against his rump, he sank back into his chair and indicated the biscuit tin. 'And go on, then, give yer man another of them things if you must.'

Twenty minutes later, he and The Divil left the yard. As his battered red van made the turn into Sheep Street, a similar van, with blacked-out rear windows, drew up beside him. The street was now blocked in both directions. Fury and the driver of the other van lowered their windows and leaned out.

'There you are, Fury. What's the story?'

'Tippin' along, Terry. Nothing new.'

'The Divil all right?'

'Sound out.'

A driver attempting to get down Sheep Street honked his horn aggressively. Fury glanced in his mirror, saw it was a man in a suit, and paid no attention. Instead he enquired after Terry's hens.

'Ah, they're all right, but I don't know, I'm not getting many eggs. 'Tis the time of year.'

'Well, that can't be right. Don't they lay more in springtime?'

'Maybe I ought to show them a bloody calendar.'

The man in the suit put his hand on his horn and, this time, didn't take it off. Fury simply raised his voice and continued speaking to Terry. 'You wouldn't have an offcut of carpet to fit a ten-be-twelve room?'

'What kind of colour?'

'Something hard-wearing I'd say she'd want. Maybe brown. Could be patterned.'

'I'd say I'd have a bit of sisal that might do.'

'Ah, Name of God, man, have you nothing better than sisal?'

'You can't beat the sisal for the wear, Fury. With a rubber back it won't want lifting for nigh on twenty years.'

'Well, poor Pat Fitz hasn't twenty years left in her. Could you not come up with a decent bit of twist?'

'I could, of course, if it's for Mrs Fitz. Would she want it dropped in?'

'Not at all. I'll come round and collect it.'

By this stage, they were both shouting above the blaring horn, and several passers-by had stopped to stare. The man in the suit got out of his car and marched towards Fury, who reached for his handbrake. 'Right so, Terry, ten-be-twelve. I'll see you, boy.' To raucous barking from The Divil, the two vans shot off simultaneously, leaving the roadway empty except for the furious man in the suit. He swung round, glared at the sniggering onlookers and, controlling an impulse to shake his fist, strode back to his car.

*

The woman from the St Vincent de Paul had said she couldn't take worn socks or underwear. Having given her so many bags of good clothing, Pat had hoped she'd remove the rest and dispose of it. But instead the woman had told her there was a clothing bank in Carrick, and driven away, leaving her to cope with the rejects. Pat knew Cassie would deal with them for her, but that didn't seem right. So she'd caught the bus and found when she'd got to Carrick that the bulging bin bag she'd carried wouldn't fit into the heavy iron chute.

The thought of bringing it home was too much for her so, in the end, she'd pulled the pants and vests out in handfuls and thrust them in, along with the socks, despite the large, torn sign that read 'NO UNBAGGED CLOTHING'.

Afterwards she'd felt so shaken she'd gone to the Royal Vic to sit down before catching the bus home. PJ, the barman, must have seen the state she was in because he'd asked if she'd like a wee drop of gin. Pat had said no, but the coffee she ordered came on a tray with a little tot of whiskey on the side. It was no more than a tablespoonful, and PJ called it medicinal, so she'd tipped it into the cup and, in fact, it had warmed her up. The last time she'd heard whiskey referred to as medicinal had been in a book-lined bedroom in Resolve.

This morning she'd woken feeling relieved to know that task at least was behind her. The next job she had to face was clearing Ger's desk before his office room could be done over. Frankie was coming to deal with the desk shortly, and Fury, who'd offered to do the decorating, had just rung to say he'd be round to drop off a grand piece of carpet. Stupidly, Pat had found her eyes full of tears. People called Fury cross-grained and a hard man to pin down, but here he was, coming round on a Saturday, saving her trouble just as he'd done before.

Having found the right key on Ger's ring, she unlocked the roll-top desk and pushed back the lid. The desk had stood in the parlour of her own childhood home. Its writing slope was of worn leather and the bank of small drawers at the back had handles of turned ebony. It felt strange to be opening them. They were full of dockets and cheque stubs with rubber bands around them, so she supposed the business files were kept in the big drawers below, and in the filing cabinets. To the left of the pen tray was a square box, which had come from Ger's family farmhouse. It had Chinese designs carved into the top, which was lacquered, and back at the farm it had stood on a shelf by the range. Ger's mam had used it as a tea caddy, and the squat silver spoon that was once kept inside it was now in Pat's own cutlery drawer. Opening the box, she found it contained a few business cards and the end of a pencil Ger must have picked up at some agricultural show.

She had just put the lid back on the box when she heard Frankie on the stairs. She hadn't heard his key turning in the door below, so, though the sound of his tread was familiar, it made her jump. He stumped onto the landing, his Burberry flapping open and a waxed hat, like a fisherman's, pulled down on his head. When he reached the door to Ger's room he asked if she had any cardboard boxes, explaining that he'd need to carry stuff down to the car. Pat put the tea caddy back on the desk and said she'd ask Des. There were likely to be some boxes in the sheds.

When she got downstairs Fury and The Divil strolled into the shop. Fury was carrying a roll of carpet on his shoulder and Pat's first thought was that the timing was unfortunate. Still, after the last time, she felt pretty sure that Frankie would behave. He'd been civil enough to Fury once he'd got a slice of cake down him, and he'd even given a bit of a laugh when The Divil stuck his whiskers into the milk jug. All the same, she thought she'd better mention that Frankie was here. Fury didn't seem bothered. 'Will I take this straight up, so? It's a nice bit of brown patterned twist I got from Tintawn Terry.'

Des asked if she'd mind the shop while he went out to the shed to look for the boxes, explaining to Fury that they were wanted upstairs. Fury propped the carpet in a corner. 'I tell you what we'll do, Mrs Fitz. The Divil and I will go out and get your boxes. Then you can go on back upstairs and Des needn't leave the shop.' He winked at Des. 'I take it the bould Mr Frankie wouldn't know how to carry a box.'

Des made no comment and Pat felt embarrassed. Why didn't Frankie come down for the boxes himself? What right did they have to be treating poor Des as an errand boy? Never mind about getting things done in the flat, what she ought to do, she told herself, was concentrate on finding a lad for the shop. It wasn't fair to have Des trying to run it alone. She'd half thought that she and Frankie might talk that through together, but perhaps he'd been right to get the desk sorted first. And it was she who'd been eager to move on and get the room decorated so, really, he wasn't to blame. But, between The Divil, the twist and Des, she felt flustered, and with Frankie waiting, and Fury here with the carpet, now was the wrong time to be trying to think the whole thing out.

When she got back upstairs the floor was covered with piles of Manila folders. Frankie had used Ger's keys to open the desk and the cabinets, and the little drawers with the ebony knobs had been pulled out and left askew. Instinctively, Pat reached for the keyring, knowing Ger never let it out of his sight. But the impulse seemed silly, so she left the ring where it was on top of the desk. Frankie had taken his coat off and was kneeling on the floor, going through the files. He looked up and asked where the boxes were.

'They're coming. You know, I've been thinking, I'll need to get a lad for the shop.'

'That's another salary.'

'I know it is, Frank, I'm not a fool, but we can't have Des down there on his own, turning the sign on the door whenever he needs to step out the back.'

'I'll see what I think when I've been through these files.'

Pat felt herself going pink. She looked at him kneeling there on the floor with the waxed hat pushed back on his head and the hairs on the backs of his hands wiry and black. He had just the same look he'd worn as a boy when she'd tell him to do one thing and he wanted to do another. Back then, he'd slip down and ask Ger to overrule her. And Ger always would. From the day she'd brought Frankie home as a baby, Ger had been a fool for his eldest son.

There was a shrill bark and, looking round, she saw The Divil. Fury was climbing the stairs behind him, the boxes balanced on his head. Frankie's chin went up when he saw Fury on the landing but he gave a grunt of thanks and began filling the boxes with files. Fury lounged against the wall, watching. Pat could see that

Frankie didn't like him there but, as the boxes filled, she was encouraged to hope that nothing unpleasant would happen. Then, when Frankie stood up, Fury offered to give him a hand taking them down to the car. 'You can put your shoulder under a roll of carpet for me when we're done.'

That didn't go down too well, but the boxes were full to overflowing so, eventually, Frankie nodded. Pat hoped that he hadn't noticed the glint in Fury's eye. Everyone knew Frankie had notions about his own importance, so getting him to carry the carpet upstairs was something Des would enjoy and probably share with half the town. Though the joke was mild and Frankie deserved it, Pat felt a twinge of sympathy, and as she did so her eye fell on the tea caddy. Laying her hand on Frankie's arm, she asked him if he wanted it. 'I'd say your dad was fond of it, son, and it belonged to his mam. Maybe Fran would like it, to hold knickknacks?'

Frankie, who had hefted a box and thrust it at Fury, shook his head. 'That wouldn't be the class of thing Fran would go for.'

'Well, you might like it yourself? You could have it on your desk, like he did.'

'Lookut, I said no, Mam. Thanks all the same.'

The thanks were so dismissive that Pat bit her lip.

First he wouldn't take his father's pullover, and now this. After Frankie and Fury had left, with The Divil under Fury's jacket, she went upstairs, and put the keyring into the tea caddy, along with the odds and ends that Ger had left there. Then she carried the box downstairs and stood it on a shelf above the range. She was glad that only Fury and The Divil had heard what Frankie had said. Fury might joke about getting him to carry a roll of carpet, but he knew the respect due to the dead and he'd never been one to gossip. He wouldn't go shaming Ger's memory by telling the world that Frankie Fitz had turned down a memento of his father from his mam.

CHAPTER TWENTY-SIX

THE MAKEOVER IN THE SALON WAS progressing. Aquamarine gauze drapes now hung at the doors and the velvet cushions with the gold tassels were gone. In their place, black and white satin bolsters graced the banquettes and the colour of the drapes was echoed in ruched curtains in the beauty parlour. Margot looked thoughtfully at the ruching. 'Definitely more *Grease* than *The Great Gatsby*. I dunno what the designer thinks he's doing.'

Cassie considered the balcony doors. 'Well, that's pretty *Gatsby*, isn't it? Fluttering drapes and a pool with a view of the ocean?'

'Did Gatsby's pool have an ocean view?'

'Didn't it? I only saw the film on late-night TV.'

Margot giggled. 'Me too.'

'Sounds like we ought to sign up for a Brad Miller cultural cruise.'

'A what?'

'That first client I had here when I started. His

name's Bradley Miller and he fixes cultural cruises. Literature, and wine tasting, and medieval castles.'

'Oh, right. Personally, when I get a holiday I prefer to lie on a beach.' Margot stopped inspecting the curtains and concentrated on Cassie. 'So how come you know so much about him?'

'I met him the other day and we got talking.'

'And when you say "met", do you mean "met by appointment"?'

'No, I don't. We bumped into each other. He's looking for suitable places to take tour groups.' Aware that she was sounding aggressive, Cassie laughed. 'Actually, it happened twice. Once when I was out for a walk and again at the Patrick's Day parade in Lissbeg. Though, as Pat said, the world and his wife were there, so it wasn't surprising. I don't suppose I'll ever see him again.'

'You will, you know. Very soon.'

'What are you? A fortune-teller?'

'No, but I've seen the appointment book. You're giving him a trim at twelve fifteen.'

*

When Brad sat down he winked at Cassie in the mirror. 'Don't scalp me.'

'I'm not sure how to avoid it.' She ran her fingers through his hair, which had hardly grown at all since she'd last trimmed it. 'Let's get it washed first.'

'Do you do head massage?'

'Kate does.'

'But you don't?'

'That would be the difference between your stylist and the junior who washes your hair.'

'See, these are the technicalities that only professionals know. Let's skip the wash, then, and do a dry cut.'

'No problem.'

Adept at dealing with clients' flirting, Cassie whipped a gown around him, waiting for the inevitable invitation to dinner. The question was, did she want to accept? By the time the cut was finished she'd almost decided she did but, to her chagrin, he just stood up and said thanks. As she shook out the gown, she could see him chatting with Margot at the desk. Then, when he'd gone, Margot bounced over, beaming. 'Well, your boyfriend's coming out on the boat tonight!'

'What?'

'I asked if he wanted to join us and he said yes.'

Cassie had arranged to spend the evening with Margot and Paul on Paul's boat. They'd fixed to take a bottle of wine and watch the sunset. Full of enthusiasm, Margot explained that Brad had just agreed to come along. 'The poor guy's lonely.'

'Oh, Margot!'

'What? It's just a boat trip. I thought you said there's nothing going on.'

'There isn't. It's no big deal.'

'Well, if it's no big deal, why make a big deal of it?'

'I'm not.'

'Look, he's here on his own and his cruise ship's sailed so he hasn't got friends to spend time with.'

'I know. I said. It's no big deal.'

'And Paul will be glad of another hand on deck.'

'Brad fixes tours. I don't think he's a sailor.'

'Actually, he's done lots of sailing. He told me his dad has a yacht.'

Cassie shrugged. 'Well, he didn't tell me. Man of mystery.'

Margot looked abashed. 'Are you sure you don't mind? Maybe I should have checked with you.'

'God, no! Why should you? I'm glad he's coming along. It'll be great.'

As Margot sent a text to Paul, Cassie called Kate to sweep the floor – though, actually, there was hardly any need to. Brad hadn't needed a haircut. She could have sworn he'd made the appointment because he'd intended to ask her for a date. So what was going on? Was he playing some complex game? Or had her instinct simply been wrong?

Lunch in the hotel's staff canteen was one of the perks of the job, but this morning, because the weather was fine, Cassie had brought two wholemeal scones and some cheese to eat on the beach. She was booked in to work a full day, which was why Margot had arranged the sunset boat trip, so now she took an early lunch break and strolled down to the pier. A steep flight of stone steps and a scramble over rocks brought her to shingle, and she crunched over broken shells and stones till she came to the sand. Though the sun was shining, the sand looked damp, so she retraced her steps, took off her jacket, and spread it on the stones. She was wearing a heavy sweater in anticipation of the evening, and the brisk wind from the ocean was invigorating rather than cold. Unwrapping the scones, she sandwiched each with a lump of red Cheddar and, taking an apple from her bag, settled down to enjoy her solitary lunch.

A fishing boat was moored in the harbour and, above it, the air was thronged with scavenging seabirds. For a while Cassie watched them circle and dive, disappearing behind the pier and swooping back up with entrails in their beaks. The catch now being gutted on the boat would feature on the hotel's menu that night. Many of the smaller hotels and restaurants used frozen fish brought in by the trawlers, but in the Spa Hotel 'catch of the day' meant just that. Cassie knew Brad had his room there courtesy of the management, but now, for the first time, she wondered about his family. If his dad kept a yacht somewhere in California, maybe his clothes, his muscles and his self-confidence spoke of privilege, just as her own silk sweaters and the rest of her edgy, urban wardrobe did. She'd supported herself since graduating from high school, but her sense of being a citizen of the world came from the hardly acknowledged fact that, if things went wrong, she could always scuttle home.

Gazing out at the foam-topped waves, she realised she'd come back to the question of where her roots were. Certainly not in the family home in Toronto, from which she knew her mom and dad were planning to downsize soon. She'd moved on from that. But increasingly in the last few weeks she'd wondered if home might be Finfarran. And, although Jack Shanahan had never crossed the Atlantic, it seemed that he felt the same visceral tug. Friday's conversation hadn't been a total disaster, or at least it hadn't ended after she'd made that second gaffe. By reverting to the subject of Mullafrack, they'd re-established common ground. Jack had loved her description of the ruin on the hillside. 'It sounds awesome. Like Stephen King's *Dark Tower* books.'

'I thought *The Lord of the Rings*.'

In fact it was Brad, not she, who'd brought up Tolkien, but Cassie had had the sense not to mention him again. Having nothing to offer but a kids' book she hadn't finished, she hadn't mentioned *Elidor* either. But apparently Stephen King's *Dark Tower* series had been influenced by Tolkien so she'd sat back and listened while Jack talked. Charmed by his enthusiasm, Cassie realised that everything she encountered in Finfarran seemed to be linked to other things in ways she'd never had any reason to think about. She could never have imagined she'd find herself part of a library book club. Or that she'd meet a guy in Ballyfin who'd remind her of just how much she loved her footloose, adventurous life. Or that she'd sit propped up on a bed in Pat's guest room describing the glory of Finfarran's landscape to a guy she'd met on the other side of the world. When she'd got a word in edgeways, she'd returned to that. 'Mullafrack's incredible. Really windswept.'

'And no village?'

'No sign of one. Just windswept and empty and stunning. Nothing to see but the mountain and the tower.'

'Wow. Imagine going back and building a house there.'

'Do you think you might?'

'Me? I dunno. My grandpa used to talk about it. He'd never been to Ireland either, though.'

'Did you know him well?'

'Pretty well. He owned a landscape gardening firm. Started out with a big old electric mower, cutting lawns.'

'The American Dream.'

'I guess. Back in high school I used to work for him on weekends. Driving round in a pickup getting my hands into the dirt. We'd go fishing together too, up at North Lake, and birdwatching. He talked a lot about Finfarran. His dad was in construction but the guy who came over in eighteen eighty-something had been a farmer. My grandpa said the yen to work on the land came down from him.'

'I think that's a thing. Stuff skipping generations. I mean, my dad doesn't seem to feel any need to come back here, but I've felt drawn to Ireland ever since I was a kid.'

'Someday I'll do what you did. Drop everything and come over.'

'For good?'

'No. Just to take a look.'

'Well, you could find yourself wanting to stay here and put down roots.'

'In a cottage by the ocean? Hey, if I won a fortune in a lottery I could buy the dark tower.'

Their eyes had met on the screen and Cassie had felt her whole body tingle but, after that, things had gone wrong again. They'd talked on about Mullafrack and, increasingly, she'd found herself struggling to avoid saying Brad's name. It was as if he kept appearing out of nowhere, just as she'd come upon him when she'd walked around the tower. The effort not to mention him made her edgy, and Jack had stopped in mid-sentence. 'Look, I'm sorry, I'm keeping you far too long.'

'No, really, no. I'm enjoying myself.'

But she knew she'd sounded false and that her body language was strained, so she must have given the impression that she was longing to get away. He'd ended the call abruptly with no suggestion that they'd talk again, leaving her feeling as if they'd had a row and he'd walked out.

And tonight she had a date with Bradley Miller. Well, not a date because he hadn't asked her for one. But they'd be drifting on the waves together, watching a golden sunset, and his presence was going to make the whole thing odd. Theoretically, this was just going to be a group of friends hanging out together. She and Margot and Paul were mates by now, and she never felt like a wallflower when she was with them. But the wine would be chilled and Margot had said that Paul had been given oysters by a guy at the marina. So, with all that and a blazing sky, how could it not feel like a double date?

CHAPTER TWENTY-SEVEN

MARY CASEY SAT ON HER GARDEN BENCH with *The Case of the Late Pig*, observing with disapproval that the book's cover had changed. The copy Tom had borrowed from Carrick Library for his aunt Maggie had been a green Penguin paperback, with the intriguing words 'Murder follows the funeral' on the front. This book had a lilac-coloured cover. Not that it didn't look intriguing, with its two menacing birds flapping in the foreground, but if she'd glimpsed it on a shelf, she wouldn't have recognised it. Which was upsetting. Once an object or a subject entered her awareness, she liked to keep a firm grip on it. Changes like this one, Hanna's divorce, and her own widowed state, unnerved her.

The garden had really been Tom's. After he'd died, she couldn't be doing with all the work it involved, so she'd asked Johnny Hennessy to lay the centre to lawn, but she'd kept the shrubs Tom had planted in beds along the fence, and the pots of night-scented stocks he'd had on the patio. They'd always sat there of an evening, she with her little martini and he with his glass of Guinness, before she'd go indoors to dish up the dinner. When they'd been working they'd never had dinner at night, but Tom had agreed that retirement was all about making changes for the better. Not being tied to the kitchen in the mornings gave you great freedom ... though, on the other hand, the days could be very long.

When Hanna was growing up Tom had had notions of grandchildren living nearby and running in to play in the flower-filled garden. That dream had been knocked on the head when Hanna had upped and gone off to London to be a librarian, and then married that smooth-talking pup Malcolm, who'd turned out to be faithless. And shameless. Mary's face still burned whenever she thought of the woman he'd been sleeping with. A so-called friend of Hanna's, if you please, and Jazz's godmother! And the affair going on for over twenty years!

Having fallen into mental exclamation points, she calmed herself with a sip of strong tea. The fact that Hanna had been betrayed disturbed her. It was common sense that a woman should always know where her husband was, and shocking that she should fail to sense when a friend was keeping secrets. These were basic skills, and the thought that a child she'd raised should lack them felt almost shameful. When Hanna had returned to Lissbeg Mary had stoutly defended her in public, but at home she'd given free rein to her outrage. What else could you do when your own daughter, having been made a fool of, was declaring she wouldn't accept a cent from the cheating hound she'd married? Hanna had insisted she wanted a life untainted by the past, a stance Mary had seen as idiotic. She'd never liked Malcolm Turner, for all that he came from a thoroughly decent family, and in her opinion he ought to have been cleaned out. She tolerated him now because, as Pat kept pointing out, he'd set up a generous trust fund for Jazz, but she still felt personally cheated by Hanna's adamance. When one man was permitted to get away with base treachery, the knock-on effect on womankind as a whole could only be bad. And, anyway, as soon as Hanna came home, Mary had seen how badly she'd been hurting. God knew they'd never been close but, even when she'd been telling her what a fool she was, she'd longed to reach out and give the poor girl a hug.

She looked again at *The Case of the Late Pig*. As far as she could remember she hadn't finished it last time, and she didn't think she'd bother to do so now. It was like every other book Tom had brought from the library for Maggie, set in an English village full of women wearing pearls and men in monocles. Mary sniffed. She'd only suggested it the previous week at the book club because she'd wanted to get things moving. Admittedly, she'd also been pleased to get the better of that Josie. The fuss made over people who'd gone to live in Resolve was annoying. If you'd never been further than Dublin or Cork you were left at a disadvantage. Not a real one, of course, because why should it matter? But if that was how people looked at you, you were hard put to gainsay it.

Pat hadn't liked the way she'd stepped in and organised things at the book club. But then she herself hadn't liked having to listen to all that stuff about Josie after that summer Pat had spent in Resolve. Josie's clothes were wonderful, and she drove a car, and her hair was so great, and she and Pat had gone off down the mall drinking sodas. You'd be sick to death of the stories. You'd nearly think she'd had no interest in her best friend's wedding album, or in the honeymoon Mary and Tom had spent in Cork.

When she'd finished her cup of tea, Mary went indoors to dress for the book club, reminding herself that Hanna was due to pick her up at six. Thoughtfully, she looked at herself in the mirror. She'd had her hair set the day before and a gold rinse put through it and, though she said so herself, her skin was still looking good. So was the little jacket and skirt she'd bought at the Carrick Couturier. Last week the crowd in Resolve had been all dolled up in green, and Josie had said they were wearing it in honour of St Patrick's Day. Which was way too early and only made them look daft. The Lissbeg members had cheered and said it was great, though, and someone had rushed away and come back with the string of shamrock bunting Hanna had over her desk in the library. Then Darina had got on her hind legs and started spouting something about St Patrick having a wife. That had produced all kinds of chat and laughter.

Afterwards, as Hanna drove her home, she'd asked if Mary had enjoyed herself. Mary had said nothing. There was no point. When Tom was alive she'd had no need to go out at night looking for entertainment and the question had had the effect of rubbing salt into a wound. Because of it, she'd half thought of giving tonight a miss but, with a final glance in the mirror, she told herself that the thing that mattered was getting Pat through these first few months without Ger.

When they reached the library Cassie was sitting on the step. Hanna unlocked the door and went in and, as she and Cassie began to set up the reading room, Mary wandered about running her fingers along shelves. Pat arrived shortly afterwards, saying she'd left Fury stripping wallpaper in the flat. Mary approved. She had always rated Fury highly. He was a sly fox and, at times, he'd give you a look that went right through you, but he always knew his own mind, the way she did herself. She said this to Pat, who gave her a shove. 'The difference is that Fury can keep his mouth shut.'

Mary shoved her back and asked how Cassie was.

'She's grand. I'd say she's excited about tonight.'

Whatever she might be excited about, it was evident that the child had taken care to look her best. Mary wasn't impressed by the blue fringe with sparkles on it, but she could see the effort that had gone into Cassie's eye make-up and recognised the care with which a corner of her jumper had been tucked up to reveal her belt buckle. It was hard to believe all this had been done to impress the members of the book club, whose average age was probably sixty-five. Mary wondered if Bradley Miller might be coming but, glancing round, she could see no sign of him. Grasping Pat by the elbow, she suggested they sit at the back.

Pat threw her a look. 'I thought you were all for the front row and getting a good view.'

'Well, a change is as good as a rest. Let's sit in here.'

From the back row she could see the seats filling, Hanna taking her usual place, and Ferdia at the computer. Cassie was beside him, looking over his shoulder. Darina Kelly had just come in, dragging Gobnit, who'd not yet been persuaded to release her mother's phone. The child, who was dressed in Superman pyjamas, was still wearing the smudged remains of her St Patrick's Day face paint. Shaking her head in disapproval, Mary turned her attention to the screen, where Josie, leaning on her walking frame, was carefully lowering herself onto a chair.

Peering between the backs of the heads in front of her, Mary thought Cassie's face seemed strained. It was only a couple of minutes to seven so if Bradley Miller was going to turn up he was surely cutting it fine. Ferdia's attention was on the computer. Briefly Mary wondered if that could be the problem. If Pat was right and the child was in love, had she gone and fallen for Ferdia? Surely someone of Cassie's age would have no trouble knowing he was gay. His own mother had said she'd known when he was six. And didn't all young people these days have what they called gaydars, ways of spotting if people were gay or straight? Rather pleased with herself for knowing the jargon, Mary reflected that Ferdia was a nice lad. If he'd seen Cassie taking an interest, he'd have found a way to set her right so she wouldn't go making a show of herself. Mentally, Mary dismissed him as a suspect. The evidence didn't stack up.

At exactly seven o'clock Hanna walked to the front and addressed the room. 'You're all very welcome again and it's great to see such a crowd. Please give a big wave to our transatlantic friends.'

Everyone waved with varying degrees of enthusiasm, ranging from Darina's thrashing hands and clanking bangles, to Mr Maguire's two fingers raised at chest level, which made him look like the pope blessing his flock. As soon as the response from Resolve had calmed down, Josie leaned forward. 'Hi, Hanna. I'd like to introduce our new technician. This is Ashlee Braun-Mulcahy, who owns the florist shop here in town. Jack's taken a rain check tonight so Ashlee's going to make sure we stay in touch.'

Ashlee was fat and middle-aged with an air of discreet professionalism, suggestive of equal efficiency at celebrations and funerals. She seemed to have set things up exactly as they'd been before, though Mary noted that, unlike the Shanahan lad who'd asked her to test the sound last week, she didn't expect you to move around shouting from different seats. Hanna said she hoped Jack wasn't unwell, and Josie laughed. 'No, I think he's just fine. Isn't that right, Mrs Shanahan?'

Mrs Shanahan confirmed that Jack was fine. 'Apparently he had "a thing" tonight. Lord knows what that means but he said he wasn't free.'

Mary saw Cassie slip into a seat at the end of the second row. Covertly inspecting her, Mary concluded that she must have given up waiting for Bradley Miller. One thing was certain, and that was that Pat wouldn't know, or know how to find out. Glancing at the little figure in the seat beside her, Mary decided Pat looked in good form tonight. Then she frowned. She hadn't expected Ger's death to release so many memories or that, with the loss of half of the foursome, long-established certainties would start to come adrift, making her view her familiar world from unaccustomed angles, and dragging her into this book club, which she wasn't sure she liked. Still, there was no doubt that Pat enjoyed it and, whatever you might think of Josie, you'd have to be pleased about that. You could see, too, that Cassie's love life was helping to take Pat out of herself. With a pleasant surge of righteousness, Mary concluded that, from now on, her duty lay in keeping a close eye on Cassie and Brad. She wouldn't let Pat know because the chances were that she'd get accused of being nosy or meddling. But the fact was that if you didn't keep tabs on what went on around you, you could miss your chance of giving things a useful bit of a nudge.

CHAPTER TWENTY-EIGHT

BY THE END OF ITS THIRD MEETING THE Transatlantic Book Club hadn't yet managed to open *The Case of the Late Pig*, but it had had lengthy and enjoyable discussions on how to acquire the book. Most Lissbeg members had applied for the copies Hanna had ordered for the library, though a few had found it at home and Darina had discovered it in a Carrick charity shop. At the start of the meeting, she'd launched into a dramatic description of her search, beginning with the statement that she'd had to take the bus 'because my SUV was in for its NCT'. The group in Resolve had listened and watched in increasing bafflement as the story twisted and turned and the acronyms piled up.

'The St V de P shop in the high street goes in for classic crime. But, for some reason, last week they mainly had MBS – I mean Mind, Body and Spirit, not that textbook outlet you have over in the States. My nephew studies on your side of the Pond. He's going to be a surgeon. He's very against Mind, Body and Spirit, by the way. He doesn't believe in anything you can't cut with a sharp knife. Anyway, I gave up on the V de P and went on to the NCBI. I adore blind dogs, don't you?' Here, seeing the bewildered faces in Resolve, Darina offered an aside. 'The NCBI is a charity for the blind here in Ireland. They have a collection box for assistance dogs in the shop. Anyway, it was no dice there, so I pressed on to IDF – which does wonderful work for the deaf – and what should I find, large as life, sitting on a shelf? *The Late Pig*!'

Having waved her tattered paperback, she'd sat down triumphantly, and Hanna had hastily asked Josie how things had gone over there. 'I don't suppose you had more than one copy in your collection?'

'No, but we're fine. Well, we will be. Mrs Shanahan's reading the one we have here in the library, and most of the rest of us have found it online. Ashlee's put it on her e-reader. And I got it in a thrift shop, like Darina did.'

The mention of Ashlee's choice had produced an impassioned debate about e-books. Pat, who had no opinion of them one way or the other, had spent the time looking at Mrs Shanahan, who was working on another piece of quilting. She was a dark, very pretty woman, with neat, regular features, and Jack's parents, whom Pat had met in Resolve, were dark too. So Seán Shanahan's blue eyes, red hair and freckles had skipped a generation and come down to his grandson. It was strange to think of Seán's copy of *The Late Pig* being read by his widow for the Transatlantic Book Club. Almost as strange as it had been to see his collection of crime novels in the Shamrock Club's library.

Behind the chattering group in Resolve still discussing e-books, Pat could see the glass-fronted bookcase. The enormous plaque above it said 'Gift of the Shanahan Family, in loving memory of Seán Michael Shanahan of Resolve, 1936–2009'. There were far more books in the case than Pat could remember on Seán's bedroom shelves, so he must have kept collecting crime stories all his life. When Cassie had suggested the holiday in Resolve, Pat had wondered if Seán had remained there, and whether, if he had, he was still alive. On the night of their arrival Josie had mentioned him casually. 'He married a good while after you did. His widow is very active in the Shamrock Club.' That was Josie, quick to know what was needed and always the soul of discretion. She'd gone on to discuss other friends and Pat had been glad, because she hadn't wanted to talk about Seán. She wouldn't have minded if she'd never had to think about him again. It had been a shock to see his looks replicated in Jack, though, and to sit in the Shamrock Club's library on the night of her farewell party and see the date of his death above those shelves of familiar books.

When the book-club meeting was over, Cassie and some of the others went off for pizza. As Pat let herself into the empty flat she felt bone tired. In a way she wished she'd stood her ground and hadn't allowed Cassie to fix that holiday or to talk her into the Transatlantic Book Club. It was hard enough dealing with Ger's death without having to cope with buried memories of Seán Shanahan, and strange to sit in Lissbeg beside Mary with Josie talking to them from Resolve. When Mrs Shanahan suggested they read Seán's books, Pat had seen Josie's troubled reaction. Hanna had seemed to think she was bothered about how to organise things. But Pat knew better. Josie had been a witness to all that had happened that summer in Resolve.

When she took off her coat, Pat laid *The Case of the Late Pig* on her well-scrubbed kitchen table. Then she remembered Thomas Hardy's poems about his wife. Years ago, in a second-hand bookshop, she'd bought a collection called *Poems of 1912–1913*. According to the introduction, Hardy's wife's death had hit him so badly that the past had become more real to him than the present. When she'd first read that, Pat had thought it pretentious, the sort of thing you might hear from Darina Kelly, but now, having lost Ger, she saw it made sense. Death did strange things to people left behind, so no wonder so many poets and authors wrote about it. Look at *The Case of the Late Pig*. The plot hinged on a man who appeared to have died and been buried and turned up as a murder victim five months later. Of course, it was just light reading, with an aristocratic English detective, whom Pat found a bit annoying. But Seán had said that sleuths and all the whodunit stuff weren't the point of crime stories – what they were really about was love and hatred, guilt, fear, greed, death and lost opportunities. Pat could almost see him now, sitting with a book in his hand, explaining to her. He'd been six or seven years older than she, and intense in a way that sometimes seemed boring, so Pat hadn't taken much notice. Her strongest memory of him was that he'd been kind.

Thomas Hardy had written stories, too, but according to the introduction of Pat's book, his poems were his best work. Pat didn't know. She just liked them. Now she went to the dresser and found the book on a shelf. Carrying it to an easy chair, she switched on the lamp. The pages parted at a poem called 'When I

Set Out for Lyonnesse'. Pat spoke the first two verses aloud to the empty flat.

> 'When I set out for Lyonnesse,
> A hundred miles away,
> The rime was on the spray,
> And starlight lit my lonesomeness
> When I set out for Lyonnesse
> A hundred miles away.
>
> What would bechance at Lyonnesse
> While I should sojourn there
> No prophet durst declare,
> Nor did the wisest wizard guess
> What would bechance at Lyonnesse
> While I should sojourn there.'

Closing the book with a sigh, she stirred the fire in the range and opened *The Case of the Late Pig*.

Later, she tidied the kitchen, locked up, turned off the lamp and, leaving the light on the stairs switched on for Cassie, went up to her room carrying the book of poems. By the time she'd undressed and was under the duvet she felt too tired for reading, so she left the book on her bedside table and settled herself to sleep. But as soon as her eyes closed she saw the harsh light of summer in upstate New York and Josie's tanned legs running ahead of her, the cork heels of her sandals hardly seeming to touch the sidewalk.

It was 7 a.m. and they were rushing to catch the bus to the factory. Pat had hardly slept at all in the unfamiliar second-floor back bedroom at the rooming house. Josie had rapped on her door at half six and chivvied her down to breakfast, saying she mustn't be late on her first day at work. Everything had been disorientating: the toast, which was made from bread that seemed to have no substance to it, the fact that jam was called 'jelly', and Josie asking her to get 'a stick of butter' from the fridge.

The bus, when it came, was nothing like a bus you'd see in Finfarran, and Pat had felt like a gawm for not knowing how she should pay the fare. Behind them, a whole queue of workers had pushed forward complaining as she'd struggled to find the right coins and put them into the slot. At home the driver would have offered to help her and half the queue would have chipped in with advice.

Once she'd got behind a sewing machine in the factory, though, she was fine. Mary was hopeless at dressmaking, being too impatient, but Pat had been running up clothes on an old treadle machine for years.

Getting used to the electric one in the factory was no problem. The forewoman told Josie to show her the ropes for the first day, but by lunchtime she'd worked things out for herself. All the same, she was tired at the end of the shift. It was six in the evening when all the girls streamed out of the factory and Josie suggested that she and Pat should eat at the Shamrock Club.

'Do they do meals there?'

'They do bacon and cabbage.'

'Oh, God, Josie, lead me to it! I'd kill for a plate of that.'

At home she hadn't been all that partial to cabbage, or to the mashed turnips with white pepper that often got dished up with a cut of bacon. But as they walked the short distance from the factory to the Shamrock Club, she'd found herself longing for a familiar meal that might make the place feel less foreign.

Lying in bed, with moonlight falling slantways through the window, Pat remembered that dusty walk, the sharp shadows cast by the houses, the absence of trees, and the six steps that led to the club's entrance. The whitewashed frontage with its painted sign was set back from the street's other buildings, which, in those days, had petered out a block beyond it into chain-link fences enclosing vacant lots. Even in the few months she'd spent there, the town had continued to spread, and most of the development was down to Denis Brennan.

When Josie had brought her in, Denis was sitting on a stool in the Lucky Charm bar. He was six foot two with shoulders like a prize bull's and eyes like gimlets. The strength of his handshake, which was like a vice, made Pat blink. There was a brief interrogation, to establish precisely who she was and where her people came from, before the old man jerked his head at Josie. 'Go on, then, get some food down her. She looks like she's feeling the lack of it.' Then, as Pat turned to go, he leaned towards her and said she was welcome to come and go as she pleased. The smell of whiskey and pipe tobacco had taken her straight back to little pubs on the back roads of Finfarran, where old men who'd never had the chance to make Denis Brennan's fortune held court with the same unquestioned authority, born of a lifetime's knowledge of how to survive.

The bacon and cabbage was served at long tables in what was then the club's kitchen, a steamy room at the back of the building where two middle-aged women cooked for the members on a gas hob and the Brennan memorial range. The range was functional in those days and its original plaque, which was painted wood, was hanging from a nail above it. The meal, which cost half the price of dinner at a diner, included a slice of apple tart and a mug of strong tea. Having finished the tart, Pat knocked back her tea in a few gulps. At the other side of the table was a couple of lads in paint-stained overalls, and one of them caught her eye and gave her a wink. 'They'll pour you another mug if you ask them nicely.'

Pat laughed. 'No, I'm grand, thanks. It just went down well after the dinner.'

'Are you up at the factory?'

'I am. I'm Josie's cousin. She got me the job.'

'And tell me this, are you going to be round long?'

Josie made a face at him. 'She's here for the summer and she's engaged, so you can keep your eyes off her. You'd want to stay well away from this one, Pat. He's like all the lads on the sites, mad for the girls.'

The boy made a face back. 'No great catch, that's what you mean. And she's dead wrong, Pat. Look at old Denis Brennan. That's the kind of money you can make in construction round here.'

Deciding that she didn't need Josie to speak for her, Pat said she was well-suited already.

'Oh, right, so, we'll have to take ourselves elsewhere.'

As the lads got up from the table and swaggered away, laughing, Josie threw Pat a good-humoured

296 THE TRANSATLANTIC BOOK CLUB

look. 'There's no harm in them, really, they're decent enough. But the great thing out here, Pat, is to find a man who does the hiring and firing. You don't want to marry a wage-slave. You want someone like Seán Shanahan.' With a flick of her eyes, she indicated a tall guy who'd just come into the kitchen. He was red-haired and freckled and dressed in neat blue trousers and a cream zip-up jacket. 'That's what everyone's after, Pat. A man with a growing business.'

Pat shifted her position to get a better view. The man paid for a mug of tea and, taking a book from his pocket, went to sit at a table against the wall. Josie leaned sideways and kicked Pat's ankle. 'You're interested now, aren't you? And you well-suited back in Finfarran!'

'I am not!'

'Not suited?'

'Not interested.'

They both burst into giggles and the guy at the far side of the room looked up. Pat nearly died but Josie waved at him. His blue eyes crinkled in acknowledgement, and before he looked back down at his book, Pat saw, for the first time, his gentle, lopsided smile.

CHAPTER TWENTY-NINE

IN THE SMALL HOURS OF THE MORNING, another Atlantic storm hit Finfarran. Gathering strength as it travelled across the ocean, the wind roared in and battered the northern cliffs. Raging on across the peninsula, it spent some of its force against the solid mass of oaks and pines in Fury O'Shea's forest, then swept across the motorway, threatening a high-sided lorry, and tore slates from the rooftops in Lissbeg. As the gusts struck, the trees in the nuns' garden were stripped of their topmost budding leaves despite the protection of the old convent walls.

Swirled by the furious wind, fine sleet froze as it fell and was hurled against streaming windows. In the flat above the butcher's shop, Pat woke with a start. As often happens when sleep has had to be courted, she had no idea of the time. She sat up, groped under her pillow, and couldn't find her wristwatch. Through the uncurtained window she could see the half-orb of the moon, bright as a new penny behind pewter clouds. Briefly, the sleet turned to hailstones and rattled the windowpanes violently, like something trying to get in. Pat wondered if Cassie had got home safely. Forgetting her watch, she threw back the duvet and, having fumbled for her slippers and pulled on a dressing-gown, made her way to the foot of the attic stairs. Here in the stairwell the sound of the storm was dulled. On the little landing above her, Cassie's door was closed. Pat went up and opened it gently, looked in, and breathed a sigh of relief.

Cassie was lying in bed, her face buried in her pillow and one arm thrown above her head. As the wind shook the house again, the clouds shifted and moonlight flooded the room. Turning in her sleep, she had pushed down the duvet, and the patchwork quilt that Pat had sewn lay like a multi-coloured pool on the floor. It was made of squares of velvet and the moonlight touched the nap with gleaming highlights. Pat instinctively moved to pull the duvet around Cassie's shoulders. Then she drew back, unwilling to risk waking her. The back of the cropped head was a dark smudge against the pillow and the arm emerging from the sleeve of the T-shirt curved protectively around it. On the nape of Cassie's neck, where a curl of hair flicked up like a little duck tail, was a small tattoo, a triple spiral motif in black ink. When Mary had first noticed this she'd sniffed in disapproval, but Pat thought it was nice. You'd see women these days with tattoos all over their arms and legs, and even their chests, in different colours, and all you'd find yourself thinking about was the way they were going to look in thirty years' time. As Mary had said, they'd be going round like frights. But this little design half hidden by the single dark curl was different. Though Mary had said that Pat only thought so because she was moon-struck by the child.

Bending down, Pat lifted the quilt and gently drew it up. Cassie turned her head, but her breathing was deep and regular and she snuggled down, instinctively relaxing to the warmth. Looking down at her, Pat told herself Mary was absolutely right. From the day Cassie had met her and Ger at the airport in Toronto she'd fallen head over heels in love with her granddaughter. The flight had been long and she and Ger were tired when Cassie had appeared in Arrivals waving a bunch of roses. She'd driven them home and settled them into what Sonny's wife called 'the guest suite'. Later, when Ger was resting, she'd produced milk and brownies and sat Pat on a sofa in the family room where they'd watched *Judge Judy* together in companionable silence, and Pat had felt welcomed. Then, in the weeks that followed, when it turned out that she and Ger weren't really welcome at all, Cassie had done her utmost to entertain them. It hadn't made Pat feel less unwanted, but the joy of bonding with Cassie had almost outweighed the sadness. Faced with the fact that Sonny and Jim had made lives from which she was excluded, her granddaughter's love had come as a gift that was all the more precious for being unexpected.

Closing Cassie's bedroom door, Pat returned to her own room and got back into bed. The warmth had gone from the duvet and the sheet felt chilly, so she reached for Ger's blue pullover and slipped it on. Outside, the storm had relented and the pale light of dawn was beginning to stain the sky. Soon she'd need to get up because there was plenty to do today. Fury had said he'd be round to finish laying the bit of carpet in Ger's office, and she hoped that Frankie would come and help move the furniture back. She'd decided to make the office into a guest room and thought that, from now on, they could call the attic bedroom Cassie's. Not that she wanted to put any pressure on Cassie to stay in Finfarran. She'd be back on the cruise ships before long, and her real home was Canada, but it might be nice for her to know that she'd always have a room in the flat, and even a place to leave a few things when she went off again on her travels. Happily, Pat turned on her side, and hugged herself.

Outside, as the grey sky turned pink, the house martins in the old convent eaves began to stir and sing.

*

Fury O'Shea was sitting at the table and The Divil was lapping tea from a saucer by the range when Cassie came down for breakfast. Pat reached for the teapot but Cassie shook her head and went to make coffee. Pat gave Fury a wink. 'I do always forget that she won't take tea in the mornings.'

'Is that a fact?' Fury added milk to his cup. 'And yer man The Divil will hardly stir a foot without it. Mind you, he doesn't like it strong. And he'd stick to water for the rest of the day, bar the drop of Guinness if he happened to get it. The end of a pint, say, if I'm having one myself. He's got no head for the hard stuff, though. Wouldn't touch it.'

Pat looked fondly at the little tan and white dog who had rolled onto his side with a deep sigh of contentment. 'He'd be great company. He's a great guard dog too, I suppose.'

'And a judge of character. There's many a one he'd see off that'd turn up with a suit on him, and many another he'd welcome in that hadn't an arse to his trousers.' Knocking back his tea, Fury declared that he ought to get on with the work.

Pat smiled at him. 'You're very good and so is Tintawn Terry. I know well that you shouldn't be here painting walls and laying down carpet. You're a builder, not a handyman, and I can't thank you enough.'

'Don't I know the kind of money the smart lads would ask if they saw you stuck? You wouldn't want to go running up bills at this stage. Not till you've got probate through and everything right and tight.'

It was an aspect of things that Pat had considered. And ever since the day that Frankie had taken Ger's papers she'd wondered if she ought to have checked whether or not they should have been moved from the flat. But life had to go on and it was Frankie who had to manage things, so she supposed that, among the files, there were things he needed to hand.

Cassie joined them at the table with her coffee, saying she wasn't going out in the van today. 'It's in for repairs, so I'll be helping in the library. There's a coffee and cake fundraiser thing happening this afternoon.'

Pat looked stricken. 'Do you know what it is, I forgot all about it! I'll make a pavlova and bring it over, Cassie. I do every year. What time do you start?'

'Hanna said I should come in round lunchtime to help set things up.'

By lunchtime the carpet in Ger's room was down and looked great. Des had turned the sign on the shop door from OPEN to CLOSED, and come up to the flat, to give a hand with the lifting. Pat had sent a text to Frankie and had no reply, but shortly they heard him coming up from the shop. Cassie, wearing her coat and about to go over to the library, was hunkered down on the floor scratching The Divil.

When Frankie came in he stopped dead on the threshold, his face darkening as they all looked round. Pat smiled and held out her hands to him. 'There you are, son. Aren't you good to come over? Des will give you a hand to move the furniture.'

Frankie's eyes swivelled between Cassie on the floor and Fury, who was lounging by the window. In a voice dripping with sarcasm, he remarked that Pat had a grand, hefty team already installed. Pat laughed uncertainly. 'Well, I wouldn't ask poor Cassie to go lifting furniture! And Fury's done far too much already.'

'Well, if he's done all that he has to do, how come he's still hanging round?'

'Frankie!' Horrified, Pat turned to Fury in distress,

but he didn't seem disturbed. With a flicker of a sidelong glance at Des, he said he'd love to help, but his back was at him.

Pat gasped. 'Ah, no, Fury! And you down on your knees laying carpet! You should have said.'

'Not at all, Mrs Fitz, that wouldn't take a feather out of me. I'm just explaining to Frankie why I won't be doing his lifting for him this time.'

To the others' surprise, Cassie rose to her feet and glared at Frankie. 'Fury's been very helpful to Pat, so I don't think you should be rude to him. And I'm perfectly happy to help Des with the furniture.'

'Oh, I bet you are.' Frankie returned her glare. 'Don't think I haven't seen your game, girl!'

Cassie, who'd been bristling, looked bewildered. 'What do you mean?'

'How well you've got your two feet under the table. I suppose you spotted over in Toronto the way it was with Ger, and decided to get in a plane with them and be here at hand when he died.'

Pat gave a little cry, and Cassie took a step forward. 'None of us had any idea that Ger was ill. Not then. He even kept it from Pat as long as he could. So, no, I didn't see it in Toronto. And what exactly are you saying?'

Without moving, Fury intervened. 'He's saying you only came here for what you could get.'

The Divil growled fiercely, deep in his throat. Cassie went scarlet. 'That I'm looking for *money*?' Pat reached out to Cassie, who gently pushed her away. 'No, wait, I need to understand this. Is he saying I'm here because of Granddad's will?'

Frankie shrugged his shoulders. 'If the cap fits, wear it.'

Pat spoke before Cassie could reply. 'Cassie is here looking after me out of pure loving-kindness. And you should be ashamed to say such a thing of your own brother's child!'

'Ah, for God's sake, Mam, would you have a bit of sense? Wasn't she overheard inside in the library asking straight-out questions about the will? Didn't you hear her yourself, and she fishing about the price of the very tiles on the shop walls? Weren't you there when she tried to deny she was out walking the bounds of the farm? She was totting up the value of the land, trying to guess the worth of it.'

'I was not!'

'And you didn't drive over to my place wanting to talk about sharing things out?'

Cassie turned frantically to Pat. 'I wasn't totting

up the worth of anything. It never occurred to me. I didn't ask questions about the will. I didn't! Well, I said something to Hanna about it when you and I got back from Resolve but *truly* ...' She faltered, unable to remember exactly what she'd said to Hanna on that first jetlagged day. Out of the corner of her eye she could see Fury looking at her.

But Pat's attention was on Frankie. 'What? When did she drive out to your place?'

'Oh, she didn't tell you that? She wouldn't, of course. She told me she'd sneaked out of here while you were asleep.'

Cassie was aghast. 'I wanted to talk about ways of helping Pat. I'd been worried about her, and she was asleep, and I thought you and Fran and I could sit down for a family talk ...' Her voice trailed away, and she found herself shaking. 'I mightn't have made myself clear, but that's why I came.'

Frankie raised his eyebrow at her scornfully. 'Ay, you were real careful not to spell things out. But I could tell fine well what you meant.'

CHAPTER THIRTY

CASSIE SAT IN THE NUNS' GARDEN knowing she ought to be at work but needing to process what had just happened. She wasn't even certain how the scene in the flat had ended. Frankie's accusation had left her gaping and, before she could summon a coherent response, Pat had gently pushed her out, telling her she'd be wanted in the library. Then she'd found Fury had opened the door and, somehow, she'd had her bag in her hand and was walking down the stairs. Frankie had remained in the kitchen, looking belligerent, and the door had been closed firmly on whatever was said next. But Pat hadn't seemed angry. Or, at least, not with her.

In the garden the warmth of the morning sun had been trapped by brick and stone. At Cassie's back was the wall of the old refectory, where the stained-glass windows shone beneath the martins' nests in the eaves. The birds were swooping to and fro, catching insects, darting from their roosts to skim the library courtyard, perching briefly on the telephone lines, and wheeling back across the garden. To her left, late clumps of delicate snowdrops were flowering under the row of tall cypresses, which grew parallel to the granite boundary wall. Light sparkling off flecks of mica in the stonework echoed the effect of the gleaming snowdrops under the dark trees. In the centre of the fountain, where the statue of St Francis extended its welcoming arms, someone had poured birdseed into the saint's stone hands, and fluttering wheatears and chiffchaffs were squabbling over the bounty, their wings whirring as they paused in flight.

Slumped on a bench between the herb beds, Cassie felt dreadful. She *had* mentioned the will when talking to Hanna, and Fury had known that in the pub, so the conversation in the library must have been overheard. And she'd said that the vintage tiles in the shop would be worth a fortune, these days. And when Frankie had found her and Pat picking shamrock, she'd called out that he needn't think they'd come to walk the bounds. But that had just been a stupid joke, made to cover up the fact that she hadn't been pleased to see him. And – of *course* – that was why Frankie had been creeping her out lately. Ever since she'd visited him that night when Pat was asleep, he'd thought she'd tried to involve him in a conspiracy. So his every look and word had been loaded with horrible implications, which she hadn't understood.

A footstep crunched on the gravel and, looking up, she saw Fury and The Divil approaching from the other side of the fountain. Fury was strolling purposefully, his hands buried in his torn pockets pulling his shabby waxed jacket around his skinny hips. The Divil was trotting beside him and, seeing Cassie, bounded forward, scattering gravel in his wake. Cassie wasn't in the mood for conversation but, knowing there was no point in trying to dodge Fury, she shuffled along the bench so he could sit down. Instead, he stood over her, with no discernible expression, while The Divil made a flying leap and landed on her knees. The compact little body with its warm, wiry coat was oddly comforting. Having turned on her lap a couple of times, to find an acceptable position, the dog settled down with his nose between his paws. Fury cocked an eyebrow at Cassie. 'I hope you know you're honoured. I've never seen him do that before, and I've known him all his life.'

Cassie ran her fingers along the little dog's back. 'Is Frankie still with Pat?'

'No. She showed him the door.'

'Did she? You mean she didn't believe him?'

Fury sat down beside her on the bench. 'She had more sense.' He turned his head and looked down his nose at Cassie. 'It's a pity you hadn't.'

'I know but, honestly, I never meant—'

'Of course you didn't. Only an eejit like Frankie would think you did.'

'But that's just it. I've been trying to work out what he *was* thinking. I mean, you can't change the fact that Ger left everything to Pat.'

'Ay, well, hard facts have never bothered Frankie.'

'So he thought that he and I could somehow overturn the will?'

'Ah, Holy God Almighty, girl, how do I know what he thought? I know how his mind works, though. He's always been able to get whatever he's wanted, and he's always imagined everyone else is as greedy as himself.'

'But then why blurt it all out in front of Pat?'

'Well, I'm no mind-reader but, if you ask me, he just lost his temper when you stood up to him. He's always been like that. I'm surprised he's kept his cool so long when Pat had already crossed him.'

'You mean about The Divil being in the shop?'

The Divil wriggled at the sound of his name and Fury gave Cassie a knowing grin. 'I mean about me coming in and out of the flat. That's what's been getting to Frankie.'

'Why?'

'Because when Ger was alive Frankie could always manipulate him, and now he's trying to do the same to Pat. He doesn't want me there to see it.'

Cassie scratched The Divil's ears. 'You mean, even though Ger left things to Pat, Frankie wants to take control.'

'I do.'

Cassie said she supposed that was understandable. 'After all, Frankie was in charge of things before Ger died.'

Fury snorted. 'It might be understandable if that was true. But it isn't. Mind you, like I said before, I wasn't here when Frankie, your dad and your uncle were growing up. But, by all accounts, Frankie was born lazy. He has the house and the big car and plenty of swagger, but I doubt he's done a day's work in his life.'

'Then how come Ger gave him the house and stuff?'

'I don't know, girl, and it's none of my business. They say Ger was fierce protective when Frankie was small. Maybe he wasn't born lazy. Maybe he grew up work-shy. Or maybe Ger just favoured his eldest, the way my dad did.'

'But if that was so, wouldn't Ger have left him everything? Like your dad left the forest to your brother?'

Fury shrugged. 'I told you I don't know, and it's none of my concern.'

It was Cassie's turn to raise an eyebrow. He saw it and grinned. 'You're as bad as Frankie, you are! You want to know why I'm hanging round if I've no dog in the fight.'

'Well – yeah. And before you say that's none of *my* business, the bottom line is that I'm here for Pat.'

Even though she liked Fury, her eyes had narrowed and there was a sharp note in her voice. The Divil turned to look at her reproachfully. Fury grinned. 'Don't go confusing him now that he's nailed his colours to the mast. He had you down as someone who could be trusted.'

'Well, I am. The question is are you?'

Fury turned and looked at her with no trace of his accustomed irony. 'Frankie's no drunk but he's a waster, just like my brother was. If he gets hold of the reins he'll have the farm ruined. Or he'll sell off the fields for the kind of housing locals can't afford. Nothing will matter to him but making money. At least Ger had an honest trade and knew how to work the land.'

'You mean Frankie might get rid of everything?'

'That's what I said. And you know what? Then it would be gone.'

There was a pause in which Cassie digested this idea. Then Fury chuckled. 'So he wasn't altogether wrong, was he? You do have a bit of an eye on the land yourself.'

Cassie turned on him in outrage, causing The Divil to wobble on her knee. She put her hand on his wiry head and he settled down again, snorting through his whiskers. Relaxing, she nodded at Fury. 'Okay. I see what you mean. I hadn't thought of it that way.'

'No, you think about land the same way I do. That's the difference between wanting to own it and feeling it might own you.'

She nodded again. Then she glanced at him. 'But if that's why Frankie doesn't want you there, shouldn't Pat be told? Ought I to say something?'

'If you'll take my advice, you'll keep your beak shut and stop thinking you've got all the answers. Nothing in life is black and white, and people need to work things out in their own good time.'

The Divil shifted his weight on Cassie's knee. The bench was in full sunlight and, beside her, a bee was droning in a rosemary bush. Autumn leaves still lay at the foot of the old convent wall, sheltered by protuberant stonework above them and already half rotted into the loamy soil. Beside her, Fury was watching the swooping house martins. Their glossy backs flashed in the sunlight and their white underparts gleamed as they passed overhead. He spoke again, looking straight ahead. 'Round here we tend to keep an eye on each other, though. Your gran's a decent woman and I don't like to see her having to cope on her own.'

'She's not on her own, she's got me.'

'That's true.'

In the silence that followed Cassie realised how far out of her depth she had travelled. 'Do you think I should call my dad?'

'No, I don't.' Fury's reply was emphatic. When he went on, Cassie could feel him thinking she wouldn't understand him. 'I'll tell you what it is, girl, it's always complex when people go away. Doesn't matter why they leave, if they put down roots elsewhere, they're strangers when they come home. And people who stay where they were born tend to stick together. If your dad and your uncle Jim came back and started to meddle they'd find they weren't welcome. It wouldn't matter what the neighbours thought about Frankie, or even how much everyone likes Pat. Unless Sonny and Jim have developed some kind of amnesia, they'll know that well.'

Cassie frowned. 'But there's nothing Frankie can do, really, is there? As long as Pat's alive she's going to have the final say.'

'That's true too.'

Realising what she'd just said, Cassie stiffened. Then The Divil sneezed and Fury gave her a sharp dig with his elbow. 'Frankie's as thick as two short planks, but he's not the type to push his mam downstairs. This is real life, not a detective story. Don't let your Transatlantic Book Club put notions in your head.'

'I wasn't.'

'You were so.'

Cassie admitted to herself that she kind-of-sort-of had been. For the first time since she'd come to Finfarran, she felt like a stranger lost in a strange land. She didn't really understand what Fury had meant about people who went away and those who stayed. And she still wasn't sure why her dad and Uncle Jim had never come on a visit. Despite what Fury had just said, it did feel a bit like a detective story. But she decided he could be trusted and she was glad to know he was keeping an eye on Pat. Aware that she ought to be at work, she got to her feet, tipping The Divil onto the gravel path. Then she stopped and looked down at Fury who was still lounging on the bench. 'Do you think I ought to go and check on Pat?'

'No. Because I can tell you what she's doing.'

'What?'

'When I left she was making a pavlova.' Seeing Cassie's disbelieving expression, he added, 'Did you not hear her say she was going to bring one over to the library?'

'Yes, but she's had a shock. She won't want to come out.'

'Do you know what it is, you've a lot to learn about living in Finfarran. If your gran promised to make a cake, she'll do it. And she'll carry it across Broad Street with her head held high. Someone will have seen Frankie come out her door with a face like a smacked arse. If Pat missed the do in the library now there'd be all sorts of talk going round.'

There was a pause in which Cassie fought tears. 'You don't think that my being here has made things worse for her? I was the cause of that row back there with Frankie. It wouldn't have happened if I'd kept my big mouth shut.'

Fury stretched out his long legs and looked up at

her. His habitual air of disparagement had returned. 'You're right about that. It wouldn't. On the other hand, some things are better out than in. But you needn't expect me give you absolution. You have The Divil's seal of approval, so I don't know what more you can want.'

CHAPTER THIRTY-ONE

THERE WAS A STREAM OF PEOPLE clattering up the library steps, carrying plates of homemade biscuits and tins containing cakes. Making no comment on Cassie's lateness, Hanna handed her a box of mugs borrowed from the delicatessen. 'Take these through to the reading room, will you? And keep an eye on them. People will offer to help wash up later on but there's hardly room to turn round in the kitchen and I don't want anything broken.'

Cassie said Pat would be over soon, bringing a pavlova.

'Perfect. There are paper plates in that box too, so will you help cut things up as they come, and lay them out? Everyone gets a coffee and a plate of cake or whatever, and they'll know to put some money in the box. Leave the amount to their discretion but, if anyone asks, suggest a five-euro donation. Have you got that?'

She had no time to ask why Cassie had arrived

looking so distracted. The fundraiser was an annual library event and, aided and abetted by other communities up and down the peninsula, Lissbeg always came out in force to support it. Frequently, more cakes were donated than could be consumed on the day, but most people enthusiastically bought up the leftovers. Many arrived with homemade scones or tray bakes, ate and drank very little, pushed twenty-euro notes into the collection boxes, and left with less impressive offerings than the ones they'd brought. Ultimately, in excess of a thousand euros would be raised for the struggling hospice in Carrick, which couldn't survive without this kind of support. It all took a great deal of work and coordination and, between playing hostess and trying to ensure that no one got jam on the library books, Hanna was always rushed off her feet.

Keeping people in the reading room was like trying to herd sheep. Numbers of those who came were avid readers, and Hanna hated to make them feel confined. But her primary duty was to her stock, so she tended to stalk the shelving, watching wanderers discussing books with pieces of cake in their hands. Some made it back to the reading room without disaster. Others would leave their paper plates precariously balanced on her displays. The worst offenders would try to turn pages while holding large slices of Pat's pavlova. In those cases, the only option was hasty intervention, which made Hanna feel like a hovering hawk constantly waiting to pounce.

Fortunately, the mood was always good-humoured. Even a text from Mary at 7 a.m. had made Hanna smile: DONT PICK ME UP IVE MADE A BATTENBERG.

It was followed by another, which read, STACIA HAS ME FIXED

Shooting back a thumbs-up emoji, she'd reset her alarm to snooze time, grateful to the neighbour who must have offered to drive Mary to the event.

Mary arrived, bearing her cake in a Cadbury's Roses tin. Hanna took her through to the Reading Room and handed it to a volunteer, who was rapidly slicing tea brack. Mary announced that, while some put fondant icing on a Battenberg, she had been sticking to marzipan for years. 'And if strained apricot jam was good enough for Queen Victoria, I've no call to go fiddling round with rose pistachio cream.'

Darina was standing by a trestle table, sadly watching Gobnit use her iPhone as a plate. Looking up, she remarked that the cake had been named for Princess Victoria, not the queen. 'She married Louis of Battenberg in 1884. I don't know how I know that, but I expect I must have seen it on Wikipedia. I do a lot of surfing, you know. At least, I did before Gobnit took the phone.'

Mary sniffed loudly. 'If that child were mine, I'd have that phone out of her hands double quick.'

'You may be right, but I do think children need to establish their own sense of parameters. And she does let me have it for emergencies, don't you, petal?' Darina looked hopefully at Gobnit, who ignored her. 'Well, I'm sure she would, if one arose. And we *have* talked about it. Talking things through with little ones is important, don't you think?'

Aware that Mary about to tell her exactly what she thought, Hanna intervened: 'The cake is lovely, Mam, you were good to make it.'

Mary inclined her head graciously. 'I like to do my bit.'

'It looks delicious. Would you like a coffee?'

'Well, I would.'

Having steered her towards Cassie, who was serving coffee, Hanna went to welcome a photographer, whose annual spread in the *Inquirer* tended to increase the final sum raised for the hospice. He was a middle-aged man known for his sweet tooth, so a cake was regularly slipped to him on leaving, with the result that his photos of the library event were far better than most of the shots on the paper's *What's Happening?* page. This year's cake had been made by a cheerful woman who, when Hanna approached her, had laughed. 'No problem at all, love. My daughter says the amount of sugar I put in my lemon drizzle cake would melt every last tooth in your head.'

Having shaken hands with the photographer, Hanna was cornered by an elderly farmer holding a slice of seed cake, which he presented for her inspection. 'Tell me this and tell me no more, what do you think of that?'

It looked boring but innocuous, so Hanna said that caraway seeds weren't everybody's favourite. The farmer's expression became so grim that she feared he might have made the cake himself, so she hastily added that the hospice was always delighted by people's generosity. Then, longing for a mug of coffee, she tried to move away. He immediately took a step sideways, cornering her again. 'Talk about crimes crying to Heaven for justice! Isn't this just the same as the case of the pig?'

Feeling at a loss, Hanna tried to place him. He was wearing an ancient cloth cap and a very new jacket, as

if his wife had smartened him before he'd driven her
into town. Apparently reading her mind, he gestured
at the crowd. 'There's my wife over there. She makes a
lovely flan.'

'Does she? How nice of her to bring one.'

'Two.'

'I'm sorry?'

'Two flans. Plum compôte and apple snow. Pure
butter in the mix, mind, and a jug of whipped cream
on her knee all the way into town.'

'How lovely.'

'Lovely, is it?' His voice rose in outrage. 'It's the case
of the pig! Am I right?'

Guessing that he must be a member of the
Transatlantic Book Club, Hanna reminded herself
that she generally sat at the front of the room. Perhaps
he'd been at the back, where she hadn't noticed him.
Tentatively, she asked if he'd enjoyed reading the book.

His shaggy eyebrows drew together aggressively.
'What book?'

'The Margery Allingham.'

'Ah, would you not be trying to change the subject!
I've read no book!' He flourished the cake so angrily
that she took a step back. 'What I'm talking to you
about is a crime.'

Hanna looked for, and failed to find, an escape. As she hesitated, a small woman came elbowing through the crowd. 'Ah, Weeshie, would you mind your good tweed when you're eating!' She tucked a paper napkin into his collar and, turning to Hanna, rolled her eyes in mock resignation. 'If husbands had to do their own laundry, we'd see a difference then! But, sure, there's no consideration for the women.'

Her husband turned on her fiercely. 'Amn't I just saying that my poor mother was heart-scalded like you are? Six months of every year she was up morning and evening, boiling pots of scraps for whatever pig we were rearing out the back. Every kind of delicacy she'd feed to them creatures, and each year the result would be the same. When the time came, we'd kill a grand, fat, likely animal, and half the parish round would be sent a big plate of meat. As a compliment. That's how it was. And what were we left with ourselves? Feck all!'

His wife looked puzzled. 'But didn't the neighbours send some of their kill round to you?'

'Isn't that what I'm saying? They did, of course! Wasn't that the way of it? You'd each kill the pig you were after rearing, and then you'd give half your meat away to the neighbours, and have to say thanks for the "compliments" they sent you in return! Bloody great plates and pans of meat carried round and round the parish, and nobody getting the good of what he'd fattened for himself.'

'But wasn't that the custom? And wasn't it sociable? And why are you talking to Hanna about it now?'

'Because it's the same thing that's happening here, woman! And it's just as daft now as it was then. The scrawny old scraps that used to get sent round to us by the neighbours! You wouldn't credit them! And our grand fat pig carried out the door! And look at this!' He thrust the plate of cake at his wife, practically spitting with anger. 'You after pouring butter and eggs into them lovely flans of yours, and I after getting handed out *a slice of seedy cake*!'

*

Pat arrived twenty minutes later bearing a sumptuous pavlova on a tray. Hanna was about to join her for a coffee when, as usual, something more pressing caught her attention. This time it was a young man who was standing in the library, glaring at a display labelled 'Readers' Favourites'. His expression was so dejected that she thought she should see what was wrong.

'Hello, I'm Hanna Casey, the librarian. I don't think I've seen you here before?'

'I don't go to libraries.'

It sounded as if he'd been passing and seen the poster for the event. More than one of Hanna's regulars had first been drawn to the library by Wi-Fi access or a chamber-music concert and returned to become a card-carrying bookworm. Here, she thought, was another possible convert. He was still looking at the books, so she asked what he liked to read.

He sighed lugubriously. 'It's sad, isn't it? Really, really sad.'

'I'm sorry?'

'The way you can't get books by men any more.'

Hanna looked at the shelf which, admittedly, featured Marian Keyes, Louise O'Neill and the new *Aisling* book, as well as an acclaimed collection of women's poetry. The young man hunched his shoulders and told her that men all over the world were downtrodden. 'It's a well-known fact that our voices are systematically being suppressed.'

'But lots of books are written by men. Overall, I'd say it's the majority.'

'Yeah, but they were written back in the day, weren't they? People like Charles Dickens and Isaac Asimov.'

'Quite a few men have been published since Dickens.'

'That's just quotas, though, isn't it? Lip service. No

one wants to come out and admit that men have been deemed irrelevant. Surplus to requirements. No one will just say it out loud. It's no wonder we can't express our sense of society's inequalities.'

Controlling an impulse to introduce him to the man with the seedy cake, Hanna attempted to formulate an acceptable response. Before she could find one Mary appeared, scrubbing her hands with a wet wipe. 'That little Gobnit's been using whipped cream to create an art installation.'

Hanna's mind leaped into overdrive. 'Oh, God, no! Where?'

'Ah, you needn't worry about your books, she spooned it into Darina's snakeskin handbag. An installation was what Darina called it. If you ask me, what that child needs is a firm hand.' Having delivered herself of her verdict, Mary scrutinised the young man. 'I don't know you, do I?'

'I'm from Limerick.'

'Well, if you want a bit of Battenberg, you'd better get your skates on. It's going fast.' Dropping the wet wipe into a bin, she turned to Hanna. 'I'll say this now, and it's not because you're my daughter. You've put on a good do here today.'

Astonished by the unaccustomed praise, Hanna

smiled. 'Thanks, Mam, that's really nice. But it's all down to people like you taking time to contribute. I just provide the venue.'

Mary pursed her lips. 'Ay, now you've said it, I suppose that's true enough.'

As Hanna struggled to keep a straight face, Pat emerged from the reading room, carrying the tray on which she'd brought her pavlova. It was now piled with rock cakes, which, she explained in an undertone, hadn't been going down well.

Mary snorted loudly. 'Weren't they made by a Finch from Crossarra? None of that lot can bake.'

Unusually, Pat failed to defend the underdog. Instead she looked helplessly at the plate. Mary and Hanna were simultaneously struck by the thought that while, in previous years, Ger would have shared Pat's purchases, today she'd carry them into an empty flat. Before Hanna could think what to say, Mary took Pat's elbow, announcing that she'd walk her across the road. 'But you needn't try palming me off with one of those rock cakes. Keep them for Cassie. She's got American teeth.'

Out of nowhere, the boy from Limerick addressed himself to Hanna. 'There's one book I've been wanting to read for months.'

Refocusing on him with difficulty, Hanna asked what it was.

'Robert Galbraith's *Career of Evil*.'

'Well, I'm not sure I've got it in stock but, if it isn't here, I can order it.'

'Oh, right. Up from the dusty vaults to which it's been banished.'

'Well, no. There's an inter-library loans system—'

'Oh, come *on*! Why not admit it? It's a book written by a man so you "haven't got it in stock".'

'Er, you do know that Robert Galbraith is a pseudonym?'

'Yes.'

'For J. K. Rowling.'

'Duh! Yes. I'm not stupid.'

'And that J. K. Rowling is a woman?'

The boy stepped away from her in horror. 'Jaysus Christ Almighty, you're sad!'

'What?'

'Out you come with the party line regardless of the truth! Or maybe you believe it. Maybe you do. Maybe you're a zombie. You know what? I'm not going to stand here and take any more of this crap.'

With an air of great dignity, he marched out of the door. As it slammed behind him, there was a crash from the reading room and a chorus of voices informed Hanna that Gobnit had been sick. Grateful that Mary was dealing with Pat, she went to find a mop and bucket. Even in the face of trouble and bereavement, life with all of its incidental absurdities went on.

CHAPTER THIRTY-TWO

THE WEATHER IN RESOLVE HAD BEEN idyllic in the summer of 1962. Looking back, Pat could see herself waking each morning to bright sunlight streaming through Mrs Quinn's lace curtains. It hadn't taken long to acclimatise to the heat. Soon she was going to work bare-legged and in sandals, like Josie, wearing big round sunglasses picked up in the drugstore on the corner, and pinning up her hair to cool the back of her neck. She learned to walk on the shady side of the street, although, in fact, people in Resolve didn't walk much. Buses ran so frequently that they didn't have to, and lots of the lads had motorbikes or pickups. Josie was taking driving lessons, and one of the girls at Mrs Quinn's owned a car. It was what she called 'an old beat-up thing', passed on to her by her mother. To Pat's eyes it was luxury. No one had a car like it in Finfarran, long and low with leather seats and a roof that rolled back. The girl, who worked in an office in town, was a bit stuck

up when it came to giving lifts, though, so Pat and
Josie mostly rode the bus.

All sorts of things were different in America. You
'rode' buses instead of 'taking' them, and you 'called'
people instead of ringing. You had to remember to look
to the left before you crossed a road. But you adapted.
Although Josie had been gone only a few years from
Finfarran, she already sounded like an Irish character
in an American film and, after a week or so, Pat got a
feeling it wouldn't be long before she'd be talking the
same way herself.

The first day she walked into the Shamrock Club on
her own she must have looked nervous because Seán
Shanahan, who'd been sipping a pint at the bar, had
called across and asked if she'd like a drink. It surprised
her because, up to then, she'd hardly said two words
to him, but the Brennans and the Shanahans were the
town's foremost families so she thought that perhaps
he thought he ought to make her feel at home. She
wasn't much of a drinker so she'd asked for a lemonade
shandy, and he'd carried the drinks to a table in the
corner. The Brennans were rich but they'd only been
in Resolve for a generation, while the Shanahans had
come over back in the 1880s. Pat had discovered that
the length of time your family had been in Resolve was

seen as important so, to make conversation, she asked Seán about his. He told her his grandfather had been a lad when he'd taken the emigrant boat. 'He walked all the way to Cork from Finfarran, and they say that a white kitten from home had hidden itself in the bundle on his back.'

'Really? Is that true?'

Seán laughed. 'I've no idea. He's supposed to have got it through immigration on Ellis Island tucked in the pocket of his greatcoat. Seems unlikely to me.'

Sipping the shandy, Pat said she'd heard people had to take off their clothes when they got to Ellis Island.

'Well, they went through medical examinations, so I guess that's right.'

'The kitten story does sound unlikely, then.'

'Still, there's always been a white cat at the Shamrock Club.'

'But the club was only built about ten years ago.'

'True. But, before that, people used get together up at the Shanahan house. And when I was growing up our place was overrun with kittens.'

'All white?'

'Each and every one. My gran and my mom were always trying to get rid of them. Even the mailman didn't get away without a kitten. And the cat that's here in the club now definitely came from us.'

Pat couldn't tell whether or not he was serious, but she'd seen a white cat, which was very handsome, asleep under the range in the club's kitchen. As soon as she finished her drink she said she ought to go through and order something to eat. 'Josie's off gallivanting with her boyfriend, so I'm eating alone tonight.'

His own drink was still half full, but he raised his eyebrows at her. 'Would you like company?'

She blushed, hoping he hadn't thought she was fishing for a date. But he knew she was engaged, because Josie had told him. Anyway, she was wearing Ger's ring. So she smiled and said that company would be nice.

They brought their drinks through to the kitchen and sat at one of the long tables, eating cod in a sauce flavoured with dried parsley and served with a pile of colcannon made with kale. Pat was getting bored by the club's relentlessly Irish menu, probably because the diner up the street from Quinn's served delicious burgers and milkshakes, and Josie had introduced her to the delights of Chinese food. She wondered if Seán had his dinner here in the Shamrock Club every night. If he had a growing business, like Josie said, he wouldn't be worried about the cost of eating out in a proper restaurant. He wasn't married, though – Josie had said that too – so maybe he was a typical bachelor, having his pint at the bar each evening and eating at the club because it was convenient.

He was good company, easy to spend time with and not pushy. She asked him about his work and he told her he'd started a landscape-gardening business. 'Well, right now it's mostly cutting lawns. I've done a couple of yards from scratch, though. Design right through to completion.'

'Who does the labouring?'

'That would be me.'

'Sounds like a lot of work.'

'Yeah, but pretty soon I'll have hordes of employees.'

'And you'll just sit in an office giving out orders?'

'That's not too likely. Getting my hands in the dirt is my favourite bit.'

So he wasn't as rich as Josie had suggested, though everyone knew you could make money fast in the States. Pat had noticed that in America gardens were 'yards' and earth was called 'dirt'. She liked the way some of the words here were strange. They made you see things from different angles, the way poems did. Rather to her own surprise, she found herself saying so to Seán.

He took a sip of his pint and gave her a grin. 'Can't say I read much poetry.'

'But you do read.'

'How d'you know?'

'Because the other night you were sitting in here with a book.'

'That's true.'

'What was it?'

'Oh, just a crime thing. Dashiell Hammett. Have you read him?'

'No.'

'So who's your favourite poet?'

'Thomas Hardy.' Pat looked at him sideways. 'You've never heard of him, have you?'

'No, I haven't.' His face broke into his lopsided smile. 'Should we talk about baseball?'

'God, no! I haven't a clue about that.'

She was none the wiser a week later after they'd been to a game. Josie and Donal came with them and afterwards they ate in a restaurant a couple of blocks from the ballpark. Seán had a car and he drove them there, with Donal in the passenger seat and Pat and Josie behind them. When Josie called it 'in back' Pat kicked her. 'In *the* back! What're you saying? 'Tis far from "in back" you were reared!'

They were still messing and laughing when Seán pulled into the parking lot and they crowded into the restaurant, which had red-checked tablecloths and menus printed with crossed French flags. The stew they ate was rich with chunks of tender meat and marrowbone, tiny pearl onions, and the taste of garlic and bay leaves. Having fixed that they'd split the bill four ways, Pat decided to get her money's worth and ordered red wine, which was sweet and dark and came in a painted jug. Afterwards, she had chocolate pudding served in a little pot.

When they got home Josie dragged Pat up to her room to talk. She couldn't believe how relaxed Seán had been. 'I've never seen him that way before! He was all smiles and chat.' Bouncing onto Pat's bed, she asked what the story was. 'Did you kiss him and turn the frog into a prince?'

'You know fine well I did not!'

'You seem to be getting on fierce well with him, though.'

'He's nice enough.'

'He drives a lovely car, I'll say that for him.'

As Pat went to bed she told herself she was glad Mary hadn't been there. Josie was a bit of a tease but at least she could let a subject drop.

The following weekend Pat was alone again. Donal had won a couple of seats to a Broadway show in a raffle so he and Josie had gone off to see it and spend the night in the city. It was a stifling hot day and Pat had written her weekly letters home: one to her mother, one to Mary and one to Ger. She was sitting on her bedroom windowsill, trying to get some air, when Mrs Quinn shouted up the stairs. When Pat went down, Seán was standing waiting for her in the hall. She could tell that the car outside, and the fact he was a Shanahan had made a big impression on Mrs Quinn.

He was wearing jeans and a denim jacket, which made him look younger than usual because, though he'd told her he did all his own labouring, he was always very smartly dressed when he came to the Shamrock Club. When he saw her he smiled and asked if she fancied a swim. 'There's a lake about an hour's drive away.'

'I don't know.'

Mrs Quinn had disappeared, leaving them together, a clear endorsement of Seán's respectability.

'I just thought, it's a hot day, so if you and Josie wanted to come along ...'

'Josie's not here.' She told him about the Broadway show and he whistled. 'Wow. That's some prize.'

'Isn't it? They're going to stay the night with some

friend of Donal's. Josie says they'll probably die of the heat.'

'If you know where to go, it's always cool and shady at the north lake.'

'And you swim there?'

'Sure. There are beaches.'

'Well – okay. Can you wait till I get my things?'

There was a swimming costume in the top drawer of Josie's chest of drawers. Knowing that she wouldn't mind, Pat grabbed it and ran to her own room. She wrapped the togs in a towel and considered what to wear. In magazines, American girls looked stylish even on beaches, so she pulled on a pair of candy-pink pedal-pushers, and a white shirt which, according to Josie, ought to be tied in a knot above her midriff. Deciding that was a bit much, Pat tucked the shirt in at her waist and found her new white sandals. It was the first time she'd worn the outfit, which she and Josie had bought on a trip to the mall. Pushing the towel and her purse into a straw basket she'd also snatched from Josie's room, she tied her hair in a high ponytail, and perched her sunglasses on the top of her head. The figure that looked back at her from her mirror seemed like a stranger so, with a strange sense of being somebody else, she ran back downstairs.

Once they got off the highway, the roads were edged with trees and, to Pat's delight, they drove through towns where the houses had white picket fences, just as she'd imagined before coming to the States. The car roof was down and she sat beside Seán in her sunglasses, with a chiffon scarf tied over her hair and wrapped twice around her neck, exactly like Audrey Hepburn in *Breakfast at Tiffany's*. When they were halfway there Seán stopped and bought her a Coke from a vending machine. Before she drank it, she held the cold tin to her cheek and rolled it across her forehead, feeling the condensation dry as soon as it touched her skin.

When they got to the lake she took off her scarf and shoved it into her basket. Seán walked round the car and opened the door for her. The first beaches they'd passed on the way had been crowded but here it was quiet, with only a couple of boats on the lake and some people off in the distance, diving from a rock. Pat got out of the car and looked around. The lake was beautiful. As she followed Seán down to a sandy beach, a flight of birds skimmed above them, making a whistling sound. They had black backs and white undersides. As she pushed up her glasses to look at them, their flight path curved and dipped, and they settled on the water.

'What are they?'

'Goldeneyes. They're called Whistlers too.'

'Were they singing?'

'No, that's the sound of their wings.'

Pat found a rock where she could sit with her feet dangling in the water. She could hear the shouts of the distant divers and the sound of the wind in the trees that edged the lake. 'What did you say this place is called?'

'People just call it North Lake or North White Lake. It's proper name is Kauneonga.'

'What does that mean?'

'It's Native American. Means "two wings" or "lake with two wings" or something.'

Overhead another flight of birds was wheeling towards the water. 'What are they called?'

'Hey, I'm no ornithologist.'

'I'm sorry. It's just all so new.'

Seán hunkered down beside the rock and watched the little birds descend on the lake. 'Actually, I do know those. They're called Butterballs. Or, hang on, maybe it's Buffleheads.'

'Do they migrate?'

'Sure. Dunno where they go, but they always come back.'

'I can see why.'

'Me, too. Once you find someplace like this I guess you find it hard to forget.'

That was the way things were the whole afternoon. Easy and funny, and beautifully cool after the heat of town. Seán lay on his back on the white sandy beach and smoked a cigarette and, after a while, Pat went into the bushes and put on her swimsuit. She was glad it fitted because she hadn't tried it on before snatching it from Josie's drawer. When she came out of the bushes Seán was already in the water. You could tell by the muscles in his shoulders that he was used to lifting and digging. He rolled over on his back when he saw her, and gesticulated, urging her to come in. Then, in case she'd be hesitant, he swam back and waded towards her, the water streaming down his chest and legs. He was built like Tom, straight-legged and slender-hipped. His shoulders and arms were tanned and freckled, like his face, but the rest of his body reminded Pat of a poem she'd read about someone who looked as if he was made of white marble. There was a cedar tree by the lakeside casting shadows on the water. She waded out into the cool, dappled ripples and, seeing that she was confident, Seán turned and struck out again to where you could see a current dragging the lake into little waves.

After their swim they lay side by side on a couple of towels on the beach. Later, as they were driving home, she realised that she'd talked herself almost hoarse, telling him about her life at home and how she and Ger and Mary and Tom were planning a double wedding in the autumn.

'Here it's the fall.'

'I know. It's a much better word.'

'Shame you won't be around to see the colours.'

'Is it beautiful?'

'It's spectacular.'

'Autumn's a kind of misty time in Finfarran. There's a sort of "everything's over" softness about it.'

'Here it's an explosion of gold and crimson and scarlet and bronze. You can't imagine how vivid. Not like the end of something at all. Like the start of something really exciting and new.'

CHAPTER THIRTY-THREE

A NEW CRUISE SHIP HAD BERTHED IN Ballyfin. The passengers were having a night ashore in the Spa Hotel, and Cassie, Margot and the hotel's beauty therapists were inundated with bookings. Cassie, who'd been due to do a morning shift, was asked by an apologetic Margot to work through lunchtime. 'Actually, if you could hang on till four I'll call it a double shift. And I'll order a sandwich from the café, so you won't die of hunger.'

'No problem. I was going to buy a roll and eat it on the beach but something expensive from the café will do just fine.' The hotel's café went in for smoked salmon and rare beef, whereas the little place Cassie had intended to go to produced less sophisticated fare. But, in the event, she hardly had time to appreciate her expensive sandwich because she and Margot worked straight through from 10 a.m. till three. The sandwich was snatched in the few minutes she'd grabbed to take a loo break, and the pot of delicious coffee, which came with it, was left to go cold on the tray.

When the worst of the rush was over, Cassie saw Sharon signalling from the desk. Leaving Kate to sweep round her chair, she went to see what was up. Sharon waved a piece of paper at her. 'That American guy Bradley Miller? He wanted to speak to you. I offered to pass on a message but he said just to tell you he'd rung and you'd know what it was about.'

Cassie wrinkled her nose. 'Would you call his room and say I could see him in Ballyfin later?' She explained that Brad had asked her for an introduction to Hanna. 'I guess he wants to fix a time. The library closes at five thirty, so I'll call Hanna and see if I can bring him in around then.'

'How come he wants to meet her?'

'He's setting up some cultural-tour package and he's interested in the psalter.'

'Okay, so.' Sharon reached for the phone. 'He's quite a looker, isn't he?'

'I guess.'

'Oh, come *on*! He's gorgeous.'

Cassie grinned. 'That's because he got himself a really good haircut.'

At four forty-five, when she stepped out of the lift

into the hotel's reception area, Brad was waiting by the door. Cassie told herself that he did actually look pretty cool. He also had excellent manners: as they went out, he held the door for her and, when he heard that she'd worked through lunch, he looked concerned. 'Hey, I'm sorry. I bet you just want to get home now and chill out.'

'No, I'm good. I grabbed a shower in the staff room so I'm re-energised.'

*

Hanna had already locked the library door and was working at her desk when Cassie texted to say she and Brad were outside. She let them in and shook Brad's hand when Cassie introduced him. He was pleasant and personable and concerned not to trespass on her time. 'Your psalter sounds like the perfect focus for one of our cultural tours. I wondered if we could talk about setting up private viewings, maybe with an accompanying talk?'

Hanna smiled. 'Obviously it's a public-access exhibition but I'm sure something could be arranged. I'd have to consult the donor and the county librarian. Now that you're here, would you like to see the psalter?'

She led them through to the exhibition space and pressed the switch to illuminate the display in the centre of the room. The book, written on vellum and bound in gilded leather, stood on a carved lectern within a protective glass case. It was about the size of a novel you'd buy in an airport. Since the opening of the exhibition Hanna had turned a new page each month, sometimes revealing dense text with minimal decoration, and sometimes pages on which glowing illustrations spilled into the margins. It was a huge draw in tourist season, but local people loved it, too, and Hanna could still scarcely believe that such a treasure had been placed in her care. She gestured at the wall-mounted screens around them. 'So, the entire book has been digitised for the exhibition, with interactive images that allow you to zoom in on detail, and translations of the text accessible in six languages.'

'Quite impressive for a little public library.'

'We had a very generous donor.' Hanna led Brad and Cassie to the case. 'Obviously, the psalter isn't handled more than necessary. You can see for yourself that each page is a detailed work of art.'

They looked at the book, which lay like an open jewel-box, its vibrant colours gleaming in the low light. Though clearly impressed, Brad simply nodded appreciatively, but Cassie bent forward drawing in her breath. 'Wow! I haven't seen these pages!'

On the left-hand side were lines of text, beautifully written in black on the ivory-coloured vellum, and dominated by an initial letter densely surrounded by dots of red ink. The letter was decorated with red-brown plait-work picked out with touches of blue and gold. Hanna looked at the text over Cassie's shoulder. 'That's part of Psalm Eighteen. The second verse, I think. *The Lord is my rock and my fortress*. Look at the pictures on the opposite page.'

The right-hand page had a single line of text enclosed in a painted frame of flowers entwined on a trellis of twigs. All of the rest of the space was taken up by illustration. On each side was a tower on a rock, drawn so the viewer seemed to be looking at them from below. One was rendered entirely in burnished specks of gold and, radiating from its painted stonework, streaks of golden light encircled the building. On the opposite side, the second tower was unrelieved black and surrounded by weeds growing up through the rock. Both towers had narrow windows and crenelated ramparts from which tightly packed armed soldiers peered down. Bending closer, Cassie could see that the dank weeds round the dark tower had crimson and purple flowers and the soldiers on its ramparts had forked tails and goats' horns on their helmets.

Across the top of the page a chain of dancing animals pranced along on their hind legs, accompanied by a band of birds playing pipes and drums. There were hares in hoods and jerkins, with leather boots on their feet. Cats were dressed as fine ladies with long, streaming veils. Six hedgehogs stood on each other's heads, to be tall enough to join in the dance. There was a lumbering bear and something that looked like an elephant, and hounds in hats, with bows and arrows slung across their backs. Tumbling down each margin, on either side of the towers, was a series of little pictures enclosed, like the central text, in a flowering trellis. Birds' beaks and glittering eyes poked out between the twigs. The flowers, outlined with dots of gold leaf, combined the four seasons of the year. Marsh marigolds jostled with mistletoe, and irises with rose hips, and the pictures they framed appeared to be random vignettes. One showed a monk working at a high lectern with a white cat curled around his feet.

Cassie turned to Hanna. 'Isn't there a picture like that in one of the kids' books in the library?'

'You're thinking of *The White Cat and the Monk*. That story's based on a marginal poem in another medieval manuscript. I expect that most monasteries with libraries had cats to keep down the mice.'

The thought of children's books had produced another connection. Staring at the two towers, Cassie asked if Hanna knew a book called *Elidor*.

'Well, yes. It's a children's classic.'

'And doesn't it have a dark tower in it, and a tower of light?' She looked at Brad. 'You said the tower at Mullafrack made you think of *The Lord of the Rings*. But when we met, I'd been thinking of *Elidor*. I had it when I was a kid, but I didn't read it properly.'

Hanna nodded. 'Well, the names of the towers in *Elidor* originate in early Irish storytelling. And Tolkien said *The Lord of the Rings* has some of the same influences.'

'Jack said *The Lord of the Rings* influenced Stephen King's *Dark Tower* series.'

'That's the way storytelling works. Ideas and images influence and modify each other.'

'But where do these towers in the psalter fit in?'

'Well, the monks who made it may have known the early Irish stories about the Tuatha Dé Danann. They were a mythological race who carried treasures to Ireland from four magical fortresses, one of which, called Findias, radiated light. But, obviously, those stories were pagan. For the monks, the tower of light would have signified the Christian Heaven, and the dark tower full of devils would have been Hell. Ultimately, in both traditions, they're symbols of good and evil.'

'Is that how they work in the other books as well? Modern ones, I mean.'

Hanna laughed. 'You'll have to read them and make up your own mind. Symbols can be fluid, and different people see things differently. Anyway, life's too subtly shaded to be summed up as black and white. Even the Christian monks knew that: for all their orthodox symbolism, nuances creep in. There's nothing pious about those dancing animals – or the way the cat appears in another picture down in the corner, holding an open book in one paw and turning a screaming mouse on a spit with the other.'

Brad had walked away from the book to inspect the screens on the walls. 'I hadn't realised the text was in Latin. But you said there's access to translation, right?'

Hanna went over to demonstrate the interactive processes, leaving Cassie still bent over the book. She called across to Hanna, 'Is this the kind of writing that used to be used for the Irish language? Pat said she was taught it in school.'

Hanna shook her head. 'Not exactly. But what they call Gaelic script is descended from the script you're looking at. That's called insular majuscule. It was developed here around the time that the monks created the psalter, and you'll find it in manuscripts all across Europe.'

Brad looked interested. 'You mean it was developed right here in Finfarran?'

'No, of course not. I meant here in Ireland. But this is quite an early example.'

'And there's no proof that it *wasn't* developed in Finfarran?'

Hanna raised her eyebrows at him. 'No. And no proof that it was. I hope the material promoting your tours wouldn't suggest otherwise.'

Brad grinned. 'Cassie said you were a stickler for accuracy.'

Finding a balance between promoting the psalter as a tourist attraction and preserving its integrity hadn't been easy, and Hanna had had more than one tussle with the tourism board's marketing teams, which, at one stage, had proposed the slogan *Feast your eyes on Finfarran's Feisty Friars*. She'd once mentioned it to Cassie over coffee, and it seemed that the depth of her outrage had been passed on to Brad. Now she could see Cassie looking anxious, so she gave Brad a reassuring smile. 'Cassie's perfectly right. But facilitating tours like yours is part of my job description, so I do hope we can get something off the ground.'

Brad held out his hand. 'So do I. And perhaps, when we do, you'll be prepared to give the accompanying talk? You're clearly more than competent. And, obviously, we'd offer a suitable fee.'

It was charmingly said yet, without knowing why, Hanna stiffened. Then, not wanting Cassie to feel that things had taken a difficult turn, she relaxed. 'As I said, the decision on whether or not to give private access wouldn't be mine alone. You do know that groups can book in for our regular exhibition tours, which are hosted by volunteers?'

'Of course.' Brad shook her hand warmly and tucked his arm into Cassie's. 'And I've no doubt they're top of the range. But I'm all about exclusivity and, I have to tell you, Miss Casey, I never settle for less.'

CHAPTER THIRTY-FOUR

CASSIE WAITED ON THE LIBRARY STEPS while Brad said goodbye to Hanna. As she glanced across the courtyard, a woman emerged from the side gate that led to the nuns' garden and bustled purposefully towards the steps. It was Mary Casey. Assuming she'd come to meet Hanna, Cassie stood aside to let her in. Brad had joined her on the steps and, as they stood there side by side, Mary looked up at them with interest. 'Well, if it isn't the two of you here again! Another chance encounter?'

The archness in her voice irritated Cassie but Brad seemed amused. 'Good to see you again, Mrs Casey. How are things?'

'I didn't know you were still hanging around.'

Hanna, who'd overheard, moved to join them. 'Cassie brought Mr Miller here to meet me, Mam. About work. If you'll come inside and sit down I'll be ready to drive you home soon.'

'I've just been over the road with Pat.' Mary looked

meaningfully at Cassie. 'She said *you*'d be finished work by lunchtime.'

'I'm going home now.'

'Well, go quietly, she was on her way to bed when I came out.'

Having managed to suggest that Cassie's neglect had driven Pat to her bed, Mary surged up the steps and into the library. Hanna touched Cassie on the shoulder. 'Don't worry about Pat. I saw her earlier on and she looked fine.'

Reminding herself that Mary was Hanna's mother, Cassie said nothing. The effort it took must have shown on her face because Hanna laughed. 'You're fond of my mother, remember? She's "feisty".'

Cassie caught her eye and grinned. 'And sometimes she's really annoying.'

'Tell me about it!' Giving her a cheerful wink, Hanna went back indoors.

Brad, who'd been watching the exchange, took Cassie's elbow. 'So, how about I take you out to dinner to say thanks?'

'For what?'

'For the introduction.'

'Well, I ought to look in on Pat.'

'Oh, come on, Pat's probably exhausted after an

afternoon with Mary. There's a good chance she retreated just to get rid of her.'

'I guess.'

'Why not scoot over now and check things out? If you need to stay, that's no problem. If not, I'll buy you a meal in Ballyfin. Unless you already had plans for this evening?'

After her rushed day the prospect of a relaxing dinner was tempting. So, having checked on Pat, who said she'd like an evening in bed with a book and a cosy hot-water bottle, Cassie decided to take up Brad's offer. Even though he'd seemed less charmed by the psalter than she'd been, she still felt they were two of a kind. When they'd scrambled down from the tower in Mullafrack, he'd stopped on the hillside and stared out at the ocean. 'Don't you think it's incredible? That you've actually been beyond that horizon? Seen night skies with different constellations? That you've stared down at churning waves and known that your ship was crossing the equator, and that you were on it? Carried away to the next adventure with nothing to hold you back?'

It had been such a perfect description of her own feelings that Cassie, who had stopped beside him, had laughed out loud. The next thing she'd known, he'd grabbed her hand and they'd plunged down the hillside together, yelling, earth and shale sliding and crunching beneath their skidding heels. Birds had flown up from the spiky yellow furze bushes and, for a steep hundred yards or so, she had felt as if she, too, was flying. All around them, the high hills seemed to throw back the exuberant sound of their voices. Then they'd ended up, gasping for breath and weak with laughter, hanging over a five-barred gate, which had stopped their headlong descent.

Now, as she drove back to Ballyfin with Brad's car behind her, Cassie, who had planned a chat with Erin this evening, assured herself that her call wouldn't be missed. The breakup with Jeff was history, and lately Erin had found a new boyfriend, called Diego. Most likely they'd be out learning dynamic new skills together or sipping exotic cocktails from a single glass. Fond though Cassie was of her, the smoochy shots Erin kept posting on Instagram were getting boring. Or irritating. Or something. Anyway, even if Erin did happen to be home to take her call, she didn't fancy hearing any more Diego stories for a while.

When they reached the hotel in Ballyfin she assumed they'd park and find a place to have dinner somewhere in town. Instead, Brad suggested they order room service. 'I've got a room with a balcony and a great ocean view.'

'Really?'

'We can eat outside and watch the sunset.'

Feeling slightly wary, Cassie followed him into the lift. Hotel rooms offered as freebies to people in the industry tended to be round the back overlooking the kitchen entrance, while those with ocean views were all at the front and at the top. As the lift doors closed, Brad pressed the button for the sixth floor and, when they reached it, led her down a corridor into a room that did indeed have a wide, railed balcony, reached by sliding doors. Tossing his car keys onto the bed, Brad said he'd order a bottle of wine. 'We can decide what to eat later. Go check out the view.'

Cassie went onto the balcony, which faced the setting sun. The sky was a riot of deep blue clouds edged with streaks of burnished gold, which reminded her of the psalter. But most of her attention was on the room behind her. It was a double room with a king-size bed and space for a sofa and a coffee-table in front of the widescreen TV. As she'd gone to the balcony she'd noticed that the en-suite bathroom was huge, with a bath as well as a walk-in shower. Far below in the marina, she could see the newly docked cruise ship. It seemed very odd, with all those passengers booked for a night in the hotel, that the management would have allowed Brad to stay in this fabulous room.

He came out and joined her at the balcony rail. 'Finfarran really is stunning, don't you think? I mean, everywhere you go. Lissbeg is cute, Ballyfin's like some kind of a movie set, and the mountains and the beaches are fantastic. I can see myself spending a lot more time over here.'

'You mean vacations?'

There was a knock at the door and a waiter arrived with the wine in an ice bucket. Cassie, who recognised him from brief encounters at the staff entrance, was about to exchange a few words of conversation, but Brad just gave him a casual nod and placed a tip on the tray. The waiter gave a slight bow in acknowledgement, and left at once. Taking the glass of wine that Brad handed her, Cassie decided she needed to get things straight. She swallowed a mouthful and faced him squarely. 'Okay. I'm sorry, but this is really strange.'

'What is?'

'You work for a cruise line, right? And you set up tours?'

'That's me.'

'And the management here just hands you the key to a fancy room like this?'

Putting his glass on the table, Brad leaned forward and kissed her on the nose.

Cassie glared. 'What the hell was that about?'

'You look awfully sweet when you're confused.'

Cassie held his eyes for a moment, then threw up her hand. 'Oh, look, I'm out of here. This is way too weird.'

'Cassie, come on, wait a minute. There's a simple explanation.'

She pushed past him into the bedroom, set down her glass and grabbed her bag. 'Is there? Really? Well, you know what? I don't want to hear it. Thanks for the dinner invitation. I'm going home.'

She thought he might try to stop her but instead he took up his glass again and leaned against the open balcony door. Everything about him was so relaxed that Cassie found herself spoiling for a fight. This was exactly like the night they'd been out on Paul's boat. She could have sworn that day that Brad had wanted to ask her for a date. She'd even wasted her time trying to work out how she'd feel. But he hadn't asked her. Instead he'd crashed her boat trip with Paul and Margot, and left her wondering what was going on.

Then, as they'd all sat watching the stunning sunset, he'd put his arm around her. And later, when they'd said goodbye, he'd kissed her. Afterwards she'd told herself the wind had been cold on the water and the kiss could just have been to say goodnight. But the truth was that she hadn't known what to think. That was the thing. You couldn't tell where you were with Bradley Miller. When they'd met at the St Patrick's Day parade he'd been so laid back he was practically horizontal. At the tower in Mullafrack he'd been strange, and she'd wondered if he was laughing at her. And then there'd been that headlong dash down the ringing, echoing hillside when their yells had seemed to fill the valley and birds had flown up in alarm.

Now he raised his eyebrows and said the last thing she'd expected. 'Who's Jack?'

'Jack?'

'Yeah. You mentioned him to Hanna, back at the library.'

'He's someone I happen to know. What's it to you?'

'Nothing. I just wondered.' He pushed himself away from the door and pulled a rueful face. 'Look, you're right. I haven't been straight with you. But I haven't lied. My name is Bradley Miller, Bradley Miller Junior. I work for Your World Awaits, which is a small but very exclusive US cruise line. My job involves conceptualising the packages we offer ...'

He stopped, and Cassie glared at him. 'Well, go on.'

'But it also involves sitting on the board of directors. Because, as it happens, the cruise line belongs to my dad.'

'Your *dad*?'

'Bradley Miller Senior. So there you have it.'

Swallowing the remains of his wine, he went out onto the balcony to pour himself another. Fizzing with indignation, Cassie followed him. 'But why didn't you *say*? For God's sake, what did you think you were doing? Playing at being a prince disguised as a swineherd?'

'No. I just ...'

'Just what?'

'Oh, God. It's hard to explain. Well, no, actually, it isn't. When girls know you're rich, they can act funny. So mostly I don't mention it.'

About to expostulate again, Cassie stopped and thought, actually, that was fair enough. Surely it would have been twice as weird if he'd introduced himself as a millionaire? Which she supposed he must be. He offered her the bottle and, still trying to make sense of things, she picked up her glass and held it out to him. Then her indignation swelled again. 'And you thought I might "act funny" if I knew how much you were worth?'

'Well, I couldn't tell, could I? In the beginning. And then, when I found it mattered, I wasn't sure what to do.'

He didn't move towards her and his dark eyes were unfathomable. Cassie lost her temper. 'Oh, stop being enigmatic! What the hell do you mean?'

Suddenly, his assurance seemed to slip from him like a mask. Underneath it, to her surprise, she could see naked vulnerability.

'I mean that I really like you. A lot. And I didn't know how you were going to react when you found out who I was.'

'Yes, but I haven't, have I?'

'Haven't what?'

'Found out who you are. I mean, I know you're the prince, not the swineherd, but that doesn't tell me much.'

Behind him, out above the ocean, the golden edges of the darkening clouds were beginning to turn scarlet. Dimly aware that the setting was now ridiculously romantic, Cassie focused again on Brad's face. As Sharon had said, he really was quite a looker. But now the regular features, golden tan and movie-star teeth seemed unimportant. What mattered was the helpless look in his eyes. He truly didn't know how she was going to react and, just then, neither did she. Then she realised how badly she wanted to kiss him. Carefully, she placed her glass on the table. 'I'll tell you what.'

'What?'

'We needn't turn this into some big drama. We could just take it slowly, step by step.'

He didn't move and it was she who took the first step towards him. Then the helpless look faded and he smiled. Their hands clasped, just as they'd done on the hillside, and Cassie felt that, together, they could launch themselves into the air and fly. Reaching up, she drew his head down to hers. It was a long kiss and when she let him go they were both laughing, balanced on the edge of something yet to be defined. Brad took her by the elbows. 'Step by step?'

'That's what I said.'

'So what happens now?'

Linking her arms around his neck, she backed away, drawing him with her into the room behind them. 'This is just a suggestion, okay? Work with me.'

'I'm listening.'

'I say we take the rest of the wine to your glamorous, king-size bed.'

CHAPTER THIRTY-FIVE

PAT DECIDED NOT TO BOTHER MAKING herself any dinner. Mary had arrived for lunch with a quiche, which they'd eaten with salad, and around four o'clock they'd had tea and buns. So, when Mary left to catch her lift home from Hanna, and Cassie looked in to say she'd be out for the evening, Pat took a bowl of soup to her room on a tray. She assumed Cassie would be eating with Brad as, apparently, they'd just been into the library to look at the psalter.

She carried the soup upstairs carefully and enjoyed it sitting up against her pillows with the tray balanced on her knees. Then she put it aside and turned her attention to Thomas Hardy. The book opened at a poem she'd never liked much. It was supposed to be about 'keen lessons' Hardy had learned about love, but he must have wanted to keep it unemotional, because he'd called it 'Neutral Tones'. That reminded Pat of Ger, always playing the strong, silent man but actually churned up inside. Adjusting her glasses, she read a verse aloud.

'Your eyes on me were as eyes that rove
Over tedious riddles of years ago;
And some words played between us to and fro
On which lost the more by our love.'

Well, there was nothing neutral about that. He was saying that neither party had gained anything by loving each other. It was only a matter of who had lost the most. Strongly reminded of why she hadn't liked the poem in the first place, Pat wondered if she might go back to *The Case of the Late Pig*. But she wasn't inclined to. Despite what Seán had told her about detective stories, she couldn't see that this one explored love or hate very deeply, never mind guilt, fear, greed and lost opportunities. Anyway, it was obvious that the murderer was going to turn out to be mad, which felt like a cop-out. Most people who did terrible things to each other weren't mad. The book in its lilac jacket lay on her bedside table, its two menacing birds flapping on the cover. There was a line in Hardy's poem about a smile sweeping across someone's face 'like an ominous bird a-wing'. You had to hand it to poets, they had a great way with words. Still, thought Pat, she could do without riddles and lost love this evening and, although it was early, the soup had made her sleepy.

Sliding further down under the duvet, she gave up on books and thought again about Ger.

When she was young there'd been no question of boys and girls going to school together. The Christian Brothers' place up by the Sheep Market and the convent down in Broad Street had even been built at different ends of the town. The Brothers had had no garden and their brickwork was less ornate but, essentially, the ethos in the two schools had been the same. But while the nuns' bullying of the girls was largely subtle, the Brothers' emotional abuse of the boys was often compounded by fierce physical violence. At the time, it wasn't much talked about, and when it was, people often argued that farmers were frequently just as rough with their sons. Which was true enough, but didn't change the damage it had wrought.

Pat had no idea how badly Ger had been beaten at school, but she knew how much he'd feared violence, and how little he'd ever expected justice. The system that placed so high a value on Tom's strength on the playing field had convinced Ger that weakness of any kind would be viewed as guilt. And in his view everyone in authority hung together, from the Brothers to the guards to the politicians and all the ranks of petty officials that strutted in between. So his instinct was to get through life by staying out of trouble, and never to show his emotions lest they'd somehow give him away. Admittedly, Frankie's birth had released a passionate protectiveness, but that had been covert and inarticulate, like her own protectiveness of Ger, and Ger's deep dependence on Tom.

Unchanging and pathetic, Ger had clung to Tom, like a dog who isn't wanted on a walk but won't give up and go home. Pat had always known the reason why. Like Mary, Tom exuded confidence. That was why everyone said that Tom and Mary were made for each other. In fact, as Pat knew more than most, Mary's air of certainty concealed a vulnerability almost as deep as Ger's. But back when they were teenagers, Mary had been the sexiest girl in town. Once the gloss of her youth had worn off, not every man would have coped well with her bossiness. Ger, for example, wouldn't have coped at all. But Tom had loved Mary for who she was as much as for who she pretended to be, just as Pat had always been able to read Ger's feelings like a book.

Wriggling her toes against the cooling hot-water bottle, her sleepy mind sought to define the past. Eventually, as she slipped off to sleep, she encompassed one part of it in a sentence. Tom's protectiveness of

Ger had come from an inherent gentleness, while her own had come from a painful sense of how badly Ger had been hurt.

Hours later, she woke to the sound of a car door slamming and, going to her window, saw Cassie emerge from the shed in the yard below. Pat watched as the foreshortened figure crossed the moonlit cobbles. A little later she heard the sound of feet passing on the landing, and the creak of the attic stairs as Cassie made her way up to her room. It was late for her to be coming in, and tomorrow, Pat knew, she'd have to be up to drive the mobile library. But that was the thing about youth. You were never tired.

Sure enough, when she got up the following morning Cassie had gone to work. As Pat was finishing a leisurely breakfast there was a knock on the door. When she opened it, Fran was standing on the threshold in a jacket that had featured in the previous weekend's *Gloss* magazine. Her large, cow-like eyes were rimmed with eyeliner and her dark hair was carefully arranged in a pile on the top of her head. She ought to have looked a picture of sophisticated assurance, but instead she seemed uncomfortable, as if she feared she'd come to the wrong place.

Pat stood back and smiled at her. 'Well, this is

unexpected! You're very welcome. Come and sit down.'

Fran stood where she was, looking at a loss. Then she came into the kitchen. She was wearing orange leather gloves and carried a tiny handbag with a miniature gilt padlock on the zip. Pat helped her out of her coat and offered her an easy chair by the range. 'It's mild enough this morning, but it's still nice to sit in the warm.'

Fran sank into the chair and looked around the kitchen. 'It's a lovely room.'

'It's grand and cosy anyway.' Pat sat down opposite her, wondering why Fran was here. Having settled herself against the cushions, Fran said nothing more, so Pat filled the silence. 'Would you like a cup of tea?'

'No, I won't thanks. I had one before I came out.' There was a long pause and then Fran shook herself suddenly, like a cow someone had poked with a sharp stick. She blinked at Pat and said she hoped she was well.

'I'm grand, thanks, love. It's kind of you to enquire.'

'Because Frankie thought, well, we thought, I wondered how you were doing. If you were feeling okay.'

Pat hadn't seen or heard from Frankie since last

Wednesday, when she'd shown him the door after he'd turned on Cassie. Evidently he'd realised how badly he'd behaved and now, afraid to face her himself, he'd sent his wife around to clear the air. That was the height of him. He wouldn't come in till the ground was tested, for fear of what he'd probably call unpleasantness. Frankie had always avoided anything hard.

She was about to begin to smooth things over, when she saw a look of resolution flit across Fran's face. The wide brown eyes seemed almost to glaze over, and when Fran spoke, it was clear that what she said had been rehearsed. 'It's a real worry for me and Frankie. Knowing you're here on your own. Things might happen. You could fall. At your age people start forgetting things. You might be in here wanting help and nobody would know.' Pat looked at her thoughtfully and said nothing. Frowning in concentration, Fran went on: 'Cassie's very sweet, of course, but she'll be gone soon, won't she? So, the thing is that Frank's really worried. About not having access. In case something was wrong.'

It was as if the door had swung open and a chill wind had swept through the room. Although they were sitting by the range, Pat's hands felt cold. Obviously relieved to have finished her speech without forgetting her lines, Fran relaxed. Then she bent forward and opened her mouth again. This time Pat forestalled her. 'He's sent you here for the key to the Chubb lock.'

The words seemed to drop from her lips like icicles but, oblivious to the tone of her voice, Fran nodded. 'That's it. That's what he wants. Because he's worried.'

Grasping the arms of her chair, Pat stood up. 'Could you do something for me, dear? Would you take a message to him?'

Fran stood up, too, looking confused. 'Well, but what I have to do is bring him the key.'

'I know. Will you tell him I'm not going to give him one? Say you asked me, just as he told you to, and that I said no.'

'I think he'll be cross.'

'I suppose he will. But don't let him bully you. Tell him that I won't like it if he does.'

Meekly, Fran put her orange gloves on. As she did so, her eye was caught by the vase that stood on Pat's mantelpiece, which now held a bunch of golden forsythia. Her vacant face lit up. 'That's a lovely vase.'

'Do you like it? It belonged to Frankie's grandmother.'

'My granny had one in the hall that was just the same.' She hovered for a moment, evidently feeling that she mustn't leave without what she'd been sent for.

Pat let her out and watched her make her way down to the shop. Briefly she stood in the door to her flat, looking down the steep, twisted staircase. Then she closed the door and turned the key in the new Chubb lock.

For a long time she sat by the range, thinking things through carefully. She'd been too much of a coward to face the truth. Frankie wasn't just lazy. Or awkward. Or thoughtless. Or any of the other words she'd used to excuse his bad behaviour since he was small. Ger's will had been plainly worded: everything he had he'd left to her, as his wife. And Frankie was trying to push her aside and take control. He hadn't come round that first day to help her sort out Ger's bits and pieces. He'd had no interest in anything but the files and papers in the desk. He didn't care how his mother felt, alone in the flat and worried about security. He'd just been afraid she might have been getting advice from Fury O'Shea. And he wasn't glad that Cassie had chosen to stay and keep her company. He'd assumed that generous, loving Cassie was sneaky and acquisitive, like himself. Dropping her head into her hands, Pat began to shiver.

Then, taking her hands away from her face, she looked at the door and realised why she'd wanted her new Chubb lock. It wasn't about making her feel safer. It was about keeping Frankie from walking in when she wasn't at home. Yet why should he want the key to the door, now that he'd taken Ger's papers? Why bother to come round again if they were all he cared about? The shivering stopped, though she still felt cold all over. She knew what Frankie wanted now, and it wasn't just access to the flat. It was the ring on which Ger had kept his keys.

With tears in her eyes, she lifted the box from the shelf above the range. A reassuring clunk told her the keys were still inside. She opened it and took out the keyring. It was a plain split ring and the keys were of different sizes. With a sob, Pat recognised a couple of small ones belonging to the suitcase she'd bought for their painful holiday in Toronto. There was another small key, which she didn't recognise, several large ones and the Yale key to the flat. Presumably the larger ones were for the shop doors, and the sheds below in the yard and at the old farmhouse. Her sobs got louder and, sitting down, she fumbled for a tissue, telling herself she mustn't get hysterical. It was too late for that class of thing now.

At the bottom of the box were the pencil stub and the few discarded business cards. Blowing her nose briskly, Pat took them out and leaned forward to throw them into the range. Then she noticed that, while the others were old and grubby, one of the cards appeared to be brand new. The address was a solicitor's and the name was one she'd never heard Ger mention. Finding her glasses, she put them on to examine the card more closely. The solicitor Ger had dealt with had an office round in Sheep Street. But this firm's address was in Carrick, not Lissbeg. Frowning, Pat turned the card over and found herself looking at a single word on the back of it, written in pencil. It was her own name and the handwriting was Ger's.

CHAPTER THIRTY-SIX

PAT SAT IN THE CAB OF FURY O'SHEA'S battered van, with Fury driving and The Divil squashed between them on the seat. She had no idea how she'd got there because the last twenty-four hours were a blur. Apparently she'd phoned Fury yesterday after finding the card. Well, she must have done, because ten minutes ago she'd been waiting for him in the alley behind the yard. With Ger's keys and the business card in her handbag, she'd gone downstairs, through the shop and out the back door. Des had been dealing with the usual Saturday-morning queue at the counter, so the only eyes observing her had been those of the milkmaid and the shepherd on the painted tiles on the wall. Now, reminded that it was the weekend, she turned to Fury in distress. 'God, do you think the solicitor's place will be closed?'

Fury raised his voice over the rattle of tools in the back of the van. 'No problem. I gave yer man a call before I came to pick you up. He'll be out on the golf course but he's sending his daughter. She's a junior partner in the firm.'

Pat was troubled. She hadn't wanted to drag some woman into the office on a weekend. The Divil turned and laid his muzzle on her knee. Fury swung the wheel, deftly passing a dawdling tourist coach, and the van sped on along the motorway towards Carrick. When they reached the outskirts of town he cut through a maze of backstreets, emerging at the entrance to the Royal Victoria's car park.

As they drove into the car park Pat looked alarmed. 'Is it all right to leave the van here? Might they clamp it or something?'

'They'll have more sense.' Fury came round to her side of the cab, opened the door and helped her climb down. 'I'm halfway through a tricky repair to the roof above the kitchen. If anyone starts annoying me, they'll be serving rainwater soup.' The Divil leaped out of the van and Fury looked at him severely. 'And you'd better mind your manners too, d'you hear me? They have fierce posh businesses up at this end of town.'

The solicitor's office was in an imposing building, set in the same terrace as the hotel. As they climbed the granite steps and Fury raised the lion's head knocker, the whole thing felt like a dream to Pat. Why on earth would Ger have come here to this solicitor, having always used the man in Lissbeg whom he'd known since he was at school? Almost as soon as Fury knocked, the door was opened by a young woman wearing an expensive tracksuit. She led them through the lofty hall and into a large room, which must once have been a Victorian lady's parlour. Much of the furniture was polished mahogany but there was a modern desk set across the fireplace, which clearly hadn't seen a fire for years. There were two armchairs in front of the desk and a swivel one behind it. Having seated Pat and Fury, the woman looked dubiously at The Divil. Ignoring her, he curled himself in a patch of sunlight on the carpet where, placing his paws over his nose, he sighed deeply and appeared to fall asleep.

The woman sat down behind the desk and smiled tightly at Pat. 'I ought to apologise for my appearance.'

'No, really. It was good of you to come in.'

With a Sphinx-like glance at Fury, the woman said she'd been delighted. 'I understand that you've come to collect what your late husband left here in my father's care.'

'Do you? Did he?' Pat clasped her hands anxiously.

'The fact is that I'm not really sure what I'm here for. What did Ger give to your father? And why?'

'I can't speak to his motive, Mrs Fitzgerald – he didn't share it and, of course, we didn't ask. But I can tell you he left us this, with instructions to hand it over when you came to collect it.'

She reached into the drawer of her desk and produced a small metal box with a lock and a countersunk handle, the kind of thing that a club might buy if it wanted a cashbox in which to keep its raffle money. Pat could remember seeing them in the Euroshop in Lissbeg before Christmas. She looked at the woman blankly. 'But what is it?'

'It's your property, Mrs Fitzgerald. Will you take it and sign a receipt for it? I don't wish to be rude, but I do have an appointment at the gym.'

'Oh, of course you do. I'm sorry.' Flustered, Pat looked around for a pen. 'I'll sign for it now, if you're really sure it was left for me. But, honestly, I don't know what Ger was at.'

A pen was placed in her hand and she signed her name on a form. The Divil gave a loud sneeze and lifted his paws from his nose. Fury stood up and put his hand under Pat's elbow. 'Right, so, we won't keep poor Jacinta any longer.'

Pat stood up, rather glad of the strength of his bony hand. It struck her that they must make an odd group standing there in the woman's impressive office, she clutching her Euroshop box, Fury in his torn waxed jacket, and The Divil standing in the sunlight with his wiry hair sticking up.

Fury winked at Jacinta. 'Tell your dad I'll be round sometime next week to have a look at his boiler. I've told him before that he wants to chuck it out before it blows up. But he didn't build a high-class business by letting the moths out of his Gucci wallet.' He clicked his fingers at The Divil, then turned back to Jacinta. 'I take it, by the way, that Mrs Fitz won't be getting a bill for this?'

Jacinta gave him a level glance and said that Mr Fitzgerald had settled everything in advance.

'Right so. Well, I hope there won't be any clerical errors. I've known lawyers who've sent the same invoice twice.'

On that lofty note, he swept Pat into the hallway. The Divil pattered after them, his claws sounding loud on the parquet after the carpet. Too confused even to thank Jacinta, who shut the door smartly, Pat stood on the steps feeling bewildered. Then Fury's hand was under her elbow again and, the next thing she knew, she was back in the van with The Divil breathing hotly on her hand and the box open on her knee.

Still holding Ger's keys, she looked across at Fury. 'It's a letter.'

'So I see.'

'Addressed to me.'

'Is that his writing?'

'Yes.'

It was the schoolboy script they'd beaten into Ger back at the Brothers'.

'Do you want to open it now or will I take you home?'

'I don't want to open it.'

Fury gave her a shrewd look and started the engine. 'Right so, buckle up and I'll take you back to Lissbeg.'

CHAPTER THIRTY-SEVEN

THE QUEUE IN THE SHOP HAD CLEARED when Pat came in, but Des was sweeping up behind the counter so he didn't see her face. She climbed the stairs slowly, stopping at the dogleg turning to lean against the wall. She hadn't slept the previous night and that, she supposed, must be why she was feeling so tired. When she reached the flat and went inside she turned the key in the Chubb lock and hung her coat on a chair. Cassie was out for the day but the fire had been stoked and damped down.

Pat stirred up the flames and left the door of the range open so she could see them. She badly wanted a cup of tea but didn't have the strength to fill the kettle. Sitting by the fire, she opened her bag and took out the letter, handling it carefully, as if it, too, might burst into flame.

Back in the 1960s, Saturday night was céilí night in the Shamrock Club. You couldn't be turning up wearing the same thing week after week so, even though she'd bought it to wear on her honeymoon, she'd undone the tissue paper that wrapped it and taken out the blue dress with the daisies round the hem. When she'd walked into the club she'd felt like a million dollars wearing the dress and Josie's pearl necklace. The place was crowded, like it always was at the weekends, even though it was only 5 p.m. The bar was jam-packed with fellows drinking pints and girls having sherries, and there was a queue for the pay phone where people were making their weekly call home. The phone calls were the reason everything started so early at weekends because, with the time difference, you couldn't be ringing too late.

Up on the platform in the dancehall, the Rambling Paddies were belting out jigs and reels. Back in Lissbeg, in Devane's place in Sheep Street, you'd dance to pop tunes and Brendan Bowyer covers, with maybe a half-hearted Walls of Limerick if the parish priest came by. In Resolve it was all sets and waltzes but, as Josie said, it was great craic and kept you from putting on weight. Pat had fixed to phone home at five thirty, so she stood in the queue and watched the dancers through the half-open door. You wouldn't get more than a few words before the next person was poking you, but that didn't matter because calls cost so much that you couldn't afford to talk long. When hers went through, Pat could tell that something had happened. Not a death or anything awful like that, but her mother's voice was clipped. 'Look here to me, pet, there's something I have to tell you. And God alone knows why I agreed to break the news.'

'What is it?'

'It's Mary. She came in the other day and said she's changing the date of the wedding.'

'But how? What do you mean?'

'I mean she's taken a notion that she wants a summer do. So you and Ger will be on your own in September.'

'But wait. What does Ger say? And why didn't she let me know herself?'

'Ah, for God's sake, Pat, this is Mary we're talking about. When did she ever do anything she could get somebody else to do for her?'

Pat could tell that her mam was raging at having been used as a cat's paw. But there was hardly time for anything except the bald information, and when she handed the receiver to the next person waiting, she hadn't really taken in what she'd heard. Then, as she walked away from the phone, she realised she was feeling kind of faint. There was a bench in the passage outside the dancehall and she sat on it with a bump just as her knees gave way. Only a minute or so later, Seán came out of the hall. He smiled when he saw her. Then, hunkering down beside her, he asked if she was okay.

'Yeah. I'm fine. I just felt a bit dizzy.'

'You're white as a sheet. Have you eaten?'

'I have. I'm grand.'

He sat down beside her and looked at her as if she were a specimen in a case. 'You could probably do with a bit of fresh air. Will I take you outside?'

Pat felt it might be better if she were to ask him to find Josie, but her voice didn't seem to be working, so she nodded and let him pilot her through the bar and onto the steps. As soon as they got there, she realised it was the worst place she could be. People who knew them kept walking past, saying hi or just looking curious, and now, to her horror, she'd found she'd started to cry. Seán seemed horrified too. He sort of edged round to hide her but that made people stare. To Pat's relief, he took her by the arm and led her down the steps and round the corner, to where he'd parked his car. As soon as they got in she lost control and bawled for what felt like hours and, by the time she reached the stage of hiccuping, her face was swollen and the eyeliner Josie had lent her was smudged and streaked.

Seán, who'd sat staring rigidly through the windscreen, gave her a look. 'I guess you don't want to go back inside.'

'No.'

'Should I take you home?'

Pat shook her head helplessly. Half the girls in the house had had plans to come to the céilí later, and they'd still be running about swapping clothes and makeup. She'd never get up to her own room without somebody seeing her.

Seán frowned. 'Will we go back to my place, then? You could wash your face and stay for a while, if you like. I could give you a drink and drop you home later.'

Unable to think of what else to do, Pat nodded, praying that no one from the club would see them go.

Seán rented a couple of rooms a few blocks away. They were built on top of a lock-up where he kept his mowers and tools, as well as his car. You climbed an outside iron staircase, which led directly to a bedroom, which was also the living space, and there was a bathroom and a kitchen at the front. Pat went into the bathroom and did her best to clean her face with soap and water. The narrow kitchen she'd passed through to get to the bathroom looked as if it was never used. When she came out, Seán was sitting on the divan bed and there was a bottle of whiskey and a couple of glasses on the coffee-table. The only other table, which stood at the window, was obviously used as a desk. The walls were lined with shelves on which folders and files stood side by side with crime stories and gardening books.

She sat on a small green-upholstered chair, which, as it was far posher than anything else in the room, looked as if it might have come from his parents' place. Seán poured the whiskey and held out a glass. Seeing her reaction, he gave her his lazy smile. 'Go on. It's medicinal.' She took it and knocked it back in one slug, feeling the warmth spread from her stomach into the rest of her body. Having swallowed the shot he'd poured for himself, Seán sat with his hands dangling between his knees. 'Do you want to talk about it?'

'I just … well, I don't know … I had a bit of a shock.'

'I can see that.'

'It's about my wedding.' She tipped the glass back again, as if there was more to be had from it.

Seán didn't offer a top-up. Instead, he looked at her gravely. 'You said you and Ger and your friends were having a double wedding this fall.'

'We were. But Mary's decided that she and Tom are getting married this month.' Pat bit her lip till it hurt.

She couldn't think why this news appeared to have turned her into a jelly. After all, it was just Mary being Mary. In the beginning she'd probably thought that the foursome thing would get them a double-page spread in the *Inquirer*. But, on second thoughts, she must have decided that without Pat and Ger around, all the focus would be on her and Tom. 'Mary was always a bit self-centred. I told you about the four of us that day we went to the lake. I suppose one reason I'm a bit upset is that I won't be there for their wedding.' She swallowed hard and gripped the squat glass with both hands. 'I mean I'm just trying to take in the fact that they'll be married next month.'

Seán poured another finger of whiskey into her glass. 'You know what I think? I reckon you ought to stay here in Resolve.'

'Well, yes, I'll have to. My ticket's booked for September.'

'No. I mean I don't think you ought to go back at all.'

Pat goggled at him. 'To Finfarran? Why not? Why shouldn't I?'

'Hey, I'm no marriage counsellor, but I am a good listener. You talked an awful lot up there at the lake.'

'What did I say? I mean, what are you saying?'

'Hey, I know it's none of my business, I'm just calling it like I see it.' His eyes were still grave and his voice was very gentle. 'I just don't think it's fair to marry someone you don't love.'

There was a spurt of flame in the range and a cinder leaped out. Pat laid the letter aside and picked up the tongs. She had a mat on the floor in front of the range so there was no harm done to the linoleum. All the same, she closed the door so nothing more could roll out. Ger used always to tell her not to be careless. He'd say there was plenty of heat to be had without opening up the door. And that was true, but Pat had always loved the dancing flames. Now, sitting down again, she straightened her shoulders and picked up the envelope. She'd never let Ger down while he'd lived so, if he'd trusted her to find his letter after he was gone, she'd better open it up and see what it said.

CHAPTER THIRTY-EIGHT

MARY CASEY CLIMBED THE STAIRS TO PAT'S flat, pausing at the dogleg to catch her breath and arriving on the landing in her usual state of outrage. She tried the handle, found the door locked and knocked on it imperiously. Getting no response, she clicked her tongue and, taking her phone from her bag, banged out a text: ARE U IN THE LOO OR WHERKE ASRE YOU IM AT THEDOOR Having rapped on the door again and got no answer, she sent another text. WOULDE YOU OPEN UP

Finally, she shouted through the keyhole. 'I'm going nowhere, girl, so you might as well let me in!'

The door opened and, as Mary surged in, Pat closed it behind her and went to sit by the range. Standing with arms akimbo, Mary glared her. 'Holy God Almighty, look at the state of you!' She strode across to the kettle and switched it on. 'Tell me what's happened.'

'What are you doing here?'

'I'm here because Fury O'Shea turned up and

pushed me into his van. And I'm half choked by the stink of sawdust and linseed oil and dog, so don't be annoying me. I've better things to be doing on a Saturday afternoon, I can tell you. But Fury said I was wanted and here I am.'

Mary set about making tea, refraining from comment on Pat's placement of teaspoons and slamming cupboard doors until she discovered a packet of ginger nuts. She drew in a chair opposite Pat's and placed a stool between them with the tea tray on it. For a minute it seemed as if Pat was going to eject her, but then, as Mary thrust the tea at her, with a biscuit in the saucer, she took the cup and her eyes filled with tears. 'Ger left me a letter.'

'Did he so?'

'It was in a box in a Carrick solicitor's office.'

'And what did it say?'

Pat shook her head, unable to speak. Mary leaned forward, dunked the biscuit in the tea and held it out to her. 'Eat that, drink up, and for Christ's sake tell me. Was he hiding a wife and thirteen kids back in Cork?'

Pat put her cup down and pressed her hand to her lips. 'Ah, don't, Mary, honestly, it's dreadful.'

'Well, where's the letter? Give it here and I'll read it for myself.'

'I burned it. But I'll tell you. It's Frankie.'

'Ah, Jesus Christ, it would be. Go on.'

'He was blackmailing Ger.'

For once in her life, Mary appeared speechless. Before she could recover, Pat continued: 'That's what it amounts to. And, Mary, it was going on for years. Since one of the times Moss Canny came home to Finfarran on holiday.'

'Hold your horses, now, what's this got to do with Moss?'

'Isn't that what I'm telling you? The time Moss got sent away in disgrace he'd been mixed up in some property deal. I don't know the ins and outs but it was some way against the law.'

'I wouldn't doubt him.'

'Will you listen? Ger was mixed up in it too. They said that they'd cut him in if he'd let them put money through his bank account. I don't know how it worked, but he ended up making a rake-off.'

'How much?'

'The letter said two thousand.'

'When did this happen?'

'A bit after we were married. Round when Frankie was born. Moss would have been a few years older than we were, and the rest of the lads involved were the same, or older still. You remember the crowd Moss hung round with?'

'I do. Bowsies, the lot of them. Ger wouldn't have had the nerve to tell them where to stick their deal.'

'That was it. He didn't. And then the guards started asking questions and the Cannys got Moss away. It was the same with the other families. They stuck their lads on a boat. And Ger didn't know what to do so he just put his head down. But the two thousand was still in his account.'

'And the rest was gone?'

'Moss took it out before he left and Ger heard no more about it.'

'But where does Frankie come in?'

Pat's hands began to shake and she grasped the arms of her chair. 'One of the times Moss came back on holiday, Frankie was in his teens and he'd gone off to some bar in Carrick. Moss was there drinking on his own. He must have thought it was a great joke to pick up with Frankie and start dropping hints about Ger. And by the end of the night didn't Frankie have the whole story? And from then on he was holding it over poor Ger.' There were beads of sweat on Pat's forehead. 'Right to the day he died, Frankie had him under his thumb.'

Mary picked up the cup of tea and thrust it at her again. 'Drink that there now, before you say another word.'

Pat took a sip of tea and looked at her piteously. 'Can you believe it?'

'Was he asking Ger for money?'

'Well, no, I don't think so. But he didn't need to, did he? He'd only to say what he wanted. The farm and no work along with it, the house and the big car. I've been thinking about it, Mary, and I know how it was. He was the eldest son. Everyone knew he was Ger's favourite – God, they probably thought he was mine as well, the way I did nothing to school him.' Pat looked at Mary imploringly. 'But you know why that was!'

'I know you never had the heart to cross Ger.'

'I should have done. I know that now. But you're right, I hadn't the heart to. He doted on Frankie. But he did do his best for Sonny and Jim, Mary. He sent them to college and gave them a good start. And they *have* done well in the end of things. And they've got their health and strength, like Ger said.'

'Ay, he got rid of them because that was what Frankie wanted. And he was cute enough to make sure they didn't emigrate to Resolve because, if they had done, they might have heard the story from Moss as well.'

Pat gulped. 'I know. You're right. He was afraid of everything. Everything and everybody. Even his own sons.' With a Herculean effort Mary said nothing. Pat squared her shoulders. 'I know what you're thinking, but you never understood Ger. He wasn't like Tom. He wasn't big and beautiful and strong. He'd had every bit of courage he was born with beaten out of him. He wouldn't have lasted ten minutes in prison.'

'Ah, for God's sake, girl, he'd never have ended up in prison. He could have called Frankie's bluff and told him so.'

'But how do you know that? You don't, and he didn't either. And you can take that smug, superior look off your face! You know damn well it was you who made me marry him. You wanted him out of your own way so you dumped him in my lap.'

'I did not!'

'Mary, would you for once in your life be honest? You never fooled me.'

'Well, why did you marry him, then, if you didn't want to?'

It seemed to Mary that Pat's eyes had sunk deep in her head, and the voice in which she replied was that of a stranger. 'When I went to Resolve, I thought I was marrying Ger because I couldn't bear to hurt him.

I told myself that if I said no, or changed my mind afterwards, I'd be doing what people had done to him all his life. Knocked him down. Made a fool of him. Told him he was worthless. So there I was, working away in the clothing factory, making money and buying things for my trousseau, and for yours. And then my mam told me you'd changed the date, and that you and Tom would be married before I got home. That was when I realised the truth.'

'I don't know what you're saying.'

'No, you don't. Because I didn't know it myself until then. There was a lad I met in Resolve, though, and he made me see it. We spent one long day together by a lake that was called Two Wings. And he was good to me when my mam rang and told me what you'd done. It was because of him that I faced something I hadn't admitted before.'

'What was that?'

'He made me see who I was really in love with. It was Tom. Right from the start. It's true that I didn't want to hurt Ger. But that didn't come naturally. It was something I'd learned from seeing Tom, and from reading poems that made me feel people's pain. And from standing back and looking at life while you reached out and grabbed it. Do you know something,

Mary? I used to tell myself you and I were different. I suppose I prided myself on that, but I'm not sure I had a right to. I never grabbed things. I wasn't greedy. But I can't say I wasn't manipulative. I could have stayed over there and maybe been happy. But I came back here and married Ger because I couldn't bear the thought of never seeing Tom again.'

'Are you saying …?'

'Ah, for feck's sake, don't be a fool, of course I'm not! Tom never loved anyone but you. If I'd done right, though, I would've stayed away and made an end of the foursome. It wasn't healthy.'

Pat looked at her bleakly. Then Mary took a pull of her tea and sniffed. 'Ay, well, now you've said your spake, let me say mine. I don't know what was healthy in Ireland in them days, between the priests and the nuns and the Brothers and the poverty and the lack of opportunity, not to mention having to make up our minds whether to go or stay. But what Ger used to say was the truth of it. You play the hand you're dealt, and most of us did the best we could.'

'Are you saying you're glad I came back?'

'I'm saying I don't know what I'd have done without you.'

Pat turned her head away and looked at the dancing

flames. 'I thought the same about you the other day.'

They sat there not meeting each other's eyes. Then Mary shook herself. 'What are you going to do about Ger's letter?'

'I'll see. It's my problem, not yours. Why don't you go home now? I'd say we both want a rest.'

'Well, if you'll take my advice about Frankie—'

'I said I'll handle it. And, before you go, I've a bit of advice of my own. It's about your behaviour to Hanna.'

Mary bristled. 'Oh, right! Advice on how to be a mother from a woman whose son blackmailed his da.'

'That's right. And I'm giving it to the woman who said she was no great hand at the mothering job herself. Remember? So shut up and listen. You treated Hanna like a rival all the time she was growing up. You did, Mary, so don't try to deny it. You couldn't wait for her to leave home so you'd have Tom all to yourself.'

'And didn't I take her back with open arms when she'd made a mess of her marriage?'

'No, you didn't. You opened the door and let her in but you nagged her half to death. But that's in the past and it's not what I want to talk about. Jazz will go her own way, and why shouldn't she? And Louisa's no relation of yours, she's only Hanna's ex-mother-in-law. But Hanna's your daughter, Mary, and she feels responsible for you. So it's the future, not the past, you need to be thinking about. You know I'm right, and there's nobody else will say it to you. The fact is you're turning into a caricature.'

'*What?*'

'You heard me. Look, you're not in your dotage yet, girl. Hanna's managed to build herself a new life. Don't go claiming that the way you claimed her childhood. God alone knows what's ahead of us, but right now you don't need constant care. So pull yourself together while you've got time, or you'll end up as a millstone round her neck.'

Mary rose to her feet and picked up the tea tray. 'Is that it? Have you said your piece?'

'I have. Did you listen?'

'Text me if you want me after you've talked to Frankie.'

'I will.'

'And I'll find my own form of transport. You needn't go sending Fury O'Shea in his van.'

'I didn't send him.'

'Ay, well, that's as may be, but look at the state of me. I'm covered from head to foot in The Divil's hair.'

CHAPTER THIRTY-NINE

ATTENDANCE NUMBERS AT THE TRANS-atlantic Book Club were rising, and for the last meeting of the month extra chairs had been set out on both sides of the ocean. In Resolve, they were now arranged on either side of a central aisle and, from the look of the miscellaneous collection of different heights and comfort, they must have involved plenty of heavy lifting. Extending the seating in Lissbeg had been simpler. The reading room was specifically designed for meetings, and the stacking chairs locked together easily. There was a charm about the view of Resolve on the screen, though, suggestive of the final scene in a vintage crime movie, when everyone gathers in the library and the detective takes the floor. The Brennan memorial range, which now appeared dead centre at the rear, added the bizarre counter-suggestion of an altar, with the cat lying asleep on it, like a white marble statue.

The seats over there were filling quickly. Most

people were carrying copies of *The Case of the Late Pig* but Hanna could see that the Canny twins had arrived ostentatiously empty-handed. Evidently they still disapproved of the club's book choice but remained determined, as committee members, to keep a watching brief. Mrs Shanahan, in a patchwork jacket, was chatting to a group of ladies, and Ashlee Braun-Mulcahy, the previous week's technician, was ensconced in a wing-back armchair, which impeded the view of at least three people in the row behind her. Erin was in the front row, close to Josie and next to a dark, very handsome young man who was perched on a stool. Beside Josie, a well-dressed older couple was seated on the best chairs in the room.

Among the Lissbeg newcomers were Margot, Cassie's boss from the salon, and the small woman whose husband had been outraged by the seed cake. He was no reader, his wife explained to Hanna, but he'd brought her into town and taken himself to the pub for a pint. 'Mind you, I haven't caught up with the reading bit myself. But I've two cousins over in Resolve – I'm Mrs Breen but they'd be Courtneys on my mother's side, though one of them married a man called Dillon and one is a widow whose husband's name was Duff. Anyway, I gave them a call and told them I'd drop in here this evening.' The woman's eyes fixed on the screen and she gave a crow of delight. 'Ah, would you look at that! There they are and it's twenty years since I've seen them!'

It seemed more than likely to Hanna that this would be another meeting hijacked by reminiscences, but the club's growing numbers were proving its worth to both communities, and it wasn't her job to police what it discussed. Mary was already in the front row. Moving to greet some more arrivals, Hanna raised her eyebrows at Cassie, who'd welcomed them at the desk. 'Is Pat not with you?'

'She said she didn't feel like coming out.'

'Is she okay?'

'Fine, I think. She's been quiet since the weekend. She sent her love.'

Hanna's attention was diverted by a pile-up in the reading-room doorway, where Darina was attempting to wrest her iPhone out of Gobnit's hand. The little girl, who was wearing a unicorn onesie, was butting her mother with the silver horn protruding from its hood. As people around them became annoyed, Mr Maguire, directly behind them, employed his classroom voice: 'That's quite enough nonsense, thank you, Gobnit. Give Mummy the phone at once and move along.'

Darina cast him an anguished glance and Gobnit threw back her unicorn's head and emitted a piercing scream. Having provoked the tantrum, Mr Maguire, still in teacher mode, immediately blamed the parent. 'A little *discipline* is all that's wanted.'

By the time Hanna had calmed things down and Cassie had taken her seat at the back, Gobnit was under Darina's chair, still glued to the iPhone, and the clock on the wall said 7 p.m. Over in Resolve, Jack strolled to the back of the room and leaned against the range. Other than coping if someone knocked over a microphone, the technician's job involved no more than establishing the Skype link in advance, shutting it down after the meeting and clearing away the equipment. Ferdia was earning overtime as a council employee, but Hanna wondered if Jack had nothing better to do on what for him was an afternoon. He seemed neither bored nor interested as he lounged against the range with his long legs outstretched.

The meeting began with much discussion of the new layout in Resolve. Everyone admired the upholstery of Ashlee's wingback armchair, and the provenance of a rosewood sofa was traced back three generations. Then a piano stool was recognised as having been carried through from the Lucky Charm bar. This provoked a brief run-through of popular songs of the seventies and a chorus of 'I Will Survive' sung by Ashlee, who turned out to be an alto. Hanna and Josie had learned by now not to attempt to control this initial chat, so they sat back, awaiting a suitable break in the conversation. Then, spotting her chance, Josie called for attention. 'How about we settle down and take a look at this book?'

Hanna was about to pick up her cue when Darina clapped her hands. 'But of *course*! I've been trying to grasp the significance of the range! It's a *metaphor*, am I right? A literary reference?' On both sides of the ocean people gaped. Standing up, Darina addressed the screen. 'I mean, *why put a range in a library*? That was the question I asked myself. Because, as we all know, each little detail is part of a wider picture. And then I thought, Darina, you're looking at a library of *classic crime stories*! And I had my answer! The range is a reference to *The Franchise Affair*!'

In the stunned silence that followed, Darina beamed at Hanna. '*The Franchise Affair* by Josephine Tey, remember? It was huge. One of the top hundred crime novels of all time.' She looked again at the group in Resolve, which was sitting in stunned silence. 'I'm right, aren't I? And what could be more fitting? Such a powerful story. No sleuth, no stolen necklace or missing will. Not even a corpse. Just a forensic deconstruction of the values of its time! So evocative of privation and monotony!' Closing her eyes, she lowered her voice dramatically. '"We put the range on only on Mondays when the scrubbing is done."' The well-dressed couple in the best seats registered shocked disapproval. Hanna saw Josie glance at them in alarm.

Delighted with her theory, Darina opened her eyes. Seeing the looks on the faces on the screen, she leaned forward earnestly, her amber beads clunking against the head of a woman in front of her. 'Honestly, it's your courage I applaud. You could have chosen any kind of artwork. A collage of authors' portraits, say, or a bust of Sherlock Holmes. But instead you went for this battered relic, this nuanced installation, which demands that we question the very term "Golden Age". Is it right for us to indulge in books so essentially linked to class and social privilege? Are not the values they enshrine intrinsically corrupt?'

The well-dressed man raised his hand. Unable to think what else to do, Hanna smiled encouragingly at the camera. 'I'm sorry, I don't know your name, Mr ...?'

'Brennan.' The man rose to his feet and glared round the room. 'And that battered relic, as you call it, was a gift to the club from its founder, Denis Brennan, to celebrate our ancestry and remind us of our roots.'

Darina turned scarlet and sat down abruptly. Hanna stifled a grin. It seemed so unfair that the first valid discussion point about the club's chosen genre should emerge from one of Darina's misapprehensions. But, with a librarian's long experience of dealing with small-town sensibilities, she guessed that the faux-pas would produce more cheerful gossip than offence. The looks on faces such as the Canny twins' showed that a set-down to Brennan pride wasn't wholly unwelcome. It was evident too that old power struggles were waning, and that Erin and Jack's generation had little or no memory of the Shamrock Club's once all-powerful founder. In fact, she thought, the symbols that had defined Resolve's Irishness belonged in the world of the convent that her own library had supplanted. Already almost irrelevant in Finfarran, they had hung on in the emigrant community, mutating into anomalies, like Mrs Shanahan's four-leaved clover and the preservation of an outworn range as if it were the Holy Grail.

Intrigued by what had emerged so unexpectedly, Hanna wondered if Darina's question applied as much to that sentimental nationalism as to the values of the Golden Age detective stories with their rigid assumptions of right and wrong and unquestioned social hierarchies. It was precisely the sort of discussion that a book club might engage in but it seemed unwise to embark on it right now. Besides, who was she to pull down old gods by questioning old certainties? In his time Denis Brennan had held his community together, and allowed it to build its future by invoking a past that, though largely mythical, upheld the virtues of hard work and mutual self-help. There was much to be admired in that. But change had come, as it always does, thought Hanna. Having outlived its use in the kitchen, the range had been moved to the Shamrock Club's library and, no doubt, would eventually find its way to a skip. Or perhaps not. Perhaps time would elevate it to the rank of a museum piece and its current faintly ridiculous air would be gone.

Over in Resolve, Josie had managed to ease Mr Brennan back into his chair. To everyone's relief, Mrs Breen stood up and called out to her Courtney cousins, producing a new outburst of chat. Mentally, Hanna made a note to suggest to Josie that the club might evolve into a local history group or a conversation circle. A dynamic had asserted itself and, as she'd told Cassie, you had to keep your ear to the ground and respond to what was required.

When the meeting was over Hanna went to the front row to speak to Mary. Ferdia had disappeared to the loo and the room was nearly empty. Josie was still visible on the screen, shaking hands with the Brennans and ushering out the remaining stragglers in Resolve.

'I'll be ready to drive you home soon, Mam. Cassie's just seeing people out.'

'There's no need for that. I've ordered a taxi.'

'But I can give you a lift.'

'You can, but you don't need to. You've your own life to get on with, without chauffeuring me around.' Mary's mild tone contained an underlying warning. It was evident that any show of surprise might provoke aggression, so Hanna nodded. Mary looked up at her magisterially. 'I'll sit here and you can give me a shout when he arrives.'

'Of course. No problem. You can keep Gobnit company.' Concealing her astonishment, Hanna went through to unlock the door for the last of her own stragglers.

Still fiddling with the iPhone, Gobnit was slumped on a chair several rows behind Mary. An expression of massive disapproval crossed Mary's face. 'Where's your mother?'

'Gone to see if she can make a call from Hanna's desk.'

Gobnit didn't raise her head and Mary's annoyance increased. 'You mean you won't let her have her own phone, you bold little girl?'

'It's none of your business.'

'How dare you speak to me like that?'

Giggling, Gobnit pulled her pink hood over her face and spoke from behind the sparkly unicorn horn. 'Because you're a nosy old woman, that's why. Nosy Mrs McNoseFace!'

Mary advanced on her. 'Give me that phone.'

Gobnit slid to the floor and disappeared under the seating, scrambling up and mounting a chair when she got to the next row. 'No, I won't. You're a nosy old noseface. You go round spying all the time. You've been spying on Cassie. I saw her and that Bradley guy having coffee in Carrick at the weekend, and you were peering out from behind a fern.'

Determined to assert her authority, Mary made a grab for the phone. Holding it high above her head, Gobnit began to clamber from chair to chair. 'I saw you! And I heard you asking that guy who works in the Spa Hotel if Cassie had spent the night there!'

Scarlet as a turkey cock, Mary lunged towards her

and, still giggling, Gobnit made a leap from the chair to a table top. 'I did! I heard you. My mummy was buying a paper because I won't let her go onto the internet, and he was in the shop and you went up and asked him questions. It's no business of yours, who Cassie sleeps with! My mummy says sexual things are *private*.'

A sound from the doorway made Mary swing round to see Cassie staring at the screen. Evidently waiting for Ferdia's return before ending the Skype call, Jack was standing in the empty room in Resolve, holding the cat. For what felt like hours nobody said anything. Then Jack reached out to the laptop in Resolve and the screen went dead.

CHAPTER FORTY

PAT KNEW FRANKIE WOULDN'T IGNORE her summons. When she'd phoned him she'd spoken more briefly than she'd ever done before, and she'd known when she ended the call that he'd been worried. She'd told him to be at the flat at seven fifteen. The book-club meeting in the library would have started by then, so there was no danger of Cassie coming in, or of Mary spotting Frankie's car and wanting to know what was happening.

After Mary's departure on Saturday, Pat had been exhausted to the marrow of her bones. She'd washed the teacups, gone to her bed and wept, hating Ger for leaving her to cope with this alone. Now she sat in the kitchen, feeling numb. No wonder Frankie had tried to push her aside once the will had been read. He'd been so sure that, when Ger died, he'd be cock of the walk. And he'd had good reason. Ger had let him believe that he, not Pat, would be his executor – hadn't said so explicitly but hadn't said that he wouldn't – and never let on that his will was fifty years old. And, after all the years of getting his own way, Frank had been easily fooled. The note of triumph in Ger's letter as he described his own cunning had made Pat wince.

As the hands of the clock passed the hour, she thought again of her own lack of courage. It wasn't just that she hadn't faced her suspicions about Frankie, or even how she'd allowed Ger to spoil him. It was more. Her first reaction to Ger's letter had been anger. She'd asked herself furiously why he couldn't have taken his grubby secret with him. He'd fooled Frankie and the end result was that she'd been left in control. Why hadn't he left it at that? Why did he need to tell her what Frankie had done? As soon as the questions were formed she saw the answers. Ger had known her just as well as she had understood him. And he'd known Frankie. He'd been afraid that, little by little, she'd let Frankie take over, and that, in the end, Sonny and Jim would lose out.

Staring bleakly at her linked hands, Pat realised he'd been right. Of course he was. He, of all people, had known the comfort of someone to rely on, and who would she have turned to for help if not their eldest son?

Perhaps Ger had known, too, how grief could

numb the mind. Since she'd read his letter she'd felt she couldn't pull two thoughts together. There was so much to process. *I didn't want you hurt, Pat, and I thought that, if you knew, you might leave me. You might take yourself off to Canada and I'd be left here with him.* There was a ring of truth in that, she thought, and Ger might even have been right. She didn't know. Inevitably, on the next page, he'd given a different excuse. *I thought that a stain on the family name would affect the other lads' chances of work.* To be fair to him, back when it all started, that could well have been so. But the shame would have reflected on Frankie himself, as well as the others. Ger should have called Frankie's bluff. But if she had been in Ger's place, would she have taken the risk? The same circular argument had tormented her for the past three sleepless nights. The fact was that, whichever way he turned, Ger had found himself cornered and all he'd done was play the hand he'd believed that he'd been dealt.

Out on the landing a key turned in the lock and the handle was rattled. If Frankie was making a point, Pat had already made her own. She waited a minute before getting to her feet and going to unlock the Chubb. He came in with his trench coat swinging, playing the bully-boy, bringing a cold draught from the dark stairwell. Pat gestured to the easy chair by the hearth.

'I'd like you to sit down, Frankie, and listen to what I say.'

'Is there something wrong? Are you well? Could it not have waited?'

She didn't answer so he shrugged and took the seat. Pat stood by the table holding onto the back of a chair. 'I'm not going to say this more than once and I want no interruptions. And no denials either, Frank, because I know what you've been at.' She drew a deep breath and looked him straight in the eye. 'I'm ashamed of you. To blackmail your own father all these years. To behave like that to a man who'd have plucked the moon out of the sky for you.' Frankie reared up, as if to answer, and Pat heard her own voice crack as she talked him down. 'You had no need to do it. And you knew you hadn't! It wasn't about need, or even greed. It was power you wanted. You liked the hold you had over him. You're a mean-spirited bully, Frank Fitzgerald.'

His colour changed and Pat looked away, unable to bear the sight of him. Then she pulled herself together before he could speak. 'I know what you're going to say, so don't bother. No one can prove in a court of law that you did anything wrong. Well, I'm not going to try to prove it, Frank. I've more respect for your father's name in this town than that.' She waited until she could feel his relief, then took a step towards him. 'But this is what *is* going to happen. The gravy train stops here. You've had everything you're going to get from your father's estate, Frankie. You can keep your house and your big car and whatever money you had on the day he died. But, from now on, every cent that's made from the farm and the shop, and from all Ger's investments, comes to me. I'll do the hiring and firing and I'll pay the bills. I'll keep the books and you'll keep your distance. And don't think that you'll be on the payroll, because you won't.'

Frankie sat with his mouth open, looking like a pricked balloon. Pat let go of the chair and moved to the kitchen sink. In her mind's eye she could see the final page of Ger's letter, penned in the neat writing he'd learned at the Brothers' school. *I know I ought to talk to you now that I'm dying but I can't. I can't think of any better way to handle it than this.* At the bottom of the page, under his tidy signature, he'd scrawled a few more lines. *The truth is that, even now, I can't bear to be the one to hurt him. I'm sorry you married a failure. I would have been more like Tom for you if I could.*

Pat could hear her own voice choked with tears as she'd sat on the edge of Josie's bed, wearing her honeymoon dress. She'd kept her cool until Seán dropped her home but, as soon as she'd got in, she'd gone upstairs bawling. The rest of them were all back from the céilí at the club, and when Josie had found out what the matter was she'd been gobsmacked. 'But, dear God Almighty, girl, a proposal from Seán Shanahan! Would you not reach out and grab it?' But when she couldn't explain, Josie hadn't pressed her. Instead she'd held her hand while Pat cried her fill.

Tonight Pat's mind had been full of a jumble of possibilities, each of which had seemed to require more courage than she had. Now, to her surprise, she thought of Cassie and, clutching the edge of the kitchen sink, sent up a desperate, incoherent prayer. She couldn't bear the thought that valiant little Cassie, with her snub nose, peacock-bright fringe and air of independence, might end up as trapped and confused by life as herself.

Aware that Frankie was staring at her, Pat forced herself to concentrate. Ger's mother's vase was upended on the draining board. When she'd taken it down to wash it, there had been dust lodged in the china petals of the roses round its neck and its curly feet. One of the three feet was chipped but you could turn it to the back, where you'd hardly notice. Having scrubbed the vase with a soft brush in soapy water, she'd screwed up the corner of a tea-towel and gone round all the crevices, inside and out.

What she had to do now was put it in the cardboard box she'd brought up from the shop. She did that, and when she turned to Frankie, she saw his mind working. Once more she interrupted him before he could say a word. 'This is the last time I'll speak to you on this subject. I want every paper and file you've taken out of this house returned by tomorrow morning. I don't know what was in them so I won't know if anything's gone. But a solicitor will, Frank, so don't be a fool as well as a blaggard. Ger could never bear to hurt you, but now you're dealing with me.'

He stood up and she thought he might hit her. Then his lip curled. 'I suppose you'll be ringing Canada now, and running to little Cassie for tea and sympathy. You're the fool if you think that girl wasn't sent here for what she can get.'

'I'll tell you what she's going to get, and then you can get out of my sight. I'm going to leave her a site and enough money to build a house on it, so she can have a place in Ireland one day to call home.' As if in answer to the prayer that had been wrenched out of her, Pat was gripped by certainty and calm. 'Cassie will make her own choices, the way I wasn't able to, and she'll have the courage to take risks, the way I never did. And, no, I'm not going to tell your brothers how badly you've behaved. I wouldn't demean your father's memory. Now you take this.' She held out the box with the lustre vase in it.

Frankie stared at it blankly. 'What's that?'

'It belonged to your father's mother. Fran likes it. Give it to her and tell her I'm happy it's going to someone who'll value it. I'm telling you now that everything else will go to Sonny and Jim.'

CHAPTER FORTY-ONE

WHEN FRANKIE HAD GONE, VOICES IN THE street drew Pat to her kitchen window. She stood back behind the curtain and looked down at the cheerful group emerging from the library. Hanna and Mary were last as usual. As Pat watched, a taxi drew up and Mary got in, fussing over the whereabouts of her handbag and demanding that her coat be tucked in before the door was shut. Then, as the driver pulled away, Hanna began to walk towards the car park. A shout stopped her and several members of the club urged her to come for a drink. Hanna hesitated, watching the rear lights of the taxi disappear round the corner. Then she ran across to where they were waiting beside the flower-filled horse trough and joined them as they sauntered off to the pub.

Pat was about to turn away smiling when Cassie appeared in the library courtyard and went through to the garden. She threaded her way along the gravelled paths till she came to the central fountain, above which hosts of martins swooped and turned. Looking down, Pat could see starry jasmine glimmering in the herb beds. As the birds wheeled above the statue, their beaks gaping for insects, Cassie sat on the edge of the granite basin. Beyond her, at the far side of the garden, the colours of the stained-glass windows were dulled by the gathering twilight. She stayed where she was, her head bent, either deep in thought or bowed down by trouble, then stood up and tossed back her peacock-blue fringe. Jamming her hands into her jeans pockets, she walked on out of Pat's sight into the shadow of the trees.

*

Fury was sitting on a bench with The Divil curled at his feet. The little dog's bark alerted Cassie to their presence, and his ears pricked at the sound of her feet on the gravel. Though she'd come to the garden seeking solitude, she sat down beside them. Fury greeted her with a nod. 'I suppose your meeting's over, is it?'

'Yeah. Pat wasn't there tonight.'

'I know that. She had a visitor. I saw your uncle Frank come out of the flat.'

Cassie's shoulders twitched in irritation. 'God,

can no one do anything in Finfarran without being seen?'

Fury grinned. 'That's heartfelt. Who's seen you doing what?'

Cassie pulled a face. 'Mary Casey.'

'I see.'

'She's been sticking her nose in.'

'Of course she has. How else would she pass the time?'

Cassie snorted. 'It's no business of hers who I go out with.'

'We're talking about this filthy-rich cruise-ship chap, I assume?'

'Oh, for goodness' sake! Have you been watching me too?'

'I have not. But word gets round.'

'Evidently.' Cassie scowled. 'And how do you know he's loaded?'

'Oh, the Finfarran grapevine is far better than Google.'

Cassie's eyes widened and Fury winked at her. 'I'm hoping that you were cute enough to check him out yourself.'

Despite herself, Cassie giggled. 'Only after I'd spent the night in his room at the Spa Hotel. I googled him in the morning on the way home.'

'You might have done better to do a search before falling into bed.'

'Well, that's where you're wrong, because the money doesn't matter.'

'Oh, right. What's the attraction, then?'

'We like the same things. Travel. Being footloose and fancy-free. That's my thing. Seeing the world. Exploring exciting places.'

Fury nodded thoughtfully. 'And with Brad it would all be cushy and safe and glamorous. I see what you mean.'

'That's not what I meant.'

'And he does look a bit like a film star.'

'No, he doesn't.' Cassie glowered at the birds, which were still wheeling around the fountain. 'Okay. Sure. He's handsome, if you like cool hair and dark eyes and great teeth. He's good in bed too, in case the grapevine hasn't informed you.'

'Well, that's always handy.'

'I never said I loved him.'

'Good.'

'Why?'

'Because you don't, do you? You're in love with Jack Shanahan.'

Cassie swung round, about to deny it. Then she

frowned. 'Wait, hang on. Just a minute. How do you even know that Jack exists?'

'Ah. Well, it was down to The Divil's crab claws.'

'What?'

'The poor dog hasn't been happy, you know, on that vet's diet. He's been pining for his custard creams. So I told myself he needed a bit of variety and took him to the marina in Ballyfin.'

'For a walk?'

'Not at all, girl, he gets plenty of exercise chasing rats at home. No, I asked a mate in Ballyfin to spare him a few crab claws. There's plenty get discarded from the catch if they're too small. Anyway, I got a bagful and yer man here thought they were great.' The Divil gave a reminiscent snort, and Fury scratched him with his boot. 'And, while I was at the marina, I had a chat with Paul.'

'Margot's Paul?'

'That's the man. He told me that Margot told him that you'd been asking questions about the land back in Mullafrack.'

'What? Oh, for God's sake, I was only—'

'One night a while back I was having a pint with Tintawn Terry. And he mentioned he'd run into Ferdia after your last book-club meeting.' Fury bent down and pulled The Divil by the ear. 'Ferdia said that a crowd of you had gone out for a pizza that evening and that, though you'd been dressed to the nines, you'd looked a bit down. He told Terry his oppo in Resolve had been off that night. The name was Jack Shanahan. I used to deliver logs to a woman near Mullafrack. I remember her saying Shanahans lived there before they went off to the States.' Fury got to his feet and looked down at Cassie. 'It's none of my business, mind. I just put two and two together.'

Cassie said nothing. Then she pulled a wry face. 'Well, I can't say that I wasn't warned not to go round asking questions. I guess I talk too much.'

'Holy God Almighty, girl, that's not the point, is it? Your problem is that you haven't done your talking to the right man.'

Fury lounged away with The Divil at his heels. As they disappeared across the garden Cassie remained hunched on the bench listening to the sound of the water falling from carved flowers into the stone basin. In her mind's eye she could see herself and Fury sitting in the pub in the forest, with The Divil at their feet eating gravy and cabbage. Fury had asked if she knew what the word 'glamour' meant.

'You mean like models and movie stars?'

He'd thrown her a basilisk glance. Then he'd sipped his pint. *'What it really means is deception. A charm to make something look like something else.'*

Enchantment. That's what he'd called it. Cassie put her elbows on her knees and stared across the darkening herb beds. And that's what she'd felt ever since she'd slept with Brad. Enchanted. Confused. Carried away by what had seemed like wonderful possibilities. In the coffee shop in Carrick Brad had said he thought they had a future. She was the one, he told her, and he couldn't let her go. It had all felt magical, mad, risky and crazy, like the moment when they'd plunged down the hillside together with the earth sliding beneath their skidding heels. But was it? Wasn't the prospect of life with Brad a safe option? One that might seem exciting but which carried no real risk? Alone in the dusk, Cassie blushed for shame. She'd been charmed by the thought of the high life. She'd even imagined the looks on her family's faces when she'd swan home to Toronto with the heir to a cruise line in tow. And it was Fury who'd made the glamour fall away, as if he'd applied astringent herbs to her eyes to break a spell. In the scented dusk, with the house martins wheeling and swooping, Cassie gritted her teeth and made a decision. She was in love with Jack Shanahan. And now she was going to have to take the biggest risk of her life.

*

There was no light on in the kitchen when she climbed the stairs and went into the flat. Pat was sitting by the range with Ger's blue jumper folded over her hands. She stood up, laid it aside, and turned on the lamp. 'How was the meeting?'

'Fine. Great. Everyone missed you.'

'I'll be there next week.'

Cassie looked hesitant. 'Fury said Frankie was here.'

'He was, love.'

Only a month ago Cassie would have kept pushing. Now she didn't dare. Pat came and put an arm around her. 'There's nothing for you to worry about, truly.'

'Fury once told me that some family stuff might be none of my damn business.'

Pat gave her a gentle squeeze and took her arm away. 'Well, I wouldn't put it that way myself but Fury could be right.' She asked if Cassie had eaten.

'No, but I'm not hungry. There's someone I need to call.'

Pat, who had turned to go back to the fire, spoke over her shoulder. 'Bradley, is it?'

'No.'

Remembering Erin's break-up with Jeff, Cassie had resisted the temptation to text Brad to say she wouldn't be seeing him again. Instead, she'd resolutely called him, wincing at his polite attempt not to show he was hurt. Now she flinched, fearing an inquisition, but Pat showed nothing more than mild interest.

'Oh, right. Tell me this, love, were you thinking of going back on your travels soon?'

'Well, not immediately. But I guess so.'

'Because you're not to think you need to stay here on my account. Honestly, I'm fine, and it was you got me through the worst.'

This was too much for Cassie. 'Oh, God, Pat, I didn't. I asked all the wrong questions and I made Frankie think I was some kind of evil gold-digger.'

'What Frankie thinks doesn't matter a pin. I know you're no gold-digger.'

'And I badgered you into going back to Resolve.'

'You did. But I needed that trip. It's helped me a lot.'

Cassie hesitated again. 'Pat, are you really over the worst?'

'I don't know, love. If you've lived with someone for fifty years maybe you never get over your loss when they die. But that's how it is. Ger's gone and I have to keep living. And I've got Mary. And Hanna. They count as family too, you know.' Pat smiled. 'And you've given me back my friendship with Josie. I've missed her. I might even go over sometime and stay with her again.'

'And, meanwhile, there's the Transatlantic Book Club.'

'Yes, and that's thanks to you too. I know I could ring Josie if I wanted to – it's not like the old days when a call to the States would cost an arm and a leg. But that's not the point. The club is a reason to get myself up and out of the flat if I'm down.'

'Truly?'

'Truly. I'm going to be fine, Cassie. So you go on upstairs and talk to Jack Shanahan.'

Cassie had reached the door before she swung back in amazement. 'How did you know who I'm going to call?'

'I didn't.'

'Then how …?'

'The trouble with you is you don't read enough detective stories. I didn't know. You've just told me.'

The look on Cassie's face made Pat burst out laughing. 'Go on, give me some privacy. I've calls of my own to make.' As Cassie disappeared up the staircase, Pat crossed to the phone that stood on the dresser. She had no idea what she was going to say when she called Toronto but maybe just telling Sonny and Jim how much she loved and missed them would be enough.

CHAPTER FORTY-TWO

CASSIE SAT IN FRONT OF HER LAPTOP willing Jack to accept her call and hating Skype's insistent ring tone. She could see that he was online, which made it worse. Nothing about this was going to be easy. What Jack had seen and heard in the library hadn't even been dramatic, just ridiculous. Gobnit prancing across the room in her pink unicorn onesie, and Mary scrambling over the seating, scarlet and officious. And the idea of Mary stalking her round Finfarran, and the ghastly revelation that she'd spent the night with Brad. The thought of facing Jack after that was cringe-making but she knew that if she did nothing tonight she'd never face him again.

The insistent tone that was driving her mad stopped, and Jack's face appeared on her laptop screen. At the back of her mind she observed that, this time, he too was sitting in his bedroom. His was orderly, with no embarrassing underwear scattered about, and, compared to herself, he seemed scarily calm. But perhaps he had no reason to be otherwise? Maybe he hadn't cared about Mary's revelation. Maybe he'd cut the link in the library out of good manners, because he'd felt the conversation had nothing to do with him. But as Cassie opened her mouth she saw that, under his freckles, he seemed unnaturally pale. The surge of hope she felt was so overwhelming she couldn't speak.

'Oh, for God's sake, Cassie!'

Cassie blinked. 'What?'

'According to caller etiquette, yours is the next move.'

'Yes. Of course. Of course it is. Because I called you.' Taking a deep breath, she controlled her voice. 'So here's the thing. I wanted to tell you my news.'

'Don't tell me, let me guess. Your world awaits. You've taken a job with an exciting new cruise line.'

'No! I haven't. I think I was going to but—' She stopped in mid-sentence. 'Just a minute, that's the name of Brad's cruise line.'

Jack looked taken aback. 'What is?'

'Your World Awaits. Why did you say that? Wait, oh, my God, you googled him!' Ignoring the fact that she'd done the same thing, Cassie bridled. 'What on earth did you think you were doing?'

'Well, forgive me for being curious when you couldn't seem to stop yourself talking about him. Or sleeping with him, apparently. Though, like the kid in the unicorn outfit said, I guess that's private.'

'Yes, it is.'

'And I've no right to object.'

'Damn right, you haven't.'

They glowered at each other from either side of the ocean. Then Cassie bit her lip. 'I didn't know you were curious.'

'Well, I was.' Jack looked away and then, turning back, looked straight into the camera. 'I am.'

Hardly able to believe what she was hearing, Cassie asked the first question that came into her head. 'Did you really have a thing the night the Ashlee woman took over at the club?'

He grinned. 'I thought I could wean myself off wanting to sit there staring at you. It didn't take long to find out that I couldn't.'

Relief exploded in Cassie, like a firework taking off. 'So, do you want to hear my news?'

He nodded, and his eyes were like slivers of blue light.

'Pat's going to be fine, and I know what I want to do next. I've decided that I'm coming back to Resolve.'

She held her breath, waiting for his reaction, and it seemed like a lifetime before he spoke again.

'Good.'

'Really?'

Jack reached out and she almost felt the touch of his finger on her face. 'Yeah, really. Maybe this time, if you hang around, we'll get to know each other. '

With a shaky laugh, Cassie placed the tip of her finger on the screen over his. 'You do realise that it could turn out we've nothing in common at all?'

Thousands of miles away, Jack's face broke into a lopsided smile. 'I know. Scary, isn't it?'

'Seriously risky.'

'And yet the weird thing is that it feels so right.'

ACKNOWLEDGEMENTS

A few years ago, when I was browsing in a shop in Dingle town, I picked up a greeting card with a picture of some very cross-looking women in hats on it, and the caption 'Our book club can beat up your book club.' A lady beside me had seen the same card, we got chatting, and she told me she belonged to 'Ireland's only Skype book club'. The club met in their local library and discussed their chosen books via Skype with a group of readers in a public library in the States. The idea of people coming together to discuss books across the ocean stayed with me and, a while back, when Hachette were asking for the fifth and sixth Finfarran novels, I realised it would make a brilliant story line for Hanna Casey's library. The trouble was that, when I came to write this book, I realised I hadn't a clue how such a club would work in real life – and I'd forgotten both the lady's name and the town she'd told me she came from.

So I took to Twitter and tweeted *#Irish #Librarians*

Help! What local library hosts a transatlantic book club? Within twenty minutes I had responses from local librarians in Fingal and Sligo, putting me on to Marie Boland, a librarian in Clonmel. A week later I was driving to Co. Tipperary to visit the Skype book club. It was surreal and wonderful, and in the course of our transatlantic chat we fixed that the next Finfarran book, which would be called *The Transatlantic Book Club*, would be dedicated to the Skype club's members on both sides of the ocean. So, of course, my first thanks and acknowledgements must go to them, to Marie and the kind librarians on Twitter, who helped me to find her, and, especially, to Stacia Whelan, the lady I met in the shop.

I'm also grateful to the lovely, supportive writing community on Twitter, and to all the readers who chat to me there and on my Facebook page (which is called Felicity Hayes-McCoy Author), and who send me emails and messages about my books, and reports and photos from your own book clubs. It's wonderful to hear your thoughts and feedback, to know that you love Fury, get cross with Mary, sympathise with Hanna and recognise Finfarran's countryside, communities and dynamics from your own experiences. I love the fact that you love how my characters span generations.

And it's brilliant to see how a shared love of books, libraries and reading can bring people together from all across the world. It seems to me that the more we reach out across boundaries, these days, the better, so thank you to everyone who's contacted me, from Ireland to Alaska, London to Abu Dhabi, Australia to China and beyond.

Finally, huge thanks here at home to my editor Ciara Doorley, copy editor Hazel Orme, Breda Purdue and everyone at Hachette Books Ireland; to the lovely booksellers who welcome me in when I put my head round their doors; to my husband, Wilf Judd; and, as ever, to my agent Gaia Banks, at Sheil Land Associates UK.

ALSO IN THE FINFARRAN SERIES

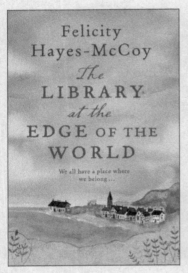

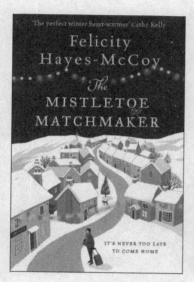

'The perfect winter heart-warmer' Cathy Kelly

FELICITY
HAYES-McCOY

The
MISTLETOE
MATCHMAKER

IT'S NEVER TOO LATE
TO COME HOME

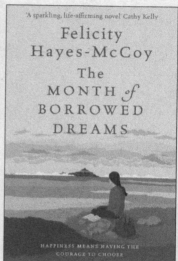

'A sparkling, life-affirming novel' Cathy Kelly

FELICITY
HAYES-McCOY

The
MONTH *of*
BORROWED
DREAMS

HAPPINESS MEANS HAVING THE
COURAGE TO CHOOSE